Y E L L O W

➤→

l e n a   n o t t i n g h a m

ISBN 978-1518869334

For the hopeful 7 year old with wide eyes and curly hair who wrote bedtime stories for her best friend's sister and never got a reply from the publisher she sent her crayon-illustrated books to.

Hey kid, you did it on your own.

I hope to make her proud.

➤➤

table of contents

➤➤

CHAPTER 1

Shiloh Everest had never loved the city. Everything was so busy and she was only one person. She could never keep up with the endless commotion happening at all hours of the day. But, the New York Academy of Art was her dream school, and when she'd gotten accepted, she decided she could deal with living in the city. After all, she was living alongside her three best friends. Everyone assumed Shiloh was living the dream.

Which she was, no doubt. After living in Miami for so long, Shiloh was itching to get out. That's why immediately following her graduation, she took off into the sunset and arrived in New York City the next day.

Moving to New York had been a dream she shared with her three best friends. Shiloh, Leah, Ryland, and Vanessa had all grown close in their freshman year of high school after working backstage on their school's production of *The Little Mermaid*. When their junior year came around, they saved up enough money, sent in their college applications, and realized that they could actually make their dream a reality.

And now here they were, two months into the fall semester of their first year of college. Shiloh loved how her life was turning out, but part of her was beginning to feel increasingly lonely. It's not like she didn't have friends, because she had plenty of them. There was just something missing. And she couldn't quite figure out what it was.

During her sophomore year, news had gotten out that Shiloh was gay. She'd expected her 3 best friends to turn away from her, but surprisingly they couldn't have cared less. They stood by her side during the incessant bullying she received. Shiloh was forever grateful for her roommates. Without them, she'd be nowhere near as happy as she was now.

But in some ways, her sexuality held her back. It wasn't exactly hard to come across another lesbian, especially in New York, but Shiloh was extremely inexperienced when it came to any type of relationship. So she kept to herself out of fear.

The moment she pushed the door open to their shared apartment, Shiloh was greeted by her three roommates. Or, should she say *two*, considering Leah was fast asleep on the couch. Vanessa and Ryland looked up from their phones and smiled in greeting to the dark haired girl.

"You'll never guess what happened today," Ryland gushed, forgetting about her phone and following Shiloh into the kitchen. "You remember that cute foreign kid in my hip hop class?" she asked, but didn't wait for Shiloh to respond. "He asked me for my number!" Shiloh's friend clapped her hands together excitedly and she couldn't help but laugh.

"I didn't doubt you for a second when you said you'd make it happen," Shiloh teased, letting her backpack slip off of her shoulder and onto the floor by the doorway.

Ryland crinkled her nose at her roommate and hopped up onto the counter. "So what's for dinner, Shy?"

Rolling her eyes, Shiloh sighed. "You couldn't have befriended a culinary major? That would've done us all a favor. I'm tired of being the only one who knows how to cook." She opened the pantry, scanning to see what she could throw together and call a meal.

"I got it!" Ryland called, causing Shiloh to turn around in confusion. She hadn't even heard anything. Forgetting about dinner, she followed the other girl towards the door, which apparently someone had knocked on moments ago. As it opened, Ryland's face held an unreadable expression, and Shiloh instantly grew confused. They rarely got visitors, and when they did, it was usually someone at the wrong apartment.

"Hi!" the cheery voice rang out from behind the door. Shiloh instantly felt sick to her stomach. She jogged over to Ryland's side to make sure she wasn't hallucinating. And she sure wasn't.

"Paisley Lowe?" Ryland asked. She was just as confused as Shiloh was. Vanessa quickly came up behind them, too, glancing at Shiloh with concern in her eyes. They all knew how Shiloh felt about Paisley.

The truth is, Shiloh hadn't come out in high school. She'd been outed by the girl standing right in front of them. Paisley Lowe, also known as the most popular girl at their high school. She was head cheerleader, prom queen, starring role in every school play. You name it, Paisley had done it. Everyone knew her name.

"Yes," the small girl on the other side of the door nodded once, confirming who it was. When she didn't say anything else, the three roommates exchanged glances.

"I'll wake up Leah," Vanessa whispered. All three of them knew their oldest roommate was the best at being friendly.

Meanwhile, Shiloh couldn't believe the girl she hated with every fiber of her being was now standing at the door of her apartment, seemingly oblivious to everything she'd done to her. Ryland and Vanessa knew exactly how much Shiloh resented Paisley. None of them had expected to see her again once they left Florida.

But now here she was, smiling like an idiot and trying to crane her neck to see into their apartment. Shiloh and Ryland looked at one another, stepping aside when Vanessa and Leah came back over to the doorway. Leah still appeared to be half asleep, but she quickly snapped out of her daze when she saw the other girl at the doorway.

"What?" she asked, looking at Paisley in confusion, and then back to her roommates. "What's going on?"

Shiloh shrugged, and Ryland and Vanessa raised their eyebrows, as if to silently say they were just as confused as she was.

"Was there something you needed?" Leah asked, turning back to Paisley, who still stood in the doorway with a smile on her face. Shiloh found it quite odd.

"Oh, yeah, that," the smaller girl giggled and pursed her lips for a moment. "I need a bed." She slipped past Leah and into the apartment, standing in the middle of the giant room and spinning in a circle to take it all in. "Do you have one of those?"

Ryland closed the door, shooting Shiloh a questioning look. All four girls turned to one another, keeping an eye on their old classmate.

"What the hell?" Shiloh was the first to speak up, keeping her voice low so Paisley couldn't hear her. Even if she did, Paisley seemed to be off in her own little world. She seemed... *different*. All four girls were confused. It was like she'd become a completely different person.

"Paisley?" Leah spoke again, giving the girls a nod to try and tell them she could handle this. The shorter girl walked over to Paisley, placing a hand on her shoulder. "Why do you need a bed? Where'd you come from?"

"My house," Paisley shrugged. She seemed completely oblivious to the fact that the other girls in the room had been at the receiving end of her reign of terror in high school. "Do you have a bed? I need one of those."

"Don't you have your own bed?" Leah asked. She shot the other girls a pleading look, realizing she couldn't handle this on her own. Vanessa and Ryland stepped forward but Shiloh stayed behind. She had too much build up resentment for the girl. She'd much rather leave Paisley out in the hallway.

"Yeah, but I have to walk a long way to get it," Paisley turned away from Leah and padded over to the couch, sitting down and picking up the TV remote. Vanessa turned back to Shiloh and made a face of confusion.

"Don't mess with that," Ryland quickly took the remote from the small girl's hands and set it on the coffee table. "Paisley, you need to go home," Ryland adopted a serious tone, standing directly in front of Paisley and crossing her arms over her chest.

After Paisley had outed Shiloh, Ryland had become increasingly protective of her green-eyed friend. She didn't know why Paisley was back, and she didn't care to find out.

"But we are friends," Paisley pouted, looking up at Ryland with pleading eyes. She pursed her lips in thought for a moment before raising her finger in the air, as if she'd come across a type of revelation. "Remember? We had chemistry together!"

Ryland raised an eyebrow. The girl was right, even though she'd only shown up to half of her classes, she remembered occasionally seeing Paisley across the classroom. That didn't make them anything close to friends, though.

"Paisley, you really need to go home," Ryland reiterated. She didn't wait for a response, instead she took the girl by the arm and pulled her up from the couch. Paisley only giggled as Ryland led her over to the door and out into the hallway.

"I have to go home?"

"Yes," Ryland nodded, pointing towards the elevator down the hallway. Paisley's smile finally faltered, but she didn't get a chance to respond before Ryland was closing the door in the small girl's face. She turned back to her roommates.

"What the hell was that?" Vanessa walked up beside Ryland and made sure the door was locked. All three girls knew what Paisley had done to Shiloh, and they knew she didn't deserve any of their hospitality.

"She was acting like an idiot," Shiloh observed, laughing bitterly.

"She's right," Leah nodded. The oldest girl suddenly grew concerned. "She was acting strange."

Shiloh shrugged and dismissed the thought. "She's probably drunk," she chuckled and walked back into the kitchen. "It's supposed to rain tonight," she added, trying to get her mind off of Paisley. What had she been doing here? Shiloh crinkled her nose, thinking back to when her high school life had taken a turn for the worse.

4 years ago

"It's funny because it's true, Shy," Ryland laughed from across the table. Shiloh looked up from her food and stuck her tongue out at her friend.

"There's no way he likes me," Shiloh rolled her eyes. She looked back down at the table and bit her lip. "Plus, he's not even cute. I'm not into guys like that."

"Or maybe you're not into guys at all."

The voice from behind Shiloh caused all four girls to look up from their phones. Except for Shiloh, who realized her phone wasn't sitting next to her on the table like it usually was. There was a sinking feeling in her stomach and she turned around, knowing exactly who the voice belonged to.

"That's interesting," Paisley laughed, scrolling through the phone in her hands. Shiloh's phone. "I knew you were gay, but I didn't know you were this gay," she sneered, raising an eyebrow and looking up at Shiloh.

"Don't you dare, Lowe," Ryland shot up out of her seat. Ryland wasn't exactly sure what Paisley was talking about, but she'd seen the look of horror on Shiloh's face, and assumed this was something important. All the girls at the table had fallen victim to Paisley Lowe at one point or another, and they knew how it felt.

"You know too?" Paisley didn't seem at all afraid of the taller girl who was now hovering over her. She waved the phone in front of Ryland's face and turned away before she could snatch it out of her hands. By now, they'd drawn the attention of the cafeteria. It was as if all eyes were on them.

"I don't know, Tori," Paisley mocked Shiloh's voice. Shiloh's heart dropped into her chest when she realized what Paisley had found. "I told him I was gay, and he seemed like he was okay with it. I don't know how I'm going to tell my mother, though," Paisley read off one of Shiloh's messages and laughed, rolling her eyes.

"I knew it," Paisley sneered. She tossed the phone in Shiloh's direction and Vanessa had to dive out of her chair to catch the device before it fell to the ground. Shiloh was still frozen.

"What the hell, Lowe?" Ryland yelled after the girl, who was already walking back to her table where the other cheerleaders sat waiting for her. Just as Ryland was about to go after her, a dark blur whizzed past her and out of the cafeteria.

Shiloh took off down the hallway and into the upstairs bathroom, knowing it would be empty at this time of day. The tears fell freely as soon as she was alone.

Shiloh had only told one person that she was gay, besides her father. She'd met her friend Tori on an online chat board, and she was the one who had encouraged Shiloh to talk to her dad. Luckily, her father had taken it well.

Shiloh wished the same could be said for the rest of her school. Except she'd never even had the chance to come out on her own. Paisley had just done it for her. And Shiloh definitely hadn't been ready.

The dark-haired girl slid down with her back against the wall, and she let her head fall into her hands as the sobs rocked through her body. What was she going to do now? She felt sick when she imagined what everyone was saying about her right now. Even her best friends were going to hate her after this.

Shiloh flinched when she felt a hand on her shoulder. "Ryland?" she whispered, wiping her eyes and looking up at the girl standing above her.

"C'mere," Ryland said softly, holding out her hand to help Shiloh to her feet. Hesitantly, Shiloh stood up. Seconds later, she was pulled into a tight hug. She felt two other pairs of arms wrap around her and couldn't hold back the second round of tears.

"I'm s-s-sorry," she managed to say once she pulled away from the hug. Her three best friends stared back at her, looking extremely concerned.

"Sorry for what?" Ryland asked, reaching out and placing a comforting hand on her friend's shoulder.

"That," Shiloh sighed, motioning in the direction of the cafeteria. "Me."

"You thought we'd be mad at you?" Leah spoke up, shock evident in her voice. Shiloh nodded slowly and Leah couldn't help but laugh. "Shiloh, we don't care if you're gay, honestly, we're happy if you're happy."

The other two girls nodded in agreement and Shiloh brought her hands up to cover her mouth. "You don't?"

"God, Shy, of course we don't care," Vanessa added. "You're still the same Shiloh that you were before, screw Lowe and whatever she thinks."

Shiloh gave them a sad smile. "Thank you guys," she whispered, and seconds later she was surrounded in a group hug. "And just so you know, I don't... you know, like any of you guys in that way."

"What?!" Ryland pulled away and pouted. "Why not? What's wrong with me?"

The girls in the bathroom all laughed and Ryland crossed her arms teasingly. Shiloh wiped her eyes, trying to make it appear like she hadn't been crying. She felt an arm link with hers and looked over at Ryland with a soft smile.

"Let's go show em' just who they're messing with, Everest."

———————————

"What do you guys want for dinner?" Shiloh bit her lip and sifted through the pantry, trying to push the bad memories to the back of her mind. She looked over at the other three girls and raised an eyebrow when she saw the unreadable expression on Leah's face.

"I wonder if she's okay," the oldest girl finally spoke up. Shiloh rolled her eyes almost immediately.

"She's either completely stoned, or drunk off her ass," Shiloh ran a hand through her hair. "Or both, who knows. Just forget about her, that's what I'm doing." She grabbed a box of pasta and held it up for the other girls to see. "Does this work?"

"Only if it's cooked," Ryland teased, and Shiloh threw the box at the younger girl. "Shut up," she laughed, pointing to the stove. "Make yourself useful and boil some water." Ryland raised a playful eyebrow at Shiloh and set the box down on the counter, bending down to grab a pot from the bottom cabinets.

Ryland and Shiloh made dinner while Vanessa and Leah busied themselves by blasting music throughout the room.

Their apartment was essentially one big room. The living room, kitchen, and office were all in the main living area of the space. Their bedrooms resided up the spiral staircase, and two bathrooms sat across the hall. Leah's father had contributed a good bit of money to help the girls afford an apartment big enough to house all of them.

"Dinner's ready!" Shiloh called, banging a spoon against the pot of spaghetti so the other girls could hear over the music. Vanessa and Leah came running in, and Shiloh handed them both of their plates. The four girls grabbed their drinks and made their way into the living room, collapsing on the couch after a long day.

"It's Shiloh's turn to pick," Ryland noted, pointing at the TV remote. Shiloh set her plate down and took the remote from her roommate. She started searching through Netflix, trying to find something to watch.

"Are you guys cool with Fr—?" Shiloh paused when she saw that her roommates' attention wasn't on her. She raised an eyebrow. "What?"

"*Shhh*," Leah whispered, raising a finger to her lips and then pointing to the door. "Do you hear that?"

Shiloh grew silent and listened along with the other girls. Just as she was about to argue that she didn't hear anything, there was a quiet noise from the other side of the door. It sounded like... *singing*?

"What is that?" she whispered, standing up from her spot on the couch.

"Don't tell me it's—," Shiloh was interrupted once more when Ryland, already at the door, waved her hand to tell Shiloh to be quiet. She slowly opened the door and peered out into the hallway. Ryland's eyes widened when she saw Paisley sitting in the hallway, leaning against the wall next to their door and humming softly to herself.

"What are you still doing here?" Ryland hissed at the smaller girl. Paisley jumped, obviously unaware that she'd been spotted.

"I need a bed," Paisley shrugged. Before Ryland could respond, she crawled under her legs and into the apartment, stumbling up to her feet and looking around happily. "Do you have a bed?"

Leah grabbed Ryland's arm and pulled her into the kitchen, along with the other girls. "Something's up," she whispered, glancing back at the girl who was now intently observing the TV remote.

"She needs to leave," Shiloh said firmly, loud enough for Paisley to hear her. She didn't care if something was wrong. She wanted her gone. She didn't want to offer any hospitality to the girl who had single-handedly made her life a living hell. "We can call the fucking cops or something."

"Shy," Leah shook her head. "Something's obviously wrong if she ended up here." She glanced at the two other girls, silently asking for some sort of help.

"We should at least try and figure out why she's here," Vanessa spoke up, placing a hand on Shiloh's arm. "Then we can take her back home or something."

Ryland and Shiloh looked at one another and Ryland sighed softly. "It's worth a try, I guess," she finally spoke, raising an eyebrow at Shiloh, who shrugged.

"Whatever," she mumbled. "I'm going to bed, I don't feel like dealing with her." Shiloh pushed past the other girls and grabbed her backpack from next to the door. Moments later, her footsteps were heard, and her bedroom door slammed shut with a bang.

As the sound echoed throughout the space, Paisley stopped what she was doing to cover her ears and look around worriedly. The three roommates quickly exchanged glances before walking into the living room. Leah sat down on the couch next to Paisley while Vanessa and Ryland remained standing.

"Where do you live, Paisley?" Leah asked, turning and looking at the confused girl.

"Here," Paisley smiled proudly, pointing to the couch and patting it gently. "This is my bed."

Ryland and Vanessa raised their eyebrows. Leah quickly shook her head. "You don't live here," she glanced at her other two roommates and then back to Paisley. "Where did you come from?"

"The plane," Paisley nodded, remembering what she had done earlier. "See?" She reached into her front pocket and frowned when she came up empty handed. Quickly, the small girl stood up and reached into her back pocket, giggling excitedly when she found what she was looking for.

Leah took the crumpled up piece of paper from Paisley and unfolded it, turning it around in her hands so it was right side up. She scanned the words and her jaw dropped. Noticing the change in her expression, Vanessa and Ryland crouched down next to her to read the writing on the paper.

"A plane ticket?" Vanessa asked, turning to Paisley. The girl nodded excitedly, practically bouncing up and down on the couch.

"I came to see my friends," she smiled, pointing to them with both of her fingers. "We had Chemistry together. I remember."

"Something's definitely up," Leah whispered to her roommates between gritted teeth. None of them had a clue what was going on. "Paisley, how did you find out where we lived?"

Paisley thought for a moment, petting her hand on her knee and feeling the material of her jeans. "This," she suddenly realized, reaching into her other pocket and handing her phone to Leah. The oldest girl studied the iPhone, unlocking it to see a picture of Paisley and two other cheerleaders.

"Are these your friends?" she asked, holding out the phone and showing Paisley the background. Upon seeing the picture, the girl's face twisted into one of confusion.

"No," she shook her head. Her eyebrows suddenly furrowed and she took the phone back, holding it inches away from her face and studying the picture even closer. "They are not my friends," she confirmed, setting the phone on the cushion next to her.

Ryland sat down next to Leah, and Vanessa sat on the coffee table so she was facing all three girls. "Paisley, cut the crap," Ryland said firmly, sending the girl a warning glare. "Why are you here?"

Paisley pouted, sticking out her bottom lip and staring up at the ceiling in thought. "Oh, yeah," she nodded, holding up her finger to show she'd remembered something. "I came here on a plane, see?"

She reached into her pocket and frowned. She went to reach into her back pocket, but Leah moved to stop her.

"You told us already," Leah reminded her, holding up the crumpled plane ticket. The flight had happened that same day, which told the girls that Paisley had flown there with the intention of seeing them. Her reason was still unknown, though.

"Oh," Paisley took the plane ticket from Leah's hands and studied it closely, running her fingers over the folded corners. "I need a bed," she nodded and pointed to the large window in the back of the apartment. "It is getting dark."

"Oh my fucking god," Ryland groaned and motioned for Leah to scoot over. The oldest girl obeyed, and Ryland switched places on the couch so she was sitting next to Paisley. Ryland grabbed Paisley by the shoulders and held her firmly in front of her. "Why are you here?" she asked, keeping her voice strong and intimidating.

Paisley lifted her shoulders, cowering under the girl's firm grip. She shook her head and pushed Ryland's hands off of her.

"Please," she murmured, shaking her head and scooting back on the couch.

"Please what?" Vanessa asked, holding out a hand to tell Ryland to pause for a moment.

"Please," Paisley repeated, shaking her head once more. Ryland and Vanessa looked at one another and Ryland groaned.

"Paisley, what's going on?" Ryland tried once more to get some sort of answer out of the smaller girl.

"It is getting dark," Paisley pointed at the window once more. "And I need a bed," she added, looking down at her jeans and patting her palms gently on her lap.

Leah placed a hand on Ryland's shoulder and the light haired girl turned around to face her. Vanessa stood up and sat on the arm of the couch so all three of them could talk.

"What are we supposed to do with her?" Vanessa was the first to speak up, glancing back at the girl on the other side of the couch, who was poking at the buttons on the TV remote once more.

Leah shook her head and sighed. "I don't know, but this feels like something out of a screwed up TV show," she ran a hand through her hair and glanced in the direction of Shiloh's room, wondering how the green eyed girl was feeling about this whole situation.

"Do you have a bed?"

All three girls jumped when they realized Paisley had stood up and poked her head into their conversation.

"I need a bed," the girl repeated, reaching up and smoothing out her own hair.

Ryland rolled her eyes in defeat and stood up. "Fine, Paisley," she sighed. "One night. You can stay for *one* night, and then you go home, okay?" She glanced at Leah and Vanessa, asking for some type of approval. She figured that if she just gave Paisley what she wanted, maybe the girl would leave the next morning.

"Yes. But I need a bed," Paisley clapped her hands together and reached up to twirl the ends of Ryland's hair around her fingers. Ryland instantly slapped her hand away and Paisley gasped, looking down at her hand and holding it close to her chest. Ignoring the small girl's dramatic reaction, Ryland bit her lip.

"Is this okay?" she whispered, bending down next to Leah and Vanessa. Leah nodded softly.

"Whatever is going on, she seems… *different.* We can at least give her the benefit of the doubt for one night, right?" Leah said, looking to Vanessa for her approval. Vanessa puckered her lips for a moment before nodding.

"I don't see why not," the dark skinned girl shrugged, glancing at Paisley. "Where is she sleeping, though?"

Ryland huffed, forgetting that one very important factor. She sighed and stood up, turning to Paisley. "You can sleep in my room for tonight," she nodded once. Paisley hopped up on her tiptoes in some sort of expression of excitement.

"Bed," she nodded. Ryland looked back at the other two girls, who looked completely shocked. She bent down next to them once more and laughed softly.

"Keep your friends close but your enemies closer, right?" she raised an eyebrow. Leah chuckled softly and shrugged.

"Just try to be nice, okay?" the older girl asked, and Ryland nodded slowly.

"Alright, Lowe, let's get you that bed you want so badly," she sighed, standing up and grabbing Paisley's hand. Before the smaller girl could respond, Ryland was pulling her towards the spiral staircase.

Paisley paused at the first stair, taking her bottom lip between her teeth.

"I don't have all day, Lowe," Ryland groaned, tugging Paisley's hand. The smaller girl hesitantly took one step on the stairs, and gripped the railing with her other hand.

"Ouch," Paisley mumbled, looking down at her feet. Thinking nothing of it, Ryland simply sighed and tugged Paisley's hand once more.

"Ouch. Ouch. Ouch," Paisley muttered with each step, but eventually they made it to the top of the staircase. Paisley immediately clapped her hands, reaching for the first doorknob she saw.

Ryland quickly grabbed her by the shoulder and pulled her back, away from Shiloh's room. That was the last thing Paisley needed to do.

"That's not my room," Ryland pointed to the next door over. "That is."

Paisley clapped her hands and jiggled the doorknob violently until it opened. She paused, walking slowly into Ryland's room and observing the memorabilia that hung on her walls. "Bed," she noted, pointing to the queen sized bed in the corner of the room.

Ryland sighed and shut the door behind them. "That's a bed, yeah," she mumbled, walking over to her dresser. "Where's your bag?"

Paisley looked at her cluelessly.

"Did you bring a suitcase or something?" Ryland suddenly realized that Paisley had been empty handed when she entered the apartment.

"I came on a plane," Paisley nodded, reaching into her pocket. Ryland rolled her eyes, grabbing Paisley's hands before she could realize she didn't have the plane ticket for the second time.

"I know. You told us," Ryland nodded, growing slightly frustrated with how she was acting. Something was definitely wrong.

"Here," she turned back to her dresser and found a t-shirt and pajama pants that would fit the smaller girl. "You can wear these for tonight."

Paisley giggled excitedly, hugging the clothing to her chest. She brought the t-shirt to her nose and inhaled, smelling their detergent. "Do I change?" she asked, holding up the shirt for Ryland to see.

The light haired girl nodded, turning to the door to show Paisley where the bathroom was. But Paisley beat her to it, and when Ryland was about to lead her out into the hallway, she turned back around to find Paisley in only her shirt, underwear, and shoes.

The girl was tugged angrily at the pajama pants, trying to pull them on over her white converse. Ryland sighed and closed the door once more, walking over to Paisley and grabbing her hands.

"You have to take your shoes off," she pointed to the white shoes on Paisley's feet.

"Ouch," Paisley shook her head and pulled away from Ryland. "Ouch."

Ryland raised an eyebrow. "Ouch?" she asked, pointing down to Paisley's shoes. Paisley nodded.

"Sit down," Ryland instructed, pointing to the bed. Paisley did as she was told, with a wide smile on her face. Ryland knelt down in front of her and pulled on the shoelaces to untie them.

"No, ouch!" Paisley protested, pulling her foot away from Ryland. The light haired girl grew frustrated and grabbed Paisley's foot again, gripping it tightly despite the girl's protests. She slipped the first shoe off her foot and gasped.

"Ouch," Paisley pouted, her bottom lip trembling. This time, Ryland nodded in agreement. Paisley's sock was stained red, with holes in the bottom where small shards of glass had wedged themselves into the bottom of her foot. Ryland checked the shoe, but it appeared as if the shoes had been put on *after* the glass was already in her foot.

"How did this happen?" Ryland asked, gripping the girl's other ankle and pulling off the second shoe.

"Ouch," Paisley nodded, as if it were a perfectly good explanation for Ryland's question. Ryland groaned.

"I'm going to try and get these out, okay?" she asked, nodding to the pieces of glass in Paisley's foot. The smaller girl shook her head furiously.

"No. Hurt," she furrowed her eyebrows.

"If I don't take them out, it'll get infected, and you'll get sick," Ryland huffed, standing up and walking over to her nightstand.

"Will I die?"

"Yes," Ryland lied, too tired to try and reason with the girl. She regretted her decision immediately, though. Paisley let out an ear piercing screech and Ryland dived across the bed to cup her hand over the girl's mouth.

"You're not going to die," she shook her head. "I was kidding. It was a joke."

Paisley pursed her lips against Ryland's hand out of confusion. "Oh," she mumbled when the other girl drew her hand away. She thought about it for a few moments before giggling at the 'joke.'

Ryland just shook her head and slipped out of the hallway, searching through the medicine cabinet until she found what she needed. Paisley was still sitting in the exact same place when Ryland came back, which she was thankful for.

"This is gonna hurt a bit, but I have to do it, otherwise it'll only end up hurting more in the long run," Ryland explained, sitting back down on the floor and laying a paper towel down next to her.

"I do not want to run," Paisley shook her head.

"You don't have to," Ryland rolled her eyes, deciding she was speaking to a child instead of Paisley.

"It may hurt, but when it's over, you can play a game on my phone, okay?"

"Game?"

"Yeah," Ryland nodded. Paisley clapped her hands excitedly and Ryland took that as her cue to keep going. Slowly, she rolled Paisley's socks off of each foot. The girl on the bed winced each time, but surprisingly kept quiet.

"Why did you come here?" Ryland asked, trying once again to get some sort of information out of the girl. Using a pair of tweezers, she lifted Paisley's foot and slowly removed a piece of glass from her heel.

"I—*ouch*—needed a bed," Paisley mumbled, crinkling her nose and trying to lean over and look down at her foot.

"I know that," Ryland said, continuing to remove the glass from the bottom of her foot, setting the pieces on the paper towel next to her. "But didn't you already have a bed?"

Paisley shook her head. "Ouch," she muttered once more. Ryland sighed, giving up on getting any answers out of her. Once she removed every piece of glass she could find, she poured a few drops of hydrogen peroxide onto a cotton ball and glanced up at Paisley.

"This is gonna sting a bit," she warned, pressing the cotton ball on the open wounds and beginning to clean the dried blood on the bottom of her foot. Paisley whimpered from above her but remained silent. "See? All done," Ryland nodded, satisfied with her attempt at cleaning the wounds.

"Game?" Paisley asked, remembering what Ryland had told her earlier.

"Not yet," Ryland shook her head. "I have to finish bandaging these," she grabbed the gauze she'd brought from the bathroom and went to work on covering the cuts on Paisley's feet, making sure to use antibiotic ointment to keep them from getting infected.

Once she was finished bandaging, she stood up and retrieved a pair of large socks from her dresser, hoping they would fit loosely over the gauze. Paisley frowned as Ryland slipped the socks over the bandages.

"Ouch," she shook her head.

"It's gonna hurt for a while, that's just how it's gonna be," Ryland took a deep breath, trying her best to remain patient. She regretted not passing the girl off to Vanessa or Leah.

"Game?"

Ryland pointed to the change of clothes next to Paisley. "Once you change," she nodded once and Paisley quickly grabbed the clothes. She stood up slowly, testing the bandages on her feet. She clapped her hands when she realized her wounds didn't hurt as badly as they did before.

Paisley struggled for a few minutes, but finally managed to get her pants and t-shirt on. Ryland had to stop herself from laughing when she realized the pants were on backwards, but decided against saying anything.

"Here," she handed Paisley her phone and crawled into her bed. Moments later, Paisley bounced up on the bed and was curled up smack dab next to Ryland. She held the phone close to her face, tapping at the screen aimlessly.

Ryland groaned and pushed the girl off of her. "This is my side of the bed," she mumbled, placing a pillow between them. Paisley opened her mouth to protest, but Ryland glared at her, causing the smaller girl to set the phone back down and burrow under the covers. Ignoring the humming noises from Paisley, Ryland turned so her back was facing the other girl and closed her eyes.

That night, all four roommates fell asleep with a million questions circulating in their heads.

C H A P T E R   2

Shiloh couldn't fall asleep knowing all that had happened earlier. So instead, she'd been spending a majority of her night with music blaring through her headphones as she lay on her back, staring up at the ceiling and trying to block out her thoughts. It didn't help much, though.

She couldn't help but wonder what Paisley had been thinking. Paisley had made all of their lives a living hell for four years, how could she expect them to be anything but bitter towards her? Shiloh had so many built up emotions against the younger girl that she was surprised she hadn't connected her fist with her face as soon as she saw her standing in their doorway.

But there had been a change in Paisley, too. Shiloh tried to continue telling herself that Paisley was just stoned out of her mind, but that wasn't a good enough explanation for everything that had been going on. There was something else contributing to this change in the girl, and Shiloh wished she could figure out what it was just to feed her curiosity.

Back in high school, everyone knew Paisley's name. She was the girl you either loved or hated, and it all depended on the way she treated you. If Paisley liked you, life was easy. If she had anything against you, though, you were screwed. Paisley had the means and the resources to turn your life into a living hell. And that was exactly what she had done to Shiloh.

News spread fast after the incident in the cafeteria. Shiloh was soon at the receiving end of countless stares, insults, and at times — physical violence. And worst of all, Shiloh hadn't even gotten to come out on her own. Someone had done it for her. Someone who she hated with every fiber of her being.

Following the incident, Shiloh was forced to tell her parents what had happened before news could get back to them. Her mother had been somewhat confused at first, but both her parents were accepting. Shiloh was forever thankful that her parents didn't give her much trouble about her sexuality. She was grateful to have a support system at home.

Her parents were infuriated when Shiloh told them what Paisley had done. They informed the school, but Shiloh knew it wouldn't do anything. Paisley lived with her uncle, and she always bragged about how he didn't care what she did. The girl could get away with whatever she wanted, and made sure everyone was aware.

So Shiloh was practically powerless. She spent the rest of her high school years eating lunch outside to avoid the slurs thrown her way in the cafeteria. Leah, Vanessa, and Ryland were her only friends. Shiloh knew that without them, those years would have been ten times more painful than they already were.

Moving to New York had been a big change for Shiloh. She decided to be open about her sexuality, since she would now have control over who she told. She was surprised when no one really cared. It was nice. She'd tell them she was gay, they'd nod in approval, and then move onto a different subject of conversation. It was totally different than it had been in high school.

Her thoughts were interrupted late that night. Shiloh jumped when she saw something move out of the corner of her eye. She squinted, seeing that her door had been left open slightly. The light from the hallway was the only thing that illuminated her room, and she watched as the figure moved over to her bed. The green eyed girl removed her headphones.

"Nessa?" she asked, sitting up and raising an eyebrow. There was no answer and Shiloh grew even more confused.

"Hi," the voice whispered. Shiloh's hands clenched into fists and she inhaled slowly. What was Paisley still doing here?

"I'm sleeping. Go away," she said firmly, rolling over on her side away from the girl. Her roommates would sure have a lot of explaining to do the next morning.

Shiloh tugged her blankets over her head and tried to convince herself that this was just some kind of screwed up dream. She didn't need Paisley haunting her any more than she already did.

"Why?" The smaller girl obviously didn't take Shiloh's hint, because moments later Shiloh felt a dip in her bed. She lifted her head and let out a frustrated sigh when she saw Paisley sitting cross legged at the end of the bed.

"Because I don't want you here," Shiloh said bluntly. She didn't see any point in hiding her feelings towards Paisley. She deserved to know how much Shiloh despised her.

"Why?"

Shiloh groaned and rolled over, sitting up and grabbing Paisley by the shoulders.

"Because I don't like you," she said loudly, but not loud enough to wake her other roommates. "Go away," she whispered between gritted teeth, grabbing her phone and slipping her headphones back into her ears.

"You do not like me?"

Shiloh ignored the girl, hoping that maybe Paisley would leave on her own if she didn't entertain her questions. What was she thinking? Coming into Shiloh's room in the middle of the night seemed like a death sentence for Paisley. Shiloh rolled her eyes.

There was a tap on her shoulder and Shiloh ripped her headphones out of her ears. "What?!" she snapped, sitting up and glaring at Paisley. "I thought I told you to leave?" she hissed.

Paisley reared back, scooting all the way against the backboard of the bed and holding her hands out in front of her. "Please," she mumbled, shaking her head. Shiloh grew confused.

"Please?" she asked, trying to keep her tough composure despite having just seen a flash of vulnerability in the girl.

Paisley nodded slowly and placed her hands back in her lap. "I wanted to talk."

Shiloh raised an eyebrow. "What?" she laughed bitterly. "Are you finally going to apologize for making my life miserable? Because I think it's a little too late for that, Lowe."

Paisley looked utterly confused. "What?"

Shiloh just rolled her eyes. "Why are you still here?" she asked, trying to change the topic of conversation. "I thought you were going home?"

"This is my home," Paisley nodded. She clapped her hands together once and looked around the dark room. "You are my friends."

"You don't live here, Paisley," Shiloh reiterated. She knew now that not even drugs or alcohol could make someone like this. It was actually starting to scare her. She was actually growing concerned.

"Can we talk?" Paisley asked, as if she hadn't heard Shiloh's previous statement. The green eyed girl rolled her eyes in frustration and sat up, crossing her legs and looking straight at Paisley.

"Why do you want to talk?" she asked, running a hand through her messy hair.

Paisley seemed to think about the question for a moment, bringing her finger to her chin and staring off into the distance. "Oh, yeah," she raised her index finger in the air. "We are friends. Friends help friends, right?"

Shiloh had to hold in her laughter. Friends? They were the furthest thing from friends. "Why?"

"Because I am scared," Paisley nodded.

Shiloh furrowed her eyebrows together. Scared? If anything, Shiloh should be the one terrified of Paisley and what she could do to her. Even though they were out of high school, Shiloh was still intimidated by the other girl. (Although, this new version of Paisley seemed like anything but intimidating.)

"Why?" Shiloh asked, trying to appear disinterested. She couldn't deny that the more she spoke to Paisley, the more concerned she became about the way the girl was acting.

"I can not sleep," Paisley nodded once and looked around the room, almost as if she was refusing to make eye contact with Shiloh. "I can not see anything."

"That's because it's nighttime," Shiloh rolled her eyes. "You close your eyes, and then you sleep. It's common sense," she shook her head.

"But I am scared," Paisley clasped her hands together slowly and took a deep breath. "I do not like new things."

"New things?" Shiloh raised an eyebrow.

"Yes," Paisley nodded once. "This house."

Shiloh was growing increasingly confused by the second. She was starting to feel worried for the other girl. Shiloh knew she had to put an end to that right away. "Get out of my bedroom," she said firmly, pointing to the door.

Paisley looked at the door and shook her head. "But it is your turn," she said, reaching out and pointing to Shiloh, placing her index finger on the spot above Shiloh's heart. Shiloh reached up and pushed the girl's hand off of her.

"My turn?" she asked, pushing away Paisley's hand again when she tried to point at her once more.

"Yes," Paisley nodded. "Right? Friends talk to friends when they are scared. Are you scared?"

Shiloh was growing increasingly more frustrated. "No, Paisley," she said bluntly. "I'm not your friend." She rolled over and scooted as far away from the girl as possible.

"But we had Chemistry together..." Paisley said softer, crawling over next to Shiloh. It was almost as if she had no sense of personal space. "So we are friends."

"We're not friends, Paisley!" Shiloh snapped, sitting up and grabbing the girl by the shoulders. "Get that through your head right now, I am *not* your friend." Her voice was low in the back of her throat.

Paisley flinched and put her hands up. "Please," she shook her head quickly.

Shiloh ignored her, pulling them both off of the bed and leading Paisley over to the doorway by her shoulders. "Go away, Paisley," she said firmly, pushing the girl out into the hallway and shutting the door before she could argue.

"Okay," the voice chirped through the door, and Shiloh rolled her eyes. After waiting a few moments to make sure she left for good, Shiloh crawled back into bed and shoved her headphones in her ears. She knew she wouldn't be getting much sleep that night.

And she was right. She hadn't gotten a wink of sleep, instead she watched an abundance of reality shows on Netflix and blasted her entire music library, trying to stop her mind from wandering back to the small girl that had appeared in her room earlier that night.

She was brought out of her daze early that morning when the door cracked open. Shiloh removed her headphones, gazing at the Leah with a look of confusion. The older girl looked anything but happy.

"What'd you say to Paisley?" Leah asked, walking over and sitting down on the edge of the bed. Shiloh rolled her eyes.

"Here's a more important question," Shiloh raised an eyebrow. "Why is she still here?"

Leah sighed softly and placed a hand on Shiloh's shoulder. "You know we can't just send her out into the city like… this," she motioned her hand in the direction of the door. "Obviously she's… changed," Leah bit her lip and fiddled with her thumbs in her lap.

"Wait, so you're seriously considering letting her stay here?" Shiloh sat up, noticeably tensing. Leah ran her hand down Shiloh's arm and placed it back in her lap, taking a deep breath.

Nodding softly, Leah studied Shiloh's face. "At least until we can figure out what's going on with her," she said cautiously.

"She's probably just high," Shiloh muttered, shaking her head and grabbing her phone from under the blankets. She looked back up to be met with an incriminating glare from Leah. "What?!" she huffed.

"You and I both know that's not the case."

"Fine," Shiloh shook her head. "But I'm not responsible for anything that happens to her if she sets foot in my bedroom again."

"Just… try and give her a chance, Shy," Leah said, squeezing Shiloh's hand. "You don't have to forgive her, I don't expect you to. Right now you just have to be the bigger person and try to be understanding."

Shiloh nodded before taking a deep breath. "Yeah, whatever," she shrugged.

"Ryland's making pancakes downstairs, if you want some," Leah added before she stood up. Shiloh lifted her head, realizing just how hungry she was.

"I'll be down in a little bit," she nodded, waiting for Leah to leave the room before she hung her legs over the edge of her bed. *Great.* What were they supposed to do with Paisley now? Shiloh couldn't bring herself to show hospitality to the girl who'd shown her nothing but hatred all these years.

Rummaging through her drawers, Shiloh became frustrated when she couldn't find anything to wear. She finally settled on a pair of leggings and a peach colored sweater, knowing that the weather was beginning to get chillier.

"Hot," she heard Paisley's voice as she descended the spiral staircase and had to stop herself from rolling her eyes once more. Once she was downstairs, she stood silently for a moment and watched the girls in the kitchen.

"Hey, no," Ryland grabbed Paisley's hand and pulled it away from the griddle. "It's hot."

"Hot," Paisley nodded once more, but obviously didn't understand because she went to reach for the pan once more. Ryland sighed and swatted her hand away.

Paisley gasped and held her hand up in front of Ryland's face.

"Ouch."

Vanessa turned around from her spot on the counter, spotting Shiloh at the bottom of the stairs. "She's alive!" she laughed, hopping down to the floor and walking over to the green eyed girl. "How'd you sleep?"

"I didn't," Shiloh mumbled, tearing her eyes away from the kitchen. She didn't wait for Vanessa to reply, she just walked over to the living room and plopped down onto the couch.

"I don't think any of us did," Vanessa sighed. She sat down next to Shiloh and shook her head. "I don't know what got her so upset."

"Huh?" Shiloh asked, confused as to what the other girl was talking about.

"You didn't hear all the commotion last night?"

Shiloh shook her head. She'd kept her headphones in all night after Paisley came into her room. "Why? What happened?"

Vanessa sighed and slumped back on the couch. "I don't know. Leah said Paisley came in her room in the middle of the night and was upset over something, but she wouldn't tell her anything," Vanessa glanced at Shiloh. "She kept asking if we were her friends." Vanessa noticed the look on Shiloh's face and raised an eyebrow at her friend. "You don't happen to know something about this, do you?"

Shiloh laid her head back and groaned. "She came in my room last night, and wouldn't leave me alone. So I just told her I wasn't her friend and then I made her leave."

"That must've been why she was so upset," Vanessa said softly. Shiloh looked at her and bit her lip, wondering if her friends were going to be upset with the way she treated Paisley. "I don't blame you, honestly," Vanessa shrugged and laid her head on the back of the couch.

"We're really letting her stay here?" Shiloh asked after a few moments of silence.

"I don't know," Vanessa turned her head to look at Shiloh. "I think the only thing we can do right now is give her a chance, right?"

Shiloh just shrugged. This was the last thing she needed on top of her already stressful schedule. She was brought out of her self-loathing when someone poked the top of her head, and she instantly whipped her head around to find Paisley standing behind the couch, holding a plate of pancakes. Wearing *her* shirt. The one she'd been looking for this morning.

"How'd you get that?" Shiloh snapped, pointing to the shirt. Paisley looked down where Shiloh was pointing and then back at Shiloh. She looked almost... scared.

"I-I found it," she nodded once.

"Where?"

Paisley thought for a moment, bringing her hand to her mouth. "In the room," she finally spoke. She pointed to the staircase.

"*My* room?" Shiloh asked, and Paisley shrugged.

"I found it," she repeated. It was silent for a few moments before she shoved the plate of pancakes in front of Shiloh's face. "Happy Birthday."

Shiloh pushed the plate out of her face. "It's not my birthday," she rolled her eyes. Paisley's expression faltered for a few moments and she glanced nervously back into the kitchen.

Ryland saw the pleading expression on Paisley's face and walked over to where she was standing, sighing heavily. "She wanted to give you pancakes," Ryland explained to Shiloh. "She thinks you're not her friend."

Shiloh ignored Ryland's pleading look in her direction and shook her head, standing up. "I'm not her friend," she said firmly before grabbing her backpack from the coffee table and tossing it over her shoulder. "I'm going out," she muttered before disappearing out of the apartment and slamming the door behind her.

Ryland made a move to go after her, but Vanessa grabbed her arm before she could. "Give her some space, Ry," the dark skinned girl sighed. All three roommates knew how Shiloh got when she was in a bad mood, and it was better just to let her have some time to think.

"Why?" Paisley spoke up, still holding the plate of pancakes. She walked over to the door and stared at it, as if she were waiting for Shiloh to come back. After a few moments, she raised her fist and knocked on the door.

Ryland quickly jogged over to Paisley and took the plate out of her hands, setting it on the counter in the kitchen before grabbing Paisley's hand and leading her back into the living room.

"Paisley?" she nodded once, making eye contact with the small girl. She decided it was time to get some answers.

"Yes," Paisley nodded, pointing to herself.

"Why did you come here?" Ryland asked, trying not to appear overly frustrated. "Did something happen to you?"

Paisley's face contorted into a look of thoughtfulness. She bit her lip and looked up at the ceiling for a few moments before looking at Ryland once more. "I had to leave," she said slowly, as if she were unsure of her words. She then nodded quickly, clapping her hands together. "I had to leave."

"Why did you have to leave?" Leah spoke up, walking and sitting down next to Ryland. Paisley thought for a moment before shrugging.

Leah sighed and ran a hand through her hair. "I guess we just have to hope that she'll tell us in time," she said quietly, looking at Ryland, who shrugged.

"Oh shit, Ryland," Vanessa sat up quickly, looking at the clock. "We have to get ready for class," she hopped to her feet and jogged upstairs.

"Who has class on a Saturday?" Leah laughed, looking at Ryland who groaned loudly.

"Anyone who's crazy enough to be a dance major," Ryland rolled her eyes jokingly. "It was the only time our teacher could get the auditorium empty, we have to practice for a big showcase coming up." She glanced upstairs where Vanessa had run off to. "Nessa! Grab my bag!"

"Way ahead of you!" a voice rang out, and a large black duffel bag was tossed over the banister. It landed on the ground with a thud.

"Please!" Paisley cried, covering her ears and cowering behind the couch. Leah and Ryland exchanged looks before Leah moved to look around the couch.

"Are you okay?" she asked the small girl, who still had her hands covering her ears. She looked up at Leah slowly, and immediately smiled.

"Yes," she nodded. Paisley stood up, watching as Ryland grabbed the bag and followed Vanessa towards the door.

"Bye Leah!" Ryland called, noticing an expectant Paisley next to her. "Uh... Bye, Paisley," she said softer, holding the door open for Vanessa before slipping out after her.

Paisley's face lit up and she waved both her hands out in front of her. "Goodnight!" she called, even though the door was already shut. Leah watched the small girl in confusion, wondering just what had happened to her. It was as if Paisley was an entirely different person.

C H A P T E R   3

Shiloh was glad none of her roommates had tried to follow her. She'd only walked across the street to the small park. Shiloh always came there when she needed to think. And boy, was there a lot to think about.

Deep down, she knew she should give Paisley a chance, but it was just so hard. When she looked at the girl, she saw the same face that had read her private texts aloud in front of the entire cafeteria. She should be allowed to resent her, right?

But at the same time, the Paisley who'd shown up at their door seemed completely different than the girl Shiloh had feared in high school. All four roommates knew something was up, but none of them had any idea what it was.

Shiloh groaned, sitting down on a bench in the back of the park and bringing her hands up to comb through her hair. She lifted her head, pausing for a moment. A patch of daisies along the edge of the path caught her eye. It was a miracle they were still surviving, considering how close they were getting to winter. Immediately inspired, Shiloh pulled her sketchbook out of her backpack and held her pencil in-between her teeth, while she flipped to a clean page.

The reason Shiloh loved drawing was because she could capture the essence of a moment. She enjoyed having to take the time and study her subject matter, to know every curve and line, every highlight and shadow, and every small imperfection. It was how she found beauty in things.

She started off with the curved stem of the daisies, making sure to highlight the glare of the sun against the grass surrounding the flowers. Her pencil scratched against the thick paper, working at an impressive speed. Her hair hung down in front of her face and she took her bottom lip in between her teeth in concentration.

Her hand froze when she looked back up, though, because her view of the flowers had been blocked by a small figure. Shiloh instantly recognized her shirt.

"Paisley, what are y—?" Shiloh's voice trailed off when Paisley turned around, holding a handful of flowers. The same daisies that Shiloh had been drawing were now gathered together into Paisley's hands. The smaller girl looked more than pleased with herself, and she held up the flowers happily for Shiloh to see.

"I found them," Paisley smiled widely, walking over to Shiloh and practically shoving the flowers in her face. Shiloh snapped, pushing Paisley's hands out of her face, which caused the flowers to fall to the ground.

"Ouch," Paisley mumbled, bending down and picking up each flower individually, holding them up to the sun as if to check if they were alright. Shiloh crossed her arms and stood in front of the younger girl.

"Why would you pick those?" Shiloh huffed, slamming her sketchbook shut and tossing it back into her backpack. Paisley stood up and hugged the flowers to her chest.

"They were pretty," she smiled, looking down at the daisies and giggling.

"Yeah, well guess what?" Shiloh asked, not waiting for a response. "You just killed them." The green eyed girl motioned to the patch of grass where Paisley had found the flowers.

"What?" Paisley whispered, looking concerned. She knelt down next to the patch of grass and patted it gently. "Oh," she muttered, shaking her head.

"Sometimes you just need to admire pretty things from far away," Shiloh sighed. As if she already wasn't frustrated, this only made things worse.

Paisley looked up from the grass for a moment, meeting Shiloh's eyes. "Like you?" she asked, tilting her head to the side like a confused puppy.

Shiloh just rolled her eyes. "Goodbye, Paisley," she muttered, grabbing her bag and storming off down the path before the other girl had a chance to respond. Paisley watched Shiloh walk away until the girl was merely a speck in the distance.

The small girl turned back to the daisies, laying them down gently next to her. She ran her fingers through the grass, feeling the remainder of the stems from where she'd cut the flowers.

"Stupid," she mumbled, shaking her head and knocking on her forehead a few times, as if to check if her brain was hollow. "Stupid," she repeated, picking up one of the daisies and trying to connect it back to the stem.

"Bad," she sighed. Her hands shook in frustration as she tried to make the daisy stand up in the patch of grass once more. "No, bad," she shook her head quickly and continued trying to get the flower to stand upright.

A drop of water on her back made Paisley jump. She looked up at the sky, trying to determine where it had come from. Suddenly there was another drop, and another, and another, until there were too many for the girl to count.

"Ouch," she muttered. Quickly bending down, she gathered up the flowers and held them tightly against her chest. She shook her head, looking around for somewhere where the water couldn't hurt her. The largest thing she could find was the forest, so Paisley held the flowers close to her and waddled off of the path, stumbling through the brush.

Meanwhile, Shiloh had just fallen asleep when someone burst into her bedroom. She'd walked back home and headed straight to her bed, intent on getting some sort of sleep in order to get the thoughts of Paisley out of her head. Ever since she'd left the park, the younger girl had been the only thing on her mind.

She groaned, sitting up and staring at the figure in her doorway. "What do you want?" she huffed, wiping her eyes and glaring at Leah.

"Where's Paisley?"

"How am I supposed to know?" Shiloh threw her hands up in the air.

"I left her in Ryland's room for twenty minutes so I could try and get some homework done, and when I came back, she was gone, Shiloh. *Gone*." Leah shook her head and sighed in frustration.

"Last time I saw her was at the park," Shiloh shrugged, running a hand through her long hair. "She picked the fucking flowers I was sketching."

Leah took a deep breath. "Okay, well, where was she?"

"At the edge of the woods by the benches," Shiloh stood up and flicked on her light. She blinked a few times to let her eyes adjust. "Why does it matter?"

"Because she could be lost, Shiloh," Leah laughed at Shiloh's utter disregard for the other girl. "Not to mention, it's pouring rain." Shiloh raised an eyebrow, drawing one of her curtains aside and realizing just how awful the weather had gotten.

"She can take care of herself," Shiloh shrugged, trying not to become too concerned for Paisley. For some reason, she was starting to feel bad for the way she was treating the other girl. But Shiloh knew what Paisley had done to her, and she continued to tell herself that she hated her.

"That's debatable," Leah mumbled, leaning on the windowsill next to Shiloh. "Did Ryland tell you about last night?" Shiloh shook her head.

"Get your keys," Leah nodded towards the door. "I'll explain while we go look for her."

Shiloh groaned. But for some reason, she grabbed her keys from the nightstand and followed Leah into the living room. She figured it was the least she could after leaving Paisley in the rain in the first place.

The girls jogged through the parking lot and slid into Leah's car as fast as they could. "So what was Ryland supposed to tell me?" The green eyed girl started the car and pulled out of the lot.

"Go left," Leah instructed. "We'll circle around the back of the park." The smaller girl started intently out the window, thinking for a few moments. "I'm not really sure," Leah said honestly. "All I know is that when Paisley was getting changed, Ryland found glass in her feet."

"What?" Shiloh's eyes widened and she turned her head to make sure Leah wasn't kidding. "Glass?"

"Yup," Leah nodded once, popping the 'p.' "She had to clean it out and everything." Leah wiped the condensation off the passenger side window as Shiloh slowly circled around the back of the park. "The weird thing is, is that Ryland said it looked like Paisley put her shoes on *over* the glass."

"What the heck?" Shiloh shook her head, becoming more and more confused at the situation they'd been put in. "This is *so* weird."

Leah just nodded in agreement. "Well she's here now, and there's not much more we can do besides make sure she doesn't accidentally burn down the apartment."

"I don't see her," Shiloh said quietly. They'd just circled the whole park without a trace of Paisley. Both girls looked at each other and Leah motioned for Shiloh to get out of the car. The green eyed girl raised an eyebrow.

"Why me?"

"You're the one who left her out here in the first place," Leah send Shiloh an incriminating look. The smaller girl *did* have a point.

"She's not my responsibility," Shiloh argued. She crossed her arms and glared out the window. This was bothering her. She was starting to feel *bad* for Paisley. She would have never expected that to happen. "She probably deserves to be out in the rain. Or worse."

"You don't mean that, Shy," Leah reached over and placed a hand on her roommate's shoulder. "She's... different," the smaller girl thought for a moment. "You and I both know that she's not the same person she was a few years ago."

"Yeah," Shiloh rolled her eyes. "At least a few years ago she knew that we *weren't* her friends," she mumbled. But when Leah glared at her, Shiloh held her hands in the air, as if she were surrendering. "Fine, okay, fine, I'll go." She reached over the backseat, feeling around on the floor. Her eyebrows furrowed together. "Where's my umbrella?"

"I think Nessa borrowed it last week."

"Well *great*," Shiloh muttered, closing her eyes and taking a deep breath. "You owe me for this." Leah smiled teasingly at her, and Shiloh took one last look at the other girl before pushing the car door open and planting her feet on the wet asphalt.

It was pouring.

The rain was pounding against the car, sounding off like a chorus of drums marching down the street. She closed the car door quickly and brought her hands up to shield her eyes from the torrential downpour. Shiloh had never, in a million years, imagined she'd be doing something like *this* just to *help* Paisley Lowe. In fact, she probably thought she would be the one to leave the girl out in the pouring rain as revenge. But now, the tables had turned.

Leah gave her a thumbs up from inside the warmth of the car. Shiloh flicked her off in return, before pushing her wet hair out of her face and hopping up onto the sidewalk. She decided the best idea would be to go to the place she'd last seen Paisley. Just as she set foot on the asphalt pathway, a loud clap of thunder caused her to jump.

Shiloh told herself she was running because she wanted to get out of the rain as soon as possible. She couldn't possibly be running because she was worried, right? Shiloh shook the thought out of her brain and skidded to a stop by the bench where she'd left Paisley. She nearly fell over from the momentum, considering the ground was already slippery.

She looked around, finding no sign of the girl. "Paisley!?" she called, cupping her hands around her mouth to make her voice travel further. She listened for a few seconds, trying to pick out any responses in the pouring rain. After a few moments with no response, Shiloh began scanning the surrounding area.

Where could she have gone? Shiloh's stomach dropped when she thought of every possible thing that could have happened to the girl. Her eyes landed on a patch of brush that had been stomped down on recently.

"Paisley?!" she called again, pushing through the brush and through the very edge of the forest. The rain was so heavy that it continued to beat down through the leaves above her. She was already soaked from head to toe. Her hair was dripping down her back and the sides of her face, and now her boots were covered in a thin layer of mud from walking off into the woods.

She wiped her eyes, looking down at her hands which now were covered in black streaks from her ruined makeup. She used the sleeve of her sweater to rub the rest of the makeup off of her face, still listening intently for any signs of where Paisley had disappeared to.

Walking further into the woods, Shiloh craned her head in all directions to try and find the other girl. The rain showed no signs of stopping anytime soon. She could only laugh at the situation she'd gotten herself into.

She stopped walking when she noticed something white on the ground, sticking out against the dark dirt. Picking it up, she realized it was one of the daisies Paisley had picked earlier. A mixture of anger and worry bubbled in her stomach.

"Paisley?! Where are you?!" she called, holding onto the daisy and walking further into the woods. The brush began getting thicker and Shiloh glanced behind her to make sure she knew the way out.

A loud clap of thunder made her jump, and moments later she heard a whimper from nearby. That had to be Paisley.

"Paisley?" she spoke loudly, looking around quicker. A flash of white behind a tree caught her eye, and she jogged over to the area, realizing the flash of white belonged to a pair of white converse.

"Paisley?" She circled the tree and her suspicions were confirmed. The younger girl sat curled up in a ball, with her hands over her ears and her head buried in her knees. Shiloh had to remind herself that this was the girl who had made her life a living hell for three years.

"*Paisley*," she said louder than before, poking the girl's leg with her foot. Paisley's head shot up and a look of terror flashed across her face, but it was instantly replaced by a look of relief when she saw Shiloh standing in front of her.

Shiloh nearly fell backwards when Paisley jumped to her feet and wrapped her arms around Shiloh's neck. Paisley Lowe was hugging *her*? This was new.

"*Lolo,*" the smaller girl hummed.

"That's not my name," Shiloh said firmly, peeling the soaking wet girl off of her. "What are you doing here?"

Paisley tilted her head to the side in thought. A few moments later, she bent down and picked up the handful of daisies she'd picked. They were soaked, flopping over dead in Paisley's tight grip. "I killed them," she mumbled, shaking her head.

The smaller girl bent down and tried to stand one of the flowers back up, the way it had been before she picked it from the grass. It fell over on its side and she huffed. "Stupid, stupid, stupid," she muttered under her breath, tapping the side of her head with her fingers.

"There's nothing you can do about it," Shiloh raised an eyebrow after observing the girl's actions. The rain was beating down even harder now, but Paisley didn't seem to care. She continued trying to fix the flowers and grew increasingly more frustrated when she didn't get the outcome she wanted.

"Paisley," Shiloh huffed, grabbing the small girl's arm and pulling her up to her feet. Paisley instantly reeled back, rubbing her arm up and down.

"Ouch."

"You're fine," Shiloh shook her head and started walking in the direction from where she'd come from. "We're going back home, come on."

"Home?" Paisley's head perked up upon hearing Shiloh's words. She quickly gathered her flowers and hugged them to her chest. Shiloh grimaced, watching as Paisley smeared even more mud over one of Shiloh's favorite band shirts. But she bit her tongue, trying to keep herself from saying anything. She just continued walking.

"Home with my friends?" Paisley scrambled beside Shiloh, breathing heavily from trying to catch up.

"I'm not your friend," Shiloh muttered, picking up the pace. She was eager to get home and change out of her soaking wet clothes and muddy boots.

"But we had Chemistry together, so we are f—,"

"We're not friends!" Shiloh snapped, turning around and throwing her hands down at her sides. "I am *not* your friend, and you shouldn't expect me to be after all the shit you put me through! So just... *just stop talking,*" she muttered.

"Oh," Paisley said quietly, hanging her head down lower and trudging behind Shiloh as they walked. The rest of the walk was pretty quiet, except for Paisley mumbling *'stupid'* to herself every few seconds. Shiloh forced herself to ignore it.

They finally reached the edge of the woods and Paisley paused, looking around slowly. She found the spot where the daisies had once been and knelt down. "I am sorry, flowers," she said softly, placing each one of the daisies back down carefully. "Goodnight."

Shiloh stood a few feet away with her arms crossed, watching Paisley's actions. The green eyed girl forced herself to ignore the guilt that was currently washing over her. Paisley stood up slowly and turned back to Shiloh, keeping quiet like the green eyed girl had told her to.

Shiloh just took a deep breath and continued walking, sighing in relief when Leah's car came into view. Paisley hurried behind her, unsure of where they were going.

"Get in," Shiloh pointed to the back seat of the car. Paisley nodded and followed her instructions. Shiloh groaned when she realized just how dirty the car was going to get.

"Where was she?" Leah asked as soon as Shiloh sat down. The green eyed girl saw her reflection in the driver's side mirror and grimaced. She looked less than appealing, that's for sure.

"In the middle of the woods like an idiot," Shiloh huffed, not even bothering to look at the girl in the backseat.

"Stupid," Paisley mumbled from the backseat, reaffirming what Shiloh had said. Leah shot Shiloh a look before turning back to face Paisley.

"Are you hurt?" Leah asked, concerned. Paisley tilted her head to the side and held her hands up in front of her face, turning them back and forth.

"It is cold," was all the smaller girl said, hugging her hands around her torso. She looked down at her lap and shook her head, sending raindrops flying all over the back seat of the car. Shiloh glared at her through the rear view mirror.

She was mad. She was mad at Paisley for hurting her. She was mad at Paisley for coming back. She was mad at Paisley for changing, as if she didn't even recall what she'd done to hurt Shiloh.

But most importantly, she was growing more and more angry with herself for not hating the girl in the back seat of the car. Because *this* Paisley was nothing like the Paisley that she'd known in high school.

CHAPTER 4

"The apartment is warm, we'll be there soon," Leah tried to comfort the girl in the back of the car, unsure of what else to do. She and Shiloh exchanged glances and Shiloh sighed heavily. This was already adding up to be a long day. They turned into the parking lot of the apartment and Shiloh parked the car, not even bothering to wait for the other two girls.

She took the stairs, sighing once she made it to their floor. They'd accidentally left the apartment unlocked, so Shiloh slipped inside quickly, leaving her muddy boots by the door and heading straight to her bedroom.

The dark haired girl changed into a pair of sweatpants and one of her favorite t-shirts. She pulled her wet hair up into a messy bun and scrubbed her face raw until all of the makeup was gone. She took a few moments to look at herself in the mirror, rolling her eyes at her disheveled appearance before heading back downstairs.

Leah and Paisley were nowhere in sight, but Shiloh could tell they were home by the muddy footprints at the door. She told herself she didn't care about what they were doing and headed into the kitchen.

"*Noooo.*"

Shiloh lifted her head out of the refrigerator when she heard Paisley's voice whine from upstairs. As much as she wanted to go see what was wrong, she forced herself to ignore it and grabbed two slices of cheese from the drawer before closing the refrigerator.

There was rustling from upstairs, followed by the opening and closing of multiple doors, but Shiloh hummed softly to herself to try and drown out the noise. She set a pan on the stove and waited for it to heat up. Just as she had finished retrieving the bread from the pantry, she heard slow footsteps coming down the stairs.

"Hi," Paisley smiled, standing across the kitchen from Shiloh. The green eyed girl turned around. Her breath caught in her throat as soon as she saw the girl in front of her. Paisley was wearing another one of Shiloh's t-shirts, which came down to the middle of her thighs. She didn't have any pants on, or socks and shoes. Shiloh noticed the bandages on her feet, which she assumed Leah had changed.

The smaller girl's hair was wet, and pulled up in a sad attempt at a messy bun. There were still a few loose stands of dark hair hanging down and framing her face. She somehow made it look cute. *Cute.* Shiloh cursed herself for using that word.

Before Shiloh could say anything, Leah came running down the stairs with a pair of Shiloh's pajama pants in her hands. "You forgot these," she handed them to Paisley, who studied them for a few moments. Leah saw the questioning look Shiloh was giving her and bit her lip. "She insisted on wearing your clothes, I don't know," Leah shrugged.

"Oh," Shiloh mumbled. Paisley pulled on the pants and patted the soft material happily. "What took so long?" The green eyed girl asked, trying to ignore the feeling that was arising in her stomach from seeing Paisley in her clothing.

"Well I discovered that she can shower on her own," Leah nodded once and motioned to Paisley, who was still petting the fuzzy material of her pajama pants. "Which is a good thing, I think," she bit her lip and studied Shiloh's face.

"Thank god for that," Shiloh shook her head. She was still extremely confused by everything that had happened in the past two days. A clattering noise snapped her out of her thoughts and both she and Leah whipped their heads around. Paisley stood next to the stove, with the overturned pan now on the floor.

"Hot," Paisley nodded once and pointed to the pan. Leah and Shiloh exchanged glances.

"Well, have fun with that," Leah winked at Shiloh. "This girl's got homework to catch up on." Shiloh glared at her, but Leah disappeared up the stairs before she could respond.

Shiloh groaned and walked over to Paisley. "Of course it's hot," she rolled her eyes and grabbed the pan by the handle. Once she set it back on the stove, she sprayed the surface with cooking spray and made sure the oven was still on. "Don't touch it," she warned Paisley, pointing to the stove.

Paisley nodded once. Shiloh hopped up to sit on the island and wait until the pan was hot enough. She started picking at a loose string at the bottom of her shirt. A hissing noise caused her to look up quickly.

"No!" she huffed, hopping off the counter and grabbing the container of cooking spray from Paisley's hand. She looked at the counter, which now had a shiny coat of grease over it. "Oh my god," she groaned, grabbing a rag and wetting it so she could clean the counter.

"It does not smell," Paisley noted, pointing to the container in Shiloh's hand. The green eyed girl put the spray back in the cabinet and shook her head.

"It's not air freshener. It's cooking spray," she scrubbed the counter where Paisley had sprayed the oil. Paisley walked over next to Shiloh and observed what she was doing.

"Cooking spray," Paisley repeated. Shiloh ignored her and tossed the rag into the sink once she deemed the counter clean enough. The dark haired girl grabbed two slices of bread and laid them on the pan, taking the spatula out of the drawer.

"What are you making?" Paisley followed Shiloh over to the stove and stood on her tiptoes to peer over her shoulder. Once she saw it was food, she clapped her hands excitedly. "I am hungry."

"I wasn't making you a—," Shiloh paused when she turned around and saw the look of excitement on the smaller girl's face. She sighed in defeat, grabbing two more slices from the bag and positioning them on the pan. She wondered when the last time Paisley had eaten was. "Do you want something to drink?" she asked slowly.

Paisley nodded. "Yellow?"

"Yellow?" Shiloh raised an eyebrow and walked over to the refrigerator. She tried to put herself in Paisley's mind, and her eyes landed on the half full jug of lemonade in the back of one of the shelves. "This?"

Paisley nodded furiously and Shiloh laughed softly, somewhat proud of herself for knowing what the girl had been referring to. She grabbed a glass from the pantry, but then glanced back at Paisley and switched the glass for a plastic cup. Once she poured the lemonade, she handed the cup to Paisley and put the jug back in the fridge.

Paisley took a sip from the cup and giggled excitedly. She leaned against the counter and continued to watch as Shiloh unwrapped the slices of cheese and laid them on top of the bread. "What are you making?"

"Grilled cheese," Shiloh responded, flipping the plain slices onto the ones with cheese, and then flipping the entire sandwich. Paisley padded over and watched, seemingly amazed by what Shiloh had just done.

"Can I try?"

Shiloh shook her head. "Maybe another time," she shrugged and pressed down on the sandwiches with the back of the spatula.

"I want to do something," Paisley leaned against the island as Shiloh turned off the stove. Shiloh turned to her and thought for a moment.

"See that door? Can you get me two paper plates from behind it?" Shiloh pointed to the pantry, and Paisley nodded. She tiptoed over to the doors, and Shiloh noticed how she wasn't putting weight on her bandages.

Paisley opened the pantry and studied the shelves. When she finally found the paper plates, she clapped her hands excitedly and grabbed the entire stack to bring to Shiloh. The green eyed girl couldn't help but laugh when Paisley handed her all of the paper plates. She grabbed two off the top and handed them back to the girl.

"Can you go put those back?" Shiloh pointed to the pantry. Paisley nodded once more and shoved the plates onto the top shelf, knocking over a few things but closing the doors of the pantry before they could fall out.

"Good job," Shiloh raised an eyebrow. She cut the sandwiches into fourths and placed one on each plate. "This one's yours," she nodded, handing Paisley one of the plates. The small girl took it happily and walked over to the living room, sitting in the middle of the floor.

Shiloh had to stop herself from making a comment about what the couches were meant for. She sat on the chair furthest from Paisley and held her plate in her lap.

"Fork," Paisley noted, pointing at the untouched food on her plate and wiggling her fingers, signifying she needed something in her hand.

"You don't need a fork," Shiloh held up her hand to show Paisley that she could pick up her food.

"Fork," Paisley shook her head and clasped her hands together. Shiloh sighed, setting her plate down and getting up to grab a fork from the kitchen. Once the younger girl had her fork, she stabbed a piece of the sandwich and held it up in front of her face.

Shiloh sat back down, watching Paisley study her food. Moments later, Paisley took a bite off of the fork and smiled widely while she chewed her food.

"Grilled cheese," she nodded once she swallowed, twirling the fork around in her hands. "You made it?"

"Yup," Shiloh nodded, already having taken a few bites of her food. She glanced at the staircase, wondering how long she would have to 'babysit' Paisley for. She needed to get back into her room, lock the door, and forget about all of this. She was supposed to hate Paisley, not make her grilled cheese sandwiches and spend time with her.

"My savior," Paisley hummed, taking another bite of the food. Shiloh raised an eyebrow at her words but decided not to question her any further. All she had to do was survive until Leah came downstairs, and then she could go back to her room. Back to hating Paisley.

The thing that scared Shiloh, though, was that she hated the *old* Paisley. The new Paisley sitting in front of her was a little harder to hate. Shiloh hated to admit it, but she found her endearing.

When Shiloh looked back up, Paisley's plate was empty. "Are you done?" she asked, wondering how she could've finished eating that quickly. Something caught her attention out of the corner of her eye, and she stood up, lifting the magazine from the coffee table and revealing the last few pieces of the sandwich.

"Why'd you hide it?" Shiloh asked. She grabbed Paisley's plate and scooped the leftover food onto it, walking into the kitchen and throwing it away. When she came back, Paisley was hanging her head down and fiddling with her hands in her lap. "What?" Shiloh asked, growing confused.

"I was full," Paisley finally looked up. She looked...scared. Shiloh didn't like it.

"That's okay," Shiloh shrugged. "You don't have to hide what you don't eat. You just throw it away. Or you could always keep it for leftovers," she tried to explain. Paisley tilted her head to the side.

"Promise?"

Shiloh was becoming more and more intrigued by this girl as time went on. She didn't like where this was going. Paisley looked at her expectantly, holding up her hand and sticking out her pinky finger. Sighing, Shiloh gave in and interlocked their fingers.

"Promise."

Paisley giggled excitedly, and then next thing Shiloh knew, a kiss was pressed to the back of her hand. Shiloh clasped her hands together and gave Paisley a slow nod. Footsteps caused both girls to turn around.

"Leah!" Paisley grabbed onto Shiloh and used her arm to pull herself up to her feet. Shiloh raised an eyebrow as Paisley hurried over to give Leah a hug. Even Leah looked surprised. "Shiloh grilled me a cheese," Paisley smiled and pointed at Shiloh, who stood frozen in the living room.

"She did?" Leah laughed, raising an eyebrow at Shiloh. "I didn't know she had a heart," the oldest girl teased. Shiloh rolled her eyes.

"Oh, she does," Paisley nodded furiously, turning to look at Shiloh. "I have seen it."

Shiloh couldn't find her words, and Leah sent her a questioning look. All Shiloh could do was shrug. What did Paisley mean? She wouldn't allow herself to ask, and instead she got up, threw her trash away, and dismissed herself upstairs without another word.

The moment her bedroom door shut, she fell face first into her pillow and groaned. She'd barely survived one day with Paisley, how was she supposed to make it through any more? Who knew how long Paisley would be staying with them? She cursed herself for being this sensitive.

Truth is, Shiloh was terrified. She was terrified of allowing Paisley to warm up to her, just to be hurt. Who knew why Paisley had shown up at their door? Maybe this was all some sort of sick joke.

Shiloh rolled onto her back, yawning and wiping her eyes. She was still exhausted, but she knew she'd just be fooling herself if she tried to fall asleep this early. Instead, she flopped her arm over and grabbed her book from her nightstand. She found her spot in *Looking for Alaska*, and continued reading from where she'd left off.

Shiloh always put her all into everything. She either loved something, or she hated something. She was extremely outgoing, or she was painstakingly shy. There was no inbetween. The word was black and white for her, there were no grays. If she did something, she did it with 100% of her being.

Which is why she got so invested in her book that she ignored the rumbling in her stomach and read straight through dinner. Ryland and Vanessa had come home from their classes bearing a brown paper bag full of takeout food. Her other roommates knew better than to bother her, though. They always gave Shiloh the space she needed, which she was thankful for.

Meanwhile, Paisley sat on her spot on the floor downstairs while the other three girls watched her curiously. Paisley poked a piece of rice with her fork, growing frustrated when she couldn't pick it up.

"Paisley, you have to scoop it," Ryland walked over and sat down next to her with her own plate. She showed Paisley how she used her fork, and Paisley quickly copied her. She clapped her hands excitedly when it worked.

Ryland, Leah, and Vanessa looked at one another. They all had millions of questions they wished they had answers for. Vanessa was the first to speak up.

"Paisley, why did you want to come see us?" Vanessa asked, setting her empty plate down on the coffee table and leaning forward in her chair.

Paisley looked up when she heard her name, pursing her lips when she heard the girl's question. "I..." she brought her fingers up and drummed them on her bottom lip in thought. "I think I wanted to see my friends."

"Are we your friends?" Ryland asked, trying to figure out who Paisley was referring to.

The small girl's face suddenly stilled, as if she were surprised by this question. "Do you want to be?" she asked, forgetting about her food and crawling over so she could sit in front of Ryland. "We had Chemistry together, I remember."

Ryland and Vanessa looked at one another. Leah sat down on the arm of the couch, trying to piece together everything Paisley was saying. She came up empty-handed each time.

"I want you to be my friends," Paisley continued, pointing to each one of them individually and then clasping her hands back together. "Are you?"

All three girls exchanged glances before Leah smiled and nodded softly, turning back to Paisley. "Of course we are." Ryland and Vanessa nodded in agreement. Even though they were still somewhat wary, they all knew that this Paisley was a completely changed person compared to the girl they knew in high school.

Paisley's face lit up and she clapped her hands together excitedly. But her smile faltered for a moment and then her shoulders slowly slumped down. "Is Lolo?" she asked, tilting her head to the side in question.

"Lolo?" all three girls asked at the same time. Paisley looked at them as if they'd posed a completely ridiculous question.

"Yes. Lolo," she nodded once and then pointed to the stairs. "The girl with the ocean eyes." Paisley pointed to her eyes and then clasped her hands together.

"Her name is Shiloh," Ryland quickly corrected her. Paisley pursed her lips in thought.

"Yes, Lolo," Paisley nodded once. "Is she my friend?"

All three roommates looked at each other and raised their eyebrows.

"I'm so lost" Ryland mouthed. The other two girls nodded and Leah just shrugged and turned back to Paisley.

"I don't know," she glanced in the direction of Shiloh's room and back down to the younger girl. "Only she knows that."

"I have to ask her then," Paisley nodded once and scrambled to her feet. Ryland and Vanessa both grabbed the girl before she could go up the stairs. Paisley tilted her head to the side in confusion. "What?"

"She's... busy," Leah quickly butted in. The other two girls nodded and Paisley furrowed her eyebrows together.

"Oh," she nodded slowly. "What do I do now?"

Ryland had an idea, and she grabbed the TV remote from the coffee table. She chose the first show she could find, which just so happened to be *Friends*. Vanessa raised an eyebrow at her and Ryland shrugged.

Paisley instantly tilted her head to the side, walking over to the TV and pressing her palm against the screen. "I like this show," she nodded once and sat down directly in front of the television.

"See?" Ryland laughed, smirking at her roommates. Vanessa shrugged and grabbed her dance bag from the door.

"That was easier than I expected," the dark skinned girl laughed, slipping her bag over her shoulder. "I've got some sleep to catch up on, I'll see you in the morning." Vanessa smiled at both of her roommates before jogging up the staircase.

Ryland and Leah both looked at each other, and then back to Paisley. The small girl was immersed in the show, giggling quietly to herself at the funny moments.

"Go on," Ryland nodded to Leah. "I'll stay down here until she gets tired." Leah nodded thankfully, shooting Ryland a grateful smile and disappearing upstairs after Vanessa.

"Looks like it's just me and you now," the light haired girl sighed and plopped back down on the couch. Paisley didn't respond, she was too interested in the television. Yawning, Ryland pulled her feet up underneath her and propped a pillow under her elbow. Both girls watched in silence, Paisley would giggle and clap her hands occasionally. Part of Ryland wondered if she even knew half of what was going on in the show.

CHAPTER 5

When the first episode was over, Paisley begged to watch another. And another. Ryland was beginning to lose track of the time.

"Please? More," Paisley pointed to the TV and nodded softly. "Yes, more."

Ryland shrugged and chose the next episode, not seeing the harm in watching one more before they went to bed. She'd almost drifted off to sleep when she felt two hands shaking her awake.

"More," Paisley whispered softly, pointing to the TV. Ryland wiped her eyes and checked the time on her phone, groaning when she realized they'd stayed up later than she had planned. She sat up and shook her head, turning the TV off with the remote next to her. Paisley tilted her head to the side.

"It's time for bed," Ryland yawned and stood up, walking over to the stairs. Paisley followed slowly, walking only on her tiptoes.

"Sleep?" Paisley inquired once they reached the top of the stairs. Ryland nodded and opened her bedroom door. Paisley stood hesitantly in the hallway.

"Cold," Paisley shook her head.

Ryland sighed and grabbed Paisley's arm, pulling her into the bedroom to avoid waking anyone up. "I have warmer clothes you can wear," she said, walking over to her dresser and searching through her drawers. "Here," she handed the smaller girl a long sleeved shirt.

Paisley looked at the shirt in her hands, opening her mouth to say something but noticing the annoyed look on Ryland's face. She quickly grew quiet.

"Remember, *this* is your side of the bed," Ryland mumbled, pointing to the side where Paisley had slept. The light haired girl didn't wait for a response before crawling under the covers and turning away from Paisley.

Paisley stood quietly, holding the shirt in her hands. She slowly slipped out of the t-shirt of Shiloh's she had on and tugged on Ryland's shirt. Frowning, she realized it didn't smell the same as Shiloh's. So instead, Paisley hugged Shiloh's t-shirt to her chest and padded over to the bed.

"Ry?" she whispered, standing at the edge of the bed and looking at the other girl. There was no response, Ryland had already fallen asleep. Paisley sighed, hugging the shirt even tighter to her chest and wiggling under the covers. She bit her lip, not happy that Ryland had put a pillow in the middle of the bed to separate them.

With a soft sigh, Paisley curled up into a ball and brought the shirt up to rest in the crook of her neck, inhaling the scent she'd already become so comfortable with. She lay for a while in silence, staring blankly at the darkness in front of her. After entertaining herself with her thoughts for what felt like hours, her eyelids grew heavy and slowly fluttered shut.

Sleep had just overtaken the small girl when suddenly her breathing intensified. Memories came back in flashes of white and red, and a bead of sweat dripped down from her brow. Paisley gasped for air, waking herself up. Her heart was beating erratically and she sat up quickly, hugging Shiloh's shirt underneath her chin and scanning the room anxiously.

Every shadow, every small beam of light suddenly adopted the possibility of danger. Paisley shook her head and squeezed her eyes shut. She didn't like this. The small girl wiped frantically at the sweat on her forehead, trying to catch the breath she didn't know she'd lost.

Cautiously, she looked over at the girl in the bed next to her. Ryland was fast asleep. Paisley considered waking her, but she knew in just the next room over, there was someone who she'd rather be with. So quietly, she held Shiloh's t-shirt tightly to her chest and tip toed quickly to the door, checking around her once more for anything that could be harmful. She peered out in the hallway to make sure it was safe before slipping out of Ryland's room.

Shiloh hadn't been able to sleep that night. She was too busy reliving her high school days, trying to make a list of everything Paisley had ever done to hurt her. The only thing Paisley had done directly, though, was read her texts. The rest of Paisley's offenses had just been caused by her cheerleader friends. This confused Shiloh even more.

Not to mention, the Paisley she knew in high school was completely different than the Paisley who had shown up at their apartment two days ago. Dare she say it, Shiloh wanted to get to know the *new* Paisley. She continued to push the thought to the back of her mind, cursing herself for even thinking of being nice to the girl.

She'd been staring at her ceiling for over an hour when a flicker of light brought her out of her thoughts. She sat up quickly, studying the crack in the door. "Wha...?" she yawned, running a hand through her messy hair and narrowing her eyes to try and see who was there.

The door creaked open slightly and a small figure entered the room. She should've known. Paisley.

"What do you want?" Shiloh sighed. When she didn't get a response, she rolled over on her side and reached to turn on the small lamp next to her bed. Her heart jumped when she turned back over and could finally see the smaller girl.

Paisley's hair was still in the same bun from earlier that day, but half of it was falling out on one side of her face. Small pieces of hair were sticking to her forehead, which was glistening with a thin layer of sweat. The small girl was visibly upset, Shiloh could tell by the pained look in her eyes and the irregular speed of her breathing.

"What's wrong?" Shiloh asked, tilting her head to the side and sitting up in her bed. Paisley tilted her head the same way Shiloh had, studying the green eyed girl in the dim light of the bedroom.

"Lolo?" Paisley whispered, taking the tiniest of steps forward and hugging the t-shirt close to her chest.

Shiloh chose to ignore the nickname the girl had given her. It was actually kind of cute. *Kind of.* But barely. In all honestly, Shiloh wished she could hate it, but she couldn't. The green eyed girl sighed and nodded. "Yeah?"

Paisley took a deep breath and glanced nervously around the room, as if she were afraid of someone watching them. "Are you my friend?" There was a pleading tone in her voice, and Shiloh could tell Paisley was on the verge of some sort of breakdown.

Letting her hands drop to her sides in defeat, Shiloh sighed heavily. "Yes, I'm your friend," she nodded slowly, suddenly feeling glad that she'd said those words. Paisley's face lit up for a second, but she quickly remembered why she was there and her expression quickly faltered.

"Promise?" Paisley mumbled, her voice barely a whisper. Her anxiousness was killing Shiloh, and the green eyed girl quickly held out her pinky in front of Paisley.

"Promise," she nodded once. Paisley sighed in relief, slowly reaching out and interlocking their pinkies. Shiloh felt how warm Paisley's hands were and only grew more concerned.

"Now what's wrong?" she asked, adopting a softer tone and patting the spot on the bed next to her.

Paisley looked surprised by Shiloh's sudden change in character, but if she was, the smaller girl didn't question it. She practically jumped on the bed next to Shiloh, landing on her knees and quickly tucking her feet underneath her. She glanced around the room once more.

The small girl leaned in close to Shiloh, as if she were telling her a secret. "There are bad things here," she whispered, before drawing her face away from Shiloh and quickly scanning the room to see if anyone had heard them.

"Bad things?" Shiloh questioned, growing even more concerned than she already was. Paisley took her bottom lip in-between her teeth and nodded quickly. "What bad things?"

Paisley shook her head violently and squeezed her eyes shut, practically making the entire bed shake. Shiloh quickly reached out and grabbed the girl's shoulders to try and still her. Paisley's eyes shot open and she almost flinched backwards, but she realized who the hands belonged to and remained still.

"There's no bad things here," Shiloh motioned around the room. "See? It's just my bedroom. I sleep in here every night." Paisley took a deep breath. Shiloh slowly drew her hands back from Paisley's shoulders and the smaller girl looked around nervously.

"There are bad things," Paisley repeated herself. She hugged the shirt tighter to her chest. Shiloh sighed and thought for a moment, trying to figure out how to calm Paisley down.

"Here," Shiloh scooted back on the bed and lifted her comforter. "It's a fort. We'll be safe under here, c'mon," she slid under the covers and motioned for Paisley to do the same. Confused but curious, Paisley crawled next to Shiloh. The green eyed girl then pulled the covers over both of their heads, using her knees to keep the blankets from smothering them.

Paisley instantly whimpered when the darkness overtook them and Shiloh quickly fished around in the sheets to grab her phone. Moments later, the phone's flashlight was turned on and she set the device between them to give them light.

"We're safe under here," Shiloh said softly. Paisley lay on her back next to Shiloh, still breathing heavily. "Why did you come in here?"

"Bad things," Paisley mumbled, pointing to her head and tapping it gently.

"Bad things in your head?" Shiloh asked, slowly catching on to what Paisley was trying to explain to her. The small girl nodded quickly, confirming Shiloh's suspicions.

"Did you have a nightmare?" the green eyed girl inquired. Paisley tilted her head to the side. "Did you see bad things in your sleep?" Shiloh rephrased her question. This earned a slow nod from Paisley, and Shiloh noticed the smaller girl's bottom lip was trembling.

"Hey, hey, don't cry," Shiloh shook her head and sat up, pushing the blankets off of them. "Everyone sees bad things in their sleep sometimes, even me."

"Even Lolo?" Paisley asked, sitting up slowly next to Shiloh.

The green eyed girl sighed and nodded. "They're called nightmares," Shiloh explained. "Sometimes they can be really scary, but want to know a secret?"

Paisley nodded slowly.

"They can't hurt you," Shiloh gave the girl a soft smile, trying to reassure her that she was safe. "They're only in your head," she reached up and tapped on Paisley's forehead like the girl had done before.

"Promise?" Paisley whispered, holding out her pinky finger. Shiloh nodded softly and interlocked their fingers, already realizing she was getting too close to this girl. But she was met with the overwhelming need to protect her.

Paisley was still breathing heavily, and Shiloh watched as she tugged at the sleeves of her shirt.

"Are you hot?" Shiloh asked, motioning to the heavy shirt of Ryland's that Paisley had on. The brown eyed girl nodded, looking at Shiloh pleadingly.

"And I'm guessing you want to wear one of my shirts?" Shiloh raised an eyebrow and sighed, knowing what Paisley's answer would be. The smaller girl smiled instantly and nodded.

Shiloh laughed. She *laughed*, surprisingly. Honestly, the older girl was just relieved that she'd somehow managed to calm Paisley down. She slid out from under the covers and opened the first drawer of her dresser where she kept her t-shirts. Grabbing a black shirt with the name of her college printed on it, she tossed it to Paisley. Luckily, the smaller girl didn't seem to have a problem catching it.

Paisley stood up, peeling off her own shirt. Shiloh turned around and nearly gasped. She hadn't expected Paisley to change in her room. But more importantly, she hadn't expected what was *under* the shirt Paisley had been wearing.

"What happened?" she asked, crossing the room and stopping Paisley before she could pull the t-shirt on over her head. Her torso was covered in bruises. Some dark purple, some light green, some large, some small. There was no pattern, they were just randomly splurged all over her body. Shiloh had to stop herself from reaching out to touch them, to make sure she wasn't hallucinating.

"Ouch," Paisley whispered, hanging her head down. She looked almost ashamed.

Shiloh bit her lip. She knew better than to push Paisley on any explanations tonight. They were both exhausted. "It's okay," Shiloh said softly, shaking her head. She took the shirt from Paisley's hands and helped the smaller girl slip it on over her head. Paisley looked down at the shirt and then smiled brightly up at Shiloh.

"We've got to get you back to bed," Shiloh nodded, turning towards her door. She paused when she didn't hear Paisley following her back to Ryland's room, and turned around to find the smaller girl already sitting happily on her bed. Sighing in defeat, Shiloh pulled her door closed behind her and walked over to the bed.

"Your hair is a mess," she noted, giving in to the temptation and reaching forwards to brush the matted hair out of Paisley's face. Brown eyes looked up at her contently. Shiloh just sighed and grabbed her brush from her nightstand. "I'll braid it for you."

Paisley didn't respond, so Shiloh just crawled onto the bed behind the girl and reached up to let the hair fall from the rest of the bun. Long, dark waves cascaded down her shoulders. In high school, Shiloh remembered that Paisley had always worn her hair up in a high ponytail, along with a bow that matched their school's colors.

As soon as Shiloh ran a brush through Paisley's hair, she realized just how knotted it was. Leah had said that Paisley knew how to shower, but she obviously didn't know how to get the tangles out of her hair.

"Ouch," Paisley mumbled as Shiloh began to slowly work the knots out from each layer of her hair. "Ouch, ouch," she huffed.

"I'm almost done," Shiloh said quietly. She tugged gently at the brush, separating the small hairs and moving onto the next knot. Paisley had more hair that she appeared to have.

Luckily, Paisley sat quietly while Shiloh finished getting the knots out of her hair. Once she was done, Shiloh realized just how much better Paisley's hair looked. It was wavy and smooth, and it lay much more flat against her head now that the tangles were gone.

"Now I just have to braid it," Shiloh explained. She slowly ran her fingers through Paisley's hair a few times, getting a feel for the texture. It smelled like her shampoo, which she assumed Paisley had used when she was showering earlier. She grabbed a section of hair at the top of Paisley's head and began a fishtail braid that extended down the back of her head and curved to the side. Braiding soothed her, and she didn't even realize she had been humming.

"Music," Paisley noted, turning to look at Shiloh. The green eyed girl had to lean forward to keep her hold on the unfinished braid, and she used her other hand to turn Paisley's head back around.

"I was humming, yeah," Shiloh shrugged, quickly finishing off the braid and securing it with a hair tie. "All done," she swept the braid over Paisley's shoulder so the girl could see.

"Pretty?" Paisley asked, turning back around to look at Shiloh. The green eyed girl nodded. Paisley yawned, still retaining the soft smile on her face.

"Tired?" Shiloh raised an eyebrow. Paisley bit her lip hesitantly, and Shiloh tilted her head to the side. "What?"

"Scared," Paisley mumbled.

Shiloh sighed and pointed to the blankets. "That's our fort, remember? Nothing can hurt you under there. Plus, remember what I told you? Dreams aren't real. I promised."

Paisley thought for a moment before nodding, remembering what Shiloh had told her. She quickly shimmied under the covers, and Shiloh sighed heavily. What had she gotten herself into?

Too tired to try and fight with herself, Shiloh crawled over to the other side of the bed and pulled the covers over both of them. Paisley scooted closer to Shiloh, and the green eyed girl noticed. It was as if the smaller girl wanted to get as close as she could to Shiloh without touching her. Shiloh knew arguing wouldn't do any good.

Her phone buzzed and brought her out of her thoughts. She glanced at Paisley, who hadn't noticed.

Shiloh grabbed her phone and narrowed her eyes to read the message on her screen.

```
[1:23 - Ryland] Have any of you guys
seen Paisley? She's not in bed.
```

Shiloh sighed, reading the message from Ryland in the group chat. She was going to have a lot of explaining to do. Her fingers tapped slowly at the keyboard, glancing over at the small girl in bed beside her.

```
[1:24 - Shiloh] I've got her.
```

She could only imagine Ryland's reaction when she got her text. Her roommate had already been on her all week about her odd relationship with Paisley.

```
[1:24 - Ryland] You're kidding me,
right?
```

Shiloh sighed, biting her lip and trying to think of a reply. Her phone buzzed before she could, though.

```
[1:25 - Vanessa] Ryland, may I remind
you that we have class in less than 7
hours? Get your ass in bed. We can
```

talk about Paisley's game of musical
beds tomorrow.

Shiloh laughed softly to herself, thankful for
Vanessa and her tendency to be a light sleeper. She set
her phone next to her pillow and rolled onto her back,
closing her eyes and trying to fall asleep. Shiloh
eventually dozed off after reliving the entire day in her
head, until she finally let sleep overtake her.

Paisley, on the other hand, opened her eyes
every few minutes to check and see if Shiloh was still
awake. Once she was assured that the older girl was
asleep and wouldn't try to sneak out on her, Paisley
closed her eyes for good. She fell asleep quickly, glad
that Shiloh didn't make a pillow barrier between them
like Ryland had done.

C H A P T E R 6

Shiloh awoke the next morning to an empty bed. It took her a few seconds to remember the events of the night before, and when she did, she sat up quickly and scanned the room. Paisley was nowhere in sight.

"Paisley?" she called, standing up and walking over to the door of her room. There was a rustling noise from behind her as soon as she went to open the door. Pausing for a moment, Shiloh turned around slowly, following the source of the noise and ending up in front of her closet. Cautiously, she opened the closet door, widening her eyes when she saw Paisley.

"What are you doing?!" Shiloh choked. She bent down and snatched her sketchbook out of Paisley's hands, glaring at the smaller girl. "Where did you get this?"

"I found it," Paisley chirped, climbing to her feet and smiling widely. Shiloh's eyebrows furrowed when she saw the streaks of marker that stained Paisley's hands. Her grip on the sketchbook tightened.

"It's *mine*," Shiloh huffed. She walked back over to the bed, sitting down and hesitantly opening to the first page. Her anger boiled when she realized that

Paisley had covered every single one of her sketches with meaningless scribbles. Hours upon hours of hard work were now rendered useless.

"What the hell were you thinking?!" Shiloh yelled, standing up and throwing her sketchbook across the room. It hit the wall, scattering her papers all over the floor. Paisley instantly flinched and covered her ears.

"Do you know how much time I spent on these?" Shiloh continued, crossing her arms and glaring at Paisley from across the room.

"They are pretty," Paisley nodded, walking over and picking up one of the drawings from where Shiloh had thrown them.

"They *were* pretty, Paisley, until you ruined them," Shiloh spat. "Just like the flowers. What did I tell you about leaving pretty things alone?"

Paisley just stared at her blankly for a few moments before holding up the drawing and walking over to Shiloh, extending it for her to see. Shiloh groaned and pushed the drawing out of her face.

Confused, Paisley tilted her head to the side. "Lolo?"

"That's not my name," Shiloh's voice was low in the back of her throat. "I don't want to talk to you, *get out* of my room," she growled, pointing in the direction of her door.

Paisley took a slow step backwards, still holding onto the drawing. "I am sorry," she held the paper up and looked at Shiloh pleadingly.

"I don't care!" Shiloh snapped, grabbing Paisley by the shoulders and shoving her into the hallway. "Leave me alone," she warned, slamming the door in the smaller girl's face and making sure to lock it. She waited until she heard footsteps walking away from her room before collapsing back onto her bed and groaning.

Shiloh's sketchbook was her prized possession. She never let anyone lay a finger on it, let alone open and draw in it. Months and months of hard work were now useless. The green eyed girl sat up and eyed the collection of papers scattered along the floor. She should've known better than letting Paisley into her room.

With a frustrated sigh, Shiloh dragged herself out of bed and began collecting all the papers that had spilled out of the sketchbook. It all appeared to be just meaningless scribbles to her. She began sifting through all of the pages, making sure Paisley hadn't spared one or two of her sketches.

Of course, she hadn't. Every page had marker scribbled over it. One drawing in particular caught her attention, though. Her half-finished daises from yesterday. It appeared as if Paisley had tried to finish drawing them, adding the flowers atop the stems that Shiloh had sketched in pencil. Shiloh closed her eyes and sighed, placing the drawings back into her sketchbook and shoving it into her backpack.

Shiloh ended up falling asleep once more on the end of her bed. She was only asleep for a few minutes, though, before Ryland knocked on the door.

"Where's Paisley?" the light haired girl called through the door. Shiloh yawned, wiping her eyes and walking over to unlock the door. Ryland stood on the other side, a look of concern on her face when she realized Paisley wasn't in the bedroom with Shiloh. "I thought you said she was with you?"

"She *was*," Shiloh shrugged. "Until she trashed my sketchbook, then I yelled at her and made her leave."

Ryland's face contorted through a multitude of emotions. She sympathized with Shiloh, knowing what Paisley had done to her. But at the same time, she was concerned for Paisley, and a bit shocked that Shiloh would just allow the smaller girl to wander off.

"Well, *great*," Ryland threw her hands in the air. "We've lost her for the second time in two days." The younger girl brought her palm to her forehead and sighed in frustration.

"She's not our responsibility," Shiloh muttered, leaning against the doorframe. Ryland lifted her head and glared at the other girl.

"Look, Shy," she sighed. "I know you're still mad at her for what she did... I am too," Ryland glanced at the floor and then back to Shiloh. "But something's changed, and I don't want her to wander off on her own and get hurt, or worse. You've at least got to admit that *this* Paisley is a hell of a lot different than the girl we knew in high school."

Shiloh rolled her eyes and shrugged. "Yeah, whatever." She went to close her door once more, but Ryland stuck her foot out to prevent Shiloh from doing so.

"You need to find her," the light haired girl said firmly.

Shiloh opened her mouth to protest but Ryland stared her down with a look of finality. Groaning, Shiloh turned on her heel and grabbed one of her hoodies from her dresser. She tugged it over her head while retrieving her keys from the nightstand.

"Can't we just drop her off at the pound or something?" Shiloh muttered, slipping past Ryland and down the stairs.

"You don't mean that," Ryland called after her, and Shiloh rolled her eyes, but remained silent because she knew the other girl was right. Ryland followed her down the stairs, watching to make sure Shiloh actually left the apartment.

"I don't even know where to look!" Shiloh huffed, shaking her head in frustration. "For all I know she could be wandering around in the middle of traffic."

"You better hurry up then," Ryland warned, pointing to the door. Sighing, Shiloh just nodded and slipped out of the door. The thought of Paisley being lost in the city was starting to scare her more than she was willing to admit.

She decided to take the stairs, hoping they'd get her to her car faster. Jogging out of the building, she scanned the area around the apartment building for any signs of where Paisley had gone. There was a construction worker sitting on a bench outside the building, and she approached him quickly.

"Have you seen a girl about my height, braided hair, in her pajamas?" she asked, biting her lip nervously. The cars whizzed past on the street and she started becoming more and more concerned.

"A while ago, yeah," he motioned down in the street in the opposite direction of the park. Shiloh nodded quickly in thanks, not saying another word before jogging over to her car and sliding into the driver's seat. Moments later, she was driving quickly in the direction the man had shown her.

She drove for a few minutes or so without any signs of Paisley. Just as she was about to turn back around, a flash of black caught her eye against the grass. She quickly pulled her car over, looking both ways and crossing the road.

Paisley was sitting cross legged in the median of the busy street, surrounded by only a few feet of grass on each side. Shiloh shivered, wondering how Paisley had managed to make it across the street safely.

"Paisley? What the hell are you doing?" Shiloh snapped, keeping an eye out for cars once she reached the median. Paisley whipped her head around, tilting her head to the side when she saw Shiloh. She didn't smile widely like she usually did, though, and Shiloh tried to act like it didn't bother her as much as it had.

Paisley stared at Shiloh for a few seconds but didn't say anything, instead she just turned back to what she was looking at. Shiloh furrowed her eyebrows and circled around in front of the girl, and Paisley quickly held her hand out to make Shiloh back up.

"Careful," she mumbled, making sure Shiloh wouldn't step forwards. The green eyed girl looked down at the ground, realizing what Paisley was looking at. Two tulips had grown through the small patch of grass in the median.

"What are you doing?" Shiloh repeated, crossing her arms and trying to be intimidating. Paisley glanced up at her and then back down to the flowers.

"What you told me to do," Paisley pointed to the flowers. "I am looking at pretty things, and not killing them." She reached out and patted the flowers gently, with a look of concern on her face.

"That's not what I meant," Shiloh sighed, giving in and sitting down across from Paisley.

"Then what did you mean?" Paisley asked. She tilted her head to the side and looked up at Shiloh. "I made you yell," she added, biting her lip. Shiloh grew confused when she saw fear flicker in her eyes.

"I just don't like it when people touch my drawings," Shiloh nodded. "I meant sometimes you just have to admire pretty things from a distance, instead of trying to keep them. Love isn't about possession, it's about appreciation."

Paisley looked at Shiloh, furrowing her eyebrows together.

"Never mind," Shiloh sighed, standing up and brushing the grass off of her pants. "C'mon, it's not safe here. We have to go home." She held her hand out to help Paisley up from the ground.

"Home?" Paisley asked curiously. She studied Shiloh's hand before taking it in her own, allowing the girl to help her up to her feet.

Shiloh went to draw her hand back, but Paisley didn't let go. Instead, the smaller girl interlocked their fingers and skipped forwards. Shiloh reacted quickly, though, grabbing Paisley and pulling her backwards just as a car whizzed past.

"You have to look both ways to make sure there are no cars," Shiloh said after she caught her breath, Paisley had almost run straight into the heavy traffic. Maybe holding hands would be a good safety precaution.

Shiloh held tightly onto Paisley while she waited for the traffic to clear. Once it did, she tugged the girl's hand and led her across the street. Halfway across, Paisley planted her feet in the ground and bent down to study something on the pavement.

"No, Paisley," Shiloh said sternly, pulling the girl up and guiding them quickly over to the car. Paisley looked intently at the penny she'd picked up, turning it back and forth in front of her face.

Growing frustrated, Shiloh took the penny out of Paisley's hand and tossed it onto the sidewalk, pulling her towards the car and opening the passenger side. Paisley gasped, looking at Shiloh as if she'd just murdered someone.

"You hurt him!" she huffed, pulling away from Shiloh and scrambling over to pick up the penny. Sighing in defeat, Shiloh crossed her arms and waited for Paisley to return to her, penny in tow. "Say sorry," Paisley held the penny in front of Shiloh's face and wiggled it back and forth.

Shiloh raised an eyebrow at Paisley. "Sorry," she muttered, motioning for Paisley to get in the car. The small girl ignored her and shoved the penny even closer to Shiloh's face.

"Say it like you mean it," she nodded once.

"I'm sorry for throwing you, Mr. Penny," Shiloh laughed at her situation. Paisley, satisfied with Shiloh's apology, crawled into the passenger seat. Shiloh quickly crossed over to the driver's side, making sure to lock the doors incase Paisley would try and get out.

"I am sorry for making you yell," Paisley mumbled. Shiloh looked over at her in confusion. "*Stupid*," Paisley whispered under her breath, knocking on her forehead and shaking her head.

Shiloh suddenly grew concerned and reached over to move Paisley's hand away from her head. "It's okay," she sighed, studying the small girl's response. "They're just drawings. They can always be replaced, right?"

Paisley nodded softly and clasped her hands in her lap. "Are you mad?"

"No, it's fine, I told you that I forgave you," Shiloh reaffirmed. Paisley smiled widely and clapped her hands.

"I am hungry," Paisley announced, drumming her fingers on her lap as they drove. Shiloh sighed, thinking for a moment.

"What do you want to eat?" Shiloh asked, glancing over at Paisley, who already appeared to be deep in thought.

"Ice cream," Paisley chirped. The small girl clapped her hands together eagerly. Shiloh opened her mouth to protest that ice cream wasn't an actual meal, but she stopped when she saw the pleading look on Paisley's face.

"Ice cream it is, then," she laughed, passing their apartment building and heading to the frozen yogurt shop down the street. Paisley giggled happily. Shiloh was beginning to realize just how much she liked that sound.

CHAPTER 7

Minutes later Shiloh was opening the passenger side door for Paisley, who crawled out excitedly and began walking in the complete opposite direction of the store. Shaking her head, Shiloh ran after her and grabbed her hand.

"This way," Shiloh laughed. Paisley held onto her hand tightly, skipping behind Shiloh with an excited smile on her face. Shiloh led them both into the store, ignoring the confused stares from the other customers when Paisley continued to skip once they were inside.

Shiloh grabbed two of the bowls from the counter and handed one to Paisley. "Do you know how to do this?"

Paisley looked at her blankly and Shiloh sighed. "Here, I'll show you," she led Paisley, who was still holding her hand, over to the wall of self-serve yogurt.

"These are the flavors," she nodded to the pictures at the top of the machines. Paisley nodded and studied each one intently. Shiloh let go of her hand so she could hold her bowl underneath the machine that dispensed Cookies and Cream flavored yogurt.

"See, you just pull the lever and—," Shiloh paused when she turned around and saw Paisley already filling up her cup with banana flavored frozen yogurt. She ran over and stopped the lever just before Paisley's cup overflowed.

"That's enough for now," Shiloh laughed. Paisley pouted.

"Again," she pointed to the machine, going to fill up her cup even more. Shiloh shook her head quickly and pulled Paisley over to the Cookies and Cream machine.

"Here," she handed Paisley her empty cup. "You can fill up mine with this one."

Paisley nodded happily, taking Shiloh's bowl but walking over to a different machine. Before Shiloh could stop her, Paisley was filling her cup with Raspberry flavored yogurt. Shiloh shook her head, sighing and accepting the cup back from a satisfied Paisley.

"There's toppings over there," she pointed to the counter next to them. Shiloh grabbed Paisley's hand before she could run over and followed her. "Don't use too many."

Paisley nodded, bending down and studying all of her different options. Shiloh was adding strawberry slices into her cup when Paisley tapped her on the shoulder and proudly held up her frozen yogurt, which was now covered neatly with banana slices.

"You really like bananas, don't you?" Shiloh asked, laughing softly.

"Yes, yellow," Paisley nodded. She smiled proudly, and Shiloh led her over to the cashier. They set their cups down on the scale and Shiloh paid. She sent a warning glare to the man behind the counter when he began eyeing Paisley, who was clapping her hands in excitement. He quickly gave her the change and she thanked him.

Shiloh handed Paisley a spoon, walking over to one of the tables. Paisley saw down, crossing her legs underneath her in the small chair. Shiloh laughed, sitting down across from her and taking a bite of her ice cream. She hadn't expected to like the Raspberry flavor, but it was actually pretty good.

Paisley started eating her ice cream by picking the bananas off and popping them into her mouth one by one. Shiloh watched as Paisley happily chewed on her food. She looked up from her bowl and smiled widely at Shiloh.

"Is it good?" Shiloh asked, raising an eyebrow.

"Yellow," Paisley nodded, as if it were a completely reasonable answer. By now, Shiloh had realized that it was to Paisley.

"Pink," Shiloh pointed to her cup. Paisley nodded excitedly, smiling at Shiloh as if she'd just unlocked one of the deepest secrets of the world. Shiloh liked that feeling.

Paisley finished half of her ice cream before she looked up at Shiloh nervously. Noticing this, Shiloh pointed to her cup. "Are you full?"

Paisley nodded slowly. Shiloh just nodded and took both of their cups, throwing them away. She saw the smaller girl sigh in relief, wondering why it bothered her so much to tell her when she was full.

"You don't have to be scared of me, y'know," Shiloh broke the silence as they were walking back to the car. Paisley was walking beside her, looking straight up at the sky and watching the clouds.

"I know," Paisley turned to look at Shiloh. "You are Lolo. You have a big heart," she reached out and knocked on Shiloh's chest, as if to show her that her heart was there. Shiloh's breath caught in her throat and all she could do was nod.

Once they reached the apartment, Paisley skipped inside and looked around happily. Shiloh checked the time, realizing they'd been out for longer than she thought. Rushed footsteps came down the stairs and Shiloh turned around to find Ryland studying them both.

"You found her?" Ryland glanced at Paisley, who was now sitting on the floor and flipping through one of the magazines from the coffee table. Shiloh nodded. "What took so long?" The light haired girl plopped down on the couch.

"Lolo got ice cream," Paisley spoke up, smiling widely and holding up the yellow plastic spoon that she'd saved from the store. Ryland raised an eyebrow at Shiloh and smirked.

"What?" Shiloh shrugged, sitting down on the couch next to the other girl. She tried to play off the time she spent with Paisley as merely something she had to do, but she was starting to realize that she enjoyed the company of the younger girl.

"Nothing," Ryland gave Shiloh a knowing smirk. The green eyed girl rolled her eyes, pulling her phone out of her pocket and checking the time. She sat up quickly when she realized she had classes the next day.

"Shit," Shiloh shook her head, groaning. She was supposed to turn in three sketches for her first class tomorrow. She had finished them all, until Paisley got to them with a marker. Ryland raised an eyebrow at her, silently asking for an explanation.

"I have some... *homework* I need to work on," Shiloh said, trying not to let Paisley know that she had inconvenienced her by ruining her sketchbook. Ryland looked at her questioningly, but didn't say anything, allowing Shiloh to disappear up the stairs and leave Paisley under her roommate's watchful eye.

The rest of Shiloh's night was spent sprawled out on her bedroom floor, trying to recreate the sketches she had planned to turn in. After multiple hours of frustrated groans and crumpled up pieces of paper, Shiloh finally produced three sketches that she considered mediocre, but she was too exhausted to try again. Telling herself they were good enough, she changed into an old shirt to wear to bed.

Just as she was about to turn her light off, a noise in the hallway caught her attention.

"No," Paisley's voice rang out. Shiloh heard footsteps and then her doorknob jiggled, but it stopped moments later.

"Paisley, my room is this way," Ryland huffed, trying to pull the small girl in the direction of the other door.

"N*ooooo*," Paisley groaned, shaking her head and reaching for Shiloh's doorknob once more. "Lolo."

"She doesn't want you in her room, Paisley," Ryland sighed in frustration.

Unable to listen to their power struggle for any longer, Shiloh got up from her bed and opened her door slightly.

"Lolo!" Paisley smiled widely, wiggling out of Ryland's grip and walking over in front of Shiloh's door. "Knock knock."

Shiloh raised an eyebrow. "Who's there?"

Paisley stared at her blankly. Shiloh and Ryland exchanged glances, and Ryland grabbed Paisley's wrist, trying to pull her away from Shiloh's door.

"N*ooooooooo*," Paisley mumbled. She shook her head and tried to pull away.

"Paisley, I swear, s—," Ryland started.

"It's fine," Shiloh sighed, opening her door wider and motioning for Paisley to come in. Ryland looked shocked, but Shiloh simply shrugged. "If you want sleep, this is the only way you're going to get it."

Obviously not buying her excuse, Ryland smirked and winked at Shiloh. Clapping her hands excitedly, Paisley ran into Shiloh's room and dived onto her bed. Shiloh quickly picked her art supplies off of the floor and hid them in the top shelf of her closet — where Paisley wouldn't find them. Once she turned back into her room, Paisley was rummaging through her dresser.

The small girl held up a yellow shirt that Shiloh had gotten from a school fundraiser. She tilted her head to the side. "Yellow?"

"You can wear it, yeah," Shiloh sighed, walking over to her bed and sitting down. Paisley nodded, tugging off her shirt and revealing the same bruises Shiloh had seen the night before. The thought of someone doing that to Paisley made her sick to her stomach, so Shiloh tried to tell herself they were probably just from cheerleading.

"Do they hurt?" Shiloh asked before she could stop herself. Paisley looked at her, tilting her head to the side. The green eyed girl stood up and ran her fingertips over one of the bruises on Paisley's shoulder. "These, the bruises, do they hurt?"

Paisley looked at her arm and bit her lip. She blinked a few times, trying to remember if they hurt or not. "Once upon a time they did," she looked back up to Shiloh, trying to explain as best as she could.

Shiloh nodded softly. "Did someone do this to you?" she asked, being driven by general concern for the younger girl. She saw Paisley's face drain of color and instantly regretted it, but before she could apologize, the smaller girl spoke.

"Bedtime," Paisley nodded once, keeping her voice calm. Shiloh decided not to push anything else, and helped Paisley pull the shirt on over her head. Both girls crawled into bed, and Paisley lay in the same spot as the night before, staying as close to Shiloh as she could without actually touching her. It was as if there was some invisible barrier between them. Shiloh fell asleep fairly quickly, exhausted from a long day of chasing Paisley around.

Shiloh broke the barrier.

She was awoken a little after midnight by panicked whimpers. She rubbed her eyes, lifting her head and looking at the trembling girl beside her. Paisley was in same state as she had been the night before when she came into Shiloh's room.

"Paisley?" Shiloh whispered, nudging the girl's shoulder. There was no response.

"Paisley, wake up," she said louder, grabbing the girl's face in her hands. Paisley's eyes opened instantly, and a look of terror crossed her face. Shiloh quickly let go of her, not wanting to scare her. The smaller girl instantly relaxed when she saw who it was, though.

"Lolo," her voice trembled. Paisley sat up, hugging her pillow to her chest and looking around frantically. "Lolo there are bad things," she whimpered. Shiloh sat up and shook her head quickly.

"There's no bad things," Shiloh reached out and set her hand on Paisley's knee, being cautious incase physical touch would scare the girl. Paisley looked down at Shiloh's hand, gently taking it between her own two hands and bringing it up to her face. She pressed the palm of Shiloh's hand against her cheek, causing the green eyed girl to shiver.

"There's nothing to be afraid of," Shiloh said after a few moments of silence, Paisley was still holding the older girl's hand against the side of her face, and Shiloh ran her thumb over Paisley's cheek soothingly. "There are no bad things here, I promise."

"Will you keep the bad things away?" Paisley asked slowly, as if she were considering each word carefully. Shiloh bit her lip and nodded softly. "Promise?"

"Promise," Shiloh whispered. She saw Paisley attempt a small smile, but it faltered. She could tell the small girl was still scared, and it was killing her. All she wanted to do was figure out what was hurting Paisley and make sure it never hurt her again. The smaller girl looked anxiously around the room and her bottom lip began to tremble.

"Paisley..." Shiloh whispered, feeling horrible that she didn't know what was bothering her. The smaller girl continued holding Shiloh's hand against her cheek, as if it held some sort of magical healing powers.

"Lolo," Paisley mumbled, squeezing her eyes shut. Shiloh saw how close she was to crying and gave in.

"C'mere," Shiloh said softly, using her free hand to pull Paisley closer to her. Paisley looked up in shock, but quickly crawled closer to Shiloh, still looking at her hesitantly.

"You're safe here, okay?" Shiloh nodded slowly. Paisley nodded, trying to believe the older girl, but she was still trembling in fear. The first tear broke against her waterline and ran down her face.

"Hey, hey, no tears," Shiloh shook her head and pulled her hand away from Paisley's face. The smaller girl whimpered, but silenced when Shiloh wrapped her arms around her waist and Paisley was pulled into her lap. The green eyed girl hugged Paisley close to her chest, feeling just how fast the girl's heart was beating.

Paisley melted into Shiloh instantly, knowing Shiloh had broken the invisible barrier between them by allowing her to be held. She sniffed, hiding her face in the crook of the girl's neck.

"I don't know what's scaring you so badly, Paisley," Shiloh sighed, rubbing circles in the younger girl's back. "But if it helps, I'll try and help you get rid of the scary things."

Paisley looked up slowly. Shiloh's heart broke when she saw the small girl's face. Tears were streaming down her cheeks, but she wasn't making a sound. It looked as if she was trying to cry silently, not to disturb anyone. It made Shiloh's heart ache.

"Lolo," Paisley whispered, reaching out and pressing her own palm against Shiloh's cheek. "Lolo is good," she nodded, reaffirming the fact to herself. Shiloh's breath caught in her throat and she felt her cheeks blush red.

Paisley reached up and scratched her face, becoming frustrated when her tears didn't go away. Shiloh noticed this and used the sleeve of her hoodie to wipe the tears from the younger girl's cheeks. "Do you want to try and sleep?" Shiloh asked after they sat there for a few minutes in silence.

Nodding slowly, Paisley sniffed and wiped her eyes just as Shiloh had done. The older girl grabbed her phone, turning on soft music in hopes that it would soothe Paisley to sleep.

Shiloh lay down, only to find Paisley curled up against her side moments later, with her legs wrapped around hers. It was as if Paisley couldn't get close enough to her. Sighing, Shiloh realized she was already in way too deep.

Both girls feel asleep very easily, comforted in knowing that the other was right beside them.

CHAPTER 8

"Lolo," Paisley whined, wiggling out of Shiloh's arms and tapping the older girl on the shoulder. "Up, Lolo, up." She nudged Shiloh's side and huffed.

Paisley's face lit up as soon as Shiloh's eyes fluttered open. "Lolo! There is light, Lolo!" She pointed to the window happily, showing the older girl that the sun had just made its way over the buildings around them.

Yawning, Shiloh sat up and tried to recall what had happened the night before. What was today? *Shit.* She had class in less than an hour.

"Thank you," she nodded to Paisley and rolled out of bed, frantically digging through her drawers to find something presentable to wear. Paisley sat quietly on the bed, observing as Shiloh changed into a pair of jeans and a light sweater.

"Leah?!" Shiloh called, jogging across the hallway and into her bathroom. Paisley followed closely behind her, standing in the doorway and watching as Shiloh put on a thin coat of makeup, trying to make herself seem more awake.

"Huh?" Leah peered her head out of her doorway. Vanessa and Ryland were already in class, and Leah didn't have class until later that night. Shiloh got home from her classes around noon.

"I have class," Shiloh nodded in Leah's direction before crossing the hallway and grabbing her backpack out of her room. Paisley continued following her as she busily shoved her belongings into her bag. "So you have to watch Paisley."

Leah just nodded, running a hand through her hair and following the other two girls downstairs. Shiloh grabbed her keys but paused just as she was about to open the door and leave. Paisley was directly behind her, looking at her expectantly.

"You can't come with me," Shiloh raised an eyebrow at Paisley. "You have to stay with Leah."

"No," Paisley shook her head.

"Yes, Paisley, I have class," Shiloh tapped her foot impatiently.

"Yes," Paisley nodded once, causing Shiloh to groan. She sent Leah a pleading look, and the older girl grabbed Paisley's arm.

"Paisley, we can make pancakes for Shiloh when she gets back," she offered, nodding to Shiloh to leave while the girl was distracted. Shiloh mouthed a '*thank you*' and slipped out the door, just in time to hear Paisley whimper as the door shut.

Trying to shake off any guilt she had about leaving, Shiloh tossed her backpack into the passenger seat of the car and sped off down the street. The short drive to her school gave her time to think about everything that was going on with Paisley. She didn't quite understand how she was becoming so attached to the girl.

Eventually, she arrived outside of the building. She realized she was five minutes late, mentally cursing herself for forgetting to set her alarm the night before. Shiloh had been too distracted by Paisley.

She grabbed her backpack and jogged into the building, noticing her teacher had already begun teaching. Sighing, she opened the door slowly and felt everyone's eyes on her. Her teacher stopped what he was doing and turned to look at her. She winced, knowing he was one of the strictest teachers in the school.

"Looks like you've finally decided to join us, Ms. Everest," he nodded once at Shiloh, who stood quietly in the doorway. "I've already collected the pieces we had due, so please put yours in your folder and bring over an extra set of brushes for yourself."

Shiloh nodded quickly, thankful that she hadn't gotten in too much trouble. She was rarely late to class. She jogged over to the back of the classroom, sliding her backpack into her hands and searching for the sketches she had made the night before. They were nowhere in sight.

"*Shit,*" she huffed, bending down and digging further into her bag.

"Something wrong, Ms. Everest?"

Shiloh quickly shook her head and looked up at her teacher, Mr. Robertson, apologetically. "No sir, I just couldn't find my sketches for a second," she lied. She must've hid them in her closet with the rest of her supplies instead of putting them into her backpack after Paisley came into the room.

Unsure of what to do now, her eyes landed on the papers sticking out of her sketchbook. The sketches that Paisley had scribbled on were the only thing she had. Anything would be better than a zero, she decided. She picked three of the drawings that Paisley had tried to finish and slipped them into her folder, biting her lip and throwing her bag back over her shoulder. Once she was done, she grabbed a set of brushes and jogged to an open seat.

Halfway through the class, Shiloh's teacher allowed the students the rest of the time to work on their assignments for the week. Shiloh pulled out her sketchbook, flipping to a blank page and sketching aimlessly.

All of the other students were using different mediums. The girl next to her was using paint and the boy across from her was using clay. Shiloh, however, always stuck with pencil. It was what she was comfortable with.

She glanced over at Mr. Robertson's desk, noticing that he had collected all of their folders from the back of the classroom. She held her breath. This meant that he was grading their assignments during class. She continued to sketch, but kept peering over to try and see if he was responding negatively to anything he was looking at.

By the end of class, she'd drawn nothing special. Her sketchbook was mostly just filled with various shapes that she'd absentmindedly doodled. The teacher dismissed them, and Shiloh quickly gathered her things. Before she could slip out of the door, the teacher met her eyes.

"Can I see you for a few minutes, Shiloh?" he asked, pushing his glasses up on his nose and looking down at something in his hands. Shiloh swallowed hard, watching as the other students filed out of the classroom. Hesitantly, she stood in front of his desk and stared down at her shoes.

"I'm impressed, Ms. Everest."

Shiloh's head shot up. "Wh-what?" she nearly laughed, knowing exactly what she had just turned in.

"Your pieces," he spread out the three pictures on the table between them. "I was expecting another one of your drab sketches, but the... these are incredibly thoughtful, balancing out the darks of your sketches with the bright colors and childish shapes. They capture the essence of imagination perfectly."

Shiloh bit her lip, somewhat offended that he had called her sketches drab.

"I don't know what's gotten into you, Shiloh, but I think you should continue working with different mediums," he slid the papers back into her folder. "You've always been one of my more serious students, constantly turning in the same sketches week after week. This is a pleasant surprise."

"I... Thank you," Shiloh had to stop herself from laughing. Apparently Paisley had just saved her from being a 'drab' sketch artist in her teacher's eyes. And anything that was worthy of his approval was a big deal.

"You've got some potential in you that I didn't realize was there, Shiloh. You're dismissed," he nodded towards the door and smiled. *Smiled.* This was the first time Shiloh had ever seen him smile.

"Uh, Mr. Robertson, may I borrow an easel? I have an idea for my next assignment," Shiloh bit her lip, going out on a limb for once.

"Take whatever you need," he nodded, motioning to the back of the classroom where all the supplies were stored.

"Thank you, thank you so much," she grabbed her bag, finding the easels stacked in the back of the classroom and grabbing one to take out to her car. She silently thanked whatever forces had caused her to forget to pack the original sketches that morning.

Her next two classes passed by slowly. Art History dragged on and on, and she found herself constantly checking the clock to count down the minutes until she could leave and go back home. Back to Paisley.

Shiloh was worried that Paisley had gotten into trouble while she was gone. Paisley could have broken something, or hurt something, or hurt herself, or ran away. Shiloh bit her lip, becoming more anxious to get home and make sure everything was alright.

After a long and boring lecture about the Impressionist Movement, Shiloh's teacher finally dismissed them. She was the first one out the door. On the way home, she stopped by the grocery store and bought groceries for the week. (Shiloh might have paid special attention to the yellow colored foods, as well.)

Eventually, she pulled into the apartment parking lot and made sure to bring all the grocery bags in one trip so she wouldn't have to leave Paisley twice. She knocked on the apartment door with her foot, since her arms were filled with bags.

"Knock knock!" Paisley's voice chirped from the other side of the door. Shiloh bit her lip to keep herself from smiling.

"Who's there?" she replied, tilting her head to the side and blowing a loose strand of hair out of her face. Seconds later, the door flew open and Paisley stood there with a wide smile spread across her lips.

"Lolo," she hummed contently. Shiloh quickly slipped inside so she could set the bags down on the island before they fell out of her arms. Leah appeared by her side moments later.

"We have a problem," Leah whispered. Paisley was already distracted by the bags Shiloh had brought. The small girl was digging through them and clapping her hands excitedly at every new item. Shiloh raised an eyebrow and turned to Leah.

"What's up?" The green eyed girl asked, suddenly growing concerned.

Leah led Shiloh into the living room. Both girls sat down on the couch and Leah took a deep breath. "Paisley has bruises like... *everywhere*," she bit her lip.

"I know," Shiloh admitted. "I saw them the other night... I forgot to say anything to you guys." Just as she finished, the apartment door opened and Ryland and Vanessa arrived, back from their classes.

"Guys," Leah motioned for them to come join the conversation. All four roommates gathered in a small circle while Paisley continued observing the food Shiloh had bought.

"What's going on?" Ryland asked. Vanessa nodded in agreement. Both girls looked concerned.

"Paisley has bruises everywhere," Leah repeated what she had just told Shiloh. The other two girls looked surprised.

"What? Why?" Vanessa spoke up. Leah and Shiloh both shrugged.

"I asked her about them last night," Shiloh admitted. "She wouldn't say anything, I don't think we'll be able to get anything out of her until *she* wants to tell us." She looked down at her hands in her lap.

"Speaking of last night, Everest, what's gotten into you?" Ryland raised an eyebrow and Shiloh groaned, slouching back in her chair. The other three girls all exchanged glances and then turned their attention back to Shiloh.

"You're whipped," Vanessa mumbled under her breath. Shiloh's head shot up, looking at all three girls giving her knowing glances.

"What?" Shiloh asked, rolling her eyes and trying to avoid their gazes.

"You see the way she looks at you," Leah piped up. Shiloh furrowed her eyebrows and glanced back to Paisley in the kitchen, growing confused at what they were talking about.

"Paisley? She looks at everyone the same," Shiloh shrugged. "Plus she can barely brush her own hair, so I doubt she knows what's going on."

"Then how come she only wants to sleep in your room?" Ryland asked, trying to coax some sort of answer out of Shiloh.

"And how come you let her call you Lolo?" Vanessa added.

Leah nodded. "And why does she only wear your clothes?"

"I don't know!" Shiloh huffed and threw her hands up in the air. "I have nothing to do with that."

"Oh really?" Leah raised an eyebrow. "Then how come she spent all day today telling me about how you cuddled last night? And how you helped her get rid of the 'bad things'?"

Ryland and Vanessa both adopted shocked expressions at Leah's words, knowing how Shiloh barely showed affection for anyone. Shiloh's face burned red and she slumped down in her chair.

"I dunno," she mumbled, avoiding eye contact with the other girls. Her roommates took that as a good enough answer from Shiloh, knowing not to push her any further.

"So I guess our plan of action is to just wait until Paisley opens up to one of us?" Leah turned back to the other two girls, nodding in Shiloh's direction, knowing that Shiloh would be the first to know anything important to Paisley.

"That's all we can do, right?" Vanessa asked, keeping an eye on the girl in the kitchen who was now studying the magnets on their refrigerator. Leah and Ryland nodded.

"Lolooooooo," Paisley's voice rung out from the kitchen. Ryland, Vanessa, and Leah all turned to Shiloh and smirked, causing the green eyed girl's face to turn bright red. She bit her lip, forcing herself to ignore Paisley. She didn't want to give her roommates the satisfaction.

"Lolo?" Paisley tilted her head to the side, wondering why the girl wasn't responding to her. "Lol*ooo.*"

"Alright, alright, I'm coming," Shiloh sighed in defeat. She pushed herself up from the chair and ignored the looks she received from the other girls in the living room. For some reason, she found it impossible to ignore Paisley.

C H A P T E R 9

"Lolo!" Paisley hummed happily once Shiloh walked into the kitchen. She shuffled over to the green eyed girl and held up a banana. "We missed you."

Shiloh glanced back at her roommates, who were all watching their interaction from the couch. She raised an eyebrow at them, and they all turned away, knowing they'd been caught.

"Do you need me to peel that?" Shiloh asked, eyeing the banana that Paisley was holding up.

"No," Paisley shook her head. She stared at the banana for a few moments before bringing it to her mouth and trying to bite into it. She quickly pulled the banana away and stared at it in disgust. "I broke it," she gasped.

Shiloh laughed and shook her head. "You didn't break it," she took the banana out of Paisley's hands and peeled it halfway, handing it back to her. "You just have to peel it first."

"My savior," Paisley hummed happily, looking down at the banana and then up at Shiloh. "Want some?" she tilted her head to the side and held the fruit up in Shiloh's face.

Shrugging, Shiloh leaned over and took a bite of the banana. Paisley giggled excitedly.

"Thank you," Shiloh laughed at Paisley's excitement.

"*Thank you,*" Paisley repeated. She nodded once and took a bite of the banana, humming in approval.

"No, you're supposed to say you're welcome," Shiloh pointed to Paisley to explain. "If someone thanks you, you say '*you're welcome*'."

"Thank you, you're welcome," Paisley nodded happily and turned around, walking over to the counter and sitting on one of the stools. Shiloh giggled at Paisley's attempt, leaning against the counter and glancing back in the living room. Her roommates looked away quickly, but Shiloh was well aware that they were still watching her.

"You have a pretty laugh," Paisley observed. She leaned across the counter and placed her fingers on Shiloh's lips, as if she could hear her laughing through touch. "I like it when you laugh," Paisley reaffirmed with a nod.

Shiloh's cheeks grew red and she knew the other girls were all surprised by how easily she and Paisley were getting along.

"I guess I should do it more often, then," she shrugged, smirking when she saw Ryland mouth '*oh my god*' to Vanessa out of the corner of her eye.

"Yes, you're welcome," Paisley smiled with a mouthful of her banana. Shiloh giggled, which caused Paisley to smile even wider.

"What's for dinner?" Ryland strolled into the kitchen, pretending like she hadn't just watched the entire encounter between Shiloh and Paisley. The green eyed girl shrugged and started putting the groceries away.

"This is dinner," Paisley announced, holding up a box of mac and cheese for Ryland to see.

"Good choice, Paisley," Ryland laughed, holding out her fist in front of Paisley. The smaller girl stared at it questioningly. "You're supposed to bump it with your fist, like this," Ryland laughed, holding her fist out to Shiloh, who returned the gesture.

"Oh," Paisley nodded, bumping both of her fists together. Shiloh and Ryland laughed, and Ryland shook her head.

"No, bump *my* fist," she explained, holding her fist out in front of Paisley. Paisley nodded once and held out her fist to bump Ryland's. Once she did, Ryland pulled her fist back and made an exploding noise with her mouth. Paisley giggled excitedly and then did the same.

"Make the girl her dinner, Shy," Ryland teased, tossing the box of macaroni and cheese to Shiloh. The green eyed girl made a face at Ryland before grabbing a pot and filling it with water. She set the pot on the stove to boil.

Vanessa and Leah both got up to join them in the kitchen. Paisley engaged them in an animated conversation about her banana. Shiloh stood back and watched, realizing the effect Paisley had on people. Paisley's smile was contagious.

Shiloh jumped when the pot started boiling over, and she quickly turned down the heat so she could add the noodles. Stirring the boiling mixture, she set the timer on the stove. When she turned back around, Paisley was right behind her, trying to look over her shoulder.

"What are you doing?"

"I'm making dinner," Shiloh pointed to the box of macaroni and cheese. Paisley clapped her hands together excitedly.

"Yellow," she giggled and held out her fist. Shiloh rolled her eyes and bumped Paisley's fist, causing the smaller girl to make an exploding noise with her mouth and turn around to look at Ryland for approval.

"Look at what you've taught her," Shiloh laughed, raising an eyebrow at Ryland. Paisley shuffled over to Leah and Vanessa and held up both of her fists eagerly. The other two girls laughed and bumped them, and Paisley continued making exploding noises.

Shiloh was enjoying this. Normally, she and her roommates spent their time in their bedrooms, or out doing their own thing. It was nice to have some down time with her friends and be able to joke around. She'd missed that. They all got so caught up in their daily lives that sometimes they forgot to check in on each other. Maybe having Paisley here was good for them.

Once dinner was ready, Shiloh scooped even amounts into five bowls and set them on the counter. Paisley clapped her hands and picked the yellow bowl, as Shiloh had suspected she would. The smaller girl happily followed them into the living room, where Paisley assumed her usual position in the middle of the floor.

Ryland, Vanessa, and Leah all purposely took up the open seats before Shiloh could. The green eyed girl glared at them, and they all smiled knowingly. Shiloh knew exactly what they were up to.

Sighing, Shiloh sat down on the floor a few feet away from Paisley and poked at her food. Paisley practically finished her entire bowl before Shiloh could even take a bite of her own.

"Still hungry?" Shiloh asked, pointing to Paisley's bowl. Paisley nodded quickly, and Shiloh handed the small girl her bowl. She wasn't hungry in the first place.

"You're welcome," Paisley smiled, taking the bowl from Shiloh. "Thank you, you're welcome," she repeated, taking a bite of the new bowl and smiling innocently. Shiloh ignored Ryland, who was whispering *'whipped'* from behind her.

Throughout dinner, Paisley would itch her head occasionally. Shiloh felt her phone buzz in her pocket, reading the new text in the group chat.

[6:58 — Leah] She needs a shower.

Shiloh glanced up at Paisley and bit her lip.

[6:59 — Ryland] I volunteer Shiloh.

[6:59 — Shiloh] I am not giving her a shower!!

Shiloh turned around and glared at Ryland, who just stuck her tongue out at the older girl.

[7:00 — Leah] You don't have to. All you have to do is sit in there with her so she doesn't get scared by herself.

[7:00 — Vanessa] Ryland and I can take her shopping tomorrow. We don't have class and you know she's going to need regular clothes eventually.

[7:01 — Leah] That's a good idea.

[7:01 — Shiloh] Fine. I'll do it. But this means Ryland has to cook for the rest of the week. And do my dishes.

[7:02 — Ryland] Rude.

Shiloh laughed softly, turning around and sticking her tongue back out at Ryland. Paisley set her bowl down in front of her, catching Shiloh's attention.

"All done?" Shiloh asked, standing up and bringing the dirty dishes to the sink. Paisley nodded, scrambling to her feet and following close behind Shiloh. "You have to shower tonight, yeah?"

Paisley tilted her head to the side for a moment before realizing what Shiloh was talking about. "Yes," she nodded once with a soft smile. "You join me?"

Shiloh nearly choked on thin air. She heard the other three girls laughing behind her, and ignored them. "No, silly. I'll sit in there while you shower, though," she explained. Paisley just nodded and grabbed Shiloh's hands.

"C'mon Lolo," she hummed, pulling the dark haired girl towards the stairs. Shiloh had to jog to avoid being dragged by the excited girl.

"Have fun!" Vanessa called from behind them. Shiloh flicked her off before they disappeared up the stairs. Her three roommates burst into laugher once Shiloh was out of sight.

"You know how to shower, right?" Shiloh asked once they were in the bathroom that sat across the hall from her bedroom. Paisley studied the room for a few moments before nodding.

"Yes. Tom taught me," Paisley said casually, walking over and turning on the knob of the shower. Water squirted out of the nozzle and she held her hand underneath it. "Cold," she mumbled, turning the knob slightly and holding her hand in the water once more. "Warm," she nodded happily.

Shiloh grew confused when Paisley mentioned 'Tom', but she decided to ask later, considering that Paisley was in a good mood and willing to take a shower.

"Alright, you get undressed and get behind the curtain, and I'll be right back, okay? I need to get you a towel and pajamas," Shiloh motioned to the shower.

"Lolo's shirt?" Paisley asked with a shy smile. Shiloh sighed and nodded.

"If that's what you want, sure," she said. "I'll be back."

"Goodnight!" Paisley waved as Shiloh slipped out of the room. A minute or so later, Shiloh returned with a towel and clean change of clothes for the girl.

Paisley was already in the shower, and Shiloh sat down on the toilet.

"*Happy birthday to you, Happy birthday to you*," Paisley hummed contently, washing the soap suds out of her hair just like she had been taught to. Shiloh raised an eyebrow from the other side of the shower curtain.

"Is that the only song you know?" Shiloh laughed.

"It is a good song," Paisley replied. She moved under the stream of water and scrubbed her face with her hands, rinsing off all the extra soap that had run down the sides of her face. Leah had given Paisley her own bottle of 2-in-1 shampoo and conditioner to make it easier on the girl.

"But it's repetitive," Shiloh ran a hand through her hair.

"Yes," Paisley nodded once. She felt her head, making sure she'd gotten all the shampoo and conditioner out before turning off the water. "I am done, Lolo."

"Alright," Shiloh stood up and handed Paisley the towel overtop of the shower curtain. "Your clothes are on the toilet, dry off and get changed and I'll be across the hall, okay?"

"Okay," Paisley nodded once. Shiloh slipped out of the room and into her bedroom. She felt her phone buzz in her pocket.

[7:32 — Ryland] Whipped.

Shiloh rolled her eyes and tossed her phone onto her bed. A few minutes later, she heard the bathroom door open and close, and footsteps shuffled across the hallway.

"Knock knock," Paisley stood in the doorway with a sleepy smile on her face. She yawned, wiping her eyes and looking at Shiloh contently.

"Who's there?" Shiloh asked. Paisley just shrugged and padded into the room. Shiloh noticed her hair hadn't been brushed, and was tangled and swept to the side.

"Do you want me to braid your hair again?" the older girl asked, grabbing her brush from the nightstand. Paisley nodded and hopped onto the bed, remembering how she had sat the last time Shiloh had done her hair.

"Yes. You make me pretty," she smiled.

"You were already pretty," Shiloh said softly, scooting behind the girl and beginning to brush out her wet hair.

"Like you?" Paisley asked, turning around to look at Shiloh. The older girl bit her lip.

"Keep your head still," she avoided the question and moved Paisley's head back around so she could continue brushing her hair.

Paisley didn't repeat her question, which Shiloh was thankful for. The older girl eventually got all the tangles out of Paisley's hair and began French braiding it down the back of her head.

"Music?" Paisley asked, keeping her head forward but tilting it to the side slightly. Shiloh reached for her phone but Paisley grabbed her wrist to stop her before she could. "No, Lolo's music."

Shiloh realized Paisley wanted her to sing and bit her lip. But no matter how badly she wanted to say no, she just couldn't bring herself to say no to Paisley.

"Fine, but I get to sing something better than happy birthday," she joked.

"You're welcome," Paisley nodded once. Shiloh laughed, wondering what Paisley believed Shiloh had thanked her for. She slowly realized that she did have a lot to thank the smaller girl for. In reality, she owed Paisley an infinite number of thank you's.

"Let's see," Shiloh thought for a few moments before she began to sing. Her soft voice filled the room and Paisley smiled contently.

Shiloh finished Paisley's braid while she sang. Once she finished the song, Paisley scooted around on the bed so she was facing Shiloh. The small girl reached up and pressed her fingertips against Shiloh's lips.

"Pretty," Paisley said softly, swaying back and forth subtly. "*Lolo*," she cooed. She drew her hand back and kissed her fingertips before pressing them back to Shiloh's cheek. The gesture made Shiloh's stomach flip.

Paisley smiled, yawning loudly and rubbing her eyes.

"Are you ready for bed?" Shiloh asked, even thought it was way earlier than the time she would usually go to bed. Paisley nodded, and without another world, she crawled to her usual spot in Shiloh's bed and curled tugged on the covers.

"I guess Ryland's bed is a thing of the past, then," Shiloh stated with an eyebrow raised.

"I like Lolo's bed," Paisley nodded and grabbed Shiloh's hand, urging her to lie down. Giving in, Shiloh lay back. As soon as she did, Paisley's legs were tangled up with hers and the smaller girl was nestled up right next to Shiloh's torso.

"You're welcome, Lolo. Goodnight, Lolo," Paisley sighed softly and nuzzled her head in the crook of Shiloh's neck.

"Goodnight," Shiloh whispered, reaching over to turn off the light next to her bed. Once the room was dark, she lay back down and pulled the covers over them. "Thank you, Paisley."

CHAPTER 10

Leaving Paisley didn't get any easier the second time around. If anything, it became more difficult now that Paisley understood what was happening.

"I go with Lolo," Paisley whined to Ryland as the light haired girl held her back from the door. Shiloh stood in the doorway, biting her lip and hesitating to leave.

"You're coming shopping with us today, Paisley," Vanessa piped up. "Shiloh will be back soon." Ryland waved her hand at Shiloh, motioning for her to leave. Shiloh sighed and slipped out the door while Paisley was distracted.

"Lol*oooo!*," Paisley cried, trying to wiggle out of Ryland's grasp. Ryland held on tightly to the small girl. She glanced at Vanessa questioningly.

"It's like we're raising a child," Vanessa mumbled. Paisley was still trying to run for the door, and Ryland was struggling to hold onto her.

"Shiloh's gone, Paisley," Ryland said firmly. She was growing increasingly frustrated with the fact that Paisley was so persistent on being by Shiloh's side 24/7.

The small girl turned around and looked at Ryland angrily.

Ryland's hands were still tightly gripping Paisley's wrists, so the smaller girl settled on kicking her legs forwards and hitting the leg of the small table by the door. The wood cracked easily under the force of her kick, causing the table to fall over and bring the glass vase on top of it crashing to the floor. Vanessa and Ryland both gasped as glass scattered everywhere. Paisley immediately cried out and covered her ears with her hands, which Ryland had released out of shock.

"Why the hell would you do that?!" Ryland yelled, turning around and glaring at Paisley. The smaller girl took a few steps back and brought her hands up in front of her face.

"Please," she shook her head violently. Ryland and Vanessa exchanged confused glances as Paisley continued to take slow steps away from them.

"Bad," Paisley mumbled, knocking on her head with her fist. "Bad, Stupid," she shook her head and hit her head even harder. Ryland raised an eyebrow at Vanessa, who was just as lost as she was.

"Stupid," Paisley uttered under her breath. "Stupid, stupid, stupid," her voice grew louder and she began violently pummeling her head with both fists. Her back slid down against the wall and she continued punching herself with her balled up fists.

"Paisley, don't do that," Ryland quickly ran over to the girl and slid down next to her. "Hey, hey, you're not stupid," she grabbed Paisley's hands and held them away from her face.

Paisley looked up at Ryland, her bottom lip trembling. The light haired girl felt extremely guilty for snapping at her. She glanced back at Vanessa, who was already using the broom to sweep up the shards of broken glass.

"Stupid," Paisley shook her head and tried to bring her hands back to her face. Ryland kept a firm grip on her wrists, and Paisley whined in frustration. "Stupid, Bad, Bad Paisley."

Ryland bit her lip and sat down next to the girl. "You're not bad *or* stupid," Ryland said softly, unsure how she should go about comforting Paisley.

"I killed it," Paisley whimpered, pointing to the vase and table by the door. She began to cry softly, tears flowing down her cheeks and spotting her shirt.

"It's okay, Paisley, it's just a vase. We can just buy a new one," Ryland shook her head. "It's okay, I promise. Do you want something to eat?" She tried to distract the smaller girl, hoping food would take her mind off of what she'd done.

Paisley shook her head violently, sobbing even harder than before. She dropped her head onto her knees and covered her face with her hands as the sobs became uncontrollable.

"Paisley, you don't have to cry," Vanessa piped up, joining Ryland on the floor next to the girl. "It's all cleaned up, see?" She pointed to the doorway. Paisley didn't respond to their attempts at comforting her, she just continued crying into her hands.

Ryland and Vanessa exchanged glances. Neither one of them knew what they were supposed to do. Sighing softly, Ryland motioned towards the door.

"Go ahead, she doesn't need to be there when you buy her clothes," Ryland said. "Just get whatever you think she needs, I'll stay here with her."

Vanessa nodded silently. Ryland scooted closer to Paisley and slowly reached out to place a hand on the small girl's back. Paisley continued crying, and the two roommates felt completely powerless. Sighing, Vanessa grabbed her purse and gave Ryland one last sympathetic wave before slipping out the door.

For the next hour, no matter what Ryland said, Paisley continued crying. Ryland sat quietly next to her, even considering texting Shiloh for help a few times. But she refrained, knowing it was a bad idea.

"My Lolo," Paisley whispered, looking up slowly and scanning the apartment. Ryland glanced over at the girl, whose cheeks were now tear stained. Paisley looked pleadingly at her.

"Shiloh's at school right now, Paisley," Ryland sighed. There was no way she could fix that problem for the other girl. She saw the look of disappointment on Paisley's face. Without another word, Paisley crawled to her feet and shuffled up the stairs. Confused, Ryland followed close behind.

Paisley tiptoed into Shiloh's room and went straight for the bed. Ryland peeked her head in the door, finding the smaller girl nestled under the covers. Sighing heavily, Ryland closed the door to Shiloh's bedroom to try and give Paisley some peace and quiet.

Meanwhile, Shiloh was aimlessly scrolling through her phone in the library of her college. She had a 20 minute break in between classes and never knew how to occupy her time. While scrolling through Facebook, she saw a familiar face on her '*Recommended Friends*' list.

She quickly clicked on the user's profile, recognizing Sydney Marx as one of the cheerleaders that Paisley was friends with in high school. Shiloh had never thought of contacting them before.

For some odd reason, she felt guilty for looking through Paisley's past life. But she decided that she needed some sort of explanation for how Paisley had ended up on their doorway. Sydney's profile was public, so Shiloh began scrolling through her photos.

Paisley wasn't featured in anything recent, but Shiloh finally recognized the younger girl's face in an album of photos from the first party of the summer, celebrating their high school graduation. Shiloh and her roommates hadn't been present. They were already on the road to New York.

It was obvious that everyone at the party was either drunk or high. Or both. Shiloh bit her lip as she scrolled through the pictures, going back even earlier.

She found pictures of Paisley with the cheer team, smiling brightly. Shiloh got the chills from looking at these photos and thinking just how different Paisley seemed, compared to how she'd been in high school.

She paused on a certain picture, though, raising her eyebrows. It was a picture of all the cheerleaders and their boyfriends, Paisley included. Shiloh had completely forgotten that Paisley was dating someone at the time that they graduated. She furrowed her eyebrows together, thinking for a moment. What was his name? *Scott.*

His name had been Scott, Shiloh remembered. She crinkled her nose at the mention of his name, wondering when he and Paisley had ended.

She reached the end of Sydney's photos, and slumped back in her chair. She was still dying for information. Checking the time, Shiloh realized she had ten minutes left until she had to leave for her next class. Gathering her things, she made her way over to the computer in the corner of the library.

Taking a deep breath, convincing herself that this was the right thing to do, Shiloh opened a new tab and started hesitantly at the screen. A few moments later, she typed 'Paisley Lowe' into the search bar and hit enter before she could change her mind.

Seconds later, the results popped up and Shiloh scanned them with baited breath. The first news article that appeared made her gasp. She quickly looked around to see if anyone had heard her, and luckily she hadn't caught anyone's attention.

> *"Car accident leaves Miami student in fatal condition, authorities are still on the search for the students involved. "*

Shiloh had to remind herself to breathe and she quickly scrolled down. She nearly gasped again when she saw the picture of the completely totaled car. Upon further inspection, Shiloh realized the car was upside down at the bottom of a ditch. Surprisingly enough, she knew exactly where the picture had been taken.

She hesitated before scrolling down to the actual article. Did she want to know? Of course she did. She was just scared. Shaking it off, Shiloh scrolled down and leaned in closer to the screen.

> *"Last night, a Miami Trooper called in an overturned car at the bottom of a ditch bordering Grove Street. Police believed the car to be abandoned, but upon further inspection they found the body of 18-year-old Paisley Lowe, a student from Miami.*
>
> *Lowe was revived at the scene and rushed to the hospital, where she remains in critical condition. The other occupants of the car are yet to come forward. Any information regarding the accident should be reported directly to the Miami Police. "*

Shiloh brought her hand to her face, wiping the tears that had brimmed her eyes. Things were starting to slowly make sense, but she was still left with millions of unanswered questions. She scanned the related articles out of curiosity and quickly clicked the first one that caught her eye.

"UPDATE: Miami students involved in severe car crash provide critical information"

Taking a deep breath, she prepared herself for what was to come. As she leaned in closer to the screen, Shiloh found herself praying that this was all some sort of screwed up dream.

"The car accident that left 18-year-old Paisley Lowe in critical condition last Tuesday is still undergoing investigation. The students involved in the collision have been brought forward and questioned.

Police revealed that two cars had been involved in a reckless driving incident while coming home from a school party. Both students at the wheel were under the influence of alcohol at the time. The vehicles were racing around the corner when the car Lowe inhabited lost control and rolled into the a ditch on the side of the road. The other car involved in the accident has yet to be found.

The driver of the car, Lowe's alleged boyfriend, survived unharmed. He claimed he hadn't realized Paisley was in the car, due to his drunken state. Instead of calling for help, Lowe's boyfriend simply fled the scene. Lowe was found over an hour later by a Miami Trooper and revived on the way to the hospital. Lowe is said to have been completely sober upon arrival at the hospital.

Lowe remains in critical condition. Sources revealed that she suffered from a broken leg, a severe cut that required over 100 stitches, and a fractured skull. The doctors also believe that the accident was so violent that it caused a traumatic brain injury. The Lowe family has yet to speak out regarding the accident."

Shiloh's blood boiled when she realized who had been driving during the accident. Paisley had been sober, too. Everyone at school knew that Paisley didn't drink. She never had said why, though. Checking the time, Shiloh groaned.

She slung her bag over her shoulder, and exited out of the tabs and trudged to her next class. Now, a million new questions began circulating in her head. She wanted to get home. She couldn't keep this to herself for much longer, and she knew she needed to show her roommates what she had found. More importantly, she needed to talk to Paisley.

While Shiloh suffered through her last class, Vanessa was out shopping for Paisley as Ryland stayed home with the distraught girl. Pulling into the parking lot of the shopping mall, Vanessa jogged inside just as it started to rain.

She wasn't exactly sure what to get Paisley. All the girl had worn since she'd been there were Shiloh's t-shirts. Vanessa strolled into Urban Outfitters and purchased a few baggy t-shirts, hoping they'd do the trick.

As she continued shopping, she ended up in Forever 21. There was a rack of adorable summery dresses against the wall, and Vanessa immediately thought of Paisley. Giving into temptation, she bought a couple dresses and a pair of comfortable converse.

She made her rounds through the store, and ended up buying a few pairs of leggings and pajama pants along the way. Once she was finished, she had a handful of bags and a long list of receipts. Vanessa headed back to her car, hoping that she'd done a good enough job.

Once she made it back to the apartment, she found Ryland in the kitchen, poking at a leftover piece of pizza. She looked just as exhausted as Vanessa felt.

"Hey," Vanessa sighed, placing the shopping backs on the island. "Where's Paisley?"

"Where do you think?" Ryland raised an eyebrow. Vanessa laughed softly, not responding since she knew exactly where the smaller girl was.

"She cried for over an hour, Nessa," Ryland sighed and leaned against the counter. "I couldn't get her to calm down."

"Are you sure this is a good idea?" Vanessa asked, biting her lip and hopping up on the counter so she could face Ryland. "Letting her get this close to Shiloh and all… I mean, you know how Shiloh is."

Ryland nodded, knowing what her roommate meant. "We can talk to Lo once she gets home."

"Lo?" Vanessa smirked.

Ryland raised an eyebrow. "What? It fits," she laughed, knowing she'd accidentally used Paisley's nickname for Shiloh. There was a long pause of silence, and then the sound of keys jostling in the front door.

"Speak of the devil," Vanessa mumbled, causing Ryland to laugh. Shiloh appeared moments later, tossing her backpack onto the couch.

"Where's Paisley?" she asked, jogging into the kitchen and looking around anxiously.

"Upstairs," Ryland nodded once and grabbed Shiloh's arm before she could run off. "We need to talk to you about something, Shy."

"Me too, actually," Shiloh breathed out a nervous laugh and motioned for the girls to follow her into the living room.

C H A P T E R 1 1

Once all the girls sat down, Shiloh took it upon herself to talk first, knowing they needed to hear what she had found out as soon as possible.

"I did some... *research*, today," Shiloh said cautiously. Her two other roommates looked at her in confusion and Shiloh sighed. She dug around in her backpack until she found the articles she'd printed out before she left.

"We wanted an explanation..." she said softly, passing the papers over to the girls. Both of them gasped as soon as they saw the picture of the overturned car.

"Paisley was in there?" Vanessa asked in shock. Shiloh nodded and scooted closer to them on the couch.

"Yep," she pointed to the passenger side of the car. "Right there. See that section? That's the part they had to saw off to get her out." She saw the other girls shudder at the thought, just as she had done.

"I knew that Scott guy was an idiot," Ryland mumbled under her breath. Her grip on the papers had become so tight that Shiloh had to reach over and pry her fingers away. "How could he just leave her there?"

"Your guess is as good as mine," Shiloh sighed. Vanessa turned the paper over and continued reading, her jaw dropping open.

"Traumatic brain injury?" The dark skinned girl tilted her head to the side.

"What's that even mean?" Ryland added, raising her eyebrows in shock.

Shiloh had already done her research, and she handed them another paper she'd printed out that afternoon. Both girls read over the paper and Ryland shook her head.

"This isn't English, Shy, how am I supposed to know what a *'Diffuse Axonal'* is?" Ryland scoffed. Vanessa shook her head, shooting Shiloh an apologetic look.

"That's the specific type, I think," Shiloh pointed to the bolded words on the page. "I don't really know much either... it's confusing." Both girls nodded in agreement.

Sighing, Shiloh slumped back in her chair. "What did you guys have to tell me?" she asked, remembering what her roommates had mentioned earlier.

Ryland and Vanessa exchanged glances. They both had just seen how much work Shiloh had put into trying to figure out what was going on with Paisley. It seemed rude of them to say anything now. Silently, they agreed to keep their mouths shut for the time being.

"Nothing," Ryland shook her head. "Paisley's in your room, by the way. She was... well... she cried for a long time after you left," the light haired girl answered honestly. Shiloh bit her lip and stood up.

"Take those bags with you," Vanessa added, pointing to the shopping bags in the kitchen. "Those are all Paisley's."

Nodding, Shiloh grabbed the shopping bags and glanced in them. "Can you guys fill Leah in when she gets back?" Shiloh asked, standing at the bottom of the stairs. She didn't want to have to explain everything for the third time that day. Both girls nodded and Shiloh sent them a thankful smile.

Ascending the stairs, Shiloh began to wonder just how Paisley had gotten there. How had she managed to get on a plane and wander here on her own? What was the glass in her shoes from? And the bruises?

Sighing, Shiloh opened her bedroom door slowly. Paisley was asleep on her bed, and the older girl decided against waking her. She set the bags on the floor by her closet and crossed her arms, wondering where she should put the clothes.

She realized just how much effort she was putting into accommodating Paisley when she began moving the clothes in her closet around to make room for Paisley's things. This was a new feeling for her, and she wasn't sure how she felt about it.

Shiloh laughed softly when she saw the dresses Vanessa had purchased. She couldn't help but envision how adorable they would look on the younger girl. Just as she hung up the last piece of clothing, a dark blur collided with her and sent her stumbling backwards. She grabbed onto the wall to keep her balance.

"Lol*ooo,*" Paisley cooed, burying her head in Shiloh's chest and keeping her arms wrapped tightly around her.

"Well hello to you too," Shiloh laughed, taking aback by the girl's abrupt greeting. Seeing that Paisley had no intention of letting go, Shiloh peeled the smaller girl off of her and took a few steps back. She immediately noted Paisley's red eyes and puffy cheeks. Guilt slowly sunk in when she realized this was because of her.

"I am sorry, Lolo," Paisley whispered, looking up at Shiloh with a look of uncertainty on her face. Shiloh tilted her head to the side in confusion.

"I killed it," the smaller girl murmured, shaking her head and walking over to the bed. Shiloh followed her cautiously. "Stupid," Paisley huffed. She burrowed back under the covers, trying to hide from the older girl.

Shiloh felt her phone buzz in her pocket just as she sat down on the end of the bed.

[4:39 - Ryland] Oh, and also, Paisley broke the table and vase by the door after you left. I guess that's what caused her to break down.

Sighing, Shiloh set her phone down and scooted closer to the figure nestled under the covers.

"Paisley, I'm not mad at you," Shiloh said softly. She realized now that a day or two ago, she would've been furious. But the table and vase were replaceable, Paisley wasn't. She had been able to learn that in their short time together.

The smaller girl slowly peered out from under the blankets. She studied Shiloh intently for a few moments before sitting up.

"Promise?" Paisley tilted her head to the side, holding out her pinky finger. Shiloh laughed softly and nodded, locking their fingers together.

"Promise," the green eyed girl nodded once. Paisley looked down at her hands in her lap, still somewhat upset. Shiloh noticed this and grew concerned.

"Paisley? Do you want to talk about it?" Shiloh reached out and placed one of her hands on the smaller girl's knee. At this point, Shiloh was one hundred percent aware that she was in too deep, but for some reason her compassion outweighed her fear.

"Talk?" Paisley asked. She looked down at Shiloh's hand in her lap, studying it carefully for a few moments. Shiloh watched as Paisley gently placed her own hand atop Shiloh's, playing with her fingers aimlessly. The small gesture was still somehow able to make her stomach flutter.

"Yeah, talk," Shiloh nodded slowly, trying to think of how she could explain the idea to Paisley. "Friends talk to friends about their problems, remember?"

"Oh, yes," Paisley nodded once. Shiloh gave her a reassuring smile before scooting back on the bed and leaning against the headboard.

"Then what was bothering you this morning that made you so sad?" Shiloh asked softly. She patted the spot next to her and Paisley crawled over eagerly. "Were you mad that I left?"

"I am scared you will not come back," Paisley bit her lip and looked over at Shiloh. "And I like you here."

Shiloh couldn't help but feel guilty, but she knew there was no way around this. She had to go to class. And bringing Paisley with her didn't seem like the best idea. She sighed and looked up at the ceiling.

"You know I'll come back, Pais, I'll always come back."

Paisley smiled at the nickname, scooting closer to Shiloh and finding her hand again. "I did not mean to kill it…" she mumbled under her breath. Shiloh barely caught what she had said.

"You didn't kill it, Paisley," she shook her head and squeezed the girl's hand. "Next time, you just need to find a way to control your emotions, right? Like punching a pillow or something." Shiloh grabbed the pillow next to her and punched it to demonstrate, which caused Paisley to giggle.

"There's other ways to control your anger, too," Shiloh nodded softly. "Whenever I get mad, I draw in my sketchbook. We just need to find you something that helps calm you down."

"Eating?" Paisley tilted her head to the side. Shiloh giggled and shook her head.

"Something besides eating," she pursed her lips and thought for a moment. "What do you like to do?"

Paisley shrugged. "I am not good at things," she sighed. Shiloh quickly shook her head, not wanting Paisley to believe that.

"Of course you are," Shiloh gave her a soft smile. "We just haven't found your true passion yet, but we will."

"You think so?" Paisley bit her lip.

"I know so," Shiloh smirked. She sighed softly when she remembered why she had come upstairs originally. Taking a deep breath, Shiloh sat up slightly and squeezed Paisley's hand. "Can I ask you a question?"

Paisley nodded softly, not knowing what Shiloh was referring to.

"Okay, so… I found out something today," she paused. "About you…" Paisley still appeared confused and Shiloh took that as a good enough reason to continue. "Do you know you were in a car accident?"

Paisley's eyes widened and she scanned Shiloh's face, trying to figure out her true intentions. After a few moments of tense silence, she nodded slowly. "I got hurt," she mumbled.

Shiloh saw the fear in the girl's eyes and kicked herself for bringing it up. But there was no going back now. "What happened, Paisley?"

"Ouch," Paisley nodded as if it were a completely reasonable answer. She scooted back and pulled up the leg of her pajama pants, shifting her position to reveal a long, raised scar that ran from the middle of her thigh to the back of her knee. "See? Ouch."

"Damn," Shiloh whispered. Paisley pulled the pants back over the cut and nodded softly.

"I... uh, do you remember Scott?" Shiloh bit her lip. Paisley's face tensed, and the small girl furrowed her eyebrows together.

"Scott left," Paisley muttered. "He left. Stupid," she shook her head and glanced up at Shiloh. "Mad."

"You're mad?" Shiloh asked. Paisley nodded slowly. "Why are you mad?"

"Scott," Paisley balled her fists and stared intently into space for a few moments. Shiloh waited patiently, trying to make this as comfortable for the other girl as possible. "Scott... left. Friends left." She brought her hands to her face and groaned.

"Hey, hey it's okay," Shiloh quickly moved Paisley's hands away from her face. "We don't have to talk about it anymore, okay? It's alright." Paisley looked up at her shyly. Their eyes stayed interlocked for a few moments before Paisley broke their eye contact, only to scoot closer to Shiloh and burrow her head into her neck.

Shiloh, surprised by the gesture, quickly pulled Paisley closer to her and held her tightly. By the dampness on her shoulder, she could tell the smaller girl was silently crying. So she continued to hold her, rubbing circles in the small of her back.

Shiloh would've done anything to see inside Paisley's mind right then. She wanted to know what Paisley remembered, or what she thought of the accident. She wanted to know what had happened with Scott. Or how Paisley had ended up in New York. There were so many unanswered questions that wouldn't be fair to dump onto the smaller girl.

They lay there like that for a while, Shiloh holding the small girl. Absentmindedly, Shiloh began singing softly to fill the silence. She wasn't even aware that she was singing. It was such a habit for her.

"Pretty."

Shiloh jumped mid-song, realizing Paisley had been watching her for some time. The smaller girl gazed intently up at her, a shy smile on her face.

"I, uh... thanks," Shiloh stumbled over her words. She felt her cheeks flush red and quickly looked away. Paisley furrowed her eyebrows and sat up slightly, leaning over so she could see Shiloh's face.

"Do you know?" Paisley tiled her head to the side, showing concern. "Lolo, do you?" She reached out and turned Shiloh's face so she was looking back at her. Shiloh swallowed hard when Paisley locked her caramel eyes with her own.

"Do I know what?" Shiloh asked, biting her lip and forcing herself to take her eyes off of Paisley. She sat up slowly, trying to distance herself from the girl. Obviously Paisley didn't get the message, because she only scooted closer.

"You are pretty, Lolo," Paisley nodded once. When Shiloh didn't respond, Paisley reached up and placed her fingertips on Shiloh's lips. "I want you to know."

Shiloh's breath caught in her throat and she had to remind herself to breathe. "I-I, uh..."

"Do you know?" Paisley tilted her head to the side, genuinely concerned that Shiloh wasn't aware of just how pretty she was. The younger girl reached up and cupped Shiloh's face with both hands, studying her up close.

"You have ocean eyes," Paisley whispered, as if it was a secret that only they could know. Shiloh couldn't remember the last time she had been this nervous around anyone. Paisley had this effect on her, and it scared her knowing what it could do.

"Your heart is pretty, too," the younger girl nodded, placing her hand directly under Shiloh's collarbone. "I have seen it."

CHAPTER 12

Before Shiloh could respond, the bedroom door burst open, causing the older girl to immediately scramble away from Paisley. Unfortunately, this caused her to fall backwards onto the floor, groaning in annoyance.

"Dinner's ready," Ryland smirked from the door. Shiloh glared at her, only to earn a wink from the light haired girl.

At the mention of dinner, Paisley clapped her hands excitedly. Without another word, the small girl hopped out of bed and shuffled down the hallway.

Ryland walked over, extending a hand to Shiloh to help the older girl off the floor. Shooting her roommate an annoyed glare, Shiloh accepted the help and brushed off her pants once she got to her feet. Paisley was already long gone. Ryland held out her hand for Shiloh to wait before they went downstairs.

"What did I interrupt?" Ryland raised an eyebrow.

"Nothing," Shiloh snapped, shaking her head. "What are you even talking about?"

Ryland sighed, crossing her arms and giving Shiloh a knowing look.

"What?" Shiloh huffed.

"Obviously something's going on between you two," Ryland nodded in the direction Paisley had gone. "It's pretty obvious."

Shiloh's face faltered for a moment but she quickly composed herself. "There's *nothing* going on," she said firmly, nodding once before walking past Ryland and out of the room.

"If you say so," Ryland sighed. She followed Shiloh down the stairs, but grabbed her hand before they reached a kitchen. "But if there was something going on, I'd make sure to tell you to be careful," she whispered.

Shiloh's stomach dropped, and she turned to face Ryland. "Well then good thing there isn't *anything* going on," she said simply before disappearing in the direction of the kitchen. Ryland sighed at her friend's stubbornness.

"Lolo, look!" Paisley hopped in front of Shiloh and held up a yellow bowl of mac and cheese. Shiloh raised an eyebrow at Ryland, who only shrugged.

"It was all we had," Vanessa passed Shiloh her own bowl over the counter. The older girl sighed, grabbing a fork and following her roommates into the living room.

Before Paisley had shown up, the four roommates usually ate dinner at separate times in separate places. Now, they all ate together. Shiloh hadn't realized how much she'd missed spending time with them.

As usual, Ryland, Vanessa, and Leah all took up the couches, purposely leaving no room for Shiloh. Not that she minded, though. The green eyed girl sat down on the floor a few feet away from Paisley, who smiled widely at her with a mouthful of food.

"Someone's in a better mood," Vanessa commented, nodding towards Paisley. Ryland and Leah both nodded in agreement.

"It's cause Shiloh's home," Ryland smirked. Shiloh glared at her, but it obviously didn't affect the younger girl. "It's pretty obvious how much Paisley loves Shiloh."

"Yes," Paisley nodded once, as if she were confirming what Ryland had said. "I love Lolo. I want to kiss Lolo," she said casually, taking another bite of her food. Shiloh, however, nearly choked on her own food. She looked to her roommates, who looked just as shocked.

"What did you say, Paisley?" Ryland glanced at the other girl. Paisley looked up and tilted her head to the side.

"What?"

Sighing, Ryland sent Shiloh a look of confusion, which the older girl quickly returned. Shiloh's heart was pounding against her chest, and she swore everyone in the room was able to hear it. Had Paisley really just said that? She couldn't have. Shiloh looked over at the younger girl, who was happily eating her dinner.

Quietly, Shiloh took her bowl to the sink. Without another word, she slipped upstairs and closed herself into her bedroom. As soon as she was alone, she ran her hands through her hair and began pacing back and forth.

What was she doing? Did she really have... feelings? For Paisley? She couldn't.

She could.

Shiloh groaned and fell back onto her bed. This was bad. This was more than bad. She was doomed. Why did she allow herself to get this close to the younger girl? Since when did she become so soft?

Since Paisley.

The green eyed girl rolled over and buried her head in a pillow, groaning in frustration. Shiloh hated feelings more than anything. But now here she was, being pulled towards Paisley.

Paisley! Of all people. Shiloh was falling for the girl who she had labeled as her sworn enemy for all these years. But no matter how hard she tried, there was no way she could find a trace of the girl she had once hated in Paisley.

This needed to stop. She needed to block herself off. This couldn't go any further than it already had. Suddenly, the image of kissing Paisley's soft pink lips flashed into her memory and Shiloh felt her heart flutter.

She had to stop this. She couldn't fall for Paisley. For all she knew, Paisley didn't even have any idea what *love* was. Shiloh forced herself to pull out her phone, her fingers quickly tapping across the keyboard.

[7:32 — Shiloh] Can one of you make Paisley sleep in your room tonight? I don't want her in mine.

Shiloh bit her lip. She knew it was harsh, but she couldn't risk getting hurt. She couldn't allow her feelings for the girl to develop even more.

[7:34 — Ryland] I'll take care of it. You okay?

The older girl quickly got up, locking her door just in case Paisley got any ideas. She sat down on the floor in the middle of her room and pulled her sketchbook out of her bag, staring at it blankly.

[7:39 — Shiloh] I will be.

She locked her phone and spun her pencil around in her hand a few times. Nothing interesting came to her mind as she tried to think of something to draw. She needed to distract herself from Paisley.

Shiloh lay down, propping her head up with her hand as she began aimlessly doodling on the paper. A few minutes later, an eye appeared, and Shiloh studied it for a moment before groaning and slamming her pencil down. Paisley's eye.

Paisley's eyes. Paisley's face. Paisley.

That was all Shiloh could think about. She quickly ripped the piece of paper from the sketchbook and sent it flying across the room. Forcing her eyes back down on a new piece of paper, Shiloh bit her lip as she began sketching once more.

Lips. Paisley's lips.

Paisley.

Paisley. Paisley. Paisley.

Shiloh huffed, giving up and shoving her sketchbook across the floor. She rolled onto her back and stared up at her cracked ceiling. This wasn't good. These were new feelings for her, and no matter how euphoric they felt, she wouldn't allow herself to take them any further. She would not get hurt. She wouldn't.

After staring at the ceiling for god knows how long, Shiloh dragged herself off of the floor and into her bed. She put in her headphones, blasting her music so she wouldn't have to hear Paisley's disappointment when Ryland wouldn't let her into Shiloh's room.

Eventually she fell asleep. Of course Paisley was in her dreams. *Of course.* Shiloh couldn't even control her feelings in her dreams. She was awoken by a buzzing. At first, she thought she was delusional and ignored it. But a few minutes later it happened again, and she lifted her head slowly. Two new messages flashed across the screen of her phone.

[1:02 — Ryland] We have a problem.

[1:04 — Ryland] Shy, please.

Confused, the older girl sat up, tearing out her headphones. The sound of her music was instantly replaced with the sound of sobbing from the other side of the wall. Paisley.

All of her defenses were thrown aside and she quickly got to her feet, slipping out of her room and slowly pushing opening the door to Ryland's room. Paisley sat curled up in the corner with her head in her legs. Ryland stood a few feet behind her, unsure of what to do. When the light haired girl saw Shiloh enter the room, she breathed a sigh of relief.

"I *finally* got her to sleep, and not even ten minutes later she wakes up screaming," Ryland shook her head and sat down on the end of her bed. "You were my last resort."

Shiloh nodded. She hesitated by the door for a moment, but eventually the sight of a distraught Paisley became too much for her. Slowly, she padded over to the smaller girl and knelt down next to her.

"The bad things aren't real, remember," Shiloh whispered. Paisley's head lifted slowly and Shiloh's heart shattered when she saw just how miserable the girl appeared to be. As soon as Paisley saw Shiloh behind her, she shot up and clung to the older girl for dear life. Shiloh quickly slid back against the wall and pulled Paisley into her lap, rocking the small girl back and forth. She completely forgot about Ryland's presence in the room. Making sure Paisley felt safe was her only priority.

Paisley's arms hung around Shiloh's shoulders and her face was buried in the crook of the neck. She continued sobbing into Shiloh's shirt, and the older girl wondered just how long she'd been crying for.

"Shhh," Shiloh whispered, rubbing circles in Paisley's back. "You're okay, I've got you." She rested her chin on the top of the smaller girl's head, staring at the wall and continuing to rock back and forth. Continuing old habits, she sang softly to try and get the smaller girl to calm down.

Shiloh's voice slowly faded out at the end of the song, and she looked down at the girl in her arms only to realize that she had fallen asleep. The older girl sighed in relief. Suddenly, she became aware of a pair of eyes on her and cursed herself for not remembering they were in Ryland's room.

"Nothing going on *my ass*, Everest," Ryland smirked. Shiloh just shook her head, freeing one of her hands and standing up carefully with Paisley still in her arms. As she stood up, something caught her eye in the dim light of the room.

"What happened?" Shiloh asked, nodding to the scratches on Paisley's exposed legs, with blood spotted here and there. She immediately grew concerned.

"She kept scratching at them," Ryland shrugged and bit her lip. "I finally got her to stop." Shiloh quickly realized what Paisley had been scratching at. The scar from the car accident was in the same exact spot. She shuddered at the thought.

"Next time, come get me right away," Shiloh nodded towards Ryland, not waiting for a response before slipping out of the room and carefully carrying Paisley back into her bedroom. God, this girl was like her weakness.

Shiloh laid the small girl on the bed before crawling over her and lying on the opposite side. She checked the time, thankful that she didn't have classes tomorrow. The moment her head hit the pillow, she felt a small figure curl up next to her. Shiloh couldn't help but smile.

"Thank you, Lolo," Paisley mumbled into Shiloh's shoulder. Shiloh was thankful the lights were off, otherwise Paisley would be able to see how bright red her cheeks had turned.

"G'night, Pais," Shiloh whispered before closing her eyes and falling asleep to the steady breathing of the small girl next to her.

CHAPTER 13

Shiloh couldn't help but be <u>relived</u> that she didn't have any classes when she woke up. All of her other roommates did, though, so it was only her and Paisley left in the apartment. She realized that the younger girl loved sunsets when she was awoken by a soft voice.

"Lolo," Paisley whispered, tapping Shiloh's arm softly. "Lolo, look."

Shiloh groaned, wiping her eyes and checking the time. It was earlier than she was used to. She yawned, looking over at Paisley. The small girl was sitting on the edge of Shiloh's bed and gazing through the window only a few feet away. She turned around with a wide smile on her face when she heard Shiloh sit up.

"Look, Lolo, look at the sky," she chimed, pointing to the window. Shiloh couldn't help but smile at Paisley's excitement this early in the morning. She crawled next to the girl and widened her eyes when she saw just what Paisley was looking at.

"It's pretty," Shiloh whispered, and she was right. The sunrise was amazing that morning. It was bright orange, illuminating the sky and even leaving orange tinted streaks of light across the floor of Shiloh's bedroom. There were flecks of pink sprinkled throughout, too. If the sky was this gorgeous every morning, Shiloh wouldn't mind waking up so early.

Paisley nodded softly. "Colorful," she added, turning to Shiloh with a genuine smile. Shiloh laughed quietly and ran a hand through her messy morning hair. Paisley's comment suddenly gave her an idea and she stood up.

"I'm gonna go get something, okay? I'll be right back."

Paisley turned to look at her, concerned. She held up her pinky finger and bit her lip. "Promise?" she asked, tilting her head to the side.

"Of course," Shiloh smiled and locked their fingers together. She pointed out the window. "See that black car, right there?" she asked. Paisley nodded. "I've gotta get something from inside it, but then I'm coming right back up here."

"Okay," Paisley smiled softly. She stood up and pressed her palms against the window. "I will wave to you."

Giggling, Shiloh nodded. "I'll wave back," she laughed. Paisley watched her as Shiloh slipped out of the room, and the green eyed girl was soon on her way down the stairs of their apartment building.

Normally, she wouldn't leave the apartment in her pajamas. But Paisley made her do crazy things, and for some reason she didn't mind it. Once she was in the parking lot, she looked up, trying to see if she could find where their apartment window was. She noticed a flash of white and giggled, waving back to Paisley from the ground.

She probably looked like an idiot in the moment, but Shiloh couldn't care less. She finally got to her car and popped her trunk, gathering the easel and paints she'd borrowed from her professor. Locking her car, she jogged back into the building.

Before she could even get her key in the door, it was flung open. Shiloh giggled when she saw Paisley smiling widely on the other side.

"I saw you! You waved!" Paisley chimed. Shiloh nodded and slipped inside the apartment. She made her way over to the wall of windows in the back of the room and began setting up her supplies. Paisley followed close behind.

"What is this?" Paisley asked. She bent down and picked up a paintbrush, waving it back and forth in front of Shiloh's face. The green eyed girl quickly took it from her and laughed.

"My paintbrush," she set the brush on the sill of her easel. She began opening the tubes of paint and mixing small drops together to create the colors she needed. Paisley watched in awe.

"You are painting?" she asked, tilting her head to the side.

"I'm painting the sky," Shiloh pointed to the window and then down to the colors in her palette. "That way I don't forget it."

Paisley clapped her hands excitedly. She stood over Shiloh's shoulder, watching as the older girl quickly started blending the mix of oranges, pinks, and yellows together on the canvas in front of her.

"Pretty," Paisley murmured, mesmerized by what Shiloh could do with a brush. The green eyed girl laughed softly and dipped her brush in the darker shade of orange. Swiping it across the material quickly, she added the streaks at the bottom of the canvas.

When she looked back up at the window, there was a figure in the way. This reminded her all too much of the time in the park when Paisley had picked the daisies she'd been sketching. Shiloh bit her lip.

Without another thought, she bent down and grabbed a few new tubes of paint. Soon, Paisley's small silhouette was appearing in the middle of the canvas, with her palms outstretched. In real life, Paisley had her hands pressed against the glass. But in the painting, she was reaching out and touching the sunset.

"*Happy birthday to you, Happy birthday to you*," Paisley hummed softly. Shiloh looked up from her painting and smirked.

"Don't you know any other songs?"

Paisley turned around to look at Shiloh and tilted her head to the side. Shiloh laughed softly and motioned for Paisley to come towards her. The small girl smiled widely and watched as Shiloh scrolled through her phone. She walked over to the speaker and plugged her phone in, pressing the play button. Paisley's eyes widened as music started to play throughout the apartment.

Shiloh sang along to the song, grabbing her paintbrush and using it as a microphone.

Paisley giggled wildly when Shiloh accidentally smeared orange paint on her nose. The older girl crossed her eyes to try and see the paint, causing both of them to laugh even more. Shiloh shrugged it off and continued to sing.

Paisley still stood by the easel, and Shiloh held out her hand and motioned for come towards her. The younger girl tilted her head to the side as she padded over. Shiloh grabbed her hand and pulled her closer, setting her paintbrush down and twirling Paisley around.

Both girls laughed as the song continued playing. Paisley grabbed the paintbrush and placed a dot on Shiloh's forehead. The green eyed girl, in return, swiped a dot of yellow paint on Paisley's nose. The smaller girl gasped, causing both of them to erupt into giggles moments later.

The song ended and both girls collapsed back onto the couch, out of breath from dancing around for so long. Paisley looked over at Shiloh and giggled, scrunching up her nose when she smiled. Shiloh couldn't remember the last time she'd had this much fun. Pure, innocent fun. She'd missed that. Paisley brought out a side of her that she never knew she had.

"See, now wasn't that better than happy birthday?" Shiloh raised an eyebrow at the younger girl. Paisley laughed even harder, grabbing a pillow and burying her face in it.

"I'll take that as a yes," Shiloh joked.

"You are fun," Paisley giggled, looking up at the older girl. Shiloh's heart fluttered and she had to turn away to hide how red her cheeks had grown. Paisley had this effect on her that she couldn't explain.

"Same goes to you," Shiloh smiled, pushing herself up off the couch. "Are you hungry?" Paisley nodded furiously at Shiloh.

"I'll make us waffles, then," Shiloh nodded and headed into the kitchen. She gathered the ingredients she would need and placed them all on the counter. Paisley didn't follow her, but Shiloh assumed she was still watching the sunset. She mixed the batter and poured the first small amount into the waffle iron, flipping it and setting the timer.

"They're cooking right n—," Shiloh froze when she walked back into the living room and saw Paisley standing in front of the easel with a paintbrush in her hand. "What are you doing?" she asked frantically, running over to the small girl.

Paisley turned around and pointed to the canvas. "More pink," she motioned back and forth from the sky to the painting. Shiloh narrowed her eyes, looking where Paisley had added a few extra streaks of pink. It actually didn't look too bad. She'd been expecting a tornado of colors.

"Not too bad," Shiloh smiled softly, taking the paintbrush from Paisley and setting it down. "But next time, ask me before you add something, okay?" Paisley nodded softly.

"Waffles?" the small girl asked, wandering off into the kitchen. Shiloh laughed at how easily she flowed from subject to subject, and quickly followed her.

"This one's almost done," she checked the timer on the waffle iron, flipping it over and grabbing a plate. She used a fork to peel the waffle out and plopped it down onto the plate. Sliding the plate across the counter to Paisley, she grabbed the syrup and passed it over as well.

Paisley clapped her hands excitedly and popped open the syrup bottle. Shiloh went to work on pouring more mix into the machine and setting the timer. When she looked back up, Paisley had completely drenched her plate in syrup, and was now eating the waffle with her hands, peeling small pieces off and popping them into her mouth.

"So I'm guessing you haven't had waffles in a while, huh?" Shiloh sighed, shaking her head at the girl, who now had syrup all over her hands and dribbling down her chin. Paisley only giggled and smiled widely, with a mouthful of food.

The timer went off, signifying that Shiloh's waffle was done. She tossed it onto a plate and poured a small puddle of syrup on the side.

"Who needs forks, right?" Shiloh shrugged, peeling off a piece of her waffle and dipping it in the syrup. Paisley watched her and giggled. She attempted to do the same, but her waffle was already soaked in syrup, which caused Shiloh to laugh with a mouthful of food.

They finished their breakfast and Shiloh put their plates in the dishwasher. She checked the time and laughed when she realized that if Paisley hadn't woken her up, she probably would've still been asleep.

"Here," she giggled, walking over to Paisley and helping her clean off her hands with a damp towel. She swiped the syrup off the smaller girl's chin, which made both of them laugh.

"Pretty," Paisley murmured, bringing her hand up and running her fingers down Shiloh's jawline. The older girl shivered at the contact and took a deep breath. Paisley smiled widely and skipped into the living room. Shiloh, however, gave herself a minute to compose herself before following Paisley. She plopped down on the couch and pulled her phone out of her pocket.

[9:38 - Ryland] How's everything there? ;)

[9:43 - Shiloh] I don't know what that winky face is for.

[9:44 - Ryland] Hush. You've got it bad, Everest.

[9:45 - Shiloh] Too bad, I've got to go. Paisley just trashed your bedroom ;)

[9:45 - Ryland] What?!

Shiloh smirked and slid her phone back into her pocket, ignoring the multiple buzzes that followed. Paisley scooted over near Shiloh and studied the older girl.

"Lolo?"

Shiloh tilted her head to the side. "Yeah?"

Paisley pursed her lips in thought. The smaller girl also took the opportunity to not-so-sneakily scoot even closer to Shiloh. "I do not want to get hurt," Paisley mumbled. Shiloh could tell she was trying her best to stay calm.

"Hurt?" Shiloh questioned. She grew concerned. "Who would ever hurt you?"

The smaller girl's whole body stilled, as if she was frozen. Shiloh could tell she'd stuck a nerve, and she knew she had to run with what she said if she wanted to get an answer out of Paisley.

"Paisley, what are you talking about?"

Playing with her hands nervously, Paisley shook her head. "No. Bad."

"What's bad?" Shiloh bit her lip.

"Me," Paisley pointed to herself, knocking on her chest with her fist. "Stupid."

"Hey, don't call yourself that," Shiloh said softly. Her instinct took over and she pulled Paisley closer to her, letting her lean against her. "You can talk to me, Paisley."

Paisley swallowed hard and pulled down the collar of her shirt slightly. Her fingers traced one of the many bruises that lined her torso and she shivered. "I don't want to get hurt again," she mumbled.

"Again?" Shiloh held her breath when a sudden possibility crossed her mind. "Paisley, did someone hurt you?" She watched as Paisley's hands froze and the small girl's eyes darted back and forth around the room, as if she were scared someone could hear them.

"Yes," Paisley nodded once, but not looking directly at Shiloh. The older girl ran her fingers up and down Paisley's arm in an attempt to keep her calm. She took a deep breath and tried to choose her next words very carefully.

"Did the person who hurt you... do these?" Shiloh asked, pointing to the bruises on Paisley's stomach where her shirt had ridden up. The small girl quickly tugged it down to cover the bruises and proceeded to nod hesitantly.

The thought of someone hurting Paisley like that made Shiloh's blood boil, but she forced herself to remain calm for the sake of the younger girl. She took a few moments to collect herself before speaking again.

"Can you tell me who?" Shiloh asked gently. She saw Paisley's breathing quicken and crossed her fingers that she wouldn't scare the smaller girl into secrecy. A few long moments of silence passed.

"Bad Tommy," Paisley whispered. Shiloh almost didn't catch what she had said. Tommy. The name sounded familiar.

Tommy. Tom. Tom Maverick. One of her father's business partners. *Paisley's uncle.*

Shiloh sat up straighter and took both of Paisley's hands in hers. "Paisley, can you try to tell me what you remember?"

"Bad. Stupid," Paisley shook her head and pulled her hands out of Shiloh's. "I was bad. It hurt. He hurt," Paisley's voice softened and she looked back at the older girl with tears in her eyes. Shiloh immediately decided that she had done enough digging for the day.

"Okay, okay, c'mere," Shiloh whispered, not waiting before scooping Paisley up into her arms. "We don't have to talk about it now." Paisley wasn't crying, but Shiloh could tell she was scared by the way the smaller girl was practically shaking in her arms.

"I won't let him hurt you again, okay?" Shiloh pressed a soft kiss into Paisley's hair, rubbing soft circles in her back. "I've got you. You're safe here."

"Sing?" Paisley lifted her head and looked at Shiloh hopefully. The older girl reached up to wipe the few tears from Paisley's face and bit her lip.

"Only for you," Shiloh sighed. She hated singing around people, mostly because as a child her parents had forced her into voice lessons when she would have rather been drawing. But now, she was thankful for them, if her singing somehow helped calmed Paisley down.

Shiloh sighed softly when she finished singing, noticing that Paisley had calmed down significantly. The smaller girl lifted her head from Shiloh's shoulder and smiled softly.

"Pretty, Lolo," she murmured. Paisley pressed three fingers against Shiloh's lips and studied her green eyes intently. "Ocean eyes," she whispered, leaning in even closer and gazing into her eyes. Shiloh's heart sped up.

Paisley just giggled and curled back up beside Shiloh. The older girl wondered if Paisley knew the effect that she had on her. Shiloh remembered what the smaller girl had said the previous night, about wanting to kiss her.

What if Paisley *did* try to kiss her? Would Shiloh let her? The green eyed girl sighed and gazed up at the ceiling. She might as well admit it. She had feelings for Paisley. *Oh god.*

CHAPTER 14

She had feelings for Paisley.

Shiloh looked down at the smaller girl next to her and bit her lip. Of course. She couldn't have fallen for the friendly girl that always smiled at her in Starbucks, or the blonde haired girl in her Art History class.

No, she just *had* to fall for Paisley. The eccentric, messy, human tornado that had shown up on their doorstep.

But Paisley was so many other things to Shiloh. Adorable, affectionate, endearing, genuine, cuddly, goofy, enchanting, and yellow. *Yellow.*

Shiloh understood why Paisley liked that color so much. Paisley was the human equivalent of the color yellow. Bright, cheery, and joyful. Yellow was also the color of sunshine, which Shiloh considered ironic.

So to answer her own question, yes. Shiloh would let Paisley kiss her. There was only one problem, and that was the fact that Shiloh had no idea if Paisley even knew what kissing meant. What if Paisley just wanted to kiss everyone she met?

It was obvious that Paisley was capable of love. Shiloh could tell by the way the smaller girl would give the gentlest of care to even something as trivial as a flower. Paisley loved. Paisley loved everything.

But did Paisley know how to *love*?

The fact that Shiloh could see herself loving Paisley surprised even Shiloh herself. She had never seen herself falling in love. In fact, Shiloh had basically sworn off any type of relationship before she met Paisley.

Shiloh didn't like people. *Most* people. She liked her family, her roommates, and now Paisley. That was about it.

She was always afraid that someone was trying to befriend her for the wrong reasons. Or that someone was being nice to her as a joke. She hated secrecy, and lies, and everything else that most people considered to be just a normal part of life.

But now, there was Paisley. Paisley was pure, Paisley was innocent. There wasn't even a word to describe Paisley. She was just so genuinely *Paisley.*

There was no way of knowing if Paisley returned her feelings, really. Shiloh sighed heavily, realizing that she would just have to wait and see what happened.

Paisley lifted her head and furrowed her eyebrows when she felt Shiloh sigh.

"Lolo?" she tilted her head to the side. "Are you sad?"

Shiloh laughed softly and shook her head. "No, silly," she crinkled her nose. "I'm just tired." She noticed Paisley yawn and realized the smaller girl was probably still exhausted from the night before. They both hadn't gotten much sleep.

"Goodnight, Lolo," Paisley mumbled, before burying her head in Shiloh's shoulder. Shiloh bit her lip to stop herself from smiling. She stared up at the ceiling for a while, continuing to cycle through her thoughts about Paisley.

Paisley's hand twitched and Shiloh giggled when she realized she was asleep. She scooted over a bit so they could both fit longways on the couch. She laid her head back and sighed softly, inviting sleep to overtake her. Eventually her eyelids grew heavy and she drifted off to sleep.

Meanwhile, Ryland and Vanessa were being dismissed from their last class of the day. Ryland wiped the sweat from her forehead and took a big gulp from her water bottle.

"I'm beat," Ryland huffed as Vanessa grabbed her bag and slung it over her shoulder.

"Same. And I'm starving," Vanessa patted her stomach for emphasis. Ryland nodded in agreement.

"Hey, why don't we meet Leah at DiClaudio's for lunch and discuss this whole... *situation*?" Ryland asked, following her roommate down the school hallway and into the parking lot.

"I'll call her and ask," Vanessa nodded, throwing their bags into the car and whipping her phone out of her pocket.

Ten minutes later they were being led to a small booth in the back of the diner, where Leah already sat waiting for them. She greeted the girls with a soft smile. Ryland and Vanessa slid into the booth.

"So what's up?" Leah asked. She was a tad oblivious to the entire situation with Paisley. And Shiloh and Paisley. Her two roommates exchanged glances and Ryland sighed.

"Paisley," Ryland nodded once. "Her and Shiloh are getting... rather, close."

Leah smiled and nodded. "I know, isn't it great? They're getting along way better than I thought they would." The oldest girl dipped her straw into her drink and took a sip. She noticed the concerned look on Ryland's face. "Is there something wrong with that?"

"You heard what Paisley said the other day," Vanessa spoke up. "About wanting to kiss Shiloh and all... I think... *We* think that Shiloh's starting to... to develop feelings for her."

Leah raised an eyebrow. "Wait, you're serious?" Both girls nodded.

"Paisley obviously like... idolizes her," Ryland drew patterns in the condensation on her glass. "But this is Shiloh we're talking about, you know?"

Leah nodded. All three roommates knew well enough that Shiloh was not one to do feelings. Or emotions in general. The green eyed girl wouldn't even let the other girls — whom she'd known for years — see her cry.

The waiter came over and took their orders, and soon they arrived at the table. Leah sipped a spoonful of her soup and furrowed her eyebrows.

"Do we talk to Shiloh about this?" she asked. "I mean, that might not go over so well with her..."

"She denies there's anything going on whenever I try to get it out of her," Ryland sighed and shook her head. "Stubborn ass," she chuckled.

"What do we do, then?" Leah asked. Ryland and Vanessa exchanged glances before turning back to Leah.

"Well we don't want Paisley to get hurt," Vanessa nodded softly and thought for a moment. "I think all we can do right now is keep an eye on them and make sure they don't get too close, right? We could get Paisley to sleep in another room."

"I think that's a little extreme, Nessa," Leah sighed and shook her head. "I mean, I hope Shiloh is

smart enough to know that if she *does* get involved…
it's going to be… *different*."

Ryland sighed. "Leah's right. Y'know we'd get
our asses kicked if Shiloh even finds out we were
talking about this right now." Both her roommates
laughed softly. "I say we just drop a few hints to Shiloh
to make her realize the… *intensity* of Paisley's
situation."

The other two girls nodded, finishing their
conversation just as their check arrived at the table.
They paid, thanked the waiter, and left.

"I'll see you when I get home," Leah waved
from the parking lot. The smaller girl had more classes
that day, while Vanessa and Ryland were heading
straight back to the apartment. All three girls said their
goodbyes and went their separate ways.

"What do you think they're doing right now?"
Vanessa joked as they ascended the stairs up to their
apartment. Ryland laughed and pursed her lips in
thought for a moment.

"I bet Paisley's made a giant mess and Shiloh is
still asleep," Ryland smirked, and both girls burst into
laughter. Both of them knew how accurate Ryland's
guess was. Which is why when they opened the door to
their apartment, their jaws dropped open in shock.

Shiloh and Paisley were both asleep on the
couch. Paisley was completely on top of Shiloh with her
head tucked into the crook of the girl's neck. Her hands
were balled up in the sleeves of Shiloh's hoodie, as if

she was holding onto her to make sure she was still there. Meanwhile, Shiloh's arms were wrapped around Paisley's torso and holding her close against her chest.

"That's kind of adorable," Vanessa admitted, biting her lip and turning to Ryland. The light haired girl laughed softly and walked into the kitchen. Vanessa followed and hopped up to sit on the counter.

"You don't think Shiloh really has feelings for her, do you?" Ryland asked suddenly, turning around and facing Vanessa. The dark haired girl shrugged and glanced back at the pair in the living room.

"It sure seems like it," Vanessa bit her lip.

"I just…" Ryland sighed. "Shiloh *hated* her, and now," she motioned to the girls on the couch. "It's just hard for me to see her forgiving Paisley when Paisley hasn't even given her an apology. And I know it's horrible because we don't even know if Paisley even remembers doing that to Shiloh, but…"

Vanessa nodded in understanding, knowing how protective Ryland could get of Shiloh. The light haired girl had practically been Shiloh's bodyguard after she was outed in high school.

"I think anyone that can somehow turn Shiloh from hating them to… cuddling with them on a couch… must be pretty special," Vanessa joked. Ryland smiled softly and nodded.

"Yeah, I guess you're right," she ran a hand through her hair. "I'm gonna go get a shower, I'm all smelly after class."

Vanessa giggled and nodded. "Let me know when you're done," she watched as Ryland jogged upstairs. Just as she turned to walk in the living room, the bathroom door shut rather loudly. She saw Paisley stir on the couch and quickly ducked back into the kitchen.

Paisley yawned, pushing her palms into the couch and looking around. When she saw Shiloh underneath her, she giggled happily. Vanessa watched from behind the wall as Paisley studied Shiloh's face for a few moments. Just as Vanessa was about to turn away, Paisley leaned down and pecked the sleeping girl on the lips.

Vanessa had to cup her hands over her own mouth to stop herself from gasping. Had Paisley really just kissed Shiloh? The green eyed girl remained asleep, and Paisley carefully rolled off of the couch and headed towards the kitchen. Vanessa quickly acted busy, pulling out her phone and scrolling aimlessly through it.

Paisley jumped when she entered the kitchen and saw Vanessa, but she smiled widely and waved at the other girl. Vanessa laughed nervously and watched as Paisley skipped over to grab a banana.

"Sleep well?" Vanessa bit her lip to hide her smirk. Paisley turned around and nodded happily.

"Lolo is warm, yes," she smiled and held the banana out to Vanessa. "Help?"

Vanessa peeled the banana and handed it back to Paisley. The small girl smiled happily and climbed up to sit cross legged in the middle of the island.

"How was your day?" Vanessa asked, setting her phone down and tilting her head to the side. Maybe Paisley would reveal something without even being asked. Paisley looked up at the ceiling and thought for a moment.

"Lolo painted," Paisley pointed to the window in the back of the apartment. Vanessa took a few steps to the side and studied it, realizing that the silhouette in Shiloh's painting looked familiar. She smirked. Shiloh had it *bad*.

"How was your day?" Paisley repeated Vanessa's previous question.

"Good," Vanessa smiled softly. Paisley took a bite of the banana and giggled. "Ryland's home too, she's showering," Vanessa added and pointed upstairs. As if on cue, Ryland's voice filled the apartment.

"Nessa! Shower's open!" Ryland jogged down the stairs and cursed when she realized Shiloh was still asleep on the couch. The dark haired girl didn't stir, so she shrugged it off and turned into the kitchen. The minute she did, she was already being dragged into the other room by Vanessa.

"Paisley kissed Shiloh," Vanessa whispered when they were out of earshot. Ryland's eyes widened.

"What?"

"Yeah, Paisley woke up and kissed Shiloh, and then just came and ate a banana like it was nothing," Vanessa nodded towards the sleeping girl on the couch.

"Well shit," Ryland laughed, running a hand through her hair and thinking for a moment. "Do you think they've kissed before?" Vanessa shrugged.

At the same time, Shiloh whined, stirring on the couch and rolling over. She realized she wasn't on her bed as soon as she hit the ground with a thud. Groaning, the green eyed girl sat up and wiped her eyes.

Ryland and Vanessa retreated back into the kitchen as soon as they heard Shiloh wake up. Groggily, Shiloh pushed herself up to her feet. When she realized Paisley wasn't there, she grew worried.

"Pais?" she called, wiping her eyes and looking around. Paisley's face lit up when she heard Shiloh, and she hopped off the counter.

"Lolo," she hummed, finding the green eyed girl in the living room. "Look, banana," she smiled and held up her food for Shiloh to see.

"*Pais*?" Ryland whispered from in the kitchen. Vanessa raised an eyebrow at the nickname.

"We should probably make our presence known," Vanessa mumbled. Before Ryland could argue, she walked into the living room.

"Oh, h-hey Nessa," Shiloh smiled, taking a step away from Paisley to try and drown the girl's suspicions. Paisley only took another step closer to Shiloh and offered the girl a bite of her banana.

"No thanks," Shiloh couldn't help but giggle at how happy the smaller girl appeared to be now that she had the fruit. "I didn't know you guys were home," Shiloh bit her lip when Ryland soon followed Vanessa out of the kitchen.

"Have a nice nap?" Ryland teased, shoving Shiloh playfully.

"Hey!" Paisley gasped, pulling Shiloh away from Ryland and holding onto her arm protectively. "Be nice to Lolo," she said firmly, patting Shiloh's shoulder.

Shiloh laughed softly and shook her head. "It's okay, Pais, they're just joking around," she crinkled her nose at the smaller girl, who seemed to be thinking over what she had just said.

"*Pais*?" Ryland questioned, taking the opportunity. Vanessa bit her lip to try and stop herself from laughing. Shiloh's face turned bright red, but she quickly composed herself.

"Yeah, Pais. It's easier than saying *Pais-lee*," she stressed the syllables before shrugging softly.

"Mhm, sure," Ryland smirked, plopping down on the couch. Vanessa couldn't help but laugh at how blunt the light haired was being. Shiloh sent Vanessa a questioning glance.

"Can we tell her?" Vanessa whispered, leaning over and cupping Ryland's ear. The light haired girl pursed her lips in thought and shrugged.

"I guess so," Ryland glanced at Shiloh. "Go ahead. I'll watch the banana princess," she nodded towards Paisley, who was sitting in the middle of the floor and smiling contently. Vanessa nodded and motioned for Shiloh to follow her. She led the green eyed girl upstairs, just incase there was a reaction larger than they would have expected.

"What's going on?" Shiloh asked, growing more concerned by the second. Vanessa sighed and sat down on her bed, patting the space next to her for Shiloh to sit down. Shiloh shook her head and stubbornly remained standing up.

Sighing, Vanessa chose her words carefully. "We got home right before Paisley woke up," she explained, running a hand through her hair. "And when she did… she… she sort of… *kissed* you."

Shiloh's hand immediately shot up to feel her lips. "What?" she asked quietly, feeling her heart speed up in her chest. How had she not woken up?

"Yeah," Vanessa nodded, unsure of what else to say. She saw a blush form on the other girl's cheeks and couldn't help but laugh. "Bet you wish you would've been awake for that," she smirked.

Shiloh's eyes widened and she quickly moved her hand off of her lips. "I-I... I don't know what you're talking about."

"Shiloh, we all know," Vanessa laughed softly. "It's *okay*."

Sighing, Shiloh sat down on the bed and ran a hand through her hair. "What am I supposed to do?" she asked, finally giving up on denying her feelings for the girl downstairs.

Vanessa scooted over slightly and turned to face Shiloh. "What do you mean?"

"About Paisley," Shiloh bit her lip and glanced down at her hands in her lap. "I mean, I have these... *feelings*, or whatever they are, for her... but she's just... Paisley. How am I supposed to know if she... y'know?"

Vanessa raised her eyebrows in surprise. She hadn't expected that. "So you're scared she doesn't... return your feelings?" the dark skinned girl asked carefully. Shiloh nodded and sighed heavily.

"Lolo?!" a panicked voice came from downstairs. Shiloh stood up quickly, biting her lip and glancing at Vanessa.

"Go ahead," the other girl laughed, and Shiloh jogged downstairs.

"Yeah?" she asked, sliding to a halt in the living room. Paisley whipped her head around when she heard Shiloh's voice. She ran into the green eyed girl's arms and clung to her.

"I lost you," Paisley mumbled into Shiloh's shirt. The green eyed girl bit her lip when she saw Ryland stand up from the couch. The light haired girl mouthed

'*Did she tell you?*' and pointed upstairs. Shiloh nodded slowly.

"I'll give you two some privacy," Ryland grinned, disappearing up the stairs before Shiloh could argue. Sighing, the green eyed girl placed her hands on Paisley's shoulders and took a step backwards.

"Hey, I was only upstairs," Shiloh said softly, feeling bad that she'd scared Paisley. The smaller girl nodded and bit her lip. "C'mon," Shiloh led Paisley over to the couch and sat down next to her. "We should talk."

CHAPTER 15

Meanwhile, the moment Ryland appeared upstairs, Vanessa had practically dragged her friend into the bedroom and closed the door behind them.

"Shiloh admitted it," Vanessa smirked. Ryland tilted her head to the side.

"Well, not exactly, but close enough. She definitely has feelings for her" Vanessa explained. "And we were completely wrong."

"*Wrong*?" Ryland asked, sitting down on the bed. "How were we wrong?"

"We were all concerned about the feelings not being returned by *Shiloh*, right?" Vanessa asked, earning a nod from the other girl.

"Well that's not the case. Shiloh's scared that *Paisley* doesn't return her feelings." Vanessa laughed and sat down. "She's got it bad, Ryland."

"What? That's insane," Ryland shook her head and laughed softly. "It's obvious Paisley adores her, you see the way she looked at her?" Vanessa nodded in agreement.

"Out of all people, Shiloh chooses *Paisley*," Ryland laughed and ran a hand through her hair. "I see why, though, now that I think about it."

Vanessa raised an eyebrow in confusion.

"Shiloh hates fake people, Nessa," Ryland explained, gesturing to the stairs. "Paisley's the complete opposite of fake."

"Damn," Vanessa laughed, realizing how accurate Ryland was. "We've got to tell Leah."

Ryland nodded in agreement. "Maybe Shiloh will actually talk to us about it now," she stood up and ran a hand through her hair. "C'mon, let's go see what the lovebirds are up to."

Both girls giggled when they got to the bottom of the stairs and saw Paisley cuddled up in Shiloh's side on the couch. Shiloh looked up and felt her cheeks turn red when she caught sight of her two roommates looking over at them.

"Is she okay?" Vanessa asked, trying not to make Shiloh feel uncomfortable. The green eyed girl nodded slowly.

"She didn't know where I was," Shiloh answered honestly. Ryland and Vanessa exchanged glances and both smirked.

"That's adorable," Ryland commented, plopping down on the other side of the couch and raising an eyebrow at Shiloh. The green eyed girl glared at her, but

Ryland knew she wasn't serious. Paisley looked up at the other girls and smiled shyly.

"What're we doing for dinner?" Ryland asked, raising an eyebrow at Shiloh.

"I don't know, *Ryland*, I thought *you* were supposed to be in charge of dinner tonight?" the other girl smirked and Vanessa high-fived her.

"Pizza?" Ryland shrugged. Paisley's eyes widened.

"Yes, pizza, yes please," Paisley clapped her hands together, causing the other three girls to double over in laughter.

"Pizza it is then," Ryland nodded once. Paisley giggled excitedly and smiled over at Shiloh.

"Too cute," Ryland muttered under her breath and shook her head. Shiloh shoved her playfully and Paisley giggled.

"Oh, so you stick up for *her*, but not for me?" Ryland crinkled her nose at Paisley. "I see how it is," she teased. Paisley giggled and hid her head in Shiloh's shoulder.

"Hey Paisley, wanna come get the pizza with me?" Ryland asked, nudging Vanessa. Paisley looked up at Shiloh questioningly.

"Go ahead," the green eyed girl motioned for Paisley to follow Ryland. "I'll be right here when you get back." Paisley nodded with a soft smile and hopped up to her feet, engaging Ryland in an animated conversation about pizza as they exited the apartment.

"So…" Vanessa started, falling back on the couch next to Shiloh. "Continuing our conversation from earlier… you're really scared that *Paisley* is the one not returning the feelings?"

Shiloh raised an eyebrow. "Yeah, I mean, why wouldn't I be?"

"To be honest, we were sort of more concerned that you didn't return *her* feelings," Vanessa admitted. Shiloh looked surprised.

"*Her* feelings?" the green eyed girl asked. Vanessa nodded immediately, surprised that Shiloh appeared to be this oblivious.

"She's completely attached to you, Shy," the other girl said with a laugh. "That girl absolutely adores you, I don't get how you don't see it." Shiloh's cheeks flushed red and she quickly looked away.

"But she isn't… well at least in high school, she wasn't attracted to girls," Shiloh bit her lip and looked back up. "What if she isn't?"

"Who says she wasn't? Either way, she is now, because trust me — the way she looks at you says it all," Vanessa said firmly, wanting Shiloh to believe her words. "Besides, wasn't *she* the one who said she wanted to kiss you?"

"Yeah…" Shiloh's face grew even redder. "But what if us kissing doesn't even mean anything to her? What if she doesn't underst—,"

"*Shiloh*, stop thinking to much," Vanessa laughed and shook her head. "You need to stop thinking about everything that could possibly go wrong and try to focus on something good that could come out of this, okay?"

Sighing, the green eyed girl nodded slowly. "I guess I do, yeah."

Vanessa smiled and shoved her friend playfully in the shoulder. "Just give it time, Shy," she stood up and ran a hand through her hair. "I'm gonna go shower really quick before they get back with dinner." Shiloh nodded and watched as her roommate disappeared up the stairs, leaving her all alone in the living room.

Sighing, Shiloh wandered over to the easel in the back of the apartment and began adding the smaller details into her painting.

———————

Meanwhile, Ryland and Paisley had just left the pizza place, and were now on the way back to the apartment. Paisley smiled happily, holding the warm box of food on her lap and watching the buildings whiz by.

"So, Paisley," Ryland bit her lip and glanced over at the other girl. "You and Shiloh seem to be getting along pretty well."

"Yes," Paisley nodded once. She smiled and turned to look at Ryland. "Lolo is my friend."

Ryland laughed softly. "Do you think, maybe... you like her as more than a friend?" Paisley tilted her head to the side and Ryland continued. "Like... romantically. Like you wanna kiss her and hug her and be her girlfriend and shit."

Paisley's eyes widened and she shook her head quickly. "No, please," she brought her hands up as if she were surrendering. "Bad. Stupid Paisley."

"Paisley, you're not stupid?" Ryland raised an eyebrow in disbelief. She saw how distraught Paisley had grown and quickly pulled over to the side of the road, parking the car and turning to the smaller girl. "What's wrong?"

"Please," Paisley shook her head, cowering back against the car door, as far away from Ryland as possible. "Stupid," she muttered under her breath.

"You're not stupid, Paisley," Ryland repeated, reaching out and taking one of Paisley's hands. The smaller girl flinched, but allowed it to happen. "The reason I asked, well... Vanessa saw you kiss Shiloh when you woke up an—,"

"Please!" Paisley cried, covering her face with her hands and tucking her head down. "Sorry, sorry, bad, sorry," she mumbled, shaking her head.

"*Paisley*," Ryland said softly, trying to get the smaller girl to calm down. "Paisley, you're not in trouble or anything," she bit her lip, wondering just what exactly was going on in the smaller girl's head.

"Sorry," Paisley's small voice cracked and she looked up slowly. Ryland cursed herself for bringing it up, because now she'd have to tell Shiloh about Paisley's minor breakdown, which also meant admitting to questioning the smaller girl about her relationship with Shiloh.

"Paisley, there's nothing wrong with you liking Shiloh like that," Ryland reached out and squeezed the smaller girl's hand. "You love who you love, no one has control over that. Did… did someone make you think that was bad?"

Paisley just nodded slowly. Ryland decided not to push her any further.

"Okay, well whoever told you that was wrong, okay? I promise. You can't tell your taste buds to love broccoli, right?" Ryland asked, trying to use food as a reference for the smaller girl. Paisley nodded.

"Well, see? It's the same thing. You can't just tell yourself to love someone you don't want to love. Just like you can't control how much you love bananas, you can't control if you're attracted to girls instead of boys.

It's just who *you* are," Ryland said firmly, poking Paisley's nose and making the smaller girl giggle.

"Promise?" Paisley whispered, holding out her pinky finger hesitantly.

"Duh," Ryland flicked her hair out of her face and locked their fingers together. "You don't need some stupid promise to tell you that, either. Your body already tells you when you see someone you like, right?"

Paisley tilted her head to the side in confusion.

"Like... when you look at Shiloh, how do you feel?"

Paisley thought for a moment. "Happy," she nodded once.

"Do you get butterflies in your stomach?" Ryland asked with a small smile. She saw Paisley ponder the saying and then nod quickly.

"Yes, like this," Paisley wiggled her fingers in front of her face. "When she is happy, my cheeks..." she pressed her hands to her face "They get happy."

Ryland laughed at the girl's innocence. "And so... you like her? In the way where you want to kiss her and hold her hand and that kinda stuff?" She felt ridiculous explaining it like this, but she knew Paisley understood.

She noticed the small girl's hesitation and squeezed her hand. "Hey, remember what we just talked about? There's *nothing* wrong with it, Paisley, promise."

"I like her," Paisley said softly, tasting the words on her tongue for the first time.

"There we go," Ryland laughed, giving Paisley a thumbs up and starting the car once more. Paisley was smiling like an idiot as she pulled back onto the street and got back onto the course for the way home.

"I like her ocean eyes," Paisley continued, looking down at her hands in her lap.

"Yeah?" Ryland smirked.

"Yes," Paisley nodded once. "I like her ocean eyes. And her lips. They're pink." She gazed out the window. "Pink like… the flowers, at the park."

Ryland giggled.

"And I like her smile. She smiles with her lips," Paisley continued, and Ryland realized she didn't plan on stopping anytime soon. "And it makes me happy. And she giggles, and that makes me happy."

"Sounds li—," Ryland was interrupted.

"And her nose is cute. She laughs, and her nose laughs too. It crinkles," Paisley poked her own nose, giggling softly to herself. "Lolo sings, too. It is pretty."

"I've created a monster," Ryland mumbled under her breath, looking over at the smaller girl who continued talking, mostly to herself.

"Lolo is like an angel," Paisley pressed her palms against the cool glass of the car window. "And she is nice. Lolo is nice and funny and yellow. Lolo is very yellow."

"Yellow?" Ryland spoke up.

"Yes, yellow," Paisley nodded once, as if that was enough of an explanation. "And I like Lolo."

"Well w—," the light haired girl groaned half-heartedly when Paisley continued talking over her.

"Lolo is… like a flower," Paisley nodded, proud at herself for the reference. "She smells good. Like a flower. And… and she's pretty. Flowers are pretty, too."

Ryland nodded softly as they pulled into the apartment parking lot. "Hate to burst your bubble, Paisley, but we're home."

"Lolo is at home!" Paisley's face lit up and she scrambled out of the car. Ryland bit her lip when she realized the smaller girl was now holding the pizza box upside down. Sighing, she followed Paisley through the two glass doors and into the elevator.

"I love pizza," Paisley smiled, shaking the box in front of Ryland as the elevator made its way upwards. Ryland gave in and took the box from her hands, holding it tight in her own. Paisley didn't seem to mind, she just wandered over and traced patterns in the metallic wall of the elevator.

The elevator dinged and the doors slowly rolled open. Paisley skipped down the hallway, knocking on each door. Ryland cursed, quickly unlocking their own apartment and pulling the girl inside before the annoyed neighbors answered their doors.

"Lolo! Pizza!" Paisley called, looking around the apartment for the green eyed girl.

"I'm coming!" Shiloh called, jogging down the stairs and running her hand through her long hair. Paisley smiled widely when she saw Shiloh, and padded over to her.

"*Lolo*," she hummed, poking Shiloh's nose and giggling.

"Pizza's not getting any warmer!" Ryland called from the kitchen. Shiloh laughed when Paisley sprinted into the other room, and she followed close behind. She raised an eyebrow when she saw how disheveled the pizza was. Just as she was about to ask Ryland what happened, Paisley turned to her.

"I carried it myself," Paisley said proudly. Shiloh nodded, her question already answered.

Ryland handed them each plates and they thanked her, picking a slice and heading into the living room. Vanessa joined them a few minutes later, and then the familiar jingle of keys signified that Leah was home.

"Two of our neighbors are in the hallway arguing over a ghost knocking on their doors," Leah giggled, shutting the door behind her. Ryland glanced over at Paisley, who seemed completely oblivious.

"Pizza's in the kitchen," Vanessa mumbled with a mouthful of food, making Paisley giggle wildly.

"What's so funny?" Shiloh teased, also with a mouthful of food. Paisley turned to her and laughed even harder. "*M' just trying to eat m' pizza*," Shiloh mumbled before taking another bite. Paisley giggled and covered her face with her hands.

Leah soon joined them and Paisley begged to watch an episode of *Friends,* which had quickly become her favorite TV show.

"I am Rachel, Rachel is me," Vanessa laughed, sprawled out on the couch. "She always thinks she's doing the right thing and ends up screwing things up even more." The other roommates laughed, nodding in agreement.

"I think Ryland is Joey," Shiloh spoke up, pointing to the screen. Ryland gasped in fake shock.

"Why am I Joey?" she huffed, making Shiloh laugh.

"Cause he eats a lot and always makes a fool out himself in front of the opposite sex," Shiloh teased. Ryland shoved her playfully. Paisley glared at her from her spot on the floor.

"If I'm Joey, then you're obviously Chandler," Ryland rebutted. "Always making jokes that no one else understands."

Shiloh laughed, holding up her hands as if she was surrendering. "I won't argue with that."

"Leah's totally Monica," Vanessa spoke up. "She's the responsible one, and also a complete neat freak." Everyone but Leah laughed, and they all received a playful glare from the girl.

"What about me?" Paisley turned around and looked at her friends. In return, they all looked to Shiloh for an answer. The green eyed girl bit her lip.

"You're like Phoebe," Shiloh pointed to the blonde actress who had just appeared on the screen. "She didn't really live with them at first, but they befriended her anyway. And she's funny, but sometimes people don't understand her jokes. But that's okay, because she's really good at making people laugh despite that. And she sees the beauty in everything. And she isn't afraid to be herself."

When she finished, she received smirks from Ryland and Vanessa, and she rolled her eyes.

"Okay," Paisley hummed happily, turning back to the screen.

"You're sure the charmer, Everest," Ryland teased. Shiloh threw a pillow at her roommate and stood up from the couch.

"I'm gonna take a quick shower," Shiloh announced, making sure her roommates heard her before slipping up the spiral staircase. She hummed quietly to herself as she stepped into the shower, letting the hot water relax her muscles.

Fifteen minutes later, Shiloh wiped her eyes and reached out from behind the curtain to grab a towel. She wrapped the fluffy towel around her body before stepping out of the shower. She gasped moments later.

"Hi," Paisley smiled, sitting on the counter and kicking her legs back and forth aimlessly.

"Uh, hi," Shiloh stuttered, holding the towel tight around herself. "What are you doing in here?" she asked, tilting her head to the side.

"I was waiting for you," Paisley smiled. Shiloh narrowed her eyes when she saw Ryland smirking from the crack in the door across the hallway. She sighed and grabbed her hairbrush from the counter before walking into her bedroom. As always, Paisley followed close behind. Shiloh stopped her at the door.

"Can you wait here? I need to get changed," she bit her lip. Paisley nodded slowly and sat down in the middle of the hallway. Shiloh held up a finger, signaling for her to wait. She grabbed one of her hoodies and a pair of pajama pants and tossed them to Paisley. "Go change in the bathroom."

Paisley brought the hoodie up to her face and smiled eagerly. She loved Shiloh's clothes. Nodding, she tiptoed into the bathroom and closed the door.

Shiloh quickly got changed into a hoodie and pajama shorts. Moments later, there was a knock at her door. Paisley didn't bother waiting for a response, she just smiled and wandered into the room.

"Hey," Shiloh laughed, sitting down on the edge of her bed. She heard her phone buzz from the nightstand and grabbed it. Paisley sat down next to her and hugged a pillow to her chest.

[8:21 - Ryland] Forgot to tell you - Paisley had a freak out in the car when we started talking about her... 'liking' you (don't hate me I had to). Apparently someone didn't exactly want her liking girls.

[8:22 - Ryland] But she definitely likes you, ocean eyes ;)

[8:22 - Ryland] You can thank me later.

Shiloh furrowed her eyebrows and set her phone down.

"Hey Paisley, can we talk?" she asked, scooting back on the bed and patting the space next to her. Paisley crawled over and sat cross legged, tilting her head to the side.

"Did your uncle ever hurt you because of someone you liked?" Shiloh bit her lip, hoping she wouldn't scare the smaller girl into silence. Paisley looked down at her hands and took a deep breath before nodding.

"Why?"

Paisley bit her lip. "I do not like boys," she mumbled and looked up at Shiloh. "Boys are not pretty."

Shiloh couldn't help but laugh softly. "Your uncle has an ugly soul, you know that? Because there's nothing wrong with you liking girls," she took a deep breath and thought for a moment. She couldn't imagine someone hurting her for who she liked. If her parents hadn't been supportive when she came out, she had no idea where she would be.

"When I told my dad that I liked girls, he was confused when I started crying," Shiloh started, sharing a part of her life she didn't share with many people.

"He told me there was no reason to cry. He said he saw it as just discovering something new about his daughter... That it was no different than me telling him about a new band I liked, or showing him a new project I did in art class. It was a part of who I was, and nothing to be ashamed of. He told me he didn't think it was a big deal because it didn't define me. I was still his daughter, no matter who I loved."

"He is nice?" Paisley asked, tilting her head to the side. Shiloh giggled and nodded.

"Yeah, he's awesome."

"You…?" the smaller girl looked down at her hands. "You like… girls, too?"

Shiloh nodded once more. "Yup," she laughed softly, realizing that Paisley had no clue that she had been the one to out Shiloh. It was comforting, in a way. She saw the smaller girl yawn. "Tired?"

Paisley looked hesitant, but nodded anyway. Shiloh leaned over and turned out the light, crawling under the covers and patting the bed, signifying for Paisley to do the same. Once the small girl was curled up beside her, Shiloh laid her head down.

"Goodnight, Pais," she whispered.

"Wait," Paisley blurted out. Shiloh, confused, lifted her head and looked at the smaller girl. The only light they had was the dim moonlight streaming through the window. Paisley looked almost angelic.

"What?" Shiloh asked, biting her lip at the lack of space between them.

"I like you, Lolo," Paisley whispered. Before Shiloh could respond, Paisley leaned up and planted a quick kiss on the older girl's lips. Without another word, Paisley laid her head back down on her pillow and closed her eyes.

Shiloh felt a rush of adrenaline surge though her, and quickly brought her hands up to her lips to make sure that had actually just happened. She looked at Paisley, who seemed completely oblivious. Her cheeks flushed pink and she slowly lay back down with her back to the smaller girl. Paisley had just kissed her.

A few minutes of silence passed and Shiloh assumed Paisley had fallen asleep. She, on the other hand, was now too wired to sleep. Even the smallest kiss from Paisley drew the most intense feelings out of her.

"Please do not be mad," Paisley sat up abruptly, unable to hold it in. She bit her lip and averted her gaze from Shiloh. Startled, the green eyed girl sat up slowly, tilting her head to the side.

"I'm not mad?" she raised an eyebrow. "You think I would be mad at you for kissing me?" Paisley nodded slowly.

Shiloh laughed and shook her head, reaching out and pressing her fingers to Paisley's lips, mimicking an action the smaller girl had done multiple times before. "I like you too, Pais," she said with a soft smile. She saw a flash of hope in the girl's eyes.

"Promise?" Paisley asked, holding out her pinky eagerly. Shiloh giggled and locked their fingers together, bringing their interlocked fingers to her lips and planting a soft kiss where their hands met.

"Promise."

"Thank you," Paisley smiled widely, crawling over and tackling Shiloh in a hug. Surprised, Shiloh laid back on the bed, still holding onto Paisley. Both girls giggled.

"No, thank *you*, Paisley," Shiloh whispered. She kissed Paisley's forehead, feeling relief wash over her. She hadn't realized how tolling it had been to hold those feelings in for so long.

She scooted over slightly so she could pull the blankets back over them. Paisley's small hands combed aimlessly though Shiloh's hair, giving her the chills.

"And next time, you can wake me up whenever you want to kiss me," Shiloh smirked. Paisley lifted her head and her eyes widened. "Ryland told me," the green eyed girl quickly explained.

"Sorry," Paisley quickly shook her head and tried to sit back up, but Shiloh tightened her grip on the girl.

"Never apologize for kissing me," Shiloh whispered, rubbing Paisley's back to soothe her. The smaller girl sighed and laid her head back down on Shiloh's chest.

"Sing?" Paisley whispered hopefully. Shiloh sighed and nodded.

"Only for you," she trailed her fingers up and down Paisley's spine. She began singing quietly, and was surprised at just how quickly Paisley seemed to calm down.

She paused for a moment, feeling Paisley's slow breathing against her neck. Shiloh smiled softly, kissing the sleeping girl's forehead and laying her head back on her pillow. She could get used to this.

C H A P T E R 1 6

Shiloh awoke the next morning to find Paisley still asleep. She laughed softly, realizing that the smaller girl had snaked her arms up the sleeves of Shiloh's hoodie to keep her hands warm. The events of the night before played in her head like a movie scene and she couldn't help the smile that spread across her face.

"Pais," she whispered, nudging the smaller girl softly. "Pais, I have to get up," she laughed, looking over at the clock and remembering that she had class that morning.

"*Hmmm*," the smaller girl hummed, fluttering her eyes open and smiling widely the moment she saw Shiloh next to her. "Hi," she beamed.

"Morning," Shiloh laughed, sliding out from underneath the girl and sitting up.

"I have class today," Shiloh explained, walking over to her closet and digging through her clothes. "Which means you get to stay home with Leah until I'm back, okay?"

Paisley nodded softly. She'd been getting better at realizing that Shiloh does, in fact, come back home when she leaves in the mornings. That didn't mean she liked it, though.

Shiloh slipped into the bathroom and changed into a comfortable outfit for class, wearing an old t-shirt because she knew they'd be painting that day. Paisley waited patiently outside the door and smiled like an idiot when Shiloh re-emerged.

"Someone's in a good mood," Shiloh giggled. Paisley just nodded.

"Yes, I kissed you," she chimed, reminding Shiloh of the night before.

Shiloh's cheeks grew red. "That you did," she laughed and ran a hand through her hair. "You can always do it again, y'know," she raised an eyebrow. Paisley's face lit up, as if she hadn't even considered the idea.

"Okay," she nodded once. Without another word, Paisley grabbed Shiloh's face and gently planted kisses all over her face, finally pecking her lips once before taking a step back and smiling widely. Shiloh's face was blood red by the time she was done.

"Your turn," Paisley smiled.

"My turn?" Shiloh laughed. Paisley just nodded, and Shiloh pulled Paisley closer to her. The smaller girl giggled excitedly, which made Shiloh's stomach flutter. She placed one hand on the back of Paisley's neck and closed the gap between them, slowly bringing their lips together.

This kiss lasted longer than their ones they'd shared before, if only by a few seconds. Kissing Paisley was different than anyone else Shiloh had ever kissed. The smaller girl was soft and gentle, and it made Shiloh's heart skip a beat. They pulled apart and moments later were interrupted by the flash of a camera.

"What the...?" Shiloh whipped her head around, spotting Leah peering out of her doorway. "Oh my god," Shiloh's cheeks grew red and she covered her face. Paisley giggled.

"Vanessa and Ryland are never going to believe this," Leah smirked, walking over to them and tucking her phone into her pocket. Paisley clapped her hands excitedly.

"C'mon Shy, it's cute," Leah laughed and nudged her roommate. Shiloh took her hands away from her face and scowled at the older girl, but couldn't hold back her smile.

"I hate to interfere, but you're gonna be late for class if you don't hurry your ass up," Leah pointed to the clock and Shiloh cursed under her breath. All three girls ended up downstairs, and Paisley wandered into the kitchen.

"So you two..." Leah smirked once she and Shiloh were alone. "How'd that come about?"

Shiloh shrugged, grabbing her bag from the couch. "She kissed me and it just sorta happened," she bit her lip to hide her smile when Leah clapped her hands happily. Just then, Paisley padded back into the room and handed Shiloh a banana.

"Breakfast," she smiled softly. Shiloh giggled, finding the small gesture extremely adorable.

"Thank you," Shiloh tossed her backpack over her shoulder. "I'll be back after lunchtime, okay?" Paisley nodded softly. Shiloh bent down and placed a kiss on the younger girl's cheek. "See you soon," she smiled softly, waving as she slipped out the door. Once she was gone, Paisley sighed and sat down on the couch.

"You like her a lot, huh?" Leah giggled. Paisley looked up and nodded happily. "I'm glad," the older girl added, walking into the kitchen. "Are you hungry?"

The pair made breakfast together and Paisley was about to wander back upstairs when she noticed something out of place in the living room, she quickly found Leah in the kitchen and tugged on her sleeve.

"Lolo's painting," Paisley pointed in the living room. Leah tilted her head in thought for a moment before realizing what Paisley meant.

"She needs that for her class, doesn't she?"

Paisley nodded. Leah grabbed her keys from the counter and motioned for Paisley to go grab her painting. "Let's go pay her a visit, then," she smiled. Paisley's face lit up and she eagerly followed Leah out of the apartment, painting in hand.

Meanwhile, Shiloh sat in class, cursing herself for forgetting her required project for the second time in two weeks. She knew she wouldn't hear the end of this. She laid her head down on her desk as her professor droned on and on about the difference between oil and acrylic paints. She had nearly fallen asleep when she heard the class fall silent. Lifting her head, she looked around to see what had caused her teacher to stop speaking.

"Uh, hi, I just needed to drop this off for Shiloh."

Shiloh looked over at the door when she heard Leah's voice. She sighed in relief when she saw her roomate holding her painting, and silently thanked her.

"You can set it in the back of the classroom, over there," her professor pointed behind him. Leah nodded and hurried over to place the painting in the back of the classroom. Shiloh met her eyes and mouthed '*thank you*,' Leah smiled and gave her a thumbs up.

"Lolo?"

Everyone's heads turned back to the door, including Shiloh. Paisley recognized her and waved violently. The small girl glanced at Leah before slipping inside the classroom and running over to Shiloh. The older girl's heart sped up and she felt everyone's eyes on her.

"Hi," Paisley beamed, running over to the table where Shiloh sat and smiling widely. Shiloh bit her lip to hide her smile at how enthusiastic Paisley appeared.

"Hey," Shiloh said softly. Leah turned around and saw Paisley, cursing herself for not making the girl wait in the car.

"Paisley, c'mon," Leah hissed, motioning quickly for Paisley to stop disrupting the class.

"Go," Shiloh giggled and nodded towards Leah. Paisley pouted but nodded slowly.

"Bye Lolo," she mumbled, turning to leave but pausing for a moment. Paisley turned back around, cupped Shiloh's cheeks, and planted a quick kiss on her lips. Shiloh's face grew bright red and she heard Paisley giggling as she ran back over to Leah, who had just apologized to the teacher. Both girls were soon out of their sight and Shiloh heard the whispers of her classmates.

Shiloh bit the inside of her cheek in an attempt to hide a smile on her face. She looked down at her sketchbook as her teacher started his lecture once more, but the only thing she could focus on was the sensation of Paisley's lips against her own.

Eventually, after what felt like forever, the class was dismissed. Shiloh tried to escape out of the door first, but her teacher motioned for her to come over to his desk. Biting her lip, Shiloh prepared herself for the worst. Eventually, all of her other classmates filed out of the room and she was the only one left.

"You're just full of surprises, aren't you Shiloh?" her teacher chuckled and placed her painting on the desk in front of him, studying it closely. "You've gone with a different medium for the first time, and I have to say, I'm impressed."

"Wow... I, uh, thank you," Shiloh laughed softly to herself, flattered by his compliment.

"I can't say I'm surprised anymore, though," Mr. Robertson pulled her sketches out from last week and laid them next to her painting. "After seeing your interaction with your visitor today, that is."

Shiloh bit her lip, wondering if she was in trouble.

"Looks like you've found yourself a muse, Miss Everest," he chuckled and nodded to the artwork on the table.

"A what?" Shiloh asked, tilting her head to the side.

"A muse," he pointed to the silhouette of the girl in the painting. "Someone who you use as inspiration for your art. She looks familiar, does she not?" he asked, nodding for Shiloh to look at where he was pointing. Shiloh's cheeks grew red.

"I... I-I..."

"Pablo Picasso had many muses, out of his many romantic interests," he continued, ignoring how flustered his student had grown. "Manet found his muse in a stranger on the street, and has over eight paintings of her."

"I didn't mean for her to interrupt y—,"

"Does she make you happy?"

Shiloh swallowed hard. "Yeah," she said softly.

"Then all is forgiven," her teacher smiled and stacked her sketches back into her folder. "I don't say this often, Shiloh, but you have potential. You just needed someone to bring it out of you."

Shiloh looked down to the ground to try and hide her smile. Paisley seemed to be helping her in every aspect of life. "Thank you," she said softly, looking back up and running a hand through her hair.

"You're dismissed," he nodded towards the door. "Keep up the good work."

"Thank you, again, thank you," Shiloh adjusted her bag on her shoulder and glanced at the clock, realizing she had to be at her next class soon. She exited the classroom without another word and quickly hurried to her Art History class.

Time dragged on and eventually Shiloh found herself tossing her bag into the backseat of her car and heading back to the apartment. When she was about halfway there, she made a rush decision and quickly pulled off onto a different road. Ten minutes later, she ended up at the shopping mall and made it inside just as it started to rain.

About twenty minutes later, she sprinted back to her car with a few shopping bags in her hands. It was pouring down rain, and as she pulled out of the parking lot, a loud clap of thunder startled her. Seconds later, lightning flashed across the sky.

It took Shiloh a bit longer to get home than usual because of the storm. Eventually, she made it back to the apartment parking lot and pulled her hood over her head to try and protect herself from the rain. It didn't help much, though, because it was pouring down so hard that she was soaking wet by the time she made it inside the elevator.

She heard thunder rumbling in the distance as she was walking down the hallway to her apartment. Immediately afterwards, she heard someone cry out — someone who sounded exactly like Paisley. She quickly ran to their door and fumbled with her keys. When she finally got the door unlocked, she burst inside and scanned the apartment.

"Shiloh, thank god," Leah sighed in relief. Shiloh turned to look in the corner of the apartment, feeling her heart drop when she saw Paisley curled up in the corner with her head in her knees. "She started freaking out when the storm started," Leah explained, standing up from where she'd been sitting next to Paisley.

Shiloh nodded, dropping her bag on the floor and jogging over to Paisley.

"Pais, Pais it's me," she said softly as she knelt down next to the shaking girl. Paisley lifted her head slowly.

"Lolo?" she murmured, reaching up and placing a hand on the girl's cheek, as if she was making sure she was real. Shiloh could tell how scared the smaller girl was by the way she was shaking, and it broke her heart.

"Yeah, I'm here," Shiloh whispered, scooting next to Paisley and pulling her into her arms. "You don't like storms?" she asked carefully, biting her lip. Paisley nodded slowly and didn't hesitate to bury her head in Shiloh's neck.

"Neither do I, but I've got you, we're safe here, okay?" Shiloh rubbed small circles in Paisley's back, trying to soothe her. "I promise, nothing's gonna hurt you," she whispered, resting her chin on the smaller girl's head and watching the rain pour down outside.

Another clap of thunder sent Paisley's hands scrambling to ball themselves in Shiloh's shirt, clinging onto her for dear life. Leah sent Shiloh a sympathetic look, which Shiloh returned. She sighed and continued to run circles in Paisley's back.

"Do you want me to sing?" Shiloh asked, biting her lip and looking down at Paisley. The small girl didn't look at her, but she nodded with her head tucked in Shiloh's shoulder.

"Only for you," Shiloh sighed.

As she finished singing, Shiloh took a deep breath. Leah had slipped away upstairs to give the girls some privacy. Paisley looked up at her slowly just as another clap of thunder startled both of the girls. The smaller girl immediately hid her face once more.

"More," Paisley mumbled into Shiloh's hoodie. The older girl sighed softly and began to sing again.

An hour, and a lot of songs later, Paisley fell asleep in Shiloh's arms just as the thunderstorm was dying down. Leah came downstairs a few minutes later and laughed softly at the sight of the two girls.

Shiloh glared at her playfully before slowly rising to her feet, keeping Paisley in her arms and walking over to the couch. Leah turned on an episode of *Friends*, which all the roommates had now become addicted to thanks to Paisley. Halfway through their second episode, the door swung open to reveal Ryland and Vanessa.

"How are my little lovebirds?" Ryland cooed, walking over to Shiloh with a wide grin on her face. Shiloh rolled her eyes and nodded to the sleeping girl in her lap, glaring at Ryland to signify not to wake her.

"She was scared of the storm and Shiloh sang to her the entire time until she fell asleep," Leah swooned from her spot on the couch, causing Vanessa and Ryland to both clap their hands happily. Shiloh felt her cheeks turn red and she quickly looked down.

"Y'all are adorable," Leah laughed. The other two roommates nodded in agreement.

"We bought stuff for dinner," Vanessa added, holding up a shopping bag. "We've gotta shower cause' we just kicked ass in hip hop class, but then we can eat and watch a movie or something to kick off the weekend." Ryland fist bumped the other girl in agreement.

"Well then hurry up, you know when Paisley wakes up she's gonna be starving," Leah motioned towards Shiloh, who nodded in agreement. They all had quickly grown aware of Paisley's never ending appetite.

Vanessa and Ryland disappeared upstairs, and another episode of *Friends* later, all five roommates headed into the kitchen where Ryland had spread out all of the ingredients she'd bought to make sandwiches.

"Lolo, look!" Paisley beamed, holding up her sandwich. Shiloh narrowed her eyes and burst into laughter.

"Paisley, you only put bananas in there," Ryland laughed from across the counter. Paisley tilted her head to the side in question, unsure what the problem was. Shiloh laughed, turning around and grabbing a jar of peanut butter from the pantry and unscrewing the lid.

"Let's at least add something besides bananas," Shiloh took the top slice of bread from Paisley's sandwich and spread a thin layer of peanut butter on the underside before placing it back on her sandwich. "There, try it, you'll like it," she giggled.

Paisley looked at the sandwich in her hands for a few moments, studying it before taking a bite. She immediately smiled widely and shot her fist out in Shiloh's direction. The green eyed girl laughed and bumped her fist, which made Paisley giggle happily with a mouthful of food. Things were different, <u>Lauren</u> realized. Paisley had somehow managed to work her way into their hearts and bring them all closer together.

CHAPTER 17

All five girls sat on a circle on the carpet in their living room, deciding to talk instead of watching TV during dinner.

Shiloh suddenly remembered something and got up, jogging over to the door and grabbing the shopping bag from earlier that day. She sat back down with a small smile on her face and plopped the bag on the floor in front of Paisley.

"I got you something," Shiloh smiled softly. Ryland, Leah, and Vanessa all collectively '*awwww*'-ed from their spots on the carpet.

"For me?" Paisley asked, a small smile appearing on her face. Shiloh nodded and Paisley clapped her hands excitedly. "Open?"

"Go on," Shiloh motioned to the bag. Paisley giggled and pulled the bag into her lap, digging inside and pulling out the bright yellow hoodie Shiloh had bought.

"Yellow!" Paisley squealed. She immediately hugged the sweatshirt to her chest and smiled widely. "Thank you, you're welcome," she crawled over and tackled Shiloh in a bone-crushing hug.

Shiloh laughed, nearly falling backwards when Paisley wrapped her arms around her. "You're welcome," she giggled. Paisley pulled away and looked down at the hoodie, giggling excitedly before leaning in, cupping Shiloh's face, and planting a kiss on her lips. This earned various hoots and hollers from their other three roommates.

"Damn," Ryland raised her eyebrows at Shiloh when Paisley pulled away. Shiloh's cheeks grew bright red when she saw her roommates' eyes on her.

Paisley stood up with the hoodie in her hands, peeling off her shirt with no shame and changing into the bright yellow sweatshirt.

"So... what are you guys?" Vanessa asked, turning to Shiloh while Paisley got changed. Shiloh bit her lip, unsure of how to answer the question. Before she could say anything, Paisley beat her to it.

"Mine," Paisley nodded once.

All of the other girls grew confused. Paisley tugged the sweatshirt over her head and padded back over to Shiloh, sitting down in her lap contently.

"Mine," Paisley repeated, wrapping her arms around Shiloh's neck and smiling widely. "My Lolo."

Shiloh's heart fluttered and she quietly wrapped her arms around Paisley to keep her in her lap. "You heard her," Shiloh nodded towards her roommates. "She's my Paisley." Paisley giggled eagerly and hid her head in the crook of Shiloh's neck.

Ryland and Vanessa both made gagging noises while Leah smiled widely, pulling out her phone and snapping a picture of the two.

"Y'all are too cute, I'm gonna puke," Vanessa groaned, sending a playful glare Shiloh's way. The three roommates weren't used to Shiloh being affectionate with anyone. It was a big change, but one that they considered monumental for the girl.

"Shut up," Shiloh muttered, trying, but failing to hide her smile. Ryland hopped to her feet to throw away her trash. Paisley took that as a sign that dinner was over, and she grabbed the remote from the couch.

"Are we really going to watch *Friends again*?" Shiloh laughed, raising an eyebrow at the girl in her lap. Paisley nodded excitedly and picked another episode, focusing her eyes intently on the screen.

Four episodes of Friends and a bag of popcorn later, all five girls were exhausted. Shiloh and Paisley were the only ones still awake.

Paisley yawned, turning over and smiling sleepily at Shiloh. The green eyed girl couldn't help but lean down and kiss the smaller girl's forehead.

"Y'ready to go to bed?" Shiloh said quietly, not wanting to wake her other roommates. Paisley nodded and pried herself out of the older girl's grasp, shuffling towards the stairs. Shiloh followed close behind.

The minute the door to the bedroom was closed, Paisley placed her hands on Shiloh's shoulders and stood on her tiptoes, capturing the older girl's lips in her own. Shiloh was taken aback, but quickly caught on.

"You're good at that," she whispered when the kiss broke. Paisley giggled and hopped onto the bed, laying on her back and staring up at the ceiling. Shiloh changed into a big t-shirt and sleep shorts and joined Paisley on the bed.

Legs entwined, hearts beating, chests rising and falling; both girls fell asleep almost instantly in each other's arms.

A scream pierced through the silent air, jolting Shiloh out of her slumber. The green eyed girl bolted upwards, darting her eyes around the room and trying to figure out what was going on. The trembling figure beside her quickly made her realize.

"Pais," Shiloh whispered, shaking Paisley's shoulder to try and wake her up. It was no use. Unsure of what else to do, the green eyed girl pulled Paisley's sleeping body into her lap. As soon as she did, the smaller girl began breathing heavily, pushing her fists into Shiloh's chest.

"Hey, hey, shhh," Shiloh said softly, hugging Paisley against her chest and ignoring the punches that were being thrown at her. Moments later, a gasp was emitted from the younger girl's mouth and her body stilled. Realizing where she was, Paisley burst into tears and buried her head in Shiloh's neck.

"Please..." Paisley's small voice cracked. "Please," she shook her head and clung to the material of Shiloh's shirt.

"I've got you, Pais," Shiloh whispered, stroking the smaller girl's hair. "I'll keep you safe."

"Promise?" Paisley looked up at Shiloh, who reached out and wiped her eyes with the pad of her thumbs before locking their pinkies together.

"Promise."

Paisley sighed heavily and laid her head on Shiloh's shoulder. The older girl shivered at the feeling of Paisley's warm breath against her neck, giving her goosebumps.

"Sing?" Paisley whispered, looking up at Shiloh with a glimmer of hope in her eyes. As always, Shiloh nodded softly and began to sing quietly.

Before the song was finished, Shiloh paused when she heard a faint rumbling noise downstairs. Paisley lifted her head, wondering why the older girl had suddenly grown quiet.

"Lolo?" she whispered.

"Shh," Shiloh held up her hand to signify for the girl to be quiet. A few moments later, there was a loud knock at the front door. Shiloh raised an eyebrow in confusion. Who could possibly be looking for them at two in the morning?

There was a groaning noise from the next room over and Shiloh heard Ryland's heavy footsteps leave the bedroom.

"Yeah, '*Ryland, you don't have to get the door,*' they said," the light haired girl mumbled grumpily. Shiloh heard her jog down the stairs and glanced at Paisley questioningly.

"Who is here?" Paisley asked, slithering out of bed and walking over to Shiloh's bedroom door. Shiloh quickly ran after her and grabbed her hand, pulling her back and pressing her ear to the door to try and eavesdrop on what was going on.

"Listen, I don't know who you are, but it is 2 in the fucking m—," Ryland's voice slowly faded when Shiloh heard the door open. "Uh, hi?" Ryland suddenly adopted a more polite tone, but still incriminating.

"Is Paisley Lowe home?" the low voice grumbled. Shiloh tensed. A million worst case scenarios ran through her mind.

"I-I… I don't know a Paisley," Ryland quickly answered.

"Me," Paisley whispered, tugging on Shiloh's sleeve. "That is me."

"I know, shh," Shiloh warned her, pulling Paisley closer to her and pressing her ear against the door, cupping her hand to try and hear them more clearly.

"Hey, you can't just do that!" Ryland's voice grew louder and Shiloh heard multiple loud footsteps enter the apartment. "What the hell are you doing?!"

"We have a warrant to search the premises, ma'am," one of the stern voices replied. Shiloh's heart started beating rapidly in her chest and she turned to Paisley, placing her hands on the smaller girl's shoulders and looking her straight in the eyes.

"Paisley, I need you to *stay here*, okay? I will be right back. Don't leave this room. Do you hear me?" she said firmly, trying to stress the importance of her words. Paisley nodded slowly, worry flickering in her eyes.

Shiloh pressed a quick kiss on Paisley's forehead before quietly slipping out of the room. She rushed downstairs, nearly gasping when she saw the three men in uniform practically tearing their house apart.

Ryland and Shiloh made eye contact and Ryland's eyes widened. Shiloh quickly looked around the apartment, noticing one of the officers digging through her backpack.

"Hey!" she yelled, running over to him and tugging her bag out of his hands. "What the hell are you doing?!"

"Ma'am, I'm going to have to ask you to step away," another one of the officers put a hand on her shoulder. Shiloh whipped her head around and shoved his arm off of her.

"Don't you dare lay a hand on me," she hissed, clutching her bag to her chest. "What are you doing here?"

"You don't happen to know where Paisley Lowe is, do you?"

Ryland shook her head furiously from behind the officer, and Shiloh did the same. The officer that had been searching her bag before appeared beside her and tried to take the bag out of her arms.

"Don't touch me!" Shiloh yelled, yanking her bag away and looking to Ryland for help.

"Lolo?!" Paisley's panicked voice rang out from upstairs. Ryland and Shiloh both cursed under their breath.

"Go back to bed!" Shiloh called, trying to act casual.

"Lolo?" Paisley's voice appeared again at the top of the stairs. By this time, all three officers were already heading towards the staircase, and Shiloh panicked.

"Stop!" Shiloh threw her bag to the ground and ran towards them, sliding to a stop in front of the staircase and blocking them from going any further. "It's three in the morning, what do you think you're doing here?"

Shiloh internally cursed when she heard soft footsteps coming down the stairs.

"Lolo?" Paisley whispered from directly behind Shiloh.

"That's her, that's Paisley," one of the cops pointed to Paisley and suddenly Shiloh was shoved aside, almost falling to the ground. She grabbed onto the wall to regain her balance just as Paisley started screaming.

"*Get off of her,*" Shiloh growled, watching as the officers appeared from the staircase, holding Paisley firmly by the shoulders. The smaller girl was whimpering, struggling to escape their grip.

"Paisley Lowe," one of the officers pulled a pair of handcuffs out of his pocket and passed them to the man holding Paisley. "You're under arrest on the charge of murder in the second degree."

Shiloh's heart dropped in her chest and Ryland sprinted over to the green-eyed girl to hold her upright.

"Murder?" Ryland spoke for Shiloh, who still couldn't find her words. "You've got to have the wrong person, Paisley wouldn't hurt a f—,"

She was cut off by an ear piercing scream from Paisley as the handcuffs snapped shut around her wrists. The smaller girl shook her head, trying desperately to pull her hands out of their reach.

"Lolo!" Paisley cried, looking straight at Shiloh, her eyes pleading for help. Shiloh snapped back into reality and put one hand on the wall to steady herself.

"You can't just do that!" Shiloh yelled, motioning to the cuffs around Paisley's wrists. The officers ignored Paisley's cries and shoved her towards the door, practically dragging her by her collar.

"Lolo!" Paisley cried again. Shiloh's hands shook.

"What are you doing?!" Shiloh yelled at the third officer who stood in front of them. "You can't just take her away like that!"

The man sighed heavily and pulled a business card out of his pocket, handing it to Ryland because he knew Shiloh wouldn't take it.

"I'm just doing my job, ladies. Call the number on that card tomorrow and you can find out about your friend. For now, there's nothing we can do."

Shiloh's knees crumpled beneath her and Ryland quickly grabbed her to keep her upright.

"Get the fuck out of our apartment," Ryland growled, staring the officer straight in the eye. Moments later, the door of the apartment slammed shut and Shiloh fell to her knees on the floor in tears. Paisley's cries could still be heard down the hallway and each one plunged another dagger into Shiloh's chest.

Two sets of footsteps came heavily down the stairs.

"What the hell is going on?" Vanessa asked worriedly, sliding to her knees on the floor beside Shiloh and trying to comfort the distraught girl. "Where's Paisley?"

Vanessa's question only sent Shiloh into another round of hysterics, causing the girl to slam her fist into the wall and sob violently into her hands. Leah stood frozen at the end of the staircase, taking it all in.

"I-I don't know," Ryland breathed, sliding down against the wall and sitting next to Shiloh. "They came looking for Paisley — three officers — and they said... they handcuffed her... and said something about murder."

"Murder?" Leah gasped, finally joining the group circled around Shiloh on the floor. "Paisley wouldn't hurt a fly!"

"That's what I said..." Ryland said quietly, shaking her head in disbelief and trying to keep her own tears back. All four roommates — not just Shiloh — had grown exceptionally close to Paisley in the time they'd spent together.

"They can't just... they can't... it's *Paisley*!" Shiloh cried, lifting her head and leaning back on the wall next to Ryland, allowing herself to sink down and curl up into a ball, resting her head on her knees. "She's... she's *Paisley*..."

"All we can do is call in the morning and see what they say," Ryland sighed, trying her best to be the voice of reason. "Fucking with the cops... won't get us very far."

"Murder..." Leah whispered under her breath, still trying to understand it herself. "Do you think—,"

"Paisley would never do that!" Shiloh snapped, lifting her head. Her eyes were blood shot and makeup was streaming down her face. She brought her hands up, grabbing fistfuls of her hair and letting out a noise of frustration. "She wouldn't…" Shiloh whispered, letting her head fall back into her hands.

All the girls grew silent after Shiloh's sudden outburst. Vanessa rubbed circles in Shiloh's back to try and calm her down. Ryland and Leah exchanged glances, both as lost for words as Shiloh was. None of them knew what to do.

Shiloh's thoughts were racing. Paisley had needed her. She'd promised to protect Paisley and she'd failed. The girl had been screaming *her* name, and she hadn't been able to do anything about it.

"Oh my god…" Shiloh whispered, lifting her head and staring blankly ahead of her. "Maybe… oh my god," she shook her head and felt her breathing speed up.

"What?" Vanessa glanced over at the distraught girl. Shiloh took a deep breath, trying to contain her sobs as best as she could.

"The bruises, her… her uncle… he…" Shiloh brought her hands to cup her mouth as she slowly connected the dots. "I need to go to Miami," she said abruptly, scrambling to her feet and grabbing the remains of her backpack from the floor.

The other three roommates all exchanged glances, confused at Shiloh's sudden outburst. Vanessa quickly got up, following her and putting a hand on the green eyed girl's shoulder.

"Miami?" the dark skinned girl asked cautiously.

Shiloh nodded, grabbing her wallet and frantically counting her money. "I need to... *shit*... seventy five... eighty," she cursed under her breath and restarting counting the bills. "They don't know... about Paisley. They need to know... I need to... I need to know," Shiloh stammered, curling her lip in concentration.

"That's not enough," she huffed, tightening her grip on the crumpled bills in her hand. She dropped to her knees, digging through the contents of her bag desperately.

Ryland exchanged glances with her two roommates before stepping forward and reaching into her back pocket. She pulled out a collection of bills and sifted through them before handing Shiloh everything she had.

"Wha...?" Shiloh stood up, looking at the bills in her hand. Vanessa and Leah both did the same, adding to the collection of money in Shiloh's hand.

"Go," Ryland whispered, pulling Shiloh into a hug before the girl could see the tears forming in her eyes. "I'll call you as soon as we find anything out." Leah and Vanessa both nodded in agreement.

"You guys..." Shiloh's voice cracked and she quickly wiped her eyes with the sleeve of her hoodie.

"Thank you so much," she shook her head and hugged her two other roommates before slipping the money into her wallet. "I owe you."

"You don't owe us anything," Vanessa spoke up. "We'll figure this out, okay? It's *Paisley* we're talking about. We'll find a way."

"I hope so," Shiloh whispered, biting her lip and looking around the room hesitantly.

"Get your ass on a plane, Everest," Ryland laughed sadly, nudging her friend's shoulder. Shiloh swallowed hard, nodding and grabbing her bag.

"If I don't answer my phone, call me until I do," Shiloh nodded, throwing her bag over her shoulder and heading towards the door. "I love you guys, okay? Thank you…"

All the other girls nodded. Ryland turned away to hide her tears and Shiloh decided not to call her out on it, just this once. She slipped through the door of the apartment without another word.

C H A P T E R 1 8

Shiloh crossed her arms, tapping her foot impatiently as she waited by baggage claim. Her plane had just landed. She was exhausted. No, she was more than exhausted. She hadn't been able to get a wink of sleep, though. Her mind was too preoccupied with thoughts of Paisley.

Second degree murder.

At first, Shiloh had thought the idea was utterly ridiculous. But she knew she needed to do this. There were too many unanswered questions, and maybe by taking a trip back into Paisley's past she could figure out what was going on.

Eventually she caught sight of her bag, throwing it over her shoulder and jogging out the large glass doors. It was then that she realized she had no clue where the hell she was going.

Still, Shiloh was ignoring her feelings about the whole situation. She had a one track mind. She needed to find out what had happened to Paisley. She needed answers to her questions.

She hailed a cab, sliding into the backseat and giving the driver the address of her old house. If she remembered correctly, Paisley had only lived a few streets over from her.

Her head rested against the window as they drove, giving her time to replay the entire events prior in her head. The sound of Paisley screaming out her name wouldn't leave her mind, and Shiloh hadn't realized how painful it would feel.

Those officers... they didn't know how to treat Paisley. She was *Paisley*. Truthfully, only Shiloh truly knew how Paisley thought, how her brain worked. She winced at the thought of Paisley being alone with all those strangers.

Suddenly, a house caught her eye. She knew the owner. *Sydney*. One of Paisley's former cheerleader friends. A rush decision pushed Shiloh to stop the cab, thanking the man and handing him a wad of bills, not bothering to count. She waited for him to drive away before turning and facing the house.

Moments later, she found herself on the porch, knocking gently on the door. She bit her lip when she heard footsteps approaching, and the door opened slowly to reveal an older version of the girl she had once known in high school. In pajamas.

Shit. Shiloh quickly checked the time, only to realize it was barely past eight in the morning on a Saturday.

"Shiloh?" the girl sounded confused.

"Uh, hi," Shiloh took a deep breath. Why was she still intimidated? They were out of high school, popularity didn't exist.

"Shiloh the lesbian?"

Oh god. Shiloh clenched her fists and chose to ignore the comment. "Can we... talk? It's about Paisley."

She saw the girl's face drop and grew concerned. Sydney placed the small dog in her arms on the ground and stepped aside, opening the door and allowing Shiloh to come inside.

"M'sorry about the whole lesbian comment," Sydney laughed nervously. Shiloh just shrugged it off, standing awkwardly in the foyer of the large house and looking around. Sydney's parents had always been filthy rich.

"We can go sit in the living room," the blonde motioned for Shiloh to follow her down the hall, leading her into a large room lined with windows. It was so clean that Shiloh was afraid to touch anything. She sat down on the edge of a black leather couch, running a hand through her hair nervously.

"Do you want water or something? We have lemonade, too, and tea, if you l—," Sydney started, but Shiloh quickly interrupted.

"I'm fine, I just..." Shiloh shook her head. Sydney sat down, nodding for her to go on. "What do you know about Paisley?"

Shiloh watched as Sydney's face underwent a series of different emotions before her lips curled into a slight frown.

"She was my friend," the blonde shrugged. Shiloh knew she was trying to play dumb and immediately put an end to it.

"You know what I'm talking about," Shiloh raised an incriminating eyebrow at her. In fact, it worked. She was proud of herself, feeling powerful that she was able to intimidate the girl who once made her high school life a living hell.

Sydney sighed and relaxed back into the couch, knowing they'd be there for a while. "What do you want to know?" she asked, dropping all hopes of making Shiloh leave right away.

"Everything. From the day we graduated."

"Okay," Sydney sighed and thought for a moment.

Flashback - First Day of Summer

"I'm not drinking, Scott," Paisley stood next to the table lined with various drinks, already feeling uneasy. Even the smell of alcohol could put her on edge. Her boyfriend scoffed, already halfway done with his

first cup. They'd only been there ten minutes and she wanted to leave.

"Don't be such a wuss, Lowe," her boyfriend chuckled, shoving a drink in her direction. She set it down on the table and shook her head.

"I told you not to call me that," she mumbled.

"C'mon, Lowe. It's cute when you get frustrated."

"You shouldn't have a fucking girlfriend if all you want to do is pick on her and piss her off," Paisley huffed, running a hand through her hair. Her heart was already pounding.

She'd never been a partier. Sure, she was popular. But only because she was pretty and she could get away with whatever she wanted. Most of the time, at least.

Paisley rubbed her arm, feeling the bruises that had appeared there that night. She'd asked her uncle to go to the party. But unfortunately, he was already drunk out of his mind. He didn't take her 'disrespect' very well, and she ended up having to ice her bruises while hiding in the bathroom. The last place she wanted to be was here, but Scott had convinced her to sneak out.

"Paisley, c'mon."

The small girl felt a tug on her arm and turned around to find one of her best friends, Sydney, standing behind her.

"I'm offering you a distraction, come on," Sydney whispered, nodding towards Scott. Paisley smiled thankfully, following the blonde girl outside and sitting on the stone wall of the patio.

Paisley liked to consider Sydney her best friend. Granted, if Paisley wasn't a cheerleader she knew Sydney wouldn't give her a second look. But since she was, Paisley tried to make the best of it.

"You okay?" Sydney asked, noticing Paisley's distant gaze. The smaller girl bit her lip, looking up at the other girl and nodding.

"I snuck out," Paisley sighed, shaking her head. For some reason, she could shake the guilt that boiled in her stomach. It made her sick.

"So?" Sydney laughed, taking a sip from her cup. *"Your uncle won't care. He doesn't care about anything you do, right?"*

Paisley nodded reluctantly. "Right," she mumbled. Because really, no matter what she did, he always found an excuse to hit her. Especially when he was drunk. Paisley was terrified to go home that night and possibly be caught.

"Does he still drink a lot?" Sydney asked carefully. She knew about Paisley's uncle after witnessing him lashing out on his niece at a sleepover.

Paisley swallowed hard and nodded.

"Has he hurt you r—?" She was interrupted.

"Sydney!"

Both girls turned to look at the door, where Sydney's boyfriend was calling her. She glanced at Paisley, who nodded for her to go on, eager to not have to answer her question. The blonde giggled, stumbling to her feet as the alcohol kicked in. Paisley sighed, watching as she disappeared into the house. This was going to be a long night.

"No one knows what she did for the rest of that party," Sydney explained, running a hand through her hair and looking down at her hands in her lap. "She just sort of… disappeared. I remember looking for her once or twice but I never did find her."

"So you knew about her uncle?" Shiloh asked, finding it hard to picture Paisley in that situation. The girl she knew now was so different that the girl Sydney had described.

Sydney nodded. "I was over at her house one night and he came home drunk, and flipped out on her. She… she begged me not to tell. So I didn't. I was too scared to. "

Shiloh clenched her fists but tried to remain calm. "What about Scott?" Sydney sighed and scooted back on the couch. Shiloh slowly began to realize that she had a lot of catching up to do.

Flashback - Later that Night

"Paisleyyy," Scott whined, tugging on his girlfriend's arm.

"No, Scott, I'm driving," Paisley said firmly, keeping her feet planted to block her boyfriend from getting inside the driver's side of his truck. She was the only one at the party who hadn't gotten drunk that night. She hadn't even had a sip of anything.

"Yeah, well it's my car."

She whimpered when she felt a tight hand grab her arm and yank her back into the street. Paisley cowered back as she watched Scott slide into the driver's side of the car, slamming the door behind him. The window rolled down moments later.

"Are you coming, or what?"

"You're drunk," Paisley reiterated, biting her lip and taking a step forwards. She glanced around the front lawn, watching everyone else pile into their cars. There was no other way she could get home.

"Loosen up, Paisley," one of the girls in the other car called out. Paisley sighed, realizing this was her only way home, and her only chance of not being caught by her uncle. She reluctantly crossed over to the passenger side, making sure to buckle her seatbelt.

Scott pulled out onto the street, leaning forwards and narrowing his eyes to see the road through his blurred vision. Paisley took a deep breath, telling herself to calm down.

"Hey Scott!"

A truck pulled up next to them and revved the engine. Paisley immediately put a hand on Scott's arm.

"Don't," she warned.

"You heard what they said, Paisley," Scott chuckled, revving the engine back and glaring challengingly at the truck next to them. Paisley noticed Sydney in the backseat, sticking her head out the window and laughing. "Loosen up."

Before Paisley could respond, the car next to them took off down the road.

"Those bastards," Scott huffed, slamming on the gas and making Paisley jolt backwards in her seat. She grabbed the handle above the passenger side door and shook violently as the car tore off down the road.

They raced around the block for a while, and when nothing bad happened, Paisley calmed down slightly. A thought crossed her mind.

"Were those girls from our chemistry class at the party?" she asked, biting her lip.

"Nah, they took off for New York with the lesbian as soon as they got their diplomas," Scott scoffed, rounding a corner and throwing Paisley into the wall. She groaned and clutched her side. "I guarantee you they'll be back within a month."

"You never know," Paisley mumbled, grabbing the handle once more as the car accelerated further forwards.

"I've got em'," he took one hand off the wheel and pointed to the car in front of them. Paisley saw blonde hair waving in the wind, realizing Sydney was sticking her head out of the sunroof.

Just as they were about to catch up to the speeding car, the car full of teenagers ahead of them made a last minute turn, making a complete 180 degree rotation, now racing off in the opposite direction.. Paisley's eyes widened and she saw the determination on Scott's face.

"Don't you d—," she started, but her voice was cut off when Scott threw the wheel to the left, causing the back end of their car to completely lose control. Paisley was thrown into the passenger side door. The back of their car continued to spin, and Scott turned the wheel violently to try and gain his control back.

It was no use, though. The back of the truck flew off the road, flipping the entire vehicle over and throwing them down into the ditch. The last thing Paisley remembered was being thrust towards the front windshield.

"Oh my god," Shiloh whispered, unable to fathom what that must have been like for Paisley. She looked over at Sydney, who was nearly in tears, and was suddenly filled with rage. "You just *left* her there?" she felt her voice grow deep in the back of her throat.

"I-I didn't know... none of us saw them wreck," Sydney sniffed and took a deep breath. "We were too far ahead of them. We just assumed they gave up and drove home."

Shiloh grit her teeth and forced herself to take a long, deep breath to try and control her anger. "What happened to Scott?"

Flashback - The Morning After the Accident

Sydney knocked impatiently on the door, glancing back at her car and taking a deep breath. She'd just received the news that one of her best friends was in the hospital after a car accident. The driver of the car had yet to come forward, but Sydney knew exactly who to go to.

Scott opened the door, furrowing his eyebrows when he saw the cheerleader on his doorstep. Before he had a chance to talk, Sydney pushed her way into his house and slammed the door behind him.

"Do you have any idea what you've done?!" she yelled, feeling the anger boil in her stomach. She felt increasingly guilty for allowing Paisley to go with him. She felt even guiltier for not being there when the accident happened. The scariest part, though, was that Sydney had no idea what condition Paisley was in. All she knew was that her friend was in the hospital after a car accident.

"What?" Scott mumbled, wiping his eyes. It was obvious he had just woken up.

"You fucking idiot!" Sydney yelled, shoving Scott backwards. That woke him up quickly, and he held his hand up in front of him defensively.

"Woah, woah, what did I do this time?" he chuckled, running a hand through his hair.

Sydney had to force herself to stay still, instead of pummeling the older boy to the ground. "You really don't know what you did?" Scott shook his head, still completely clueless.

Deciding against saying anything else, Sydney whipped out her phone and showed him the text from their school, asking them to keep Paisley in their thoughts. Scott's eyes widened.

"Do you even remember?" Sydney hissed.

"I thought I walked home," Scott shrugged, handing her back the phone. Sydney was infuriated at how casual he was acting about this.

"You're an asshole, Scott, did you know that?" Sydney growled, shoving him backwards once more. "Do you even care what you did to her? What if she died? It should've been you. You don't even have a fucking scratch on you."

"My arm sorta hurts," Scott shrugged.

That was it. Sydney punched him straight in the jaw, sending him stumbling backwards.

"When the police get a hold of you, you're gonna be in a lot of shit," Sydney huffed, clenching and unclenching her fist before storming out of his house and slamming the door behind her. Her next stop was the police station, where she told them everything she knew.

When the police went to Scott's house. He was gone. From the appearance of his bedroom, he had packed a bag and fled. No one had a clue where he was.

Sydney was infuriated. But now, she was growing concerned about Paisley. She had just assumed it was a fender bender, and her friend had a few stitches, at the worst.

Little did she know.

"When's Paisley getting discharged?" she asked one of the officers while she sat at the police station, waiting on a report back to see if Scott had been found.

The officer chuckled, as if she'd made a joke.

"What?" Sydney asked, placing one of her hands on his desk. Her eye landed on a folder with the words 'Medical Report', printed in bold black letters. Before she could think, she grabbed the folder and opened it.

The officer snatched it out of her hands moments later, but the damage had already been done. She'd already seen the pictures of the completely totaled car, and the small girl lying nearly lifeless in a hospital bed, connected to all sorts of wires and machines. She felt physically sick.

"Oh my god," her voice came out barely a whisper and she had to sit down. This was a million times worse than she thought it would be. "I need to go see her," she shook her head and stood up, running out of the police station before someone could convince her otherwise.

Twenty minutes later, she burst through the front doors of the hospital and ran to the front desk.

"Paisley Lowe?" she asked, breathless. "Where's her room? I need to see her."

The nurse typed something into the computer, furrowing her eyebrows at the screen and typing something else. Sydney tapped her foot anxiously.

"Her guardian won't allow her to have visitors at this time," the nurse continued looking at something on the screen. "In fact, he won't even allow anyone to have contact with her besides himself."

Sydney slammed her palms down onto the counter, feeling completely powerless. She heard footsteps behind her and froze when she realized who it was. Tom Maverick, also known as Paisley's uncle.

"Mr. Tom, you have to let me go see Paisley," she said breathlessly, turning around and clasping her hands together. He just stared blankly at her.

"Who are you?" he slurred. Sydney smelled the alcohol on his breath and grew increasingly furious.

"Sydney Marx, I'm Paisley's friend," she tried her best to remain calm.

"Oh good, I was looking for one of you," he spat, leaning down and looking her straight in the eye. "You stay away from my niece, you hear me? You and all your little friends, too. Or you'll regret it."

Sydney took a step backwards, realizing she was shaking slightly.

"But—," she started.

"You know what I'm capable of," he glared at her. "Get out, and don't you dare get any ideas."

Unsure of what else to do, Sydney ran out the door of the hospital and collapsed into tears in the front seat of her car.

"Please tell me someone got to go see her," Shiloh's voice rasped as she tried to hold in her anger. "Did you even tell anyone about what her uncle did to her?"

Sydney shook her head and sighed. "When she got out of the hospital me and some of her teammates tried to go to her house and see her, but he answered the door and threatened to call the cops if we came back."

Shiloh stood up with her fists balled at her sides. "And you just let her stay there? Knowing what he did to her *before* she had brain damage?!"

Sydney quickly stood up and held her hands up as if she was surrendering. "I know, I know," she sighed, shaking her head. "I just... listen—I already beat myself up over it every day, you don't have to tell me how stupid I am. I already know."

"Good," Shiloh huffed, running a hand through her hair and thinking for a moment. "So... did she really..."

"Kill him?" Sydney finished her sentence. Shiloh nodded slowly. Both girls sat down once more and the blonde took a deep breath.

"Honestly, I think so," Sydney bit her lip. "I don't know... how she *is*, now, but he could get pretty violent. What if she shot him in self defense?"

"She shot him?" Shiloh raised an eyebrow. All she knew what that Paisley was charged for murder and that the prime victim would be her uncle.

Sydney pulled out her phone, typing something and then reading off of the news article. "*Gunshot wound to the chest, fired from less than 12 inches away,*" she bit her lip and set her phone back down.

"Oh my god," Shiloh brought her hands up and hung her head down. "What're they gonna do to her?"

"You don't think they'll send her to jail, do you?" Sydney said after a few minutes of tense silence.

Shiloh sighed, standing up and shaking her head. She had to suck it up for now. "Not if I have anything to say about it," she said, looking around and biting her lip. "You don't mind giving me a ride to her house?"

"There's no use, they've got the place covered in caution tape and warning signs."

"Then you'll give me a ride to the woods *behind* her house so I can sneak in," Shiloh nodded her head, grabbing her bag and walking towards the door. She wasn't going to accept no for an answer.

"Fine," Sydney sighed, searching around for her keys and jogging to catch up with Shiloh. As they walked to her car, questions began circulating in her head.

C H A P T E R 1 9

"How do you know Paisley?" Sydney asked, looking over at Shiloh once they were on the road. Shiloh shifted uncomfortably in her seat.

"She's my… uh," Shiloh cleared her throat and looked out the window. "My girlfriend."

The car nearly ran off the road when Sydney heard Shiloh's words. "Your *what*?"

"Girlfriend," Shiloh bit her lip.

"Wait, but didn't she like… read your texts to the entire school and out you?"

Shiloh nodded.

They pulled up next to the woods behind Paisley's house and Sydney parked the car, signaling for Shiloh to wait for a moment.

"And you're sure she's not just going along with it because she doesn't… understand?" the blonde asked carefully. Shiloh grew confused. "Like… she had a *boy*friend before, not a *girl*friend, y'know?"

Shiloh bit her lip as the thought crossed her mind. She didn't have an answer. Sighing, the dark haired girl shook her head and exited the car. "I'm not worried about that right now," she said, leaning down so she could see the other girl. "My main concern is getting her back home safe. Thanks for the ride, but you can go now."

She closed the door and stormed off without another word. Shiloh was reminded of why she left this town. Everyone was so close minded. She heard Sydney's car speed off just as she reached the start of the woods. The back of Paisley's small brick home could be seen through the trees, and Shiloh wasted no time in pushing her way through the brush.

There was caution tape draped all across the back door, as well as the windows. They really hadn't left anything up to chance.

Then something else caught Shiloh's eye. The storm cellar. Glancing both ways to make sure no one was watching her, she crossed the yard and pulled on the handle of the cellar. Shit. Locked.

She was desperate now. Desperate for answers. She kicked the door in frustration, about to turn back around when she heard a cracking noise. The hinges.

Shiloh quickly kicked the door again. And again. And again, until the hinge of the door snapped off and hung down. She quickly crawled down into the cellar, pulling out her phone and turning on the flashlight.

Luckily, the cellar seemed to be connected to the house. Shiloh climbed the small metal ladder, pushing the trap door above her open. She pulled herself up, shining the flashlight around and realizing she was in the garage. Mission accomplished.

Quietly, she entered the house. Right away, she was greeted with a scene that made her gasp. The white tile floor of their kitchen was stained with blood. Glass was shattered everywhere, and Shiloh was thankful she wore boots with thick soles.

Glass.

Ryland had mentioned something about how there had been glass in Paisley's feet when she showed up at their apartment. She couldn't have possibly fled straight to their apartment after this happened, could she? Shiloh bit her lip.

All she knew, and all she was sure of, was that Paisley wouldn't kill someone unless it was absolutely necessary.

The kitchen reeked of dried blood, and Shiloh headed towards the rickety wooden staircase. Each step felt as if the floor would give out any second. The house was a mess. No one would suspect that mega-popular cheerleader Paisley Lowe lived here.

She found Paisley's bedroom right away. Bright yellow. Shiloh bit her lip to hide the smile, realizing that some things really hadn't changed.

Bumping the door open with her hip, Shiloh took a moment to study Paisley's old bedroom. The walls were yellow, the same yellow that Paisley still adored. The same color as the hoodie Shiloh had given to her.

Her bed was a mess, and books were lined neatly along her shelves. Shiloh wondered how long Paisley had lived here after the accident.

Kneeling down, something caught her eye underneath the bed. She lay down and grabbed the box, pulling it out and examining it. The words '*High School Memories*' were written on top in black marker, and it was dated the date of their graduation. The date of Paisley's accident. The day Shiloh had left for New York.

It made Shiloh's heart drop. Paisley must have done this before the party. Suddenly, a part of her felt extremely guilty for snooping through her things. She tried to tell herself that Paisley would have wanted her to do this. Paisley would want her to understand.

Slowly, Shiloh lifted the lid from the box and couldn't help but laugh softly when she saw what was inside. A small, yellow stuffed monkey. A bow from cheerleading, striped in her school colors. A handful of string friendship bracelets. A report card.

Shiloh unfolded the report card, scanning it over carefully. Straight A's all year. Damn. Shiloh had just assumed Paisley was a typical uneducated cheerleader that only cared about painting her nails.

She slipped the report card back in the box just as she felt her phone vibrate in her pocket. She answered it quickly, hoping it was Ryland with good news.

"Hello?" she bit her lip, standing up and sitting on Paisley's bed.

"Shiloh? It's Ryland."

"What's going on?" Shiloh quickly replied, tapping her foot nervously.

"Paisley has trial in a week, they're saying she… killed her uncle…"

"I know," Shiloh sighed. "I think she did."

"You *what*?!"

"Yeah," the green eyed girl took a deep breath and composed her words. "He was an alcoholic, he was abusive, and when she got in the accident… I just think… if he was *this* bad to her before, things would only get worse after she had a brain injury."

There was silence on the other line and then a long sigh of realization from Ryland. "They're holding her there until her trial… I-I don't know what's going to happen to her."

Shiloh shivered of the thought of Paisley in a prison cell. It was utterly ridiculous. "We just need to prove it was in self defense, right?"

"We talk to her lawyer on Monday," Ryland explained. "That's when we need to give them as much information as possible that will help her."

"What about evidence?" Shiloh glanced down at the shoebox.

"Evidence?"

"Like proof that he was abusive or something," Shiloh explained. In the bottom of the shoebox sat a leather bound journal, and she bent down to pick it up, turning it over in her hands.

"I mean, yeah, that'd help," Ryland finally spoke. Shiloh nodded and placed the journal in her lap.

"Great," she bit her lip. "Call me if you know anything else, okay?"

"Got it, be safe, okay?" Ryland's voice was laced with concern. Shiloh could tell she was just as worried as she was.

"Yes ma'am," she chuckled, trying to lighten the mood. "You too, okay? I'll be home as soon as I find what I need."

The girls said their goodbyes and Shiloh sat her phone on the bed. She looked at the leather journal in her hands, running her fingers over the worn edges. Once she opened this, she knew there was no going back.

After taking a deep breath, she flipped to the first page of her journal.

It's Paisley. Again.

Uncle Tom took my old journal on Christmas because I was writing in the living room, and he threw it in the fireplace. I mean, I guess that's better than him taking it and reading it. I'm sure he'd get a kick out of all the shit I said about him in there.

I don't understand why he hates me so much. I mean, what happened to my parents wasn't my fault. I didn't ask for them to go out that night. I didn't ask for the road to be icy. The last thing I wanted was to lose them.

But apparently it's easier for him to blame a six year old instead of coming to terms with the fact that his sister is dead.

He hit me again today. I was an idiot and accidentally forgot to turn on the dishwasher last night, so he hit me and then made me wash them all by hand.

School is alright, I guess. Scott is Scott. I know I've been dating him for a while, but I keep feeling pressured to feel something towards him. But... I don't. He's more like a good friend. Sometimes he's not even that.

I'll write tomorrow. It's the first day at school after winter break. Wish me luck.

- Paisley

      Shiloh traced her fingers over Paisley's handwriting, trying to burn it into her brain. Paisley's parents must have died in a car accident, she realized.

Swallowing the lump in her throat, she flipped to the next page.

Do you ever see someone who is sad and it makes you more attracted to them?

That probably sounds really twisted, oh my god, just let me explain.

I wrote about this in my old journal, but since that's now just ash in the fireplace, I'll explain it again in case future Paisley doesn't remember.

There's this girl in my grade, Shiloh.

Shiloh's hands froze and she felt her heart speed up. She scooted back on the bed and continued reading.

Her dad and Uncle Tom work in the same field, and their businesses were merging. They were supposed to be partners, but Uncle Tom hates all people, so he wanted to get rid of her dad somehow.

I guess that's where I came in. I got home from school one day and he pulled me aside and told me I had to do something to his daughter. Shiloh. I was supposed to start a rumor or something to make her hate me, so in return, her dad would hate Uncle Tom. And knowing her dad, he wouldn't want to work with my uncle. In some twisted way, my uncle would end up getting the job by himself and getting paid even more because of it.

I didn't really know this Shiloh girl too well. I mean, she was super pretty. I had nothing against her, you know? But if I didn't listen to him... god I don't even know what he'd do. So I did it.

I don't even know what happened. I picked up her phone and these messages were there about her being gay... so I read them. It's all a blur because afterwards I felt so sick that I went to the bathroom and threw up. I hate myself. I hate myself for doing that to someone.

Now, it's our senior year, and she still hates me. I don't blame her.

There's one tiny problem now, and that's the fact that I think I have feelings for her.

The journal fell out of Shiloh's hands and she had to dive forwards to grab it before she lost her place. She took a deep breath, not being able to believe the words she had just read. She slowly leaned down and continued reading.

Just let me explain, okay? I see her walking around the hallway... and she just looks so vulnerable. Like I said before, somehow it made me more attracted to her. Like seeing that she was human and she had emotions made her more real.

And I don't even know, because she's a girl. But when I think about it, when I look at her, the things I feel are totally different than when I look at Scott. And not even sexual feelings, either. Like I just want to hug her. Or hold her hand. Or kiss her.

Oh my god. What am I going to do? I need a friend. A real one. I just need someone to talk to me, someone who will listen.

"I would've been that friend," Shiloh whispered, tracing her fingers across the curly letters.

I don't even know if I'm gay, or if it's just Shiloh, or what. But you know, the universe does a great job of fucking things up for me because the one girl I want is also the girl that hates me more than anything in the world. I don't blame her though, what I did to her is unforgivable.

Shit. Uncle Tom just got home. I'll write more later.

- Paisley

Shiloh sat on the bed in utter shock. Paisley… the *old* Paisley, had developed feelings for her. She wondered if Paisley still remembered any of that. This changed everything for her. What Sydney said surely couldn't be true, because Paisley had been attracted to a girl before the accident. A girl that just so happened to be Shiloh.

She took a deep breath and turned the page.

I'm gay.

I am gay. Paisley is gay. Paisley Lowe is gay. I think. Oh my god, I don't know.

I saw Shiloh in the hallway today. She was wearing yellow. My favorite color. God, it looks even better on her. Maybe it's my favorite color because she's the only one who can make a yellow sweater look attractive.

She's in my chemistry class. It's the only class we have together. We're in the same lab group, too. I try to be nice to her, I really do. Part of me wants to tell her why I did what I did, but what if she tells her dad? I can't risk it. I wish I could, but I just can't.

She sucks at Chemistry, though.

Shiloh raised an eyebrow questioningly.

I mean, I think she tries. But she really just sucks. We have to put our papers into our group folders at the end of class and it's my job to turn them in to the teacher. So I may or may not change her answers for her so she doesn't fail. I mean, come on! It's the least I can do.

The green eyed girl bit her lip, running a hand through her hair. And all this time she'd believed she was just really good at Chemistry. Good thing she didn't go to college for science.

Uncle Tommy hit me today. Well, after he threw an empty beer bottle at me. Luckily it missed my head by a mile cause his aim is shit when he's drunk. I asked him if I could borrow his car so I could go out and buy the supplies I needed for a project we had due the next day.

Bad idea, obviously. He flipped out on me, threw the beer bottle, called me irresponsible, and then pinned me up against the wall and punched me in the face.

Fun, right? Yeah, not.

I don't know what to write about anymore, so I guess I'll see you later.

- Paisley

Shiloh's heart was slowly breaking. Knowing that she could've helped Paisley deal with all of this instead of having her deal with it on her own. She could have been there for her. There were still more pages filled with writing, and Shiloh continued to read.

Uncle Tom hates Scott.

He always tries to set me up with the student interns from his job. My question is, how does he still have a job? Haven't they realized how much of a scumbag he is?

Anyway, he brought two of the interns home last night to work on one of their projects. He made me come downstairs and talk to them, which wasn't that bad, until he started trying to get one of them to ask me on a date. He was literally like - "You can have her! Do whatever the hell you want with her, I don't care."

None of them did anything about it, either. Maybe if one of them would have stood up for me things would have turned out different.

After they left, I went to go back up to my bedroom and hide as I always do, but he grabbed me and pinned me against the wall and started yelling about how I don't "put myself out there" and that I choose horrible boyfriends. I don't even remember. But I remember I was just so tired and exhausted that I ended up screaming back at him and somehow the words "I'm gay" slipped out.

Long story short, he beat the shit out of me. When I tried to run upstairs, he caught up to me in the office, and grabbed his gun out of one of the drawers. (Which I didn't even know was there, to be honest)

He started swinging it around and threatening me with it. I was scared to death. Eventually he let me go, and I made sure to take the bullets out of the gun once he fell asleep.

And now I'm here. And I'm thinking about everything he said to me. About how I was an abomination. A disgrace. A mistake. I could list them on and on.

I don't know what I'm gonna do anymore.

- Paisley

Shiloh brought her hand up to face and felt the hot tears on her cheeks. She wiped her eyes and took a deep breath. She had to make it through the rest of this journal. Hopefully this was more than enough to prove Paisley's act had been in self defense.

Tomorrow is the last day of senior year.

Shiloh's heart dropped in her chest as soon as she read the first line. She immediately knew this would be Paisley's last entry. The thought that Paisley wrote this having no idea what was to come made her feel sick to her stomach.

I want to apologize to Shiloh. I wish I could. But I'm too scared. I heard Uncle Tom loading his gun again last night. If I take the bullets out again, he's sure to catch on. I shouldn't be terrified to live in my own house, should I?

Anyway, I'm feeling very nostalgic today. One more day, and then I'm free from the public education system. Free to start the rest of my life. Free to move out.

Part of me is hoping that Shiloh will stay here and go to community college, just like I am. Maybe we can be friends or something. I'd really like that. I really like her.

But I doubt she'll want to stay here. I've made her life miserable, she'll probably want to get as far away from me as possible.

That's not all, though. I know she's not going to stay here, in this shitty little town, because she doesn't belong here. I might have looked through some of her artwork while me and the cheer squad were hanging up posters in the art room. She's amazingly talented.

If only Uncle Tom had picked to work with someone else... who had a less attractive daughter. Then maybe I could get to know Shiloh. We all know that's never going to happen.

- Paisley

Thinking what she had just read was the last entry, Shiloh went to close the book, but noticed the indented writing on the next page. She bit her lip when she saw the date on the next entry. The date of the accident.

It's 4 am. I'm graduating today. Everything is going to change, and hopefully for the better.

"Everything sure changed alright," Shiloh whispered, fighting back another set of tears.

Maybe I'll really get my life together after this. I mean, everyone thinks I have it together, but I really don't. If only they'd look past the whole 'perfect cheerleader' image they seem to have of me. But no one cares enough to.

You know what makes my day even better? Our graduation gowns are blue and yellow. Which means, Shiloh will be in yellow today. My favorite girl in my favorite color.

Scott wants me to go to a party tonight. I don't even want to go, cause everyone's going to be drinking. But I guess I have to. I need to loosen up, right? Plus, it's the last party I'll be going to in a while.

I need to break up with Scott, I know. I just haven't found the right time. Plus I'm also slightly terrified of what may become of me if I do. He doesn't have a good reputation with ex-girlfriends.

If I'm reading this in the future, I hope I'm happy. I hope I have a warm home, a comfy bed, good friends who will stick up for me. I hope I'm safe. Away from toxic people like my uncle. I hope I can be myself. I hope I don't have to hide who I am just to fit in. And maybe, I hope I'm in love. And maybe if I get really lucky, I'll be in love with Shiloh. But hell, I don't deserve someone as good as her. She deserves the world, and I can't give her that.

- Paisley

"You already have," the girl on the bed whispered. Shiloh didn't even try to fight the tears anymore, they fell freely.

Maybe Paisley was happy.

Shiloh read over the list again. Paisley did have a warm home, a comfy bed, and good friends. She was safe. She was away from her uncle. And she definitely didn't try to hide who she was any more. And maybe, just maybe, she was in love.

But all those things would be thrown to shit if Shiloh couldn't get Paisley back.

She closed the journal, slipping it into her backpack. Using her phone, she snapped a few pictures of Paisley's room, just so she could remember it. Just as she turned to leave, something caught her eye.

A small bump underneath the covers on the bed.

Slowly, she peeled away the covers and giggled when she saw what was underneath. A yellow (of course), stuffed puppy. It was ragged, and patched in some places. It had sure seen better days, but Shiloh could tell it was beloved to whoever owned it. She felt a smile spread across her face when she imagined giving it to Paisley.

If she ever got the chance to.

Shiloh took a deep breath, stuffing the toy into her backpack along with the journal. This would have to be enough evidence, right? She jogged down the stairs, grimacing at the blood stain on the floor.

Her phone rang just as she crawled out of the storm cellar, standing up and brushing the dirt off of her knees. She quickly answered it, jogging into the woods for cover.

"Hey, what's up?" she said, catching her breath and leaning against a tree.

"Ryland wanted me to call and check up on you," Leah replied on the other line. Shiloh smoothed out her shirt and began walking back through the woods.

"I just left Paisley's house," Shiloh answered truthfully. "I've got what I needed, so I'm coming home."

"That was quick," the other girl answered.

"I don't want to stay here any longer than I need to," Shiloh began walking down the sidewalk, hoping she could catch the bus back to the airport if she walked fast enough. "Too many bad memories."

"What about your family?"

"I don't want to have to explain all of this to them right now," Shiloh sighed. Luckily, her friend understood. It wouldn't be the easiest thing for Shiloh to explain her relationship with Paisley to her parents, who knew exactly what Paisley had done to her in high school.

Shiloh and Leah talked for a while longer until Shiloh finally reached the bus stop. She sat down once she and Leah finished talking. Millions of questions were still buzzing around her head at light speed. Most importantly, what was going to happen to Paisley?

CHAPTER 20

Shiloh pulled Paisley's journal out of her backpack. She traced the worn leather cover, wondering how many times Paisley had held this same journal in her hands. It was hard for her to grasp the fact that the same girl who had written in this journal was the one Shiloh had kissed only a few days ago.

Her phone buzzed a minute or so later, and Shiloh furrowed her eyebrows when she realized it was a Facebook message from Sydney.

Sydney Marx: Hey, I just remembered something. The entire cheerleading squad had to come back to the school gym the day after graduation to clean out our lockers. Paisley never got her things. If I remember correctly, they still should be in a box next to the Lost and Found in the library. Just thought you'd want to know.

It was worth a try, Shiloh decided. She pushed herself up from her spot on the curb and began walking in the direction of the school. It would be a long walk, but she didn't feel like waiting for the bus. She needed something to occupy her time.

Over half an hour later, her old high school finally came into view. Shiloh cringed at the sight, remembering all the bad memories she'd associated with the building. Swallowing her pride, she slowly realized that no one was at the school. It was a Saturday.

Remembering something, Shiloh jogged around the back of the school and found the loading docks. The food was delivered to the cafeteria on trucks, which would park at the loading dock and be carried into the kitchen. Lucky for Shiloh, she'd gotten detention in her sophomore year and had to help carry crates back and forth. And now, she remembered the code they'd used to unlock the door.

6022.

She tapped the numbers in on the keypad and hit enter. Moments later, there was a low beeping noise and the click of the lock. Shiloh glanced around her one last time before opening the door and slipping inside.

The library was on the opposite side of the school from the kitchen. She jogged her way there, breathless by the time she reached the rows and rows of bookshelves. A large sign read 'Lost and Found' in the back corner.

Once Shiloh made it there, she found the box Sydney had been talking about. She knelt down next to it, biting her lip and hesitating for a moment. Did she really want to do this? What if she found something even worse than what she had already found?

Doing her best to dismiss her concerns, Shiloh slowly lifted the flaps of the box and peered inside. She pulled out a packet of papers stapled together, eyeing them curiously.

"If you were to write the story of your life until now, what would you title it and why?"

Shiloh furrowed her eyebrows when she read the heading of the paper. Upon further inspection, she realized it was a college entrance essay. This should be interesting. Shiloh took a deep breath, preparing herself for what was to come.

My parents died when I was six. Whenever I tell people I can still remember them like it was yesterday, they look at me like I'm crazy. But I do. I still remember little things about them. I remember my dad always had paint on his hands, and I remember my mother would always scold him for getting turpentine on his new clothes. He was a painter, and she was an accountant.

It's funny, because no one would have expected them to fall in love. The woman who loved numbers, and the man who could barely tell time. But apparently they did. I don't know much about their past. I don't have any family to ask questions, besides my uncle. But he can get very evasive when I try and discover information about my parents, so I've given up.

The one thing I remember the most about them, though, was how much they loved color. Especially my father. I would always sit on a stool in his studio and watch him mix his paints together. The best days were the days that he would set up a smaller easel for me, and I would get to use finger paints. I always tried to paint like him, but I could never quite get it right. So I'd start over, and smear a new piece of paper with yellow.

At that time, yellow was my favorite color because it was the color of the sun, and macaroni and cheese. My mom took a sewing class just so she could sew me a stuffed yellow dog for my birthday. I named him Sunny. I still have him.

The meaning of the color changed for me one night in the dead of winter. The day before Christmas, actually. My parents had taken us up to Colorado to spend the holidays at a ski resort. I remember seeing snow for the first time, and being scared of it. Obviously I grew to love it, though.

It was Christmas Eve. I remember because my parents told me I would have to go to bed early since Santa was coming. There was a daycare at the resort, and my parents dropped me off there right after dinner. I was confused at the time, and they never told me *where they were going. I would later find out that they had forgotten one of the most important items on my Christmas list — a yellow princess dress.*

I remember one of the workers at the resort coming into the room looking very distraught, and taking me out to her car. She took me to the hospital, and then I was handed off to another nurse. She told me that my parents had been in an accident, and that my aunt and uncle were coming to pick me up.

I wouldn't stop asking her questions, and eventually another woman came and sat with me in a small room. It was yellow, I remember. And I remember feeling uneasy, because the room was painted such a happy color, but everything felt so sad.

In that same yellow room, the woman explained to me that my parents had been in a car accident, and that my mother had died instantly. I don't remember crying. I don't think I understood.

Apparently I was 'handling it well', and I was allowed to go back to see my father. All of his injuries had been internal, so he looked perfectly fine to me. I remember running out of the nurse's arms and shaking him on the hospital bed, trying to wake him up. They had to drag me out of the bedroom.

I was supposed to wait in a chair in the corner of the waiting room while my aunt and uncle flew all the way to Colorado to pick me up. I had no other family on either side.

I remember watching the daughter of the other driver in the accident being reunited with her parents. I watched her run and leap into her father's arms, giggling happy. I watched her mother, who had a pink cast on her arm, cry and talk about how thankful she was that they were alright.

And I remember being so brutally jealous of them. Because they were talking about how they would go out and get hot cocoa and go home and wait for Santa to come. All while I sat in the corner, wondering why her mother got to live, and why her father wasn't hurt. At that time, I wished I could trade places with her. She had on bright yellow snow boots.

Finally, my aunt and uncle came to pick me up. Aunt Susie was my favorite person besides my parents. My dad always called her a 'Southern Belle.' She had grown up on a ranch in Montana, and everything made her smile. She was always picking flowers and keeping them in her kitchen.

When I was little, my mom and dad always told me that Uncle Tommy didn't like kids too much. I spent most of my time with Aunt Susie, anyway, so I didn't really mind.

They took me home, and I remember them showing me around the house and telling me where everything was. I thought it was funny at the time, because I'd been in their house millions of times before.

But then they showed me my new bedroom, which Aunt Susie said we could paint yellow. And I remember crying because I realized I wasn't going to get to go home.

The day of my parent's funeral, I made the decision that I hated funerals with all of my heart. First, because their funeral just so happened to be the day of my seventh birthday. And second, because I hated the color black, and I had to wear a black dress. I cried when I had to put it on. Uncle Tom started yelling at me, but Aunt Susie made him stop, and told him that I was allowed to be sad, because it was a sad day. On the way to a funeral, she picked a daisy and let me pin it to my dress so it wouldn't be as sad-looking.

I didn't like having to go to a new school. I had to make all new friends, and I wasn't very good at making friends. I never was. When I introduced myself to the class, my teacher asked me what my favorite color was. I lied and said pink, because that's what all the other girls had said. Plus, I wanted so badly to hate the color yellow. But I didn't.

In fifth grade, I met my favorite teacher to date. Mrs. Browne always wore bright colored dresses, and always made sure to tell our whole class just how important we were to her. I'm thankful I had a support system at school, because at home, things were getting hard.

In the second month of the school year, Aunt Susie got very sick. At first, everyone thought it was the flu. She went to the doctor, got her medicine, and in a few days, she was back to normal.

She got sick again about a week later. This time, the medicine didn't work. It was the middle of the night, and she got really bad. Uncle Tommy wanted to take her to the hospital, but she refused. She told him she could wait until the morning.

She couldn't wait until the morning.

I remember skipping into her room to wake her up. I was excited because I was in the school play that day, and she had promised to help me with my makeup. I was only going to be a tree, but I was still excited.

Next to her bed, she had a little collection of buttercups and dandelions I had picked for her that summer. They were wilted and rotting, but she'd never bothered to take them out of her room. It made me feel special.

When she wouldn't wake up, I started screaming for my uncle. I kept shaking her, trying to get her to open her eyes. By now, I understood well enough what death looked like. But for some reason, I had the overwhelming need to do something to try and save her.

That was the first time my uncle hit me. He tried to pull me off of her, but I wouldn't let go. I just kept shaking her and screaming for her to wake up. And then he slapped me. Hard. Across the face. I started crying even harder, but he ignored me and picked her up and took her to his car. The hospital told us she had been dead long before I tried to wake her up.

I didn't go back to school for a week. Mrs. Browne and my whole entire class signed a card for me, and I remember it had a bright yellow bird on the front. I kept it in my bedroom for good luck.

Uncle Tom hit me for the second time on the Sunday night before I went back to school. I couldn't find my backpack, and I started panicking because Aunt Susie had always packed my lunches, and she'd always helped me put on my shoes, and I remember listing all the things that I couldn't do without her in my head.

I was running around the house looking for my backpack, and my uncle kept yelling at me to be quiet. But, I was more focused on finding my backpack. I ran into his office and started going through all the cabinets, and I must have knocked a stack of papers on his desk over.

The next thing I know, he grabbed my arm and slapped me right across the face. I remember seeing a beer bottle on his desk, and asking him if he was an alcoholic. We had just been learning about alcoholism in school, which is why I asked. That got him really mad, and he threatened to hit me again. Luckily, I ran back upstairs.

It didn't stop there, though. It continued all through high school, and it only got worse. Luckily, I'm getting out of his house soon.

So if I had to title my life story, it would be 'Yellow.' Because for some reason, that color sticks out in all of my memories. My cheer uniform for high school was yellow. My prom dress was yellow. When my first boyfriend asked me out, I was wearing a yellow *and white headband. The only Christmas present my uncle has ever gotten me was a yellow pair of earrings, when I was thirteen. They're not the prettiest things ever, but I hold them close to my heart because he gave them to me.*

I got my first kiss from a boy with yellow chains on his braces. I drank my first beer on a worn, yellow couch in my neighbor's basement. I realized I was gay when I saw the girl of my dreams wearing a yellow sundress.

To me, yellow is a happy color. You can't look at the color yellow and be sad for very long. I guess it's my mantra in life. I try and wear a smile no matter how much I'm hurting, because eventually things should get better.

[Paisley - PUT A CONCLUSION HERE BEFORE YOU SEND THIS IN, DUMBASS. OH AND ALSO THERE'S LEFTOVER CHIPOTLE IN THE FRIDGE DON'T FORGET THAT]

Shiloh giggled when she read the note Paisley had put on her unfinished essay, as she wiped the tears from her eyes. She suddenly had a lot more insight into Paisley's childhood.

She sat there for a few minutes, reading the paper over and over. It broke her heart to know everything Paisley had been through. She didn't deserve it. Shiloh wished she would have known this back in high school. Maybe she could have helped her and made sure the accident never happened.

Sighing, Shiloh folded the papers in half and slipped them into her bag. She fished around in the box, only finding a collection of hair ties, math worksheets, and a pair of tennis shoes.

Deciding nothing else was important enough to bring with her, she walked back around the school and slipped out the same door by the loading dock. She made sure to lock it before using her phone to call a taxi. She shuffled her feet anxiously at the front of the school while she waited.

A little over an hour later, she found herself waiting for her plane to board. Handing her ticket to the woman in uniform, she quickly found a window seat on the plane and sat down. She fell asleep almost instantly, exhausted from having barely any sleep in the past two days.

She was jolted awake by a nightmare. Glancing around to make sure no one had seen her miniature freak out, she took a deep breath and held her hand to her chest. Her heart was beating rapidly.

In her dream, Paisley had been in jail, and been getting messed around with by a group of inmates. Shiloh was there, but she couldn't talk or move, she could only watch. Paisley kept calling to her for help but Shiloh couldn't move. The idea that Paisley could possibly end up in a jail scared Shiloh to death.

She forced herself to take a deep breath, wiping the tears of frustration that had formed in her eyes. All Shiloh wanted was to get Paisley back, to rid the smaller girl of her past and prove to her that all people weren't as cruel as her uncle. Paisley had been through hell and back, and didn't deserve a second of it. It baffled Shiloh that somehow Paisley still retained her same childish innocence.

The rest of her flight was spent staring longingly out the window. What was Paisley doing this very second? She must be scared out of her mind. Shiloh wondered if she had a change of clothes, or had even had something to eat that day. Her worrying drove her insane, until finally the jolt of the plane landing snapped her out of her thoughts.

She waited impatiently as the passengers began to file out of the plane. Sending her roommates a quick text to let her know she had landed, she made her way to baggage claim and collected her things. A while and a lot of waving later, she finally managed to hail a cab.

She made it back to the apartment around dinnertime, thanking the taxi driver and trudging into the lobby with her bags. The elevator ride up to her floor felt like an eternity, but she finally turned her key in the door and stepped into the apartment. All three girls were sitting on the couch, and Ryland was the first to get up.

The minute Ryland's arms were around Shiloh in a tight hug, Shiloh burst into tears. Soon she was surrounded with hugs on all sides by all of her roommates, who looked exhausted as well.

"She doesn't deserve any of this," Shiloh whispered. The group hug finally pulled away and she was led over to the couch.

"Did you find anything out?" Leah asked, giving Shiloh a reassuring squeeze on her shoulder. Sighing, Shiloh nodded and dug around in her bag. She pulled out the journal and packet of papers, holding them close.

"Her uncle was abusive," Shiloh bit her lip and blinked back tears. She flipped through the pages of the journal, remembering the words Paisley had scrawled down on the worn paper. "It must've only gotten worse after the accident."

"But what about the gun?" Vanessa spoke up, trying to think logically. Shiloh nodded and scanned a few of the pages in the journal until she found what she was looking for.

"He used to threaten her with it," Shiloh swallowed hard and traced her fingers over the indented handwriting. "She said she took the bullets out, but he'd only put them back in."

"If someone threatened me with a gun, I'd shoot him too, point blank," Ryland snapped, clenching her fists in frustration.

"If I'm correct, it's his fault for having a gun unlocked and accessible to a minor, right?" Leah thought for a moment. "In class we had to study a script for a criminal investigation show, and I remember it discussed a case like that."

"I sure hope so," Shiloh closed the journal and placed it in her lap. "If he can get away with all those years of abuse, and she gets blamed for defending herself, I don't know what I'm gonna do." Her voice cracked and she wiped her eyes quickly to try and prevent the next set of tears from spilling over.

"We just have to hope it won't turn out like that," Vanessa sighed and ran a hand through her hair.

"Paisley would never hurt anyone on purpose!" Shiloh huffed and stood up, beginning to pace back and forth across the living room to try and relieve some of her built up frustration.

"They better realize that," Ryland agreed, walking over to Shiloh and blocking her from the path she'd been pacing. The light haired girl placed her hands on Shiloh's shoulders to try and make her focus. "Shy, you look like shit, you need to sleep."

"I know," Shiloh sighed and shook her head. "But I can't."

"Shiloh…"

"I'm fine, Ryland," Shiloh sat back on the couch and pulled her legs up underneath her. "Can we just watch TV? I don't want to think… or talk about this anymore."

None of the girls said anything else, Ryland grabbed the remote and flipped to a random channel, knowing none of the girls would want to watch *Friends* without Paisley. Shiloh tried her hardest to stay awake, but her head began to bob and eventually her eyelids grew too heavy. Sleep overtook her within the first ten minutes of the show.

CHAPTER 21

The next few days passed in agony for all four roommates. Shiloh, however, was taking everything worse than the three other girls. She'd just opened up and allowed herself to get close to Paisley, only for the smaller girl to be torn away from her. The impending thought that Paisley may end up in jail and never be able to come back home terrified Shiloh.

In all her years on earth, Shiloh had never suffered a loss as great as this one. Sure, she'd lost her great aunt when she was 7 years old, but she didn't remember anything about the woman. Her mother had scolded her for picking flowers at the funeral instead of mourning along with her family, but Shiloh simply couldn't bring herself to feel sad over the loss of someone she barely knew.

Now Paisley was another story. Shiloh cared immensely about the younger girl. Granted, she used to hate her. But she found it impossible now, after learning about her. Shiloh found it impossible to hate someone once she figured out enough about them. Once she learned someone's true motives, it made it easier for her to sympathize with them.

She spent the rest of the weekend in bed. Her roommates would come into her room and check on her occasionally, but after she lashed out at them multiple times, they decided it was best to give the green eyed girl her space.

It was only at 11 PM on Sunday that Shiloh realized she had classes the next day. Which meant she was supposed to turn in another one of her independent art projects. After considering just skipping class, Shiloh was eventually able to pry herself out of bed.

She flicked on the lights in her bedroom and searched her backpack for her materials. Her eyes scanned over the colors of paint she had to choose from, grimacing at all the bright vivid colors she'd brought home. Eventually, she shoved all but two tubes of paint back into her bag.

Using the black and white paints, she mixed a variety of grays in her palette. Gray. Because without Paisley, everything seemed to lose its color. Bright colors only reminded her of what she could possibly lose.

She began to search in her closet for a canvas, swearing that she had one stashed away somewhere. Her heart stopped when she found what she had been looking for. It looked a bit different than she'd expected, though.

Instead of finding a plain white canvas, Shiloh found a plain white canvas — covered in Paisley's childish scribbles. She must have done this the morning she had colored in her sketchbook, as well.

Feeling tears welling in her eyes, Shiloh slammed the painting down on her easel and began to blindly slather paint over the colorful drawings, wanting to get them out of her sight as quick as possible.

A few minutes and a fit of tears later, Shiloh looked down at her palette only to realize she'd used up all of her paint. Glancing back up at the canvas, she bit her lip when she realized just how thickly she'd layered on the colors. Paint was dripping down the canvas, down the easel, and leaving small specks on the floor.

Growing increasingly frustrated with herself, Shiloh threw her paintbrush down and groaned. She trudged back over to her bed and crawled under the covers, curling up in the same spot where she'd spent the entire weekend.

There was a knock at the door a few moments later. When Shiloh didn't acknowledge it, Ryland let herself into the room. She raised an eyebrow at the painting before walking over and sitting on the edge of the bed.

"How're you feeling?"

Shiloh sighed, sitting up and wiping her eyes. "Why can't we just go... I don't know, fucking steal her back and leave the country?"

"Cause then we'd all end up in jail, dumbass," Ryland laughed softly. "It's getting late..."

"I know," Shiloh glanced at the clock. "I have class tomorrow."

"You're going?"

The green eyed girl nodded. No matter how much she wanted to miss class, she knew she needed some sort of distraction. Sitting around and allowing her thoughts to run freely was only making her feel worse.

"What do you think she's doing right now?" Shiloh said quietly after a few moments of silence. She saw Ryland's face fall slightly and sighed. Neither of them liked the thought of Paisley in a jail.

"From what I know, they're holding her in a cell until the trial," Ryland ran a hand through her hair and glanced out the window. "And then... depending on what happens in trial, y'know..."

Shiloh clenched her jaw and nodded. She knew. She'd thought about it for hours. "I better get some sleep," she said finally, deciding not to continue the conversation and work herself up even more. Ryland nodded in understanding.

"We meet with the lawyer tomorrow," Ryland reminded her, standing up from the bed. "We'll pick you up from class and we can drive there together?"

"Sure," Shiloh sighed. "Night."

"It'll all work out somehow," Ryland said quietly, giving Shiloh a sad smile. The green eyed girl just sighed and pulled the covers over herself. Ryland slipped quietly out of the room.

Shiloh tossed and turned, but finally ended up falling asleep, only to be woken up a few hours later by the blaring noise of her alarm. Groaning, she sat up and stared at her wall, working up the willpower to get out of bed.

As she was washing her face, Vanessa appeared behind her in the mirror. She looked up, tilting her head to the side.

"Are you okay?" her roommate asked softly. Shiloh splashed cold water on her face and nodded.

"Tired," she shrugged, drying off her face and dotting concealer under her eyes. "Thank god for makeup, right?"

Vanessa laughed softly. "Yeah, really," she bit her lip. "You sure you're alright? We meet with the lawyer today and I figured it might be hard for you."

"I'm fine, Nessa," Shiloh said firmly, not wanting her roommate to push the subject any further. She was trying her best to move any emotions out of her head. Luckily, Vanessa took the hint, giving her a sad smile before leaving her alone.

Once Shiloh was dressed, she scanned her bedroom one last time. When she saw the painting, she cringed. It would have to do, though. She had no time to throw together something else. Tucking it under her arm, she jogged out to her car, tossing it into the backseat carelessly.

She drove slowly to class, wanting to put it off for as long as possible. Shiloh hadn't realized how much she needed Paisley in her life until she was gone. Paisley had brought color to her once dull skies. And now, the blue of the sky was slowly fading with each day of Paisley's absence.

Eventually, she ended up in the front parking lot of her school. She parked, circling her car so she could grab her painting.

"Shit," she mumbled, noticing the chips of paint that had rubbed against the back of her seat. She picked up the canvas, turning it over and groaning when she saw the small white spaces where the thick sections of dried paint had chipped off. Now, some of Paisley's childish scribbles were peeking through the black and gray coating.

She was too tired to try and think of a solution, so instead she tucked the painting under her arm and jogged inside to her classroom. Of course, she was late once again, and after apologizing a million times, she set her canvas in the back of the classroom and quietly took her seat.

Meanwhile, back at the apartment, Ryland and Vanessa were cooped up in Ryland's bedroom, hovering over her laptop.

"How can she not have any family?" Vanessa furrowed her eyebrows. They'd been trying to find someone who had connections to Paisley for the past hour, but they'd come up empty handed each time.

"I have no clue," Ryland sighed, shoving the laptop off of her lap. "I give up."

"Hey, wait," Vanessa lay back on the bed and thought for a moment. "Didn't she always talk about how she was Cuban?"

"I remember that, yeah," Ryland nodded and scooted back on the bed to join Vanessa. "Which means she might have family there, but..."

"They won't know her," Vanessa finished her sentence for her. "And they won't speak English." Both girls sighed in defeat.

"I can't imagine having *no one*," Vanessa said after a few minutes of silence between them. "That'd be... terrifying. I mean, the only person she had was a complete asshole."

"She had us," Ryland lifted her head and sat up. "And Shiloh."

"*Shiloh*," Vanessa raised her eyebrows suggestively.

Ryland rolled her eyes at Vanessa's playfulness and stood up, walking over to the window and staring at the city below them. "She's not taking it well. If Paisley has to leave... y'know... She'll be crushed."

"She didn't know what she was getting into," Vanessa agreed.

Across the city, Shiloh was just finishing her class. She practically ran to the door, but one of her classmates tapped her shoulder before she could leave and pointed to her teacher, who had been trying to get her attention. Shiloh grimaced, dropping her shoulders in defeat and walking over to his desk.

"Your work this week is sure... different," Mr. Robertson began, setting her painting on the table. Shiloh crinkled her nose, cursing herself for even turning it in. "You put a lot of emotion into this, yes?"

Shiloh bit her lip and shrugged. "I guess."

"To me, this looks like a work of pure grief, Miss Everest," he leaned over the painting and traced the colorful marker underneath the paint, where Paisley had drawn.

Shiloh clenched her fists. "It's none of your business, actually. All you're supposed to do is grade it," she snapped, feeling her blood boiling. She couldn't help it.

Her teacher lifted his head to look at her, surprised by her sudden outburst. Shiloh held her breath. He just nodded towards the door, signaling that she could leave. Shiloh practically sprinted out of the room, not wanting to get herself into any more trouble.

When she made it to the parking lot, she glanced around for Vanessa and Ryland's car. All four roommates had agreed to drive to meet with the lawyer together. In her backpack, Shiloh clutched Paisley's journal close to her chest.

When she couldn't spot their car, she sat down on the curb and waited. Every time she was alone, Shiloh's mind always seemed to wander to Paisley. What was the small girl doing at that very moment? What if she was hurt? Or sick? Or scared? Shiloh bit her lip and squeezed her eyes shut.

The familiar rumble of Ryland's pickup truck beckoned in the distance. Shiloh lifted her head, noticing her friends waiting for her at the back of the parking lot. Sighing, she jogged over and slid into the backseat next to Leah, who squeezed her hand supportively.

"Vanessa, it's a fucking left turn, look at the brochure," Ryland leaned over from the driver's seat and fished a piece of paper out of the glove compartment, unfolding it and pointing to the small map.

"Hey dumbass, it's only a left turn if you hold it upside down," Vanessa flipped the paper around to prove Ryland wrong. The light haired girl huffed and turned the car right, speeding off down the road.

"Calm down up there!" Leah shook her head, turning to Shiloh and rolling her eyes. "They'd been on edge all day."

"Have not," Vanessa mumbled. "We're just nervous, that's all."

Shiloh remained quiet while the girls bantered back and forth. Her mind was still on Paisley. Only a few days stood between them and the trial. And everything would become even real the moment she set foot in that courtroom.

"Shy…?" Leah said quietly. Shiloh looked up.

"What?" she snapped.

"You're crying…?"

"Oh," Shiloh whispered, wiping her eyes and turning her head away from the other girls. "I'm fine."

None of the other passengers in the car questioned her, knowing it would only make things worse. Vanessa and Ryland continued to argue over the directions until they finally pulled up in front of the large building.

They walked inside in silence, and a few minutes later they found themselves seated in a small room around a table, sitting across from a small man with a briefcase. Shiloh felt sick to her stomach. The reality of this was slowly sinking in.

"I guess we can get started then," he nodded once, pulling a stack of papers out from his briefcase and thumbing through them. "Paisley had to undergo a psychiatric evaluation as well as a medical evaluation," he started.

Shiloh swallowed hard.

"Unfortunately, she wasn't very compliant," he continued, making Shiloh's heart drop in her chest.

"Looks like we've got enough information, though, if we combine everything with her previous medical records. I'm assuming you girls know about the accident Miss Lowe was involved in?"

All of them nodded except for Shiloh, who just sat frozen. He flipped through the papers and pulled out a pale yellow sheet, sliding it across the table for them to look at.

"That's the official accident report," he explained, placing two pictures on the table in front of them. Shiloh felt her stomach flip and she had to turn away to compose herself for a moment. "Those were taken the day after the accident. You can see where her skull was fractured, which is where most of the damage to her brain was done."

Turning back slowly, Shiloh studied the picture. Paisley was connected to a multitude of wires and machines. She was so small and vulnerable in the big hospital room. Shiloh's hands shook and she had to shove the pictures back across the table for her own good. The other girls understood, just as shocked by the images as she was.

"The trauma to her head was pretty severe," he continued, slipping the pictures back into his briefcase. "Typically, a traumatic brain injury has cognitive, perceptual, physical, and behavioral affects. All of which Miss Lowe seems to be showing."

"Memory loss is evident, although it seems to be spotty in some cases. It's hard to identify the things she does remember, and the things she doesn't. She has trouble understanding others and processing her own information, as well as expressing her own thoughts, which is frustrating for her."

"But in her case, that doesn't seem to account for some of her… *problems*, to put it lightly," he sighed and fished through his papers again, reading one of them for a few moments.

"A history of abuse is evident, yes?" he turned to them. All four girls nodded.

"Her uncle," Shiloh spoke up for the first time. "It started in 5th grade."

He nodded and jotted something down. The other three girls looked at her, wondering how she knew the information. Shiloh ignored their gazes and took a deep breath.

"At first we thought her brain injury may have triggered something called non-fluent aphasia, which would explain her trouble speaking in full sentences," he cleared his throat and scanned the papers once more. "Which might be the case, but there seems to be more."

"There's a long recovery period after something as traumatic as a brain injury. Especially in Paisley's case, she would have to relearn a lot of things that she'd lost in the accident," he explained. "Unfortunately, the person she was living with at the time was not only abusive, but negligent."

"Her uncle wasn't a fit caretaker. Paisley didn't have any help in her recovery, which explains her... *peculiar* way of seeing things. Everything she knows she's most likely figured out on her own. With no socialization, this all can stunt her recovery. Are you following?"

Shiloh clenched her hands into fists. Her blood was boiling with anger towards Paisley's uncle. She settled on nodding slowly and forcing herself to breathe deeply.

"Now for her psych evaluation," he began, and Shiloh's heart was beating rapidly. As if what she was already going through wasn't enough, there had to be even more. Paisley didn't deserve any of this.

The man slid another paper out of his binder and laid it on the desk. "She showed signs of Posttraumatic Stress Disorder, most likely from the abuse that continued once she got home from the hospital."

"Basically, her brain is overwhelming itself. She already had damage done to her brain, so now having to process the abuse and any repressed memories is even harder for her than it would be for, say, me or you."

"This is so fucking stupid!" Shiloh snapped, slamming her hands into the table and standing up. "I don't get why we even have to sit here, while Paisley is out there, and we can't even help her!"

She felt a hand on her arm and looked over at Ryland, giving her a sympathetic look. No one seemed to be angry with her for being upset, and Ryland tugged on her arm to urge her to sit back down. Shiloh sighed and slouched back into her seat.

"You don't happen to be the one she calls '*Lolo*,' do you?" the man nodded to Shiloh. The moment she heard the familiar nickname, the green eyed girl burst into tears. Her roommates immediately crowded around her to calm her down.

"I'm fine, guys, I'm fine," Shiloh mumbled, wiping her eyes and sniffing. Truth is, she wasn't fine, but she could fake it for now. "I need to talk to him alone, I have…" she nodded towards her backpack. The girls understood, giving Shiloh supportive smiles and slipping out of the room.

Once the door shut behind them, Shiloh bent down and pulled Paisley's old journal out of her backpack, flipping it open and setting it on the table.

Shiloh bit her lip and thought for a moment. "She brought this with her when she showed up at our door," she lied. She couldn't confess to breaking into the house.

"She wrote about her uncle in here," Shiloh said after taking a deep breath. The lawyer nodded, signifying to her that it was okay to go on. "She talks about how he… hit her, and at one point she says he threatened her with his gun, which I think could explain how she… *you know*."

Shiloh passed the journal across the table for him to look at. She looked down at her hands in her lap, her anxiety growing by the second.

"Can I take pictures of these?" the lawyer asked, holding up a small digital camera. "This would serve as solid evidence in the courtroom." Shiloh nodded softly, watching as he snapped a couple pictures of the pages, before passing the journal back across the table.

"I just wanted to brief you and your roommates on what we've concluded so far with Paisley," he explained, beginning to store the papers back in his brief case. "We've got a solid argument, strong evidence, and proof of his abuse. I think we've got a pretty good chance."

Shiloh took a deep breath and nodded. "Thank you," she said softly, holding Paisley's journal tight to her chest and heading out to meet the other girls in the lobby. There were a million thoughts running through her head, and Shiloh knew the next few days were going to be anything but easy for her.

CHAPTER 22

After their meeting with the lawyer, Shiloh went home and headed straight to bed. She tossed and turned, but finally ended up falling asleep fairy early. She woke with a start at around 9PM, breathing heavily and bringing her hands to her face. Another nightmare about Paisley in jail.

This time, Shiloh and Paisley had been separated by a wire fence, holding hands through the small holes in the barrier. All of a sudden, Shiloh had felt a force pulling her backwards, and no matter how much she struggled, she couldn't break free. Paisley was pulled away as well, by two prison guards behind her.

Paisley was calling out for Shiloh to help her, but Shiloh couldn't respond. She tried, but every time she opened her mouth, no sound would come out. Then all of a sudden, everything went dark, and she felt as if she was falling. And that's when she was jolted awake.

Shiloh took a deep breath, scrambling to turn on her light and convince herself it had all been just a dream. Once she calmed herself down and assured herself that she was safe, she came to the realization that she would never be able to get undisturbed sleep that night.

So she went for a walk. Granted, going for a walk probably wasn't the best idea in the middle of the night, in New York City, by herself. But she was Shiloh, and she acted on her impulses. So she slipped on her shoes and silently made her way out of the apartment and outside into the fresh air.

Her walk took a dramatic turn, though, when she gazed longingly at the park across the street. That park had been where she'd scolded Paisley for picking the flowers, and where she'd found Paisley in the woods in the pouring rain. She took a deep breath, slowly forming an idea.

She walked down the street. Thankfully, she knew exactly where she could find what she needed, and if she walked at a fast pace, she could make it there just in time. Her worn converse carried her quickly down the block, and eventually she ended up right where she needed to be.

After purchasing more than she should have, Shiloh decided to get a taxi back to the park instead of having to carry everything. Ten minutes later, she found herself in the back corner of the park where Paisley had picked the daisies.

She dug. She dug out the area where the daisies had once grown. Using the collection of flowers she'd purchased from the nursery, she carefully planted them along the curve in the sidewalk, making sure the yellow ones were on proud display in the middle.

Before Paisley, if Shiloh had been told she would be planting flowers at midnight, she would laugh and think it was a joke. But now, here she was. Paisley had brought spontaneity into her life, and now Shiloh found herself doing things she never thought she would. And enjoying it.

An hour or so later, all the flowers she had bought were now planted neatly in the small corner of the park. Maybe this was her mind's twisted way of making up for yelling at Paisley for the daisies, but either way, it had kept her mind occupied for a good amount of time.

She stood back and admired the small garden she'd created, wishing Paisley could have been there to see it. Shiloh thought back to the day she had told Paisley that love wasn't about possession, and that it was about appreciation.

Looking back now, Shiloh hated the fact that that statement was true. Because hell, she could appreciate Paisley no matter how far away the girl was. But she wanted Paisley there. With her. And at the moment, that wasn't possible.

She sat on the bench for a while, just admiring her handiwork. She didn't realize how long she'd been outside until a beam of sunlight peered over the trees and nearly blinded her. Sighing, she made the decision that even though she had class that day, she deserved a day off.

The moment she walked through the apartment door, all three of her roommates crowded around her.

"Where the hell were you?" Ryland looked the girl up and down to make sure she was alright.

"I went for a walk," Shiloh shrugged, not wanting to reveal what she had actually been doing. She'd already gotten enough '*whipped*' comments from her friends, and wasn't in the mood for any more of them.

"You're fucking insane," Ryland shook her head. "We thought you got kidnapped or something. Warn a girl next time, will you?"

Shiloh just chuckled to herself and ran a hand through her hair. She walked into the kitchen, grabbing a box of cereal from the pantry and making herself breakfast. All of her roommates eyed her questioningly.

"You're late for class," Leah spoke up. Shiloh raised an eyebrow for a moment before shrugging.

"M'not going," she mumbled with a mouthful of food.

"That's a first," Vanessa whispered to Ryland, who nodded in agreement. They decided not to question Shiloh further, though. With only a few days left until Paisley's trial, they wanted to keep Shiloh in as best of a mood as they could.

Shiloh's mood plummeted downwards around dinnertime, though, when her phone buzzed in her pocket and she excused herself into her bedroom.

"Hello?" she asked, sitting on the edge of her bed and biting her lip.

"Shy? It's mom, your father just got me a new phone. How are you?"

Shiloh's eyes widened. Her mother had always been good at telling when Shiloh was upset, even over the phone. She took a deep breath.

"I'm good, mom, how are you?" she asked, scooting back on her bed and crossing her legs. It's not that she wasn't close with her mother, because she was, but she didn't exactly have a believable explanation for why she was this miserable. Luckily, her mother didn't seem to notice.

"We're all good down here, sweetie, what's new with you? I've been so busy I just haven't had the time to call," her mother explained on the other end of the line. Shiloh racked her brain for something new in her life *besides* Paisley.

"I, uh, I'm doing good in school," Shiloh offered a half-assed lie, biting her lip.

"That's all?" her mother questioned, and Shiloh could tell she knew something was up. "How are the other girls?"

"They're good," Shiloh nodded once and gazed out the window, watching as the sun slowly began its descent behind the horizon.

"Everything's '*good*' with you then, eh?"

"I guess," Shiloh shrugged. She didn't know what else to say to try and lead the conversation in another direction. She'd never been good at talking about herself.

"What about your dating life? Any hot girls in the city?" her mother teased.

"Mom!" Shiloh felt her cheeks grow red and suddenly she couldn't get her mind off of Paisley. "I... I-I... I don't know."

"So there is someone!" her mother raised her voice. "Noah, you were right!" she called to Shiloh's father in the background. Shiloh's jaw dropped and she suddenly grew increasingly anxious. Now they would bombard her with questions, and she wouldn't know how to answer them.

"Who is she? What's her name?" her mother came back on the other end of the phone. Shiloh tensed and couldn't find her words.

"I... she's... I don't know," she stumbled over her words.

"You don't know her name?" her mother laughed. Shiloh lifted her head when she heard a soft knock at the door, revealing Ryland staring questioningly into her room. When she saw the nervous look on Shiloh's face, she immediately joined the girl on the bed and threw and arm around her shoulder. Shiloh took a deep breath.

"I don't know what… *we* are, yet, I don't really want to get your hopes up for nothing," Shiloh bit her lip. It wasn't technically a lie.

Ryland raised an eyebrow and mouthed '*Paisley*?' to Shiloh, who nodded and motioned for Ryland to keep quiet. Thankfully, the light haired girl got the message.

"Oh, well that's understandable, honey," her mother sighed on the other end of the line. Shiloh bit her lip, knowing both of her parents were eager to hear about whoever their daughter had met. If only they knew.

"You'll be the first to know," Shiloh tried to reassure them. Ryland patted Shiloh's back in support and the green eyed girl sent her a thankful smile. Thankfully, her mother dropped the subject, and Shiloh said she had to go help with dinner. Once the call ended, Ryland tilted her head to the side slightly.

"You're not going to tell them about Paisley?" her roommate asked, crossing her legs underneath her. Shiloh bit her lip in thought.

"They know who she is," Shiloh sighed and shook her head. "They know what she did to me in high school, and I don't want to bring that up to them right now. Plus, without any context, telling them that she's being charged for murder isn't exactly the ideal way to introduce her."

"True," Ryland agreed and nudged Shiloh playfully. "Quit worrying so much. It'll all work out."

"Do you really believe that?" Shiloh rebutted. Ryland shrugged and laid back on the bed.

"I'm trying my best," she admitted.

"Me too," Shiloh mumbled, gazing out the window at the sunset. All the different colors reminded her of Paisley and she abruptly got up, whipping her curtains shut. Ryland jumped at the girl's sudden outburst, watching as Shiloh turned around with tears in her eyes. Immediately, Ryland held out her arms. Shiloh willingly fell into them, letting the sobs overtake her.

"I-I just want her back," Shiloh managed to say between sobs. Ryland just nodded in agreement. All four roommates felt a void open when Paisley had left.

"There's some cheesy ass quote about loving something and letting it go," Ryland said after a few minutes of silence between them. Shiloh wiped her eyes and looked up at the other girl.

"And if it comes back, it was meant to be. I know," Shiloh whispered. "Is it really true, though?" She sat up and wiped her eyes, her mind was suddenly racing. "What if you love something and it doesn't come back? What do you do then?"

"No one has all the answers," Ryland said truthfully. "You've just got to hope that the universe knows what it's doing."

Shiloh bit her lip to stop the next round of tears from falling. "Why does it hurt so much?" she groaned and lay back on the bed, staring up at the ceiling blankly. "This is why I don't get attached. Because then something comes along and threatens to ruin everything."

She clenched her fists, growing angrier and angrier at everyone who stood between her and Paisley. She jumped when she felt a hand on her arm.

"We've just gotta fight for her then, right?" Ryland said softly, squeezing Shiloh's hand. "If we go down, we'll go down fighting."

Shiloh nodded softly, forcing herself to believe the words that Ryland spoke. Paisley was hers, and she was going to make sure it stayed that way.

Hell, if love was painful, she didn't care. The pain was worth it.

Oh god, the pain was *so* fucking worth it.

Two days of absolute hell passed as slowly as they could. Shiloh spent most of her time in her room, sitting on the edge of her bed and staring out the window. Her room was positioned so she had a perfect view of the park across the street. All week she had been watching people's reactions when they saw the abundance of flowers she'd planted a few nights back. She hoped that maybe some of their happiness would rub off on her.

Shiloh found it funny how when Paisley showed up at their door, she had no idea a girl that small could cause her so much pain just by being absent in her life. She wasn't aware how painful losing someone was.

People talk about emotional pain, but they never seem to mention the physical pain of distance. Shiloh had always thought people were exaggerating when they said their heart 'hurt,' but now, she understood. It was literally as if someone had reached straight into her chest and gripped her heart, not allowing it to beat any further.

She was suspended in a world of nothingness. It was as if time had stopped, and she was trapped watching everyone else move on with their lives, while she struggled to free herself. Paisley had left and taken everything Shiloh had valued with her.

And it didn't make sense to her at all. Because she'd known Paisley for such a short period of time, and yet the time they'd spend together was so full. And god, she'd used that girl as a security blanket. Paisley brought light back into Shiloh's life and now, nothing was left but shadows.

She'd come into Shiloh's life, turned everything upside down, and disappeared once more. And Shiloh wanted nothing more than to get her back.

It was now the day before the trial, and Shiloh couldn't sleep. Nearly midnight, the moon was the only thing illuminating her otherwise dark bedroom. She rolled onto her back, staring up at the ceiling and tracing the constellations in the cracks. Maybe Paisley could see the moon from where she was. Maybe it would lead her back home.

CHAPTER 23

"Shy."

"Shiloh."

"Everest!"

Shiloh woke with a start when her blanket was tugged from overtop of her, causing her to fly off of the edge of her bed and land on the ground with a thud. She groaned, still half asleep, and glared at Ryland and Vanessa standing above her.

"You brought it upon yourself," Ryland tossed the blanket on the floor. "Today's the day, get dressed and get your ass downstairs for breakfast."

The green eyed girl waited until her roommates were gone to untangle herself from the blankets and stumble up to her feet. Today was the day. Paisley's trial. The day where things could suddenly become one hundred percent more real for her.

Telling herself not to think about it, Shiloh blasted music from her speakers to keep her mind occupied. She got changed into leggings and a band t-shirt, throwing her leather jacket overtop of it to accommodate the declining temperature.

She looked at herself in the mirror, realizing just how exhausted she looked. It matched the way she felt. Sighing, she splashed cold water on her face to try and wake herself up. It didn't help much.

The moment she set foot in the kitchen, a bowl of cereal was shoved into her hands. Leah gave her a soft smile and nodded towards their other roommates in the living room. Shiloh sat down on the carpet since the couches were full, realizing she was sitting in Paisley's usual spot. She swallowed the lump in her throat and glanced up at her roommates.

"Nervous?" Vanessa asked her. Shiloh nodded, taking a bite of her food and picking at a loose strand of carpet.

"You're not the only one," the dark skinned girl responded, motioning to the other two girls on the couch as well as herself. "None of us know what to expect."

Shiloh bit her lip. At least she wasn't alone in this. She didn't know what she would do if she had been handling this by herself. "Thank you guys," she whispered, nodding once. "I dunno what I'd do without you."

"We were thrown into this together, it's only fair that we stick it out together," Leah nodded, giving the girl on the floor a soft smile. Shiloh returned the gesture and finished the rest of her breakfast in silence. This was a bad thing, though, because it only allowed her thoughts to race.

Regardless of what happened that day, she would be in the same room as Paisley. She would see her face, and she kept trying to hold onto that one simple blessing. And maybe, just maybe, she'd get to hug her.

The car ride to the courthouse was dead silent aside from Ryland's occasional complaints about traffic. All four girls were on edge. Shiloh picked anxiously at her nails, a nervous habit she'd had since she was a child.

"Here we are," Ryland breathed out. Parking the car, the light haired girl gazed at the building in front of them and took a deep breath. The minute Shiloh saw the name of the building, she felt sick to her stomach. This was really happening, this wasn't just a dream.

The three other girls slid out of the car, but Shiloh sat frozen, running over everything in her mind. This was real. She jumped when she felt a hand on her shoulder, turning to find Ryland holding out a hand to help her out of the car. Swallowing the lump in her throat, Shiloh allowed the other girl to lead her out of the car and up the steps to the courthouse.

Ten minutes later, the four friends sat on an uncomfortable wooden bench, all scanning the room nervously. Shiloh bit her lip.

"I feel sick to my stomach," she mumbled. Leah, who was sitting next to her, placed a hand on her knee and gave her a supportive smile. Shiloh just sighed and looked down at her hands in her lap.

The sound of footsteps brought her attention back to the front of the room, and her heart dropped in her chest the moment she saw the neon yellow sweatshirt. The same one she'd gotten Paisley. The same one Paisley was wearing the night they took her away.

What made even more of an impact was the girl *wearing* the sweatshirt. Shiloh immediately felt Ryland and Vanessa grab her hands to try and comfort her, but she already felt a lump forming in her throat.

Paisley hadn't seen her yet. In fact, the smaller girl kept her eyes locked on the ground the entire time. She was dead silent as one of the officers led her to the front of the room to sit down. It was only then that Paisley lifted her head and looked shyly around the room.

Brown eyes met green and Shiloh swore her heart stopped beating. Ryland's grip on her hand tightened. Paisley studied Shiloh's face for a second, as if she was making sure it was her. Moments later, chaos broke out.

"Lolo?" Paisley stood up, starting to walk towards Shiloh. The green eyed girl was about to get up as well, but a man grabbed Paisley before she could walk any further.

That sent Paisley into panic, and she whimpered, trying to pull her arms out of his grip. This only made him hold tighter onto her, but she continued to try and run forwards to Shiloh.

"Lolo!" she cried, thrashing her arms to the side wildly and struggling to plant her feet in front of the other. Another officer appeared to help keep Paisley from running. Shiloh sat frozen. This wasn't real. This was all a dream.

"Shiloh."

"Wha…?" Shiloh snapped out of her hypnotic stare on Paisley and flinched when she saw one of the officers was now standing in front of her. She glanced at her roommates helplessly.

"We're going to need you to leave the room, ma'am, you appear to be some sort of distraction for her," the man nodded towards Paisley, who was looking straight at her pleadingly. Shiloh had to tear her eyes away.

"I can come with you," Ryland offered. Shiloh turned to look at the girl next to her and shook her head slowly. She needed to be alone. Ryland nodded in understanding, which Shiloh was thankful for. Saying another word would most likely send her over the edge.

Without another word, Shiloh got to her feet and quickly walked out of the courtroom. Truth be told, she was glad to get out of there. She didn't think she could handle reliving Paisley's past all over again. Once had been more than enough for her.

Paisley started screaming for Shiloh when she saw the green eyed girl waking away, and Shiloh forced herself to keep walking. If she turned around, she knew she wouldn't be able to leave. And that would only cause more trouble for the both of them. That didn't stop her heart from aching more than it ever had, though.

Unsure of where else to go, Shiloh walked down the courthouse steps and sat at the bottom, kicking a pebble on her way down. It was a fairly chilly day in the city, but she couldn't care less. She needed all the fresh air she could get.

The minute she thought back to what had just happened in the court room, Shiloh felt sick all over again. The image of Paisley crying out her name and struggling to run towards her was all it took for Shiloh to burst into tears. The green eyed girl let her head fall into her hands as sobs escaped her lips.

Meanwhile, Ryland, Leah, and Vanessa all sat anxiously as the trial began. The pictures of Paisley in the hospital after the car accident were presented to the jury, along with excerpts from her journal, which talked about her uncle's abuse.

Once Shiloh had left, the officers had forced Paisley to sit back down. They had to handcuff her to the table to keep her from running. The image made Ryland shiver. Paisley didn't deserve any of this. And Shiloh didn't deserve to see her go though this.

Ryland's blood was already boiling by halfway through the trial. Hearing all the horrible things Paisley had to go through was making her angrier by the second, but something else made her snap altogether.

"Shouldn't we be concerned about the threat someone like *her* poses to society?" the prosecutor turned to Paisley's lawyer and raised an eyebrow. The combination of her body language and the tone in her voice set Ryland over the edge, and she hopped to her feet before the man could respond.

"Can I say something?" Ryland called out, clenching her fists and trying to keep herself calm. She stepped into the aisle and everyone's heads turned to her. Including Paisley, whose eyes met hers pleadingly.

"And who might you be?" the judge addressed her. Ryland took a step forward.

"I'm her roommate," she pointed to Paisley.

The judge looked between Ryland and Paisley for a few moments before nodding once. "Go ahead."

Ryland took this as a cue to move forward, she marched straight to the front of the courtroom and faced the jury. She took a deep breath before she started to speak.

"When Paisley first showed up at her house, my three roommates and I *hated* her," Ryland began, keeping her voice steady. She saw Leah and Vanessa gaping at her actions, but ignored them. "We were anything *but* friends in high school, and we had no idea why she would try to come to us out of all people."

"My friend Shiloh — the girl who you saw before — resented her the most. Paisley… she… she did some things to her in high school. Although she doesn't remember them anymore," Ryland nodded towards Paisley, who was watching in confusion.

"Shiloh started out completely hating her. But then somehow, Paisley started to win her over. God, they were fucking inseparable until they had to come and take her away!" Ryland flung her arm backwards and motioned to the two police officers standing a few feet behind Paisley.

"And if you don't know Shiloh, you should know that she is the stubbornest person I've ever met in my entire life. It's unheard of for her to change her opinion about someone. But somehow Paisley did that," Ryland pointed to Paisley once more. "So I think that's a pretty good judge of character."

"And if *you*…" Ryland glared at the prosecutor. "If you think that Paisley is a threat to society, you couldn't be more wrong." She took a deep breath and tried to contain her anger. Everyone was listening to her intently, curious on what she had to say.

"Paisley wouldn't hurt a fly. She's literally the definition of innocence," Ryland ran a hand through her hair. "This is the same girl that cried for hours because she broke a vase and thought she '*killed*' it. And if you think that's a danger to society, you need to rethink your definition of danger."

Ryland finished bluntly, nodding once and not waiting to be dismissed before marching back and taking her seat. She was infuriated at the entire situation. Vanessa reached out and squeezed her shoulder, meeting her eyes and silently telling her she did well.

"Well," the judge scanned the courtroom. "With that being said, we'll have a short break while the jury comes to their verdict, and we'll gather back here in ten minutes after they make their decision."

The three girls looked at one another, and then over to Paisley, who was staring at them longingly. They knew if they left the room that it would only cause a scene with a smaller girl, so instead Vanessa tugged them both into the back corner where they couldn't be heard.

"You've got balls, Ryland," she said once they were out of earshot. Ryland just nodded and brought her hand to her chest.

"My heart is beating like crazy," she confessed, glancing back at the front of the room where she had just stood. "You don't think I fucked everything up, do you?"

Vanessa and Leah exchanged glances before shaking their heads. "It was good. You did good."

"Do you think Shiloh's okay?" Ryland bit her lip and glanced around the room. "I should go check on her." She nodded, making her decision. "Yeah, I'll be back in a few minutes."

The other girls nodded in understanding. Ryland jogged out of the room, trying to think where her green eyed roommate would have gone. Knowing Shiloh, she would be outside, so that's where Ryland checked first.

Sure enough, she caught sight of the dark haired girl at the bottom of the steps. She made her way down slowly, narrowing her eyes to see what Shiloh was doing.

"Hey loser, you okay?"

Shiloh slammed her sketchbook shut the minute she heard Ryland's voice. Once she had calmed herself down, she had realized she needed to remember what Paisley looked like if that had been the last time she would ever seen her. The green eyed girl had flipped to an open page in her sketchbook and attempted to bring Paisley to life on paper. The last thing she wanted to do was forget what she looked like.

She looked up at Ryland, biting her lip and shrugging. "M'fine. How'd it go? Is she...?" she suddenly grew worried and moved to stand up. Ryland put a hand out to stop her.

"They haven't made their decision yet. We have a ten minute break," Ryland explained, sitting down next to Shiloh, who sighed heavily. "I sort of... said something."

"You what?" Shiloh raised her eyebrows.

"They thought Paisley was a '*danger to society*,'" Ryland scoffed, making air quotes with her fingers. "Which is bullshit, and I made sure they knew that."

"Please don't tell me you punched someone," Shiloh bit her lip.

"Only with my words," Ryland chuckled, trying to lighten the mood. Shiloh rolled her eyes and let her head fall in her hands.

"I don't know what I'm gonna do if..." she shook her head.

"Don't focus on the worst possible outcome," Ryland ran a hand through her hair and glanced back up at the building. "It'll all work out the way it's supposed to, okay?"

Shiloh just nodded, keeping her eyes locked on the ground. Ryland checked her phone and cursed when she saw the time.

"I've gotta get back in there," she stood up and gave Shiloh's shoulder a soft squeeze. "Don't get into any trouble while I'm gone!" she called as she jogged back up the stairs. Shiloh turned to watch her disappear back into the building.

Once she was alone again, Shiloh slowly reopened her sketchbook. Using her pencil, she began scratching in the smaller details. Paisley's small birthmark on the side of her face, her dimples, the perfect curve of her lips. Shiloh squeezed her eyes shut and took a deep breath.

Maybe wanting to remember what she looked like was superficial, but Shiloh didn't see it that way. Looking at Paisley reminded her of other things.

Looking at her eyes reminded her of the way Paisley would smile with her entire face. Looking at her lips reminded her of Paisley's incessant laughter, and how good it felt to kiss her and feel her giggle against her lips. Looking at her eyes reminded her of the way Paisley would study Shiloh so intently, completely unashamed of the way she was staring.

Paisley was something else. And it wasn't just the *new* Paisley, either. After reading her old journal entries and getting to know the old Paisley, Shiloh had slowly fallen in love with both versions of the girl. But now, she might not get to know either one.

Sighing heavily, Shiloh wiped the few tears that had escaped her eyes and closed her sketchbook, shoving it into her backpack. She propped her elbows on her knees and let her head fall into her hands. Sleep was demanding her attention, and she was slowly losing the fight. She stared at the cars in the parking lot, absentmindedly counting their colors.

Some time passed, and the green eyed girl was now nearly asleep on the steps. She was in a half asleep, half dreaming state. Her eyelids were growing heavier by the second.

Meanwhile, four girls slowly made their way out of the front of the courthouse. Three of the girls pointed to Shiloh, nudging the smaller girl in her direction with wide smiles on their faces. When the girl saw where they were pointing, her face lit up, and her feet took off down the steps.

The minute Shiloh felt a body practically tackle hers into the grass next to the steps, she swore she was dreaming. She blinked her eyes open, growing increasingly confused.

"*Lolo*," the voice hummed contently. Shiloh's eyes widened and she felt her heart beat faster than what she thought was humanly possible. She had to be dreaming.

"Pais?" she whispered, lifting her head and wiping her eyes. The small girl was clinging to her, nuzzling her face in the crook of the neck. The moment Paisley looked up and met Shiloh's eyes, the older girl realized it wasn't a dream. This was real.

"Oh my god," Shiloh threw her arms around Paisley and held her closer than she ever had before. She was back. She was safe. She was with *her*.

"Lolo promised," Paisley mumbled, with her head still lying on Shiloh's shoulder. Both girls were practically flat on the grass in front of the courthouse, but neither cared at all.

"What?" Shiloh asked, pulling apart from the prolonged hug and wiping the tears from her eyes. The moment Paisley saw this, she grew increasingly concerned. The smaller girl reached out and pressed her palm against the side of Shiloh's face, tilting her head to the side.

"Why are you crying?" Paisley asked, concern flickering in her eyes. She reached out with her other hand and used her thumb to ever-so-gently wipe each individual tear from Shiloh's cheeks. "Are you sad?"

Shiloh shook her head furiously. "No, of course not," she laughed softly. "I'm just really happy," she explained, using the sleeves of her jacket to wipe her own eyes. "Sometimes people cry when they're really happy."

"I am happy too, Lolo," Paisley smiled widely, pulling Shiloh into another hug and sighing contently. And all at once, Shiloh felt whole again.

"What did I promise?" Shiloh asked, revisiting what Paisley had said before. The smaller girl smiled brightly and reached out to traced her fingers over Shiloh's jawline.

"You promised to keep me safe," Paisley nodded once. "You did. I am safe," she smiled widely.

Shiloh felt her eyes well up with tears again and she held Paisley close to her. "I always keep my promises," she whispered, realizing she couldn't remember the last time she'd felt this innocently happy.

After lingering in the hug for as long as she could, Shiloh pulled away and helped the smaller girl to her feet. As soon as they were both standing, Paisley clung onto Shiloh again, not wanting to risk losing her once more.

Shiloh's smile grew even wider when she saw her three roommates standing at the top of the stairs, gushing at the sight of the two other girls. The moment they made eye contact with Shiloh, they all came running down the stairs and nearly knocked over Paisley and Shiloh in a group hug.

All that was heard was their laughter, the air full of relief from the stress-filled week. All seemed right in the world.

"Together," Paisley's muffled voice rang out from the middle of the circle. "I have my friends again."

CHAPTER 24

"So she's basically free. I mean, she's not going to jail," Ryland explained to Shiloh as they walked back to the truck. "She's required to start seeing a therapist and some other special doctor, but that's about it. They said from her uncle's autopsy it was obvious that the gun had misfired. She must've been trying to get it away from him and pulled the trigger by accident."

"Damn," Shiloh bit her lip, sliding into the back of the truck.

"Lolo," Paisley hummed happily, crawling into the back of Ryland's truck and scooting right up next to Shiloh. The five girls had decided to go out to dinner to celebrate Paisley's acquittal. Shiloh was on cloud nine.

Vanessa slid into the back of the car next to Paisley, with Leah and Ryland in the front. Ryland winked at Shiloh in the rear view mirror, making the green eyed girl's cheeks flush red when she realized Paisley was practically sitting in her lap.

"Hi," Paisley smiled widely, her face inches away from Shiloh's. She didn't seem to mind that there were three other people in the car watching them.

"Hi," Shiloh giggled, feeling the now-familiar feeling of butterflies in her stomach. Paisley abruptly leaned in, kissing Shiloh quickly and then turning around to make sure everyone had seen them.

"My Lolo," she announced proudly. Shiloh was taken aback by the kiss, and moments later Paisley's lips were against hers again. This time Shiloh caught up, and kissed her back gently. She felt Paisley smiling against her lips and couldn't help but do the same. When the kiss pulled away, Shiloh's face grew red as she felt everyone's eyes on her.

"Gross," Vanessa mumbled under her breath, sending Shiloh a playful smirk through the mirror. Shiloh shoved her playfully, which caused Paisley to giggle. Vanessa moved to push Shiloh back, but Paisley threw herself in between them to stop her.

"Be nice," Paisley nodded once, taking Vanessa's hands and moving them away. The dark skinned girl raised an eyebrow.

"So Shiloh can hit me but I can't hit her back?" she and Shiloh exchanged glances. The green eyed girl burst into laughter.

"Yes. Be nice," Paisley let go of Vanessa's hands and scooted into Shiloh's side. Vanessa rolled her eyes playfully.

Once they made it to the pizza place, Paisley tugged Shiloh out of the car and practically dragged her inside the restaurant. They were taken to a large booth in the back, where Paisley insisted that she sit next to

Shiloh. (As if the girls would allow them to sit apart from each other.)

"What're we getting?" Leah asked, turning the menu over to continue reading it. Paisley furrowed her eyebrows and reached across the table, taking Leah's menu away from her and placing it on top of her own.

"Pizza," she nodded once, pointing to the picture on the menu and smiling proudly. The other four girls exchanged glances and shrugged, figuring pizza would be all they needed. The waitress came and took their order, paying extra attention to Shiloh the entire time.

Now Paisley may be pretty special, but she wasn't stupid. She saw the waitress wink at Shiloh and immediately scooted closer to the girl. By the time the waitress collected their menus and left the table, Paisley was practically in Shiloh's lap.

"What are you doing?" Shiloh giggled, wrapping an arm around Paisley. The smaller girl glared at the waitress across the restaurant and Shiloh followed her line of vision, realizing what she was alluding to.

"Her?" Shiloh asked, raising an eyebrow. Paisley looked at her, concern evident in her features. This only made Shiloh laugh and shake her head.

"Why would I want her when I've got you?"

Paisley smiled shyly. Meanwhile, Ryland and Vanessa were making gagging noises while Leah looked at the other two girls affectionately. Shiloh stuck her tongue out at them, which only made Ryland flick water off of her straw at them.

"Hey!" Paisley crossed her arms and glared at Ryland across the table. "Be nice."

"Wait, Paisley, didn't you have those clothes on when you left our apartment?" Leah spoke up, interrupting their conversation. Paisley looked at her sleeves, thinking for a moment before nodding slowly. Shiloh raised an eyebrow.

"You've been wearing those clothes the entire time?" she asked, turning to look at the girl next to her. Paisley suddenly grew ashamed, but nodded her head.

"They didn't give you a change of clothes?" Shiloh bit her lip, fighting the urge to get up and give the people who had been taking care of Paisley a piece of her mind.

"Mean," Paisley shook her head, leaning into Shiloh's side. The older girl looked at her roommates questioningly, wrapping a protective arm around Paisley and holding her close.

"How were they mean?" Shiloh asked, running a hand through Paisley's hair to loosen her curls. Paisley thought for a moment.

"They did not understand me," she replied slowly, tracing circles in the material of her jeans. Shiloh took a deep breath to calm herself down. Paisley noticed Shiloh's agitation and turned to the other girl. "But I am here now, right?"

"Exactly," Ryland spoke up, reaching across the table and squeezing Paisley's hand. "And I don't think you're gonna leave anytime soon."

Paisley nodded confidently, turning back to Shiloh and kissing her cheek. "I stay with you, yes?" Shiloh felt herself comforted by Paisley's touch and she nodded slowly.

"Of course," she smiled, kissing Paisley's forehead and earning more gagging noises from Ryland's side of the booth. She kicked the light haired girl under the table, causing Ryland to reel backwards, tipping her chair over and landing on the ground with a *thud*.

"Ouch," Paisley giggled from her side of the table, knowing what Shiloh had done. Ryland groaned, standing back up and brushing off her backside.

"Nice one, Everest," she joked, sitting back down. Vanessa and Leah both struggled to hold in their laughter, but the moment Ryland looked over at them questioningly, they both lost it.

Ryland was about to rebut their laughter with a sarcastic comment, but their pizza was brought to the table before she could. Paisley squealed excitedly, which earned a few questioning glances from the tables around them. The moment Shiloh glared back at them, though, they averted their eyes.

"Woah," Shiloh grabbed Paisley's hand just as the girl reached for the entire pizza. She giggled and shook her head, grabbing a knife and beginning to cut the pizza. "Sharing is caring, Pais."

"Oh," Paisley watched intently as Shiloh cut her a slice, holding up her plate when Shiloh asked her to. She giggled in anticipation when Shiloh slid the pizza onto her plate, and immediately took a bite.

"I like pizza," Paisley smiled widely. Shiloh giggled and cut herself a slice, passing the knife across the table to the other girls.

"I can tell," Shiloh raised an eyebrow at Paisley, who was already halfway done her slice before Shiloh had even taken a bite.

"But I like Lolo better," Paisley added, setting down her food and reaching up to press her fingers to Shiloh's cheek. Shiloh shivered. Giggling, Paisley withdrew her fingers and leaned up to kiss the same spot on Shiloh's cheek.

"Damn, Shy, she chose you over pizza," Ryland grinned from across the table. Shiloh bit the inside of her cheek to hide her smile. Paisley turned her attention back to her pizza, taking another bite and giving Vanessa a thumbs up from across the table.

A little over an hour later, the girls all arrived back at the apartment. Paisley stood hesitantly in the hallway, biting her lip when everyone else went inside. Noticing this, Shiloh turned around and stood in the doorway.

"Are you coming?" she asked softly, tilting her head to the side. Paisley took a step forward but still remained quiet. Growing concerned, Shiloh took a step out into the hallway and took Paisley's hand. "What's wrong?"

The smaller girl held onto Shiloh's hand tightly, peering into the apartment and looking down at her feet. "It is scary," she nodded towards the doorway.

"Scary?" Shiloh turned to glance back into the apartment, trying to figure out what could possibly scare the younger girl. "What's scary?"

"I do not want to leave again," Paisley proceeded to free her hands, clapping her wrists together behind her back and looking at Shiloh pleadingly. Shiloh's heart dropped when she realized the smaller girl was referring to the handcuffs that had been put on her when she was taken from the apartment.

"Hey, no, that's not going to happen again," Shiloh shook her head, stressing her words to make sure Paisley believed her. She took a step forward, taking both of Paisley's hands in her own and meeting her eyes.

"There's no more bad guys," she said, tucking a loose strand of hair behind Paisley's ear. "I'm going to make sure of that."

Paisley opened her mouth to speak, but Shiloh already knew what she was going to say. She beat her to it, lifting her pinky finger. "I promise, Pais," she giggled. Paisley crinkled her nose when Shiloh took the words out of her mouth, but proceeded to lock their fingers together.

"Can I ask you something?" Shiloh questioned, figuring now was a good of a time as any. Paisley nodded softly, allowing Shiloh to continue.

"How did you end up coming to New York? How'd you find us?" she asked, running a hand through her hair nervously. She watched as Paisley furrowed her eyebrows, biting her lip in concentration and looking down at the ground. Shiloh allowed her time to think.

"I…" Paisley looked at Shiloh nervously. "I remembered you."

Shiloh brought her hand up to her lip, toying with her bottom lip nervously. "You what?"

"I remembered you," Paisley said more confidently, reaching up and cupping Shiloh's cheek with her hand. "Lolo was in New York. I needed a friend."

Biting her lip, Shiloh nodded and looked down at the ground. "Are you happy here, Paisley?" she asked, wondering if maybe she wasn't enough for the girl.

"Yes!" Paisley smiled widely, taking Shiloh's hands in her own and swinging them gently. "I have you. I am happy." She thought for a moment before meeting Shiloh's eyes. "Are you?"

Shiloh giggled, feeling relieved from Paisley's response. "Of course I am," she crinkled her nose playfully. "I have you, I'm happy," she repeated what Paisley had just said. Paisley realized this and giggled.

"Thank you for being my friend, Lolo," Paisley pulled Shiloh into a tight hug, taking the older girl by surprise. Shiloh felt her heart melt right then and there, and she wrapped her arms around Paisley gently.

"Thank *you* for being *my* friend, Pais," Shiloh smiled as they pulled away from the hug. "Are you going to come inside now?"

Paisley nodded softly. "We will watch *Friends*," she declared, shuffling past Shiloh and into the apartment. Laughing, Shiloh followed her into the living room, where Paisley was already picking out an episode.

The other girls joined them halfway through the first episode. Midway through their third episode, Leah fell asleep. By the time their sixth episode ended, Shiloh and Paisley were the only ones awake.

"Pais," Shiloh giggled quietly when she saw Paisley grab the remote to pick another episode. "We've watched six episodes already, I think it's time for bed."

Paisley furrowed her eyebrows and set the remote back down.

"Do you think you can take a shower first?" Shiloh asked, realizing that if Paisley hadn't been given a change of clothes, she most likely hadn't been given an opportunity to shower, either. Paisley nodded softly.

"Lolo's pajamas?" she asked, tilting her head to the side with a hopeful smile on her face. Shiloh giggled.

"Sure," Shiloh got up quietly and held her hand out for Paisley, who took it gently and pulled Shiloh up the stairs. Once they reached the bathroom, Shiloh handed Paisley a towel and left a change of clothes on the sink.

"I'll be right across the hall, okay?" she said, squeezing Paisley's hand. The smaller girl nodded in understanding, and Shiloh closed the bathroom door quietly before slipping into her bedroom.

She heard the squeaking sound that indicated the shower was turned on just as she lay back on her bed. Having a moment alone made her realize how relieved she truly was. And just how painful losing Paisley had been.

It scared her tremendously — knowing how much control one person could have over her emotions. But she trusted Paisley.

Before Paisley, Shiloh had been considerably closed off. Her parents had always told her that she was in too much of a rush to grow up. Maybe Paisley was exactly what she needed. The girl made her do things she never imagined she'd ever do. And surprisingly, she liked it.

About fifteen minutes later, she was brought out of her thoughts when her door slowly creaked open.

"Knock knock," Paisley whispered, standing in the doorway. Shiloh lifted her head, feeling her breath catch in her throat when she saw Paisley. The smaller girl had on one of Shiloh's oversized band shirts, and a pair of boxer shorts underneath.

"Who's there?" Shiloh giggled. Paisley smiled widely, padding into the room and closing the door quietly so she wouldn't wake the other girls. Walking over to the bed, Paisley handed Shiloh a hairbrush, which caused the older girl to raise an eyebrow.

"Braid, please?" Paisley crawled up onto the bed, sitting cross legged. Shiloh couldn't help but smile and she nodded softly. Patting the spot in front of her, Shiloh began brushing through Paisley's hair gently once she scooted backwards.

"Lolo?" Paisley said softly, keeping her head still as Shiloh began to section off her hair.

"Yeah?" The green eyed girl asked.

"Am I bad?"

Shiloh sat up straighter, pausing what she was doing and tilting her head to the side. "What?"

Biting her lip, Paisley turned around to look at Shiloh and looked down at her hands. "They think I am bad," she said softly, lacing her fingers together.

"Who does?" Shiloh asked, reaching out and placing her hands around Paisley's. She could tell the younger girl was feeling ashamed of something, and she intended on finding out what.

"Everyone."

"I don't," Shiloh said softly. She shook her head and laced their fingers together. "Out of everyone I've ever met in my entire life, you are the furthest from bad. I promise." She held out her pinkie, but Paisley didn't move.

"I killed him," Paisley shook her head, sending droplets of water flying around them. "I am bad."

"Your uncle?" Shiloh asked carefully. She'd never exactly addressed the topic with Paisley. The smaller girl looked up and met Shiloh's eyes, nodding hesitantly.

"C'mere," Shiloh whispered, pulling Paisley into her side and ignoring her wet hair. "Do you want to tell me what happened?" she asked cautiously. She felt Paisley take a deep breath.

"He hurt me, Lolo," she said quietly, looking up at Shiloh with a look in her eyes that begged for forgiveness.

"I know, baby," Shiloh nodded softly and ran her fingers up and down Paisley's arm to soothe her. "What happened?"

"I was bad. And he was angry," Paisley clenched her hands into fists and pressed them into the bed. "There was a gun. I was scared, and I tried to stop him." The smaller girl took a deep breath and Shiloh squeezed her shoulder reassuringly.

"I did not mean to hurt him. I do not like hurt," Paisley shook her head quickly, and Shiloh reached out, cupping her cheeks to stop her.

"It is not your fault, Paisley, do you hear me?" she pressed her forehead against the smaller girl's and looked her straight in the eyes. Paisley nodded slowly, shocked by Shiloh's reaction.

"All of that stuff that happened to you, that is not your fault. I promise. I'll promise a million fucking times if it will help you realize that," Shiloh shook her head, pulling Paisley into a hug and holding her tightly.

"And I'm so sorry I couldn't keep you from going through all of that. But I'm going to do everything I can to keep you safe from now on, I swear," Shiloh took a deep breath, trying to calm herself down.

"Thank you," Paisley whispered, resting her head on Shiloh's shoulder. For some reason, Paisley's words reminded Shiloh of the Paisley she'd known in high school, and she shivered.

"I have something for you," Shiloh remembered, jogging across the room to grab her backpack. Paisley watched her questioningly from the bed.

The moment Shiloh pulled the stuffed dog from her backpack, Paisley's face lit up. She scrambled off the bed, taking the yellow toy into her own hands and smiling widely.

"Sunny!" she hugged it to her chest and looked up at Shiloh. "You saved him."

Shiloh giggled and walked back over to the bed. Paisley crawled up as well, sitting down next to Shiloh and holding the stuffed animal in her lap.

"You remember it?" Shiloh asked, pointing to the toy. Paisley nodded.

"Yes. He was mine," she held the dog up for Shiloh to see, before setting it down at the foot of the bed. "How did you find him?"

"I, uh," Shiloh swallowed hard and pulled her bag up on the bed next to them. "I had to go back to your house… while you were gone." She pulled Paisley's old journal out and sat it in front of her. Paisley stared at it blankly.

"What is that?" she asked, running her fingers over the leather cover.

"You don't remember this?" Shiloh asked, flipping the journal open and pointing to one of the many pages with writing on it. "This was your journal. At least, before the car accident."

"I do not remember," Paisley hung her head down.

"Hey, you don't have to be ashamed," Shiloh reached out and tilted Paisley's chin up so she wasn't looking down. "I don't expect you to remember anything. What's past is past, right? It doesn't matter." She tossed the journal off of the bed.

Paisley gazed up at Shiloh and smiled softly before yawning. Shiloh giggled and raised an eyebrow. "Tired?"

Paisley nodded, and burrowed under the blankets without another word. Laughing, Shiloh leaned over to turn off the lights and pulled the blankets over both of them. As always, the moment her head hit the pillow, Paisley curled up at her side.

"Goodnight, Pais," Shiloh whispered. In response, Paisley yawned and nodded before pulling Shiloh closer to her. Giggling softly, Shiloh laid her head on her pillow, falling asleep shortly after. This was the first time she'd gotten much of any sleep in the past week. Now that she was comforted by the fact that Paisley was safe, she soon faced the reality of her exhaustion.

She slept soundly for a fraction of the night, but was awoken by a set of nails digging into her arm. She rolled away groggily, lifting her head to see what was going on. The small whimpers from beside her quickly made her realize that Paisley was having another nightmare.

"Pais," she whispered, tapping the sleeping girl. No response.

"Paisley," she said louder, this time sitting up and shaking Paisley's shoulders. The girl continued to cry out, but she was fully asleep. Unsure of what to do, Shiloh lay back down and pulled Paisley next to her.

She began humming aimlessly. The small girl's hands immediately clung onto her shirt.

Shiloh held her breath when she felt Paisley stir. The smaller girl's eyes fluttered open and she gazed up at Shiloh, a worried look on her face. Instantly, Shiloh reached down and wiped the tears from her eyes.

"Are you okay?" she asked softly, pulling Paisley closer to her. The smaller girl nodded and felt around under the covers until she found Shiloh's hands, lacing their fingers together.

"More," she whispered, resting her head on Shiloh's chest. A soft smile spread across Shiloh's face, realizing her soft humming might have calmed Paisley down. She nodded softly.

A short while later, Shiloh bit her lip to hide her smile when she realized Paisley had fallen back asleep. Taking a deep breath, she pulled the covers back over them and allowed sleep to overtake her for the second time that night.

CHAPTER 25

"Lolo, look at the sky," Paisley prodded the other girl's side, trying to wake her up. Shiloh groaned and rolled over. This only encouraged the younger girl. She crawled on top of Shiloh so one leg was on each side of her torso.

"Wake up," Paisley giggled, poking Shiloh's cheek and pointing to the window. "You are going to miss it, Lolo."

"Miss what?" Shiloh's raspy morning voice finally filled the silence. She opened her eyes to come face to face with a smiling Paisley, already attempting to make her sit up. Shiloh groaned, but allowed herself to be pulled upwards.

"The sky," Paisley turned Shiloh's head and pointed to the window. "It is pretty. Like you. We have to appreciate it, right?" She turned back to the other girl and tilted her head to the side.

Despite having just woken up, Shiloh managed a soft smile. She wiped her eyes and sat cross legged, gazing out the window for a few moments.

"I guess it is pretty beautiful, huh?" she laughed softly. Paisley nodded, crawling over to Shiloh's side and leaning against her shoulder.

"Why don't we go get a better view of it, then?" Shiloh smiled softly and stood up. Paisley watched her, confused, as Shiloh dug through her drawers. The green eyed girl handed Paisley a pair of leggings and a sweater. Paisley tilted her head to the side.

"Go get dressed and let's go watch the sunrise," Shiloh nudged her towards the door. Paisley's face lit up and she nodded excitedly, scurrying across the hallway and into the bathroom. Shiloh quickly got changed into jeans and a hoodie, pulling a beanie on over her tousled morning hair.

"Knock knock," Paisley giggled, standing in the doorway. Shiloh crinkled her nose and slipped into her boots before leading Paisley out of the bedroom.

"I have a surprise for you, too," Shiloh remembered. She pointed to Paisley's converse, signaling for the girl to put them on.

"Surprise?" Paisley sat down and tugged on her shoes. She eyed the laces questioningly and then looked up at Shiloh.

Bending down, Shiloh giggled as she began to tie Paisley's shoes. "Yeah, a surprise. It's at the park," she double knotted the laces and then helped Paisley up to her feet. "C'mon, you'll like it."

"I like you," Paisley smiled proudly, grabbing the doorknob. She surprised Shiloh by turning around and placing her hands on her shoulders. "There are oceans in your eyes, Lolo. I see them."

Shiloh's breath caught in her throat when Paisley locked eyes with hers. This girl had a way of evoking the deepest emotions out of her. For someone so innocent, Paisley certainly knew what she was doing.

Both girls leaned in at the same time. Shiloh wrapped her hands around Paisley's waist and pulled her closer. She felt the smaller girl smile against her lips. It was soft, it was sweet, it was gentle. But it was perfect nonetheless.

When the kiss broke, Paisley smiled widely. "I want to see the surprise," she looked hopefully up at Shiloh, who was still recovering from the kiss. The green eyed girl could have sworn that Paisley could hear her heart pounding against her chest.

"I-I, yeah, the surprise," Shiloh cleared her throat. "C'mon, let's go to the park."

Paisley smiled excitedly and grabbed onto Shiloh's hand, tugging her towards the door. Laughing, Shiloh followed the small girl, making sure to lock the apartment door behind them.

"Slow down, Pais," she laughed, squeezing Paisley's hand and slowing her to a walking pace. "It's not going anywhere."

"What is it?" Paisley asked as they stepped onto the elevator. Shiloh grabbed Paisley's hand just as she was about to push the wrong button for the lobby.

"Press this one," Shiloh tapped the correct button, and Paisley obeyed. "And you can't know yet. That would ruin the surprise."

"Oh," Paisley giggled. The elevator lurched downwards and the small girl instantly clung onto Shiloh.

"It does that sometimes," Shiloh wrapped an arm around Paisley to comfort her. "Don't worry. See?" she motioned to the doors as they opened to reveal the ground floor of the building. Paisley sighed in relief and pulled Shiloh out of the elevator, through the lobby, and into the cold morning air.

"Cold," Paisley shivered instantly. Noticing this, Shiloh giggled and pulled the smaller girl into her side, keeping an arm wrapped around her waist. Paisley hummed contently.

"C'mon. We'll walk around the whole park," Shiloh led them towards the park entrance, knowing the surprise would be at the very end. Paisley smiled up at Shiloh and crinkled her nose.

"The whole world is asleep," Paisley observed, looking around the empty park. Shiloh laughed and ran a hand through her hair.

"Well yeah. I would be too if *someone* hadn't woken me up," she teased. Paisley raised an eyebrow and tilted her head to the side. "That's you," Shiloh explained, poking Paisley's nose. The smaller girl giggled and hid her face in Shiloh's shoulder.

"Lolo, I have a question," Paisley stopped walking suddenly. Shiloh grew worried, turning around to face Paisley and taking both of her hands in her own.

"I'm listening," Shiloh nodded, telling Paisley it was okay to go on. The smaller girl's eyes flickered down to the ground, and then back up to Shiloh. Paisley bit her lip.

"Why did I scare you?" she tilted her head to the side slowly. Shiloh grew even more confused.

"You never scare me," she laughed nervously and squeezed Paisley's hand. Paisley shook her head and shuffled her feet on the gravel pathway, frustrated with herself for not being able to get her words across.

"No, no Lolo," she shook her head and took a deep breath. "I mean… you were scared… of me. When I came here," she turned and pointed to the apartment building across the street.

"Paisley, I wasn't scared of you then, and I'm not scared of you now," Shiloh bit her lip. "What are you talking about?"

"You…" Paisley sighed and let her hands fall to her sides. "You did not… talk to me, or… or smile at me," she pointed to Shiloh's lips. "Why?"

Shiloh's mouth formed an 'O' shape. She looked down at the ground nervously and back up at Paisley, who was glancing up at her hopefully.

"Do you really want to know?" Shiloh asked, biting her lip and hoping Paisley would take back her question. She nodded, and Shiloh sighed. Leading them both over to a bench a few steps away, she sat down and took a deep breath. Telling Paisley the truth hadn't been her ideal plan, but she also didn't want to hide it. Plus, part of her was curious if Paisley remembered any of what she had done.

"I wasn't scared of you," Shiloh confessed, reaching out and taking one of Paisley's hands in her own. "I was mad at you."

Paisley's eyes widened and she sat up slightly. "Mad? Was I bad?"

Shiloh didn't respond, instead she looked down at her hands and continued talking. "Do you remember me in high school?"

Paisley tilted her head to the side and looked up at the sky, as if she were trying to remember. After thinking for a few moments, she looked back to Shiloh and shook her head slowly.

"Okay, well," Shiloh took a deep breath. "You did… something. To me. And it was mean."

"Mean?" Paisley bit her lip.

"Yeah," Shiloh glanced up at Paisley, noticing the worry in her brown eyes. "You outed me in front of the whole school."

Paisley stared at her blankly.

"You told everyone in the school I liked girls. Before I was ready to tell them that," Shiloh tried to explain it in a way that Paisley would understand. She saw understanding wash over Paisley's features.

"Oh," Paisley stood up and shook her head. "Stupid," she balled her hands into fists and brought them up against her forehead, continuing to shake her head.

Shiloh quickly stood up and pulled Paisley's hands away from her face. "Hey, Pais, look at me," she said once Paisley squeezed her eyes shut.

Slowly, Paisley looked up at Shiloh. "I am bad," she whispered, talking a step backwards and shaking her head.

"You are not," Shiloh pulled Paisley closer to her despite the girl's attempt to move backward. "You're not bad, listen to me, okay? Look me in the eyes."

"Your uncle is bad. He put you up to it, okay? You had no choice," Shiloh slowly took a step towards the bench once more, pulling Paisley with her. "I didn't know that at the time. If I had, I wouldn't have been mad at you. I would have been mad at *him*."

She sat down slowly, urging Paisley to do the same.

"I am sorry," Paisley swallowed hard and hung her head down. "I am sorry, Lolo."

Shiloh's heart dropped into her chest. The words she had wanted to hear Paisley say all those years had finally been spoken, but she felt utterly horrible. Shaking her head, she reached forwards and cupped Paisley's face in her hands.

"You have nothing to be sorry for, okay?" she said quietly, but still with finality in her voice. "Everything bad that has happened to *both* of us has only brought us here." She pointed between them. "And we're good now, right?"

Paisley nodded slowly. Shiloh felt her heart break when she saw a tear roll down Paisley's cheek.

"I forgive you, by the way," Shiloh whispered, folding her legs on the bench underneath her and pulling Paisley into her side. "I forgave you long before this, actually. I think I forgave you the day you crawled into bed with me after you had a nightmare."

"I am sorry, Lolo, I am very sorry," Paisley mumbled, burying her head in the crook of Shiloh's neck.

"Paisley, you don't have to apologize," Shiloh bit her lip and looked down at the smaller girl. Maybe telling her the truth was a bad idea.

"You have a good heart," Paisley whispered, looking up and Shiloh and studying her face intently. A few moments of silence passed between them. Paisley then reached up and pressed the tips of her fingers against Shiloh's lips.

"And ocean eyes," she whispered, moving her hand away and leaning in to kiss Shiloh gently. When Paisley pulled away from the kiss, Shiloh only snaked her arms around the girl's waist and pulled her back into another kiss.

"You…" Shiloh whispered once they pulled away from the kiss, gazing into Paisley's eyes. "You're a beautiful soul, Paisley," she nodded slowly, reaching out and tucking a loose strand of hair behind the girl's ear.

"Me?" Paisley pointed to herself. Shiloh giggled and nodded.

"Yes, you. Who else would I be talking to?" she raised an eyebrow. Paisley looked around the park and shrugged her shoulders, which made Shiloh laugh even harder.

"Do you want to keep walking?" Shiloh asked, looking down at Paisley. "There's still a surprise waiting for you."

Paisley looked up slowly as a small smile spread across her face. That was enough of an answer for Shiloh, who rose to her feet and held out her hand for Paisley.

"Thank you, Lolo," Paisley said quietly, taking the girl's hand as they continued their walk around the park.

"For what?" Shiloh kicked a pebble on the asphalt. Paisley giggled and did the same, watching the small rock bounce along in front of them.

"Being my Lolo," Paisley hummed, kicking another pebble and nearly tripping over her own two feet. Shiloh quickly grabbed her to keep her from falling, and both girls laughed.

"What do you mean by *your* Lolo?" Shiloh asked curiously, biting her lip.

"My Lolo," Paisley raised an eyebrow at Shiloh. Her answer alone was sufficient for her, she didn't understand what Shiloh meant.

"Do you know what a girlfriend is?" Shiloh asked.

"Yes," Paisley nodded once. "You."

Shiloh's heart skipped a beat and she nodded slowly. "Well, alright then," she laughed softly. "Easy as that?"

"Yes," Paisley smiled widely. "You and me, right?"

Shiloh smiled, squeezing Paisley's hand. "Me and you," she nodded once. Paisley clapped her hands excitedly. Shiloh noticed how close they were getting and stopped walking.

"Do you trust me?" she asked, walking up behind Paisley and covering her eyes. Paisley tilted her head to the side slightly but nodded.

"Walk slowly forwards," Shiloh kept Paisley's eyes covered, leading her around the corner of the park and positioning her in front of the flowers. "Ready for your surprise?"

"Yes, now?" Paisley clasped her hands together.

"Now," Shiloh confirmed, letting her hands drop away from Paisley's face. The small girl gasped the moment she saw the colorful flowers that lined the small corner of the sidewalk.

Paisley turned and smiled widely at Shiloh. Without another word, she padded over to the flowers and knelt down in front of them.

Shiloh watched as Paisley looked at the flowers intently. Turning around, Paisley reached for the water bottle in Shiloh's backpack and made her way back over to the flowers.

"What're you doing?" Shiloh asked, watching as Paisley opened the water bottle and filled the cap with a few drops of water.

"Feeding them," Paisley nodded once, turning the cap over and sprinkling the water on top of the flowers. "Feeding them, and not killing them."

Shiloh couldn't help but smile, and she sat down on the bench to watch as Paisley continued to water the flowers, one capful at a time.

As Shiloh watched her, so immersed in her own world, she realized why she was so drawn to the girl. Paisley was mindlessly innocent. She was genuine.

There were no ulterior motives to her actions; she did what she wanted to do without questioning herself. In doing so, Paisley made herself easy to love. Shiloh could easily recognize the inner workings of Paisley's mind because she was so open.

Paisley loved endlessly. Shiloh realized that Paisley didn't put up walls to prevent herself from loving. Paisley forgave eternally, which hurt Shiloh to think that someone would take advantage of that. She decided right then that she'd do everything she could to make sure that didn't happen.

The smaller girl's love of flowers was quite ironic, actually. Shiloh considered Paisley to be the human equivalent of a flower. In fact, if she hadn't known where Paisley had come from, she would have assumed that Paisley grew out of a budding daisy in the garden.

In the same way that flowers slowly rise back up, even after being stepped on, Shiloh realized that Paisley would love continually despite the things she'd gone through. Paisley was effortlessly beautiful, Shiloh knew this for a fact.

The thing that scared Shiloh the most, though, was the fear that Paisley wasn't aware of her own fragility. She saw how Paisley gave and gave without asking for anything in return. She feared someone would come along and hurt the younger girl because of that.

"Thank you."

Paisley's voice brought Shiloh out of her thoughts. The smaller girl was standing in front of her with the empty water bottle in her hands.

"They are pretty, Lolo," Paisley smiled and twirled a piece of Shiloh's hair around her finger. "Like you."

"Like *you*," Shiloh giggled, standing up and pulling Paisley into her side. "They're yellow, see?"

"Yes," Paisley pointed to the flowers. "I love them." She turned to Shiloh, standing on her tiptoes and kissing her cheek. "Thank you."

"You're welcome," Shiloh smiled softly, wrapping an arm around Paisley and kissing her forehead. "What do you say we go get some breakfast now?"

CHAPTER 26

"What is out there?" Paisley whispered, turning slightly to face Shiloh. They'd spent the day together, and were currently lying on their backs, looking up at the sky. Shiloh had spread a blanket out in their corner of the park so they could watch the sunset; which eventually turned into watching the stars slowly dot their way across the sky.

"Out where?" Shiloh asked, still staring up at the sky. Paisley pointed upwards.

"In the sky. There has to be more, right?" The smaller girl studied Shiloh's face once again. She found the older girl much more interesting than the stars.

"No one knows," Shiloh finally turned to look at Paisley, earning a soft smile from the girl. "I think that's what makes looking up at the stars so magical. There's so much out there that we don't know about yet."

"It is scary," Paisley scooted closer to Shiloh and laid her head on her shoulder.

"Nah," Shiloh shook her head. "We're safe down here, Pais," she snaked an arm around Paisley's waist and gazed back up at the sky. "The stars just remind us that we're not alone."

"I am not alone," Paisley nodded once. "I have you."

"You have me," Shiloh confirmed, smiling softly at Paisley.

"And you have me," Paisley smiled widely and turned over to her side, propping herself up with her elbow so she could study Shiloh's face. "You and me, right?"

"Me and you," Shiloh nodded once and winked at Paisley. The smaller girl giggled and let her hair hang down in front of her face.

"Hey, don't do that," Shiloh laughed softly and reached out to tuck Paisley's hair behind her ear. "Don't hide your beautiful face."

"I am beautiful?" Paisley tilted her head to the side, as if beauty was a foreign concept to her. Shiloh raised an eyebrow and turned so she, too, was now on her side.

"I think everyone's beautiful," she began, reaching out and twirling a piece of Paisley's hair around her finger. "But there's just something about you that makes you special," Shiloh smiled softly. "I've gotten to know you for more than just your outer beauty."

"I am happy here," Paisley sighed softly, turning back over on her back and looking up at the sky. "It is a new feeling, but I do like it."

"It's a new feeling?" Shiloh bit her lip, thinking back to Paisley's old journal entries. The girl had constantly wished for happiness, hoping that some day in the future she could find it.

"Yes," Paisley nodded, continuing to gaze up at the stars. "Before... there were bad things. And bad people. It was hard to be happy," she turned to Shiloh and pursed her lips. "But there is happiness here, I have found it."

Shiloh's breath caught in her throat when Paisley reached out and placed her hand above Shiloh's heart. "There is happiness here. With you," Paisley smiled contently. "I am home."

"Home?" Shiloh asked, finding it hard to form a coherent sentence. She was thankful it had grown dark, so the smaller girl couldn't seen the overwhelming blush on her cheeks.

"Yes, home," Paisley nodded. "I looked for a home. Before you," she sat up and turned so she was facing Shiloh. "But I could not find it. Because even happy houses have sad people, did you know that?"

Shiloh nodded softly, beginning to understand what Paisley meant.

"I did not understand how happy houses could have sad people," Paisley continued. Shiloh reached out and took the small girl's hand in her own.

"I thought a happy house could be a home. But if there were sad people, I could not find home," Paisley thought for a moment and looked down at their hands. "But I found you." She traced her eyes up to Shiloh's face.

"You are not a house. But you are a home, Lolo. Did you know that?" Paisley tilted her head to the side and innocently traced her fingers up Shiloh's arm. "My home. I found it here."

Slowly, Paisley reached up and placed her hand back over Shiloh's heart. "My home has a heart. I can feel it, and I have seen it." With her other hand, she reached up and cupped Shiloh's cheek, studying her face for a few moments.

"My home has a breathing heart and ocean eyes," Paisley smiled softly.

It was as if the butterflies in Shiloh's stomach would never cease. The dark haired girl reached up, placing her hand on top of Paisley's, overtop of her own heart.

"If you found your home," Shiloh started, lifting Paisley's hand off of her chest and placing her hand over Paisley's heart. "Then my home found me."

Paisley's lips parted into a smile, making Shiloh laugh softly. The smaller girl nuzzled back down into Shiloh's side and sighed contently.

"I am so happy, Lolo," she mumbled into the crook of Shiloh's neck.

"And I'm so happy that you're so happy," Shiloh giggled, feeling her heart swell up at the moment they were sharing. "You've been talking a lot more lately, have you noticed that?"

Paisley lifted her head and furrowed her eyebrows together. "What do you mean?"

"I can't explain it... you've just... you've been making a lot of progress since you've first got here. You're learning a lot, yeah?" Shiloh bit her lip. Paisley nodded softly.

"That's a good thing, Pais," Shiloh laughed quietly and ran her fingers up and down Paisley's arm. "That means you're starting to express yourself more. That's good. I want to know what you're thinking."

"I want to kiss you," Paisley whispered. Shiloh nearly jumped when Paisley spoke. "That is what I am thinking."

"Nothing's stopping you," Shiloh quickly recovered and gave the girl a soft smile. Paisley crinkled her nose and looked down shyly.

"Don't be shy," Shiloh laughed softly and turned Paisley's chin so they were facing each other once more. Leaning in slowly, Shiloh connected their lips in a soft, gentle kiss. When they pulled away, Paisley smiled widely and tangled herself back up in Shiloh's side.

Their kisses never lasted more than a few seconds, nothing too deep. Shiloh wouldn't allow that. She didn't want to take advantage of Paisley. She could wait. They had all the time in the world.

Silence overtook both the girls as they stared up at the sky, exploring the endless universe above them with their eyes. Shiloh turned her head slowly, studying Paisley instead of the sky. The smaller girl was much more enchanting.

"Sing," Paisley caught Shiloh looking at her and smiled. "Can you sing, Lolo?"

"Only for you," Shiloh leaned over and kissed Paisley's temple.

Shiloh turned her head to glance at Paisley when the girl didn't respond once the song was over. A soft smile spread across her face when she saw the girl's eyes had closed and her chest was rising and falling slowly. She'd fallen asleep.

"I didn't know I was that boring," Shiloh laughed softly to herself, peeling Paisley's sleeping figure off of her and rising to her feet. She brushed off her jeans before bending back down and gently picking Paisley up. The girl remained asleep as Shiloh tossed the blanket over her shoulder and began walking back towards the apartment.

Paisley stirred slightly when Shiloh turned around and pushed through the door to their apartment. Mumbling something inaudible, she buried her head in Shiloh's chest and sighed heavily.

"Wanna walk on your own?" Shiloh raised an eyebrow. Paisley turned her head and gazed up at Shiloh groggily.

"No," she giggled, hiding her head back in Shiloh's neck.

"You're lucky you're cute," Shiloh teased, sliding the blanket off of her shoulder and kicking it into the corner by the door. Slipping off her shoes, she adjusted Paisley in her arms and carefully made her way up the stairs.

Judging by the lack of light in the hallway, all their other roommates were already asleep. Shiloh quietly used her hip to push the bedroom door open and made her way across the dark room. Lying Paisley in her bed, the smaller girl immediately curled up into a ball and squirmed under the covers. Shiloh giggled at her actions.

"C'mon Lolo," Paisley mumbled, lifting her head and squinting groggily at Shiloh. The older girl bit her lip in thought for a moment.

"I've got some homework to finish first," she said, rummaging around in her drawers and pulling out a large canvas. "You go ahead and get some sleep, I'll be up in a little bit."

Paisley held out her hands and motioned for Shiloh to come closer. Once Shiloh was within her reach, she cupped Shiloh's cheeks and placed a kiss on her forehead.

"Goodnight, Lolo," she hummed, turning back over in the bed and burying herself under the covers. Blushing, Shiloh whispered a soft goodnight before grabbing her canvas and leaving the room.

Yawning, Shiloh positioned herself at the easel downstairs, pulling up a chair and propping her canvas up.

She never did end up going back to bed. She worked all through the night, not even realizing how much time had passed. Shiloh was only brought out of her intense state of concentration when she heard soft footsteps coming down the steps.

Wiping her eyes, she quickly turned the canvas around and looked behind her. It was only then that she realized the sun was shining through the windows, letting her know that the night had completely passed her by.

A yawning Paisley slowly padded her way over to Shiloh, studying the older girl in confusion. "Where were you?"

"Working on something for class," Shiloh's voice rasped. She cleared her throat and motioned for Paisley to come closer. The smaller girl obliged, walking over and sitting in Shiloh's lap.

"Tired?" Shiloh raised an eyebrow when Paisley sighed and laid her head on Shiloh's shoulder. The smaller girl nodded slowly and mumbled something inaudible. "What?"

"I am hungry," Paisley lifted her head and crinkled her nose. Shiloh giggled and kissed her forehead.

"I think we can fix that," Shiloh sat up and walked into the kitchen. Paisley followed eagerly, climbing up onto the island and watching as Shiloh set a pan on the stove.

"How'd you sleep?" Shiloh asked, cracking two eggs into the pan and turning the burner on. Paisley shrugged and stretched out her arms.

"I had a dream about you," she admitted, smiling shyly. "We were in the stars."

"The stars?" Shiloh laughed softly, scrambling the eggs in the pan with a spatula. "That sounds like a good dream."

"It was good because you were there, Lolo," Paisley giggled and slid off the counter, walking over to where Shiloh stood and watching her as she slid the eggs off of the pan and onto a plate. Paisley jumped when the toaster beside her dinged and two slices of bread popped out.

Shiloh giggled at Paisley's reaction. She tossed the toast onto the plate and quickly spread strawberry jelly over both of the slices.

"Breakfast for you, my princess," she said playfully, handing the plate to Paisley. The small girl looked down shyly, but not before Shiloh saw the pink tint of her cheeks.

"C'mon," Shiloh laughed, grabbing an apple from the counter and leading Paisley over to the kitchen table. Paisley sat down, studying the meal Shiloh had made her before taking a bite out of her toast and humming in approval.

"Good?" Shiloh raised an eyebrow.

"Yes. You made it," Paisley smiled, giving her a thumbs up. Shiloh laughed, taking a bite out of her apple and returning the gesture.

"I've got to get ready for school," Shiloh sighed, looking at the clock. "Leah doesn't have class today, though. So you can stay here with her."

"You will come back, right?" Paisley looked up, tapping her fork against her plate.

"Of course," Shiloh nodded once and reached out to squeeze Paisley's hand. "I always do."

As if on cue, Leah's soft footsteps could be heard coming down the stairs. Shiloh tossed the core of her apple into the trash can and planted a kiss on Paisley's forehead.

"I'm gonna go get dressed," Shiloh told Paisley, giving Leah a thankful smile before jogging upstairs. She quickly got ready, going out of her way to find a pastel yellow sweater that she had tossed in the back of her closet. Slinging her bag over her shoulder, she appeared back downstairs about fifteen minutes later.

"Yellow," Paisley chimed, walking over to Shiloh and running her fingers down the sleeve of her shirt. "You are pretty," she smiled, taking Shiloh's hand in her own.

"And you are, too," Shiloh laughed softly, ruffling Paisley's hair and making the younger girl crinkle her nose. "I've gotta go to class, I'll be back, okay?"

"Duh," Paisley giggled, raising her eyebrows.

"Who taught you that?" Shiloh laughed, walking over and grabbing her canvas from the easel in the back of the apartment. She made sure to keep the front hidden from the other girls in the room.

"Ryland," Paisley nodded once and gave Shiloh a thumbs up.

"Ryland is bad news, isn't she?" Shiloh teased, slipping on her shoes. Paisley just shrugged and walked over to the door.

"I'll be back," Shiloh gave Paisley a quick kiss on the cheek.

"I know. You said that already," Paisley giggled and shook her head. Shiloh made a face at her, laughed softly, and slipped out the door without another word.

The brisk morning air woke her up right away, and soon she found herself jogging into the school building. For once, she was on time, and she had actually remembered her project. She placed the canvas face down in the back of the room and took her seat.

Class went by slowly. Shiloh busied herself by doodling flowers in her sketchbook. For once, she used colored pencils to bring them to life. Paisley had helped her find the color in things. She was thankful for that.

"You're dismissed for today," her teacher clapped his hands together and turned off the projector. "Shiloh, can I see you before you leave?"

Shiloh took a deep breath, looking up from her sketchbook. Was he going to scold her for skipping class the week before? She resolved on nodding softly, slowly packing up her things as the rest of the class filed out of the room. Biting her lip, she made her way over to his desk.

Her teacher glanced at the door before running his hand through his hair. "Pardon my language, Ms. Everest," he started, flipping her painting over in front of them. "But where the hell did this come from?"

Shiloh tilted her head to the side, looking down at the painting she'd finished the night before. In the painting, there was a girl standing by the bank of a pond, looking down into the water at her reflection.

In her reflection, though, she was painted in dark colors, radiating sadness. The smallest details showed this. The girl in the reflection wore all black, hid her face behind her hair, and let her shoulders slump down.

In contrast, the girl above the pond was standing up tall. She had on a white sundress, and in her hand she held a small yellow flower. The trees behind her were bright and colorful, and there were clouds in the bright sky above her.

"I, uh, I painted it last night," she bit her lip.

"This is incredibly detailed," he ran his fingers over the canvas. "Normally I wouldn't approve of the mixing of two different medias, but somehow using watercolors and oil paints really worked in your favor, Shiloh."

"I, uh, wow," Shiloh cleared her throat. "Thank you," she bit her lip.

"Compared to last week's painting, this looks like the work of a completely different artist," he chuckled. "I have a feeling something changed since we've last seen each other. Am I correct?"

Shiloh just nodded slowly.

"Well I hope you hold onto her this time," he gave her a knowing smile. Shiloh felt her cheeks turn red at the thought of Paisley and looked down shyly.

He pulled a paper out of his desk and began scrawling something down. "I'm transferring you to the advanced class," he folded the paper in half and handed it to her. "It's usually only for juniors and seniors, but you have too much potential, I can't let you continue to sit around and learn things you already know."

Shiloh raised her eyebrows and looked down at the paper in her hands, confirming her transfer. "I… wow," she shook her head and breathed in slowly. "Thank you."

Mr. Robertson picked up her painting and handed it back to her. "Life is too short to love with limitations, Shiloh. Remember that."

Shiloh nodded softly. "Thank you... so much," she held the canvas under her arm and took a deep breath.

"You're dismissed now, Ms. Everest. I'll see you around."

Shiloh gave him a thankful smile, slinging her bag over her shoulder and quietly slipping out of the classroom.

On her drive home, she turned off the radio and gave herself time to think. So much had changed in such a short amount of time. Paisley had come into her life and completely turned it upside down.

If you had told Shiloh this would happen a year ago, she would have punched you in the face. But now, it was believable. And it was real.

She knew it wouldn't be perfect from then on. Paisley still had a lot of things to process, and a lot of things to work through. Shiloh was aware of that. She was more than aware. But more importantly, she was willing to wait.

Maybe that was what had changed. Before, Shiloh wanted a relationship for all the wrong reasons. She wanted a perfect relationship. No conflict, no problems; just happiness.

Granted, it was quite an unattainable wish. And she knew that now.

But with Paisley, she wanted everything. She wanted to be by her side through the good times *and* the bad. She wanted to be the one that held her when she cried. She wanted to be the one that made her laugh. Shiloh wanted to be a part of Paisley's life, for *all* of it.

It wasn't perfect, but that's what made it perfect. To her.

She pulled to a stop in the parking lot, parking her car and looked up at the tall building. A wide smile appeared on her face when she saw a movement coming from their apartment window. Waving back to Paisley, she jogged into the building.

The second she touched her key to the doorknob, the door flew open and Paisley smiled happily at her.

"Lolo," she hummed, practically jumping into Shiloh's arms. Shiloh dropped her bag down and returned the hug, kissing the top of Paisley's head and feeling a thousand butterflies erupt in her stomach. The smaller girl sighed contently.

"You came back," Paisley smiled softly, pulling away from the hug and gazing up at Shiloh.

Shiloh nodded and placed a hand on Paisley's cheek, running her thumb over the smooth skin.

"I always will."

E P I L O G U E

"*Yes*, mom," Shiloh rolled her eyes, looking over at the girl in the passenger seat. "We just left the airport. We'll be there soon."

"You'll see, mom, I told you," Shiloh bit her lip and glanced over at Paisley. The smaller girl in the passenger seat smiled softly. "Alright mom, I've got to drive. I'll see you soon."

Shiloh laughed softly once she hung up, setting her phone in the cupholder and lacing Paisley's fingers with hers using her free hand.

"You look nervous," Paisley tilted her head to the side slightly, letting her loose curls fall over her shoulder. "Are you nervous?"

Shiloh shrugged and turned her attention back to the road, following the familiar route to her childhood home. "A little, yeah. I have no reason to be, though."

"It will be fun, right?" Paisley traced her fingers around Shiloh's wrist absentmindedly.

"Of course," Shiloh smiled. "You get to meet my crazy family." Paisley giggled and flipped Shiloh's hand over, tracing circles in her palm.

Weeks had passed since Paisley's acquittal. The seasons had changed, leaving a light blanket of snow across the ground in New York. In Miami, however, it was practically the perfect temperature. It was comfortable outside no matter what you were wearing.

After she was released, Paisley was required to begin routine therapy appointments. At first, the smaller girl had been hesitant. But with ushering from Shiloh, and time, the bi-weekly visits began to show progress.

She'd never be back to 100% normal. But as her doctor had said, there was always room for improvement.

One of Shiloh's main concerns had been her and Paisley's relationship. She talked to Paisley's therapist right off the bat, firing question after question at the middle aged woman.

What she'd walked away with was a never ending list of medical terms, which basically explained to Shiloh that yes, Paisley was capable of love. And a relationship was fine as long as things were taken at a slow pace, and Paisley was well aware of where things were going.

Paisley was aware. Definitely aware. When Shiloh had discussed the future with her, she was met with a babbling Paisley, going on and on about what they would name their children, and what color they would paint their house. (Yellow, obviously.)

The thought of spending the rest of her life with Paisley gave Shiloh butterflies every time she thought about it. But she could wait. The more people she met on a daily basis, the more she realized how much she needed Paisley.

And now, here they were. Weeks later, holding hands in the car on the way to Shiloh's childhood home. Shiloh's mother had invited Shiloh and her 'mystery girlfriend' to spend Christmas with them.

So yes, Shiloh was nervous. Extremely nervous. She had no idea how her parents would react when they found out who the mystery girl actually was. Because as far as they knew, Shiloh still hated Paisley with every bone in her body.

"Here we are," Shiloh smiled nervously. She squeezed Paisley's hand and nodded towards the house on the corner of the street. A group of small children were gathered on the front lawn, kicking around an inflatable beach ball.

"I like it," Paisley smiled widely, sitting up straighter to get a better view of the house. Shiloh parked the car on the side of the road and took a deep breath, turning to Paisley.

"Y'ready?" she asked, biting her lip. Paisley nodded.

"Are you?" she rebutted, catching onto the fact that Shiloh was more nervous that she had admitted to being.

"As ready as I'll ever be," Shiloh crinkled her nose and kissed Paisley's hand. "C'mon." She unlocked the car and slid out of her seat.

"Shiloh!" A small blonde child squealed, breaking away from the group and running towards the older girl.

"Hey there, munchkin," Shiloh laughed, catching the child who practically jumped into her arms. "You got so much taller!"

"Yeah! Mommy says it's cause' I eat my 'bedgetables," the smaller girl giggled and wrapped her hands around Shiloh's neck. "Did you know that Santa's coming tonight? He's gonna bring me a b—,"

The smaller child quickly hushed and Shiloh raised an eyebrow. She turned around, realizing the girl had been staring at Paisley, who stood shyly behind them.

"Mags," Shiloh smiled softly and motioned for Paisley to come closer. "This is my friend Paisley, can you say hi?"

"*Paisleeeee*," Maggie giggled and crinkled her nose. "Hi!"

"Hi," Paisley smiled shyly, waving her hand. Shiloh smiled at her girlfriend and looked back at the child in her arms.

"Paisley, this is Maggie," she nodded to the blonde child. "She's my sister. Well, adopted."

"Her mother was one of my mom's clients at work. She passed away giving birth to her, and my mom wouldn't allow them to put her in the foster care system," she laughed softly and ruffled Maggie's hair. "She's six."

"Oh," Paisley nodded once, thinking over what Shiloh had just said. "Her hair is yellow," she whispered, pointing to the wavy blonde curls on Maggie's head.

Shiloh laughed and nodded. She set Maggie down on the ground, thinking she would rejoin her cousins on the front lawn. Instead, Maggie grabbed Shiloh's hand and tugged her towards the end of the driveway.

"You have to see the chalk drawing I made 'nesterday!" Shiloh glanced back at Paisley, giving her an apologetic smile before she was practically dragged away by the smaller child.

A few minutes later, Shiloh was finally able to peel herself away from the plethora of chalk drawings and make her way back up the driveway. Maggie skipped behind her contently.

Shiloh grew worried when Paisley wasn't where she left her. She looked frantically around the yard, sighing in relief when she saw her girlfriend surrounded by children, wearing a wide smile on her face.

"Do not kill them," Paisley shook her head and gently moved one of the boy's hands away from the flowers. "They will not be pretty if you kill them."

"Hey *Paisleeeee*, catch!" Maggie tossed a beach ball in Paisley's direction. The older girl laughed and hit the ball back. The children squealed excitedly and ran after the toy. It was bounced back in Paisley's direction, and soon a game of catch was in full swing.

Laughing softly to herself, Shiloh jogged up the front steps and hesitantly rang the doorbell. Might as well get it over with. She glanced back at Paisley, who was currently on the ground with a pile of children giggling excitedly on top of her. She had to stifle her laugh when she heard footsteps approaching. The door swung open moments later.

"Oh look! It's Shiloh and…" her mother's voice trailed off when she realized Shiloh was alone. Or so she thought. Shiloh glanced back at Paisley, who had just freed herself up to her feet and tossed the beach ball back across the yard.

"Oh my god," her mother gasped under her breath. Shiloh's breath caught in her throat when she felt herself being tugged inside, jumping when the door slammed shut behind them.

"You brought a murderer to dinner?!" her mother practically yelled, motioning to the front door. "And where's your girlfriend?"

Shiloh bit her lip. "She's not a murderer," she said quietly, glancing out the window worriedly. "And that's her. Paisley's my girlfriend."

"Shiloh, there's articles all over town about her killing her uncle! You're kidding, right?" Shiloh shook her head slowly.

"Mom, I can explain, she's b—,"

"*Lolo*?!"

Shiloh's eyes widened and she made a move to grab the doorknob. She felt her mother's eyes burning a hole in the back of her head and took a deep breath, opening the door.

"Pais, I'm right here," she waved her arm, catching Paisley's attention. The small girl sighed in relief and ran over to her girlfriend, grabbing her forearm and standing close by her side.

"Uh, mom," Shiloh cleared her throat and tugged Paisley inside the house. "I'd like you to meet Paisley. Paisley, this is my mom."

"Hi," Paisley smiled softly, offering a small wave. Shiloh held her breath when her mother didn't respond. After a few seconds of awkward silence, she turned back to Paisley and squeezed her hand.

"You can go back out and play, I've got to talk to my mom for a little. Okay?"

"M'kay," Paisley hummed, giving Shiloh a soft smile. The older girl kissed Paisley's cheek innocently and watched as she wandered back onto the front lawn. She was instantly surrounded by kids once more, begging her to play with them. Shiloh laughed softly, but her laughter quickly faded when she turned back to her mom and saw the look on her face.

"I don't approve of this at all, Shiloh," her mother crossed her arms and shook her head.

"Just let me explain," Shiloh shook her head and paced back and forth for a few moments. Her mother looked at her expectantly.

"You know about the car accident," Shiloh cleared her throat and anxiously ran a hand through her hair. "She doesn't even remember much of high school, and... her uncle wasn't... he was abusive. The whole 'murder' thing... she was trying to protect herself. They think it misfired when she was struggling to get the gun away from him... and...." Shiloh looked down at her shoes and took a deep breath.

"This is ridiculous, Shiloh," her mother sighed and shook her head. "She's practically psychotic."

"Don't you dare," Shiloh's head snapped up, glaring at her mother. "You don't even know her."

"I still don't approve of this," her mother crossed her arms and raised an eyebrow at Shiloh.

"Well you better deal with it," Shiloh snapped. She'd never been one to talk back, so her words had even surprised her. Her mother didn't respond. Shiloh didn't let her. The door slammed behind her before her mother had a chance to protest.

Shiloh exhaled heavily, running a hand through her hair and scanning the yard. She locked eyes with

Paisley, and the smaller girl immediately knew something was wrong.

"Lolo?" she tilted her head to the side and jogged over to her girlfriend. "Are you okay? You look sad."

"M'fine," Shiloh shook her head. "Just nervous."

"Do you need a hug?" Paisley smiled shyly and outstretched her arms. Shiloh giggled and wrapped her arms around Paisley. The smaller girl hummed contently and kissed Shiloh's cheek when they pulled away.

"Are you best friends?"

Both girls jumped, looking down at the smaller blonde girl next to them. Maggie tilted her head to the side, expecting an answer.

"Paisley's my girlfriend," Shiloh said softly, kneeling down next to Maggie.

"Girlfriend?" Maggie glanced up at Paisley and then back to Shiloh.

"Yeah…" Shiloh bit her lip, trying to think of an explanation.

"Yes," Paisley spoke up. "Some girls like girls, and some boys like boys. That is okay. If it makes you happy, it is okay. Right?" She glanced over to Shiloh, who was blushing slightly.

"Right," Shiloh nodded once.

"And it makes us happy," Paisley added quietly, causing Shiloh to look up at her with a soft smile on her face.

Maggie looked back and forth between them for a moment, thinking over what they had just said. "Okay!" she smiled, grabbing Shiloh's hand. "Come play with me!" She reached over and took hold of Paisley's hand as well. "You too, *Paisleeeee*."

"That was easier than I thought," Shiloh bit her lip, glancing back at the door. She followed Paisley and Maggie over to the group of kids, greeting her cousins.

"Tag!" Paisley giggled, hopping out from behind a tree and tapping Shiloh's shoulder. The older girl jumped, turning around and clasping her hands over her heart.

"You scared me!" She raised her eyebrows at the giggling girl. "That's unfair!"

"You are it!" Paisley crinkled her nose. Shiloh shook her head and took a step towards Paisley.

"You better run, then," she smirked. Paisley squealed and took off down the yard, following the group of children running in the same direction.

"Pais, look!" Shiloh called. Paisley turned around, looking from side to side to try and see what

Shiloh was pointing out. Moments later, she was practically tackled to the ground.

"Tag," Shiloh smirked, holding the girl in her lap and lying back on the grass to catch to her breath.

"That was not fair!" Paisley giggled, rolling onto her back next to Shiloh. "You tricked me!"

"Payback," Shiloh laughed.

"Get 'em!"

Shiloh and Paisley exchanged glances when they heard a stampede of footsteps in their direction. Before they could react, the group of children piled on top of them, giggling incessantly.

"Choking, not breathing!" Shiloh laughed, struggling to push herself into a sitting position. She peeled Maggie off of Paisley and tickled the small child into submission.

"You guys are ruthless!" Shiloh poked her sister's nose, making Maggie laugh and sit down in the grass next to the other kids.

"You saved me," Paisley giggled, standing up and brushing the grass off of her pants. Shiloh hopped to her feet as well, running a hand through her hair.

"I guess I won," Shiloh teased, taking a step closer to Paisley and lacing their fingers together. "I think the winner deserves a kiss," she smirked, turning and pointing to her cheek. Before Paisley could reciprocate, though, Shiloh's eyes landed on the person standing in the driveway.

"Dad?" she breathed, squeezing Paisley's hand to signify for her to stop. The smaller girl pulled back and followed Shiloh's eyes to the man in the driveway.

"I'll be right back," Shiloh bit her lip, giving Paisley an apologetic smile before jogging over to her father.

"I can explain," she breathed, studying his face nervously. "I'm sorry if I w—,"

"I talked to your mother," he said, glancing at Paisley. Shiloh nodded, biting her lip. This wasn't going to end well.

"I'm sorry," she shook her head and looked down.

"Y'know, I was gonna come out here and talk to you about this," he said, cupping the back of his neck with his hand. "But then I saw you…" he nodded in Paisley's direction. "With her. And I guess what I'm trying to say is… I think you're perfectly capable of making your own decisions."

Shiloh looked up in shock. "Wh-what?"

"Your mother… give her time. She's just not used to you being so grown up," he continued. "I can't say that I'm completely comfortable with this, but I think everyone deserves a chance, right?"

"Thank you," Shiloh let out the breath she'd been holding in. "You'll love her, I promise," she smiled shyly before pulling her father into a big hug.

"I trust you," he chuckled, squeezing her shoulder when they pulled away from the hug. Shiloh took her bottom lip in between her teeth and glanced behind her.

"Pais," she motioned for the smaller girl. Paisley looked up, smiling softly and jogging over to the two figures in the driveway. Shiloh snaked an arm around her girlfriend's waist and pulled her into her side.

"Dad, this is Paisley," she nodded towards the younger girl. "My girlfriend."

"It's nice to meet you, Paisley," her father smiled warmly, extending his hand for Paisley to shake. The smaller girl grinned, holding out her fist and looking at him expectantly. Shiloh held back her laughter.

"You are supposed to bump it," Paisley whispered, moving her fist back and forth. Shiloh just nodded at her father, signifying for him to go along with it.

He bumped his fist against Paisley's, and the smaller girl made an exploding noise with her mouth, looking at Shiloh proudly. Shiloh bit her lip, glancing back at her father and studying his face. She breathed a sigh of relief when he laughed softly.

"Your mother made a huge Christmas Eve dinner," her dad chuckled, nodding towards the front door. "I didn't even know that was a thing, honestly." He noticed the nervous look on Shiloh's face.

"C'mon girls, I'll take you to the dining room," he gave Shiloh a supportive nod. She sighed softly, keeping her arm around Paisley's waist and following her father into the house.

"Wait for us, *Paisleeeee*!" One of the younger boys called, forgetting about their game of catch and following the other children into the house.

"The dining room is this way," Shiloh giggled when Paisley started going up the stairs. "You've gotta meet everyone."

"Oh," Paisley smiled and hopped back down next to Shiloh, lacing their fingers together and following her down the hallway. "Meet who?"

"My mom's side of the family always comes and stays at our house the night before Christmas so we can wake up and open presents together," Shiloh explained, turning the corner and walking into the dining room.

"Shy!" Her brother hopped up from his spot at the table and wrapped his arms around his sister. "You look different."

"Minus the extra human I have attached to me, I don't think I've changed much," Shiloh laughed, holding up her and Paisley's interlocked fingers. Daxton raised an eyebrow, studying the girl Shiloh had brought with her.

"Hi," Paisley smiled shyly, holding out her fist in between them. Daxton eyed Shiloh questioningly, but bumped his fist with Paisley's. She made an exploding noise with her mouth before giggling quietly.

Daxton exchanged glances with Shiloh. "I like this one," he nodded once in approval. Shiloh laughed, crinkling her nose and ruffling her brother's hair.

"I do too, kiddo," she turned to Paisley and placed a kiss on her cheek, just in time for her mother to walk in the room with a plate of food. She didn't even glance in Shiloh's direction. Shiloh swallowed nervously.

"Hungry?" Shiloh raised an eyebrow at Paisley, who was eyeing the food on the table. Paisley nodded and tugged on Shiloh's hand, pulling her over to sit down.

"I wanna sit next to *Paisleeeee*!" Maggie giggled, running into the dining room and scrambling to crawl atop the chair next to Paisley.

"Looks like someone's made a new friend," A man sitting across the table smiled at Maggie. Paisley glanced at Shiloh nervously.

"That's my Uncle Gregory," Shiloh explained with a soft laugh. She saw Paisley's face freeze and quickly grabbed her hand. "He's not a bad uncle, Pais."

"Oh," Paisley took a deep breath. Shiloh ran her thumb over the back of her hand to try and comfort her. "He is good?"

"Yeah, see?" Shiloh turned to face him. "Uncle Greg, this is Paisley. My girlfriend." Paisley smiled shyly.

"So that's who Dylan was talking about," the man laughed, extending his hand. "He kept going on and on about '*Paisleeeee*', who was the coolest girl he knew," he chuckled. Paisley smiled widely and held out her fist.

"You're supposed to bump it," Shiloh laughed, noticing his confusion. He nodded in understanding and bumped Paisley's fist, causing the girl to make an exploding noise with her mouth and smile proudly.

"Dylan! Come sit next to me and *Paisleeeee*!" Maggie waved to the smaller boy that had just entered the dining room. Soon, Shiloh's relatives began filling the empty chairs around the table and engaging one another in conversation.

Surprisingly, everyone seemed more than welcoming to Paisley. Except for Shiloh's mother, that was. Throughout the entire meal, she would barely look in their direction. Shiloh was thankful that Paisley didn't notice this.

"How's school going, Shy?" Her father spoke up about halfway through the meal. Shiloh took a sip from her drink and shrugged.

"My professor moved me up to the advanced class," she smiled shyly. Paisley glanced over at Shiloh happily.

"She thinks she is bad, but she is very good," Paisley spoke up, twirling her fork around her fingers. "I watch her."

"I think that's a common trait among most artists," her dad chuckled. Shiloh crinkled her nose at Paisley, who giggled and looked away.

"You better be focusing on your education, Shiloh," her mother spoke up for the first time since they sat down. She glanced from Shiloh to Paisley and raised an eyebrow.

"Oh, she is," Paisley spoke before Shiloh could. "She is not allowed to cuddle until she does her homework, I said so." Shiloh's face grew bright red.

Shiloh's mother kept quiet for the rest of the meal, and Shiloh had to hold back her laughter over the fact that Paisley had unknowingly shattered all of her mother's suspicions.

"Mommy, can me and Dylan go to the creek?" Maggie spoke up, pointing to her empty plate and then to the child sitting next to her. "Please?"

"You can't go all by yourselves, and I don't think a—,"

"I can go," Daxton stood up, wiping off his hands. Maggie and Dylan squealed excitedly, hopping out of their chairs and running towards the back door.

"Margaret Everest, listen to your brother!" her mother called after her. The small girl hummed in agreement, and moments later the three pairs of footsteps disappeared outside. Shiloh laughed softly at their excitement.

Soon, everyone finished their meal and Shiloh's mother began carrying plates into the kitchen. Paisley got up quietly, wandering into the other room. Shiloh quickly followed after her, pausing at the doorway.

"Do you need help?" Paisley asked shyly, tapping on Shiloh's mother's shoulder. The woman turned around and raised an eyebrow at Paisley.

"I've got it," she said coldly, turning back around and leaving Paisley standing there quietly. Shiloh quickly jumped in.

"Let's go outside, Pais," she said softly, grabbing her girlfriend's arm. "It's too nice out to stay cramped up inside." Paisley just nodded and allowed Shiloh to lead her out the back door.

"She does not like me," Paisley said softly once the door closed behind them. "Did I do something wrong?"

"Of course not," Shiloh sighed and shook her head. She laced their fingers together and led Paisley towards the old swingset in their backyard. "She just needs some time."

"We can give her that," Paisley nodded once, sitting down on one of the swings next to Shiloh. She reached out and found her hand once more, swinging back and forth slowly. "I was just trying to help her."

"I know, Pais," Shiloh sighed. "My dad really seems to like you, though. And Daxton. And Maggie. And everyone else," she squeezed Paisley's hand, making the other girl laugh.

"I never gave you your prize," Paisley realized, standing up and walking in front of Shiloh with a soft smile on her face.

"My prize?"

Paisley nodded, placing her hands on Shiloh's knees and leaning down. "Yes. You won tag, so you get a kiss," she giggled softly before leaning in and capturing the green eyed girl's lips within her own.

Meanwhile, two pairs of eyes watched them quietly from the kitchen window.

"She loves her."

Shiloh's mother, Colette, whipped her head around to look at her husband. "What?" she raised an eyebrow, worry in her voice.

"Shiloh," he nodded, pointing to the two girls on the swings. Paisley had sat back down and they were holding hands, giggling about something. "She loves her."

"And how do you know?" Colette put a hand on her hip, craning her neck to get a better view of her daughter.

"I just do," Noah shrugged. "When I first saw her, there was something about the way she looked at that girl. I couldn't put my finger on it at first. But I've never seen her like this with anyone else."

"You're sure?"

"Positive," he nodded once and leaned against the counter.

Sighing, Colette turned to him and ran a hand through her hair. "I just don't want her to get hurt."

"She's old enough to make her own decisions," Shiloh's father shrugged. "I'm not too worried. Paisley seems like a good kid. I trust my daughter's judgment."

Colette just sighed and turned back to the dishes, glancing at the girls outside once more.

———————————

"Do you know what today is?" Shiloh drew her bottom lip between her teeth, remembering Christmas Eve also happened to be the day Paisley had lost her parents. She couldn't imagine having a tragic accident such as that happen to her on the day before what was *supposed* to be a happy holiday.

Paisley tilted her head to the side slightly and thought for a moment. "Tomorrow is Christmas?" she said questioningly.

"Yeah, but..." Shiloh took a deep breath. "It's the anniversary of your parents... their accident..." she bit her lip. Paisley thought for a few moments.

"Do you think... they would like me?" She asked quietly. Shiloh reached out, tucking a strand of hair behind Paisley's ear and nodding.

"Of course they would, silly," she gave her a soft smile. "You're their daughter. And you're a pretty awesome person, too."

"But I am..." Paisley looked down at her shoes and shuffled them in the grass while she formed her next words. "I am broken."

Shiloh's heart dropped in her chest and she quickly shook her head. "You are far from broken, Paisley," she turned slightly and cupped the girl's face in her hands. "Listen to me, okay?"

Paisley nodded softly.

"You are *not* broken, okay? You're Paisley. That's all you are. You can't define yourself with a word that somebody else made up," Shiloh ran her thumb over the girl's cheek. "It's up to *you* to define who Paisley is. And she's not broken."

"Lolo..." Paisley looked up at the sky.

"I'm not finished," Shiloh grabbed Paisley's hand to try and get her attention, but the smaller girl was staring up at the sky. A moment later, she felt a raindrop on her arm. Then another, then another, and another.

Soon it was drizzling lightly. Paisley giggled and turned back to Shiloh, wiping her eyes.

"Shiloh!"

Both girls jumped when they heard a scream from behind them. Two figures broke through the woods, running towards them.

"Daxton?" Shiloh stood up quickly. The rain began picking up speed. Paisley shuffled silently behind Shiloh just as Daxton and Dylan caught up to them.

"Maggie's gone," Daxton panted, leaning over and putting his hands on his knees.

"What?" Shiloh raised her eyebrows, scanning the yard to see if they were playing a joke.

"I don't know, we turned around and she was gone. We called her name and looked around but we couldn't find her *anywhere*," Daxton shook his head and wiped his mouth with the back of his hand. "You have to help us."

"I've got to tell mom," Shiloh shook her head, jogging inside and wiping the raindrops from her forehead.

"Mom? Dad?" she called once she was in the kitchen. She heard footsteps behind her signifying that she'd been followed.

"Shiloh, what's up?" her mother hurried into the room, noting the worry in her daughter's voice.

"Maggie's lost in the woods somewhere," Shiloh bit her lip. Her father appeared in the room moments later. After explaining to them what she'd learnt from Daxton, her father dialed the police on his phone.

Shiloh could hear the steady downpour of the rain outside and bit her lip. A clap of thunder made her jump and she immediately turned around to comfort Paisley.

But she wasn't there.

Shiloh's stomach instantly dropped and she turned to Daxton. "Where's Paisley?" she asked, holding her hands out in front of her and looking at him desperately.

"I don't know," he shook his head and glanced outside, where the sky was growing darker. "She didn't come inside with us."

"Shit," Shiloh shook her head and pushed past him. "Shit, shit, shit," she ran outside, ignoring the pouring rain. Where could Paisley had gone? She was just by her side a second ago. This wasn't good.

"Paisley!?" Shiloh called, standing in the middle of her yard and circling the perimeter. When she didn't get an answer, she took a deep breath and jogged into the woods.

"Pais?!" she cried, trying to make her voice heard over the beating of the rain. "Maggie?!" She pushed her way through the woods, trying to retrace the path Daxton and the kids had taken to the stream.

This reminded her too much of the first day Paisley had been with them, where Shiloh had found her in the woods at the park. Except now, there was more for her to lose.

She continued calling out their names, trying to cover every inch of the woods behind her house. Another clap of thunder sent her scrambling backwards, nearly falling. She grabbed onto a tree to regain her balance.

"Shiloh!" She heard a voice boom over the storm and bit her lip.

"Yeah?!" she called, cupping her hands over her mouth.

"You *need* to come back inside!" Her father yelled. Shiloh jogged to the clearing of the woods, hugging her arms around her torso when she saw her father waiting for her.

"I can't, I have to go f—," she was interrupted.

"It's not safe to be out here, Shiloh, the police are on their way," he grabbed her arm and started leading her inside. Shiloh glanced back at the woods, feeling her stomach boiling with anxiety.

A towel was immediately wrapped around her shoulders when they made it back to the house. She shivered and walked back over to the door, watching the rain pour down and drip down the glass windows.

"We have to go find them!" Shiloh threw the towel down and turned around, facing her family, who had gathered into the kitchen. "What if someone got them? Or… Or…?"

She shook her head, squeezing her eyes shut and falling down to her knees. She couldn't lose Paisley again. Paisley *hated* storms. She would never go out in one voluntarily. The whistling of the strong wind outside didn't help to calm her nerves, either.

"Honey, you should really sit down," her mother ushered her daughter into the living room, making her take a seat on the couch. Shiloh took a deep, shaky breath, glancing out the window once more.

She watched her other family members doing the same as she was, searching out the windows for any sign of life. Shiloh's hands shook, and she clenched them into fists to try and calm herself down.

Suddenly, the lights flickered, causing the smaller children to squeal. A few seconds later, the entire house was encased in darkness. Shiloh inhaled sharply, blinking a few times and looking around the dark room.

"It's okay!" one of her uncles called, shining his phone flashlight around the room. "It's just a power outage. No big deal."

Shiloh swallowed hard and buried her head in her knees, willing Paisley to be okay. A noise made her whip her head up.

"It's them!" Someone called. Shiloh immediately jumped to her feet, running into the kitchen just as someone slid open the glass door. Seconds later, Paisley stumbled into the room with Maggie in her arms, falling down to her knees as soon as everyone crowded around her.

Maggie was almost instantly carried off by the adults. Shiloh ran to Paisley's side, sliding down to her knees next to her girlfriend.

"Oh my god, Paisley? Are you okay?" Shiloh brushed the wet hair out of her girlfriend's face. Paisley was soaking wet from head to toe, shivering violently.

"Y-yeah," Paisley nodded slowly, wiping her eyes. "It is c-c-cold," she shivered, teeth chattering.

Without another word, Shiloh stood up, scooping Paisley into her arms. The smaller girl wrapped her arms around Shiloh's neck and shivered.

"What were you thinking?" Shiloh asked, carrying her down the hallway and up the stairs. Carefully, she led them to her old bedroom, lying Paisley down on the queen sized bed. The room was dimly lit by what little light was left outside.

"I had to help," Paisley wiped her eyes. She sat up slowly, wrapping her arms around her torso and biting her lip.

Shiloh sighed, walking over to her dresser and pulling out a change of clothes. She laid them on the bed next to Paisley and motioned for the girl to lift her arms.

"You could've gotten hurt," Shiloh said, peeling Paisley's wet shirt off of her torso and helping her slip into a dry hoodie of hers.

"I know," Paisley played with the sleeves of the hoodie, thinking for a moment. "But I did not want her to get hurt, either. I had to help."

"Where'd you find her?" Shiloh asked, biting her lip and slowly pulling Paisley to her feet. She helped the smaller girl step into a clean pair of pajama pants.

"She was hurt," Paisley pointed up to her head. "But she woke up when I was carrying her."

"Her head?" Shiloh asked. Paisley nodded.

"She was bleeding. But only a little bit," Paisley made a pinching motion with her fingers and shivered slightly.

"Cold?" Shiloh raised an eyebrow.

"Yes," Paisley laughed softly. "Very."

Shiloh gave her a soft smile, overwhelmingly thankful that both Paisley and her sister were alright. She quickly changed out of her wet clothes and into a pair of pajamas, making sure to keep her torso hidden.

A clap of thunder made both girls jump. Paisley whimpered, looking around the dark room nervously. Shiloh jogged into her bathroom, fishing around in her cabinets until she found what she needed.

She set the candle on the small table beside her bed, lighting a match and holding it above the wick. Once the candle caught flame, she flicked out the match and threw it away. Now the room was slightly better lit.

The second Shiloh sat down on the bed, she was pulled closer to Paisley, who practically crawled into her lap. Laughing softly, Shiloh laid down and Paisley immediately laid her head on her chest, curling up next to her.

"Still cold?" Shiloh asked, feeling the small girl shivering beside her. Paisley nodded slowly, and seconds later Shiloh tugged a blanket over both of them.

"Thank you, Lolo," Paisley sighed softly, burying her head in Shiloh's neck. The older girl ran her fingers up and down Paisley's spine absentmindedly.

"M'gonna have to get used to you being more independent, aren't I?" Shiloh laughed softly.

"Yes," Paisley giggled, moving her wet hair out of her face. "But I will still be yours," she lifted her head, kissing Shiloh's cheek gently. The older girl blushed.

"That's all I ask," Shiloh poked Paisley's cheek and laughed. Paisley crinkled her nose, turning over and hiding her head in the pillow. Shiloh realized she wasn't shaking anymore, and sighed thankfully.

A buzzing sound appeared, just as the lights flickered back on. Shiloh sat up and blinked a few times to adjust to the bright light. Just as Paisley sat up, the door of the bedroom opened slowly.

"Is she okay?" Shiloh's mom asked, slipping into the room and nodding in Paisley's direction. Shiloh was thoroughly surprised.

"Yeah, just a little shaken up," Shiloh smiled softly, taking Paisley's hand in her own to comfort the younger girl. "Is Maggie okay? What happened?"

"She said she was playing where she wasn't supposed to and slipped, I guess she hit her head and fell," Shiloh's mother sat down on the opposite side of the bed. "Paisley must've found her passed out somewhere."

Shiloh glanced over at Paisley and gave her a comforting smile. The younger girl returned the gesture, crinkling her nose playfully.

"Thank you, Paisley," Colette turned to look at Shiloh's girlfriend. "I think I owe you an apology."

"It is okay," Paisley shrugged. "Thank you, you're welcome."

Colette glanced at Shiloh, who just shrugged and giggled. Shiloh was surprised when her mother turned back to Paisley and held out her fist. Paisley tilted her head to the side.

"I thought you were supposed to bump it?" Shiloh's mother smirked. Paisley's face lit up and she glanced at Shiloh before bumping her fist with Colette's and making her signature exploding noise with her mouth.

'*Thank you*,' Shiloh mouthed to her mother, who just gave her an understanding nod.

"I guess I'll see you girls in the morning," Colette nodded, standing up. "Get some rest now, Santa's coming," she laughed, leaning down and kissing Shiloh's forehead.

"Goodnight, Paisley," Colette smiled, kissing the top of Paisley's head and giving her shoulder a comforting squeeze. Shiloh's jaw nearly dropped open, and both her and Paisley exchanged glances once they were alone once more. Paisley blushed slightly, and gave the girl a soft smile.

"You really know how to win Everest women over," Shiloh teased, winking at Paisley. The smaller girl giggled shyly.

Shiloh fell back onto the bed, tugging on Paisley's arm to make the smaller girl do the same. They had just snuggled up against one another when they heard footsteps approaching the door. Shiloh groaned and sat up quickly.

"Shhh," the smaller child peered her head through the door and shut it quietly behind her. "I'm a'posta be sleeping," Maggie giggled, looking at the two girls on the bed.

"Hey munchkin," Shiloh patted the space on the bed between them for the smaller girl. Maggie smiled happily, crawling next to them and sitting cross-legged. "How do you feel?"

"Good! It's all better, see?" Maggie pointed to the pink bandaid on her forehead. "*Paisleeeee* saved me," she smiled, pointing to the other girl on the bed.

"I know she did," Shiloh smiled, squeezing Paisley's hand. "Did you thank her?"

"Oh yeah!" Maggie practically tackled Paisley into a hug, giggling quietly. "Thank you, *Paisleeeee*."

"You are welcome," Paisley laughed. Shiloh pulled her back into a sitting up position and kissed her cheek.

"Did you know that tomorrow is Christmas? I asked for a bike, and a castle, and a dog, and a horse," Maggie began, counting off her list of presents on her fingers. Shiloh yawned, and Paisley noticed this.

"You should go to sleep, then," Paisley looked at the smaller girl. "Santa is going to come soon, right?" she turned and winked at Shiloh, who had to stifle her laughter.

"Right!" Maggie nodded once. "I better go back to bed," she giggled and crawled off the bed. "Goodnight, *Shiloooooh*. Goodnight, *Paisleeeee*." She gave them both a kiss on the cheek, pausing by Shiloh's face for a moment.

"I think you should marry her," she whispered, giggling as Shiloh's face turned bright red. Without another word, Maggie scurried out of the bedroom and down the hallway, leaving Shiloh and Paisley alone once more.

"M'tired," Paisley yawned, laying back down and looking up at Shiloh hopefully. "Sing?"

"Only for you," Shiloh said softly, leaning over to turn off the light before lying back on the bed next to Paisley. The smaller girl curled up beside Shiloh, a soft smile forming on her lips as her girlfriend began to sing quietly.

When Shiloh finished the song, she was well aware that Paisley had already fallen asleep. The smaller girl's breathing would slow down and her hands would slowly make their way under the sleeves of Shiloh's hoodie.

Something about this time of night made Shiloh nostalgic. Everything was calm and quiet, and she could hold Paisley in her arms without any interruption. In these moments, she could forget all about the things they had endured for the past few months.

She sighed softly, pressing a soft kiss on the top of Paisley's head. The smaller girl smelled like a mixture of the rain and Shiloh's shampoo. With a soft smile, Shiloh allowed sleep to overtake her.

Shiloh was awoken by the sound of soft giggling. Before she had time to react, she heard a stampede of footsteps approach the bed. Moments later, she was tackled by a crowd of giggling children.

"Lolo, wake up!"

And Paisley.

Groaning, Shiloh rolled over, only to be met with her girlfriend, sitting beside her and smiling widely. Maggie and Dylan giggled, bouncing up and down on the bed.

"What are you doing up so early?" Shiloh turned to her younger sister, ruffling her hair. Maggie giggled and shook her head.

"It wasn't me. It was *Paisleeeee*," Maggie pointed to the brown eyed girl sitting next to Shiloh.

"Santa came," Paisley leaned down, whispering in Shiloh's ear.

Sitting up, Shiloh rubbed her eyes and caught sight of the clock. "At six o'clock in the morning?!" she gaped, widening her eyes at Paisley. The smaller girl nodded contently.

Before Shiloh could say anything else, her bedroom door slowly opened.

"Oh good," Shiloh's mom smiled at her. "I thought I was going to have to drag you out of bed. Everyone's awake already, thanks to those three." She nodded towards Paisley and the two children, who glanced at one another bashfully.

"Might as well get a head start on those presents, right?" Colette smirked. Maggie and Dylan squealed excitedly, scrambling off of the bed and down the hallway. Paisley hopped up to follow them, but Shiloh grabbed her wrist before she could.

"We'll be down in a second," Shiloh gave her mother a soft smile. Thankfully, Colette didn't question them. Once Shiloh's bedroom door was closed again, Paisley turned back around, pouting.

"Why did you stop me?" Paisley tilted her head to the side and sat down on the edge of the bed. Shiloh just smiled and stood up, taking Paisley's hands in her own.

"I wanted to give you your present first," she squeezed Paisley's hands. The smaller girl's face lit up and she stood up on her tiptoes.

"Where is it?" she asked excitedly, looking around the room. Shiloh laughed and shook her head, letting go of Paisley's hands and taking a step backwards.

Paisley grew confused when Shiloh peeled off her hoodie, leaving her only in a tank top. Her eyes widened when Shiloh slipped the strap of her tank top downwards.

"Ouch," Paisley shook her head, taking step forwards and pressing her fingers underneath Shiloh's collarbone. "I do not understand," she said quietly, looking back up at Shiloh.

"It's a tattoo," Shiloh laughed softly and moved Paisley's fingers off of her shoulder. "Remember the day you picked the flowers and I got mad at you?"

Paisley thought for a moment before nodding softly. "You said I killed the pretty things."

"I was pretty mean then," Shiloh admitted, biting her lip and looking back down at the tattoo. "But this is different." She reached out, taking Paisley's hand and placing it back on top of her tattoo.

"Feel that?" she asked, smiling softly. Paisley nodded.

"It is your heart," she tapped on Shiloh's chest. "Why?"

"They're two daisies, Paisley," Shiloh pointed to her tattoo. "It's me and you. That way you can have your pretty things."

"Oh," Paisley's lips slowly curved into a wide smile, and she traced the outline of the tattoo. "I love it," she giggled, looking up at Shiloh slowly.

"You do?" Shiloh bit her lip to hide her smile. Paisley nodded immediately, tracing the outline of the flowers once more.

"Yes," Paisley placed her hands on Shiloh's shoulders and placed a soft kiss on her lips.

"I figured it could be like a promise ring," Shiloh shrugged. "But I know wearing jewelry bothers you, so I thought it'd mean more if I got something permanent."

"A promise ring?" Paisley tilted her head to the side and held up her pinky, remembering her version of a promise.

"Yeah," Shiloh giggled, interlocking their pinkies and keeping them intertwined. She swung their hands back and forth gently and studied Paisley's face. "It basically means that I promise to stick by your side no matter what happens."

"It's a promise to always be patient with you, even if sometimes it's hard for me to understand. It's a promise to sing to you no matter how tired I am. It's a promise to buy you as many yellow things as your heart desires. It's a promise to hold you through as many thunderstorms that come our way. It's a promise to make *us* work."

Paisley was smiling like an idiot by this point. She looked down shyly. "Really?"

"Of course," Shiloh kissed Paisley's forehead and pressed their foreheads together. "It's us, kid. Always."

"You and me?" Paisley met Shiloh's eyes hopefully.

"Yeah," Shiloh whispered. She found herself lost in Paisley's eyes for a moment before she leaned in and gently connected their lips.

She felt sparks erupt the moment their lips met, and couldn't help the butterflies in her stomach when she felt Paisley smile into the kiss. She pulled away, keeping their foreheads pressed together and gazing into Paisley's eyes. It was at that point that Shiloh realized this was the happiest she'd felt in a long time.

"Me and you."

a c k n o w l e d g e m e n t s

➤➤

To everyone who's been with me since the start —
thank you so much. You've given me confidence in
myself and in my writing, allowed me to share the little
world I've created with you guys, and hopefully
allowed me to give you a glimpse into my thoughts.

I remember being so incredibly nervous to post the first
chapter of *Yellow* on Wattpad, and being overwhelmed
with the feedback I received. You've grown just as
attached to the characters as I have, and you've made
me laugh and cry with the messages you've sent me.
Thanks for sticking it out, babes. This one's for you.

I love you endlessly. Be nice to yourselves.

lena nottingham

my social media

wattpad - txrches

tumblr - txrches

twitter - @lenajfc

435

Coming   Soon

B l u e

After a long and lengthy journey, Shiloh finally believes she and Paisley have reached the light at the end of the tunnel. But when the past comes back to haunt them, they find themselves in a completely new playing field. Change suddenly begins to overtake them, in more ways than one.

47195840R00268

Made in the USA
Lexington, KY
30 November 2015